CINDY DORMINY

right for me

To Daisy Mae. You were the right dog for me.

CHAPTER ONE
Shelby

It's about time my best friend worked up the nerve to tell the hot doctor her big news. He has a right to know they have a child together. *Talk about being a third wheel in the most awkward of situations.* But if I don't tag along, Darla will chicken out again. As if concrete encases her feet, Darla takes her sweet time walking up the sidewalk to Theo's apartment. My index fingers are going to leave a permanent mark between her shoulder blades as I prod her forward.

Bless her heart. She understands this is the right thing to do, but his reaction might break her. His emotions when he finds out he has a six-year-old daughter could range from sheer joy to complete outrage. I'm afraid he's going to be closer to the ticked-off zone, but I can't tell Darla that. She doesn't need another excuse to postpone the inevitable.

In the same voice I use when trying to convince one of my clients to lift two hundred pounds, I say, "You can do this." I pull my blond ponytail tighter then give her a thumbs up.

She exhales and bobs her head up and down so fast, I'm afraid she's going to get a concussion. "I have to do it."

Her hand pauses before rapping on Theo's apartment door. After she raises her hand three times without knocking, I take her hand and force her to tap on it. In my mind, I count off ten seconds... fifteen... twenty. *No answer. Crap.* It's taken her a month to work up enough courage, so we're not leaving until she has this conversation with Theo. We'll camp out on his doorstep if we have to, because she's not moving a muscle until she has the "we have a child" conversation. Darla and Theo are meant to be together, so I don't want anything to come between them.

She takes a step to leave. "He's not here. Let's go."

Before she can escape, I grab her arm. She's not going to give up this easily. "Maybe he's asleep. Give him a sec—"

"Can I help you?" a deep voice rumbles from behind, stopping us in our tracks. The smell of freshly baked chocolate chip cookies wafts out of Theo's apartment.

I rotate to check out a carbon copy of Theo with the same dark-blond hair, the same light-green eyes, and the same facial features. But this guy is as tall as a tree. His hair is going every which way and, lucky for me, he's shirtless. The only thing on his chest is a white powdery handprint. When I get caught gawking, I blink and shake the dirty thoughts out of my mind. *Stay on target.*

"We're here for Theo," I say to this nameless perfect male specimen.

"He's not home yet." He motions toward the apartment with his head. "Want to come in and wait for him?" He props the door open with his long arm, and a light dusting of white powder settles in the hairs of his forearm.

"No!" Darla yells.

"Yes, we do." I latch on to Darla and drag her under the guy's outstretched arm and inside the apartment. "I'm Shelby, and this is Darla." My neck hurts from the strain of peering up at the guy's face that is so much higher than mine. It's totally worth the pain.

His eyes widen. "Oh. Make yourselves at home, although I'm not sure when he'll be back. He's at the hospital."

I nudge Darla down on the couch and sit beside her.

"Let's go," she whispers to me. "I changed my mind."

Without losing eye contact with the mystery man, I say under my breath, "We're here. You are going to do this."

"I'm Tommy, by the way." He glances over his shoulder before he stuffs his hands in his jeans pockets.

"Theo's brother?" Darla's voice is a high-pitched shrill, causing him to flinch.

He grins. "Is that a problem?"

She stands and stares me down. "I can't do this."

I nudge her back down on the couch, stride over to Tommy, and wrap my fingers around his beefy arm. "Nice to meet you." Over my shoulder, I mouth to Darla, "Have mercy." Then I clear my throat. "This is a good thing." I cannot believe I just petted Tommy's bicep like he was a newborn puppy.

His expression is priceless. It's as though he can't decide if he should let me continue or snatch his arm away.

After another squeeze of his large bicep, I say to Darla, "You can... practice on him."

Tommy's deep voice rumbles with amusement. "Excuse me?"

My legs turn to jelly. *That voice. Oh my stars.*

Darla covers her face with her hands.

I flash Tommy a perky smile. "You see, Darla has something really, really important to tell Theo, and she's terrified at how he'll react. Could she practice her speech on you?" I give him my best hundred-watt smile.

He scratches his head, which releases my hold on him. "Uh... I guess. Sure."

"Good." I wave an arm toward Darla. "Go for it. Spit it out."

She opens her mouth, but nothing comes out.

In my best preppy cheerleader voice, I say, "Come on, Darla. You can do it."

Another rumble of laughter bubbles out of Tommy. He leans against the wall, arms crossed over his bare chest. "Tell me what? That I let two crazed strangers in?"

Darla points at Tommy, her face flushed. "I can't tell him first. That would be a complete slap in the face to Theo."

Tommy pushes off the wall and runs a hand through his hair. "Tell me or don't. I don't care. I've got cookies in the oven." He takes a step toward the kitchen.

I lick my lips. "Yum."

"Well, you see..." Darla closes her eyes and blows out a big breath before she continues. "Theo and I had sex in college, and he has a daughter."

I grin at her before I dare a glance at Tommy. He freezes mid-stride then whirls around. His mouth hangs open, and all the color has drained from his face. "Theo has a kid?"

Using this as another excuse to latch on to his arm, I escort him to the couch. With a shaky hand, he points toward the kitchen.

I pat him on the arm. "I'll switch off the oven."

For the next thirty minutes, I do a mental review of the steps to perform CPR. After Darla's confession, I might be called upon to save a life. All I remember from my refresher course is to push hard and push fast, and that sounds so dirty right now.

I'm not sure if Tommy has taken in a full breath since Darla started her rambling about how she met his brother and how she thought he didn't want anything to do with her and their daughter. His slumped shoulders and the worry that consumes his face tells me all I need to know about how close he must be to his brother. And all of this was because Darla accidentally sent "you have a kid" emails to Tommy instead of Theo right after they graduated college. It would be funny if it weren't for the fact that, because of that, Theo doesn't realize he's been a father for the past six years.

Darla wipes her eyes and takes a deep breath. She drags out her keys from her purse. "I have to go."

No. We can't leave yet. Worst best friend ever.

"Right now?" I practically shout. From the corner of my eye, I sneak a peek at Tommy. "I mean... he baked cookies."

Tommy chuckles.

That voice.

With renewed confidence, Darla says, "I'm going to the hospital to tell Theo right now."

It's terrible that I'm being selfish, but this Tommy person is eye-balling me. His eyes rake over me, making me feel tingly in a place I thought was covered with cobwebs.

With gritted teeth, I say, "You're right. Let's go." Helping my best friend takes precedence over a silly crush any day of the week. *But he's so cute...*

When we get to the front door, Tommy clears his throat. "Uh, Shelby. I can take you home if you want to stay for... cookies."

I freeze and side-eye Darla, who quirks up an eyebrow then nods.

"Sure." My outward expression may give off a confident, nonchalant vibe, but on the inside, I'm doing the biggest happy dance ever. After Darla leaves, I prop my wet noodle of a body against the back of the door and give myself a good talking to. The faster I fall for a guy, the worse it hurts when he leaves. I need to learn from my mistakes.

Tommy clears his throat, and I shake my head to stop my internal monologue. He motions toward the kitchen with his head. "Want a cookie?"

You bet I do. I never want this day to end, but a part of me can't wait to get home so I can sketch his chiseled face. And there is no way on earth I will throw this one away—the drawing or the man.

A few minutes later, while I'm stuffing my face full of cookies, we attempt a decent but awkward conversation. In one of Tommy's pacing episodes, he returned wearing a T-shirt, and even though I tried to conceal my disappointment, the smirk etched on his face suggested he has mind-reading capabilities.

"I'm sorry about barging in here, but Isaac and I have tried to convince Darla ever since Theo's been back in Nashville. But she's so worried how he'll take it. I mean, it's not every day you find out you're a father. Him, not you, of course."

Tommy parks his large frame in the kitchen chair next to me, and his eyebrows shoot up. "Who's Isaac?"

My stomach flip-flops with excitement. The chance that he sounds a little worried about me having a boyfriend makes me giddy. I do my best to tamp down my emotions by diving into another cookie. "He's one of my employees at the hospital fitness center. Aggravating as all get-out, perfect body, and... he bats for the other team."

Tommy's mouth curls into a smile. "Oh... good. The name Isaac means laughter, by the way."

I crack up, almost spewing cookie particles out of my mouth. "That explains so much."

He rakes a hand through his hair, and it takes every muscle fiber in my body to keep me from doing the same thing to it. Instead, I place my hand on top of his other hand, which is resting on the kitchen table. "It's not your fault. You didn't realize the emails were meant for your brother."

His long-lashed eyes drift from my face down to where our hands connect. "I hope their conversation is going well. I should call him." Tommy removes his hand from mine to reach in his back pocket for his phone.

"Not a good idea. Let her handle this."

He stares at the phone screen for a moment, blows out a breath, then places it on the table. "I guess you're right." Before I realize what he's doing, he snatches the half-eaten cookie out of my hand and gobbles it down. But it's his wink that leaves me a puddle in my chair.

"So, what do you do, Mr. Other Edwards?" I ask after I manage to catch my breath.

Tommy furrows his brow and draws out a breath.

Great. He's a leech, living off his brother. Or he can't keep a job because of a gambling habit. Or worse, he's a musician who assumes he's going to be a star any minute.

"I'm in graduate school."

Yay! He's not a musician.

"What field? I have a master's in public health." I slide the plate of cookies closer to me. He reaches for another cookie, but I land a playful smack on his hand, causing him to smile.

"Biomedical engineering. In Boston. I'm on a break. Next topic."

Ooookay. That's not odd at all. I stand to enter the kitchen. "The cookies were awesome."

With a bashful grin, he replies, "Thanks. You don't happen to be a professor's daughter, do you?"

Very odd.

"No. My father owns his own company, and my mother spends her days doing charity work."

He chews on his lip. "Good."

I pick up the cookie plate. "Let me clean up."

He jumps up and follows me. "Don't worry about it. I'll just mess it up again when I make sourdough bread later anyway."

"Did you say sour—" I jerk around, and my face slams into his big chest. I didn't expect him to be right on my heels, but oh my, that was a fantastic collision.

He backpedals, doing the hand-through-the-hair thing that I'm already learning is his nervous habit. "Sorry about that. I, uh…" Now his hair is standing up in a whole bunch of messy, sexy waves. "Aw, what the heck." He snakes one hand around my waist and cups his other hand behind my head. Tommy pulls me close, leans way down, and when his lips touch mine, I forget all about the Darla-Theo-ba-by-daddy drama.

Seconds, or minutes, or it could have been hours later, he pulls away and stares into my eyes. I'm not sure how long the kiss lasted, but it wasn't long enough. Both of us are out of breath, and he has a wild-eyed expression. He rests his forehead against mine and lets out a whimper. "I better take you home while I still have any blood supply going to my brain."

"No blood to the brain is totally fine by me." I gasp as soon as the words are out, not believing what just spilled from my mouth. He must think I'm a floozy.

He chuckles as he captures a strand of my hair that escaped my ponytail holder and slides it behind my ear. "What's your favorite cookie?"

"Anything with chocolate."

He kisses the tip of my nose. "Okay. Next time, I'll make anything with chocolate."

Woo-hoo! There's going to be a next time. I hold out my hand with my little finger pointing upward. "Pinkie promise?"

He throws his head back and belts out a chuckle. "Sure thing, Shelby."

With our pinkie fingers intertwined, I imagine other body parts doing the same thing. And from Tommy's sly grin, I would bet dollars to doughnuts that his thoughts are going down that same road. Anything chocolate can't happen soon enough.

CHAPTER TWO

Tommy

It takes all my willpower to walk away from Shelby's condo without showing her what I want to do with her. And by the faint whimper she lets out when I pull back after another serious lip-lock, I'm pretty sure she wouldn't mind if we continued. After one last tiny peck on her pouty lips, I walk backward with my eyes trained on her the entire time.

Shelby rests her back against her front door and waves to me. I return the wave, but not before my foot slips off the curb, sending me stumbling onto the hood of my car. "I'm good."

Just as she opens her front door, she lets out a slight *tee-hee* and shakes her head.

Real slick, doofus.

It would have been so easy to let myself go further with Shelby. She has those lidded eyes that were screaming "take me to bed," and we're both consenting adults. But after my fiasco in Boston, I promised myself I wouldn't jump into another relationship again... ever. But here I am, dancing the tongue tango with a girl I just met. I'll never learn.

She's not like Hazel.

I speed away, trying to figure out if I should go back to Theo's apartment or hang out with my mom. If Theo's home, he may be in a piss-and-vinegar mood and want to punch my lights out for being the dummy that kept him from being with Darla all these years, even though I didn't do anything on purpose. So Mom is the safer option, and I'm sure she will be more than happy for me to do some serious stress baking.

To avoid the noise cluttering up my brain, I phone my little sister, Heather, who is away at college, taking summer classes. When she answers, I put her on speakerphone.

"Hey, bro."

Her springy voice already has me smiling. "Hey, I need some advice."

Her giggle resonates through my car. "You're asking for advice? From me? What have you done with my brother?"

"Ha ha." I rake a hand through my hair. "I met someone."

Heather groans. "Tommy, no."

"Exactly. That's why I called you before I did something stupid again."

"Did you do anything?" Her voice rises at the end of her sentence, like the last word has hidden meaning.

"No. Yes. I mean, we kissed. A lot." The silence on the line makes me wonder if she hung up the phone, which might be a good thing. "Are you still there?"

I drive into my parents' neighborhood, and the street floods my brain with childhood memories. Theo, Jennifer, Heather, and I would ride up and down the street on our bicycles, creating havoc. It was hard to balance having fun with trying not to drive my preacher father too crazy.

Heather sighs. "Yeah, just processing. You really shouldn't—"

"That's why I ran away from her like a scared thirteen-year-old. I'm such a dork."

"Yes, you are. But Tommy..." Her whiny voice says volumes. "Why are you doing this to yourself again? After what Haz-hell put you through?"

That's a very good question, and I don't have a good answer for her. I couldn't tell her that, when I opened the door, I saw an angel standing before me, and all my senses left me acting like a silly, lovesick puppy. Shelby was adorable, and she even petted my arm. I was a goner when she decided to ditch her friend in order to hang out with me and eat cookies instead. I could get used to a gorgeous, smart girl who loves my cooking.

"Tell me about her."

A warm smile slides across my face as I pull into the driveway and cut the engine to my beat-up jalopy. "Her name is Shelby. She's friends with a girl who apparently had sex with Theo when they were in college."

Heather gasps. "No way."

"And... they have a kid together."

"Oh, holy night."

I grin even bigger because Theo is so shy around girls, even more so than me. "Yes, and don't repeat any of that because he hasn't been told yet. Anyway, I only met Shelby less than four hours ago, and I already feel like I've known her my entire life. She likes my cookies."

"Duh. Of course she does. But don't you feel it's too soon?"

Of course she'd say that, and it's exactly why I called her. She'll toss some truth bombs my way and won't hold back. "It is, but she's real, and I'd like to see where this leads."

After my craptastic year, I promised myself I wouldn't get involved for at least a decade or two, but here I am, already having feelings again for someone right out of the gate. Hazel put a bad taste in my mouth for women, especially the kind who like to do illegal things and pin it on someone else... me.

"Well, can you take it slow?"

I climb out of the car and lean against the hood. Mom peeks out of the bay window and waves for me to come inside. I hold up a finger, motioning that I'll be a minute. "Apparently, I only have two speeds: zero and sixty. I don't know what thirty feels like."

"'Bout time you find out. Can you give your libido one month for your brain to catch up?"

I chuckle as I throw my head back. "I'm not sure that's possible."

"You are such a guy. A geeky one, but a dude nonetheless. How about two weeks? If you can get through a fourteen-day cooling-off period, and you find out she's not a resident of the planet Weirdoville, then go for it."

Twenty thousand one hundred sixty minutes. That doesn't sound too bad. I've gone way longer than that without sex, but that was always because I had no willing participant. Shelby's willing, and I'm more than able to participate.

"So am I supposed to avoid her until then? Because that's the opposite of getting acquainted with her."

Heather groans into the phone. If she were in front of me, I suspect she would be giving me a serious eye roll right now. "Of course not. Get to know her. See if she's worth going down that road. Dude, you are so smart. How did you not learn any of this relationship stuff before now?"

I tap the side of my head as if she were there to see me do it. "Book smarts doesn't mean much with women. That's how I got into the last mess, remember?"

"Don't remind me. I'm googling some famous quotes about patience to help you out. Ooh. Here's a good one. It's a French proverb. 'There is no science without patience.' Or how about this one? Ben Franklin said, 'He that can have patience can have what he will.'"

I snort. "You do realize he had more mistresses than Carter's got little pills, so not the best example, but I get it. Good things come to those who wait. Yada, yada, yada. I gotta go. Mom's waiting for me. Are you coming home soon?"

"You bet. Oh, I found one more quote." She snickers. "This one is perfect for you. 'Patience is bitter, but its fruit is sweet.' That was Aristotle."

"Bye, Heath Bar."

"Two weeks. You can make it that long. I'll be home by then."

"Fine. Bye." I slide the phone back into my pocket and drag my-self up the sidewalk. I'm the dumbest dork around.

You suck, Aristotle.

CHAPTER THREE
Shelby

Giving Tommy my phone number wasn't the smartest move, but I couldn't resist, especially after the smoking-hot kisses that turned my legs into jelly. It would be pretty awesome to have a decent guy in my life for a change. But I'm sure nothing will come of it. It was a fun afternoon full of tasty cookies served by a yummy man, and that's all it will be.

Nice guys are never interested in me.

My thoughts go to Darla. I sure hope Theo takes the news well. Fingers crossed that he's not mad. She would never intentionally hurt anyone, especially him. After all, she deserves a break too. And they are such a cute couple. I really hope he laughs it off and they get married and live happily ever after.

I pull out my pencils and sketch pad, and my hands drift across the page, capturing Tommy's adorable face. *That jaw. Those adorable eyes. His wide grin.* They are seared into my memory, and I work like I've had too much caffeine as I attempt to draw every detail. I grin as I draw his messy hair and even make sure a touch of flour rests above his ear.

My phone buzzes, and I jolt out of my seat, dropping my sketch pad. It's him. He texted me.

Tommy: *Hey, it was very nice meeting you.*

I run a victory lap around the kitchen table as I reread his words ten times.

Calm down, girl. It's just another guy. Yeah, right.

Shelby: *You were a nice surprise to a rather serious situation.*

He sends me a cringy face emoji, and I giggle.

My phone rings, causing my heart to race. Tommy's calling. It's one thing to have a text conversation, but it's totally different to include voice. There is tone and inflection, and most of all, I can't type and delete a thousand times until I get the words perfect.

I swipe to answer and speak with a shaky voice. "Cookie eaters anonymous."

His deep, rumbly chuckle makes me do a wiggly dance as I sink back into my chair. "So, Shelby..."

I love the way he says my name, even if it has a tinge of uncertainty to it. He could be calling to tell me he regrets kissing me. If that is the case, I really do wish he would have stuck to text messages. I'm sure there's a "you're a sucky kisser" emoji perfect for this occasion.

"I was wondering, while I'm in town, maybe we could get lunch or go for coffee. Something casual and public."

I hold the phone away from my ear, trying to figure out what in the heck that means. "Sure. I'd like that."

"Okay. Great."

My mind goes down the dirty road, so I say, "Or you can come over, and I can make us lunch."

"Okay. No! I mean... let's start with coffee. Rain check on the lunch? Like a two-week rain check?"

Maybe I read this guy completely wrong. He sounds as if he's very unsure about me now. It's probably because he will be leaving to go back to school in the fall and doesn't want to get too serious. I get that, but we could have so much fun in the meantime.

"Coffee is good. Today?"

Silence fills the line. We've either been disconnected, or I really scared him off.

He clears his throat. "See you in ten at Bongo Java?"

I really expected him to have some sort of excuse for delaying our coffee date too. "Looking forward to it."

Woo-hoo! I can't imagine anything better to go with my coffee than a double shot of Tommy. If I can get lucky, there might be some whipped cream added to the order.

Even though I drive way over the speed limit and run a red light to get to Bongo Java, Tommy beats me there. He's standing in line, which gives me a great opportunity to check him out without him noticing.

His long, lanky legs are nothing like his brother's. Theo is maybe five feet eight at best, but Tommy is easily a good two to three inches over six feet. And I've never seen shoulders that broad on any engineer around here.

He pulls out his phone, and his fingers fly over the keypad. I jump when my phone chirps, alerting me to a text message.

Tommy turns around and spots me. With a huge grin, he says, "Hey. I was hoping you wouldn't bail on me."

Heat rushes up my neck. I hope he didn't see me checking him out. I gesture at myself. "Me? Not hardly."

He motions with his head for me to join him at the counter. We order, and while we wait on our coffees, I stand there like a bump on a log. I'm not sure if this is a date or if he's bored and wanted company.

I clear my throat. "Have you heard from Theo? I haven't heard a peep from Darla. I hope things are going well."

Tommy shrugs. "Not one word. I'm trying to stay out of sight until this whole thing blows over because if or when he finds out I was responsible for the mix-up..."

Like it's the most natural gesture, I rub his shoulder. "It's going to be okay, and I bet you anything, before you realize it, this will be one of those crazy stories you all tell at every Thanksgiving."

He snorts. "I hope so." Blowing out a breath, he mumbles something about the fruit being sweet. Then he smiles. "Tell me about Darla. You two are coworkers, right?"

"More or less. Actually, I'm her boss, but she's my best friend too, so I try not to be very bossy. But Isaac is another story. If I don't stay right on his tail, he'll goof off all day."

"All work and no play makes Jack a dull boy."

I roll my eyes. "That's exactly what Isaac says. Is that your mantra?"

He shakes his head as he hands me my coffee cup. "Yes, but I guess you would say that it doesn't matter. It is what it is." Tommy takes a gulp of his coffee and stares off. "Sorry. I have a lot on my mind. I didn't mean to be rude."

Tommy doesn't understand the meaning of the word rude. Rude is flirting with another girl right under my nose. I understand rude when I see it, and that is not what Tommy is. He's distracted.

"No apologies."

Through the uncomfortable getting-acquainted conversation over coffee, he relaxes, and I even get a chuckle and a smile out of him. As we stand to leave, his large hand engulfs mine, and his warm skin sends tingles down my arm.

At my car, I say an awkward goodbye, but not before I give him a sneak-attack kiss on the cheek. "See you soon?"

He rubs his cheek where my lips touched it. "Yes. In about twenty thousand minutes."

I giggle because he's so adorably dorky, but I have no idea what he's talking about. It must be an engineering thing. "Counting the minutes?"

"You have no idea."

"Cute. See ya, Tommy."

He watches me back out of the parking space, and as I wait to turn onto the street, I catch a glimpse of Tommy banging his head on the roof of his car. I have no idea what that's about, but he is, hands down, the most interesting person I have ever met. And I can't wait to see him again.

CHAPTER FOUR
Tommy

T-minus two weeks since I met Shelby, but since my niece has been in the hospital, I've been less fixated on counting down the days until my self-appointed time limit is up. Having a seriously ill niece is the lowest point ever for our family. Little Stella is so sick, and it's heartbreaking to see what it's doing to Darla. Plus, Theo has been a pill to deal with lately. But after a good, old-fashioned Edwards intervention, he appears to be getting his head out of his butt and doing the right thing. Theo's first impulse was to push Darla away, but he realized she didn't do anything to purposely hurt him. Now they are back on track to becoming a happy little family.

As terrible as it sounds, at least little Stella's illness has been a distraction from wanting to take my interest in Shelby to the next level. And I have needed the distraction. Heather's home now and has kept my feet to the fire on my two-week abstinence agreement. It's ridiculous how I can go months at a time without wanting sex, but one afternoon with Shelby, and all my brain focuses on is being with that cutie. I thought having this cooling-off period would put out the fire, but all it has done is fan the flames and make the desire even worse.

Thank goodness Stella is getting better, and my countdown clock shows I only have one hundred minutes left to make it to exactly fourteen days. It's finally safe to be alone in the same room with Shelby. The few times we've been in the hospital waiting room at the same time, I get all jittery if she's close to me. She's going to have a permanent scowl mark on her forehead from all the confusion I'm causing her.

I knock on her apartment door, counting down the seconds. Her infectious smile makes me wish we were in the Eastern time zone. This alarm can't sound fast enough.

"Hey, stranger. Come on in." Shelby takes my hand and walks me into her kitchen. "I took the liberty of buying some ingredients for you to make me something chocolate. You promised. Remember?" Her bright smile warms my soul.

"I sure did." I rub my hands together. "Let's see what you have in mind." I know what I have in mind, but that will have to wait another sixty-five minutes.

She waves her hand over the ingredients. "I'll make it easy on you this time. How about chocolate chip cookies?"

You are not making this easy.

"Sounds good to me."

Together, we whip up a batch of cookie dough. Her arm brushes against mine, sending tingles down my spine. I'm glad my hands are busy dropping dough onto the cookie sheet so she can't see how much they're shaking. Being at her house prior to my timer going off is more difficult than I thought it would be. Perhaps I shouldn't have stopped by her house until the time ran out.

While the first cookie sheet is in the oven, she leads me to the couch. She kisses me on the lips, and I sink down next to her, enjoying what I have only been obsessing about for the last two weeks. *Aristotle can shove it.* I wrap my arms around her waist, and Shelby lets out a soft moan.

Twenty-five minutes.

I push away from her, and she frowns. "If you're not into me, just say so."

"That is not it at all." I point toward the kitchen. "I'm a serious baker. To let cookies burn is a tragedy." I jump up and rush into the kitchen, adjusting the front of my jeans the entire way. While I slide cookies off the sheet and onto a wire cooling rack, I sneak a peek at Shelby sitting on the couch, chewing on her lip.

"Come taste the fruits of your labor," I tell her.

The fruit is sweet. The fruit is sweet. No science without patience. Aristotle and science have never met Shelby, *so they can stuff it.*

Shelby lets out a huge sigh and slogs over to the stove. I feed her a cookie, and her eyes roll back in her head. "Oh my. You are perfect." She slaps a hand over her mouth. "I mean, these are perfect."

I swing around and focus on throwing the last batch of cookies in the oven. The heat is not doing anything for my arousal. After I slam the oven door shut, I open the freezer door in hopes of cooling off my overactive male hormones. My phone buzzes, making me jump.

"It's Theo, telling me Stella is doing better."

Shelby's eyes brighten. "I'm so happy for them. She's a great kid."

"I can't wait until she gets out of the hospital so I can hang out with her." I glance down at the timer on my phone.

Ten minutes.

Shelby opens the oven a bit to check on the cookies. "I can handle the rest if you want to leave. I can take a hint."

"No." I squeeze my eyes shut and pray for the time to speed up. It wouldn't be a character flaw if I only made it to twenty thousand one hundred fifty minutes. Heather would never have to know I caved. "Shelby, I have never met anyone like you. You're smart and fun, and... you are so beautiful."

She swallows hard. "But..."

"No buts. It's just that..." I scratch my head, trying to formulate words so she'll understand why I'm being so standoffish. "This is going to sound like something a high schooler would do."

She raises an eyebrow and crosses her arms. "It's time for you to leave. If you're not into me, it's fine. I get it."

I scrub my face with my hands. "Can you give me just three more minutes?"

"What?"

I lead her back to the couch and plunk her down. "I am going to sit at the table for three minutes."

She stares at the ceiling. "You are acting so strange."

Before I lose my courage, I blurt out, "I made a big mistake one time by jumping into a relationship too soon, so I promised my sister I would wait two weeks before we…"

Shelby covers her mouth then doubles over laughing. "You're so cute."

"I'm a man of my word. Plus, Heather would figure it out if I went back on my word. She has ways."

I sit at the table with my phone in hand. My knee bounces as I focus on the numbers counting down to zero, like I'm watching the last few seconds of a football game. When the whistle blows, signaling I have successfully reached my official two-week time point, I jump up and scream, "Yes!"

I rush over to the couch and scoop Shelby up in my arms. I kiss her hard on the lips, making her melt in my grasp.

She pulls back for a breath. "Wow."

"Yeah. Let's do more wowing. Which way to your bedroom?"

She points as she covers her mouth with mine.

For the next one hundred eighty minutes, we make up for lost time.

Aristotle, you might be on to something.

CHAPTER FIVE
Shelby

Every extra second I have, I sketch a drawing of my new favorite subject: Tommy. I keep hidden supplies in my work desk for when the mood strikes, and lately, that's more often than I feel like doing my day job. I haven't been able to keep my mind, or my hands, from obsessing over him. Once I realized he'd made a pact with his little sister to take it slow and not jump in headfirst with me, his behavior was super cute. And he was completely worth the wait.

Even though we are trying to keep our relationship a secret for now, I'm sure a few people close to me have caught on pretty quickly. My goofy expression and the bounce in my step haven't gone unnoticed at work, especially by Isaac. He clears his throat as he leans against my office door, and I almost jump out of my skin. Before I am able to slide the sketch under a work document, Isaac snatches it out of my hand.

"Give that back."

His approving gaze scans Tommy's image. "Very good. I see why you're sleeping with the dude."

I jump out of my chair and lunge for the paper he holds way above my head. "If you don't give it back, I'll make you give Mrs. Owensby a fitness assessment."

He freezes and ponders my threat before handing me the drawing. Then he holds his hands up in front of him defensively. "Boss lady, you don't fight fair, but I didn't hear you deny the part about sleeping with him."

I slide the drawing in my file cabinet drawer labeled "bills," the safe place I store all my drawings I want to keep away from prying eyes. In the few short weeks since I met Tommy, I have drawn so many pictures of him, I'm going to need a bigger file cabinet to store them all. I lock the cabinet and toss the key into my purse.

Isaac groans. "First off, I don't understand why you hide your talent. You're so good. And don't play dumb. That file is not where you keep your bills."

My eyebrows rise. "You know about this?"

"Pfft. Girl, you assume you're sly, but I am the eyes and ears of this establishment. Never mind that. Why are you keeping your latest love interest on the down-low?"

"Shh." I poke my head out of my office to scan the fitness center workout area. It's a slow time of day with very few members exercising, but anyone might be lurking around. "You understand why. If my mother gets wind that I'm drawing again, she'll go from zero to sixty off the cliff." In my best exaggerated mother's voice, I say, "Oh, Shelby Lynn, don't go putting crazy ideas in that pretty little head of yours again. Art is not a career."

Isaac snorts. "Your impression of her is pretty spot on. But what about that gorgeous specimen you're hiding... or attempting to hide."

I roll my eyes. Isaac may be my employee, but he's more than that. He's technically Darla's best friend, but he's grown on me over the years. "We are trying to be considerate of the situation with Stella. Darla and Theo's little girl is really sick. I can't waltz into the pediatric ICU all lovey-dovey."

Mentioning Isaac's deathly ill goddaughter changes his expression to stoic, which doesn't happen often. "True." He peeks out of my office at the front desk. "But don't you want to tell your parents you finally found someone decent after the last disaster?"

I sneer at him. He understands as well as I do how high the bar is set in order to please my parents. No man will ever be successful enough for them.

"Let's not talk about them right now."

"Yeah, especially since Mother Dearest just walked in." He waves at her, and I rush to peer out my office door. My mom is standing at the front desk, talking to the receptionist.

"Hello, Mrs. Williams. Nice to see you."

She's never going to approve of the leggings and corporate T-shirt I'm wearing. I glance down at my worn-out sneakers. "How do I look?"

Isaac puts a hand on each of my shoulders, and when I stare into his big eyes, he calms my nerves. "Great, as always. In case you have forgotten, you manage a fitness center, not a Fortune 500 company, so you are wearing appropriate business attire." He nudges me toward my mother. "Go. Play nice."

When my mom sees me approaching, her big smile fades as she analyzes my clothes. "I was in the neighborhood and thought we could have lunch together, but I see you're about to take a Pilates class or something."

My shoulders slump. "No, Mom. This is what I wear to work, but if the lunch offer still stands, I would love to go with you." I give her a genuine smile because I really do want to spend time with her. I love her, but I only wish she would approve of my choices.

After another once-over, she replies, "I'm sure we can find somewhere that won't mind your attire."

Gee, thanks, Mom. Nice way to make me feel inadequate... again. Even if I were dressed in linen pants and a silk blouse like her or had my highlights done on a regular basis, I would still never measure up to her standards.

Isaac walks up to us, holding my purse out for me. "You two have a nice, long lunch. I've got the place covered."

Mom gives Isaac a smile, and when we reach the front door, she stage-whispers, "Such a nice boy. Does he have a girlfriend?"

I can't count the number of times I've had to remind her that he's gay, but she still believes it's a phase, that he hasn't met the right girl yet. He'll never meet the right girl.

"No, he doesn't. Remember?"

She pats my hand as we walk toward her Mercedes-Benz S 560. "Oh, yes. Maybe someday. And don't forget, he comes from a very well-to-do family."

I might as well not mention Tommy because his family is far from wealthy.

"Mom, Isaac is my employee and a friend. I'm not interested in him."

She groans. "Aren't there any wealthy doctors that exercise at your work?"

I should have locked up the fitness center and insisted Isaac come with us, but then that would have given her the impression that we were an item. While I slide into the buttery-soft leather seat of her car, I count to ten to calm my nerves. I really want lunch with my mother to be different this time.

As she drives down West End Avenue toward one of my favorite lunch spots, It's Greek To Me, I listen to her chatter about what's happening with the charity event she's organizing and Dad's latest business deal. Occasionally, I give her a smile or a courtesy "uh-huh," all the while obsessing about the awesome food waiting for me. The restaurant owners don't care if I'm gussied up for a meal, and I could really go for a gyro the size of my head right now.

"I really do wish you could find a nice man."

I chuckle. "You mean a rich man. You would rather I marry a wealthy gay man than be alone."

Mom gasps. "I did not say that."

Through clenched teeth, I say, "Every time you see Isaac, you make a comment about him and me. I'm not interested. He's not interested. It doesn't matter that his father owns a baseball team. It's never going to happen."

She sighs. "I realize I'm pushy, but you are such a sweetheart. I only wish you could find someone who is worthy of you, someone who can provide for you and make you happy."

My chest tightens. This conversation has been on a continuous loop for the past five years, and I'm going to have early-onset hypertension from her forced matchmaking attempts.

"I make myself happy. I love my job. I have great friends, and if you must know, I'm seeing someone right now." *Holy crap on a cracker.* I cannot believe I said that. So much for not mentioning Tommy. If her litmus test is being from a wealthy family, he will never measure up to her standards. Plus, we decided to keep our relationship on the down-low for the time being.

Mom parks the car, her mouth hanging open. "Why didn't you tell me?

I chew on my lip, not sure what to say or how much to leave out. "His name is Tommy Edwards."

She scrunches her eyebrows together. "Is he a nice guy?"

It's what she's not asking that is more obvious. He's nothing like the last disaster. "Yes. He's a very nice guy. And I know you want to know about his family, so his father is the pastor at the Methodist Church, and his mom is an attorney." That should give her enough information to think he comes from good people, even if they aren't loaded.

Her face breaks out into a huge smile. "Why didn't you say something?"

I throw my hands in the air and stare out the passenger window. "Because we haven't known each other very long, and I'm not sure where it's going yet."

When I dare to glance at my mother, she has the goofiest grin on her face. "You like him, don't you?"

Heat rushes up my neck. I'm not sure how to answer.

Mom claps her hands together. "Then it's settled. You and this Tommy fellow will meet your dad and me for brunch this Sunday."

It takes a few seconds for her statement to sink in. My throat almost collapses, and right as I begin to protest, she shushes me. "It's settled, Shelby Lynn. On Sunday, I want to meet this man that makes you blush like that."

Please stop!

When I am able to breathe again, I reply with the only response that will satisfy my mother. "Sure thing. I can't wait."

Tommy is going to flip out, right before he runs back to Boston and I never see him again.

CHAPTER SIX

Shelby

As I lie in bed, tangled up with Tommy, my stomach lets out a massive growl.

He groans. "Tell me you're not hungry again."

"I really would love one of your yummy omelets."

He glances over at my alarm clock and whimpers. "At two in the morning?"

"Uh-huh."

He scoots me closer and kisses the hollow between my shoulder and neck. "We should have a little fun first. Really work up an appetite." He waggles his eyebrows, but I don't respond to his advances.

I pull a pouty face. "Please." I bat my eyes for added effect.

He owes me after I played his favorite board game, Risk, last night. I don't understand his affinity for it, nor do I understand the rules, but I tried, even though I asked a million questions. It wasn't all that fun, but because he wanted to play it, I endured it, especially because I have hopes he will pay me back with his amazing baking skills.

With all that's going on in his family, we agreed to keep seeing each other in secret for now, but it's getting increasingly harder to do. I want him with me twenty-four, seven, so at some point, getting our families involved is inevitable.

I goose the tickle spot on his side, and he squirms away from my grasp. "So you're going to play hard to get?"

With one swift move, he flips both of us over so he's on top of me, and pins my arms over my head. "Don't forget the rules."

"You do love rules and games, don't you? If I was a board game, which one would I be?" When he releases me, I slide my arms around his neck.

He stares at the ceiling. "Let's see. Probably Sorry."

"What?"

"Or maybe Trouble."

I try to shove him away, but his body is three times the size of mine, so he doesn't even budge. "Mister, you better watch it."

He kisses my neck, and I purr into his ear.

"You are more like the game Perfection."

I crinkle my brow. "The one where you try to fit the pieces into the right places before the time's up?"

"Uh-huh. But it's not the race. It's the name. You are perfect, sugar."

"Aw, you're slick. It's a good thing you didn't say Risk."

He pops his head up and grins from ear to ear. "We could play it if you—"

"No."

His shoulders slump. "Oh, come on. You know you love it."

With a stoic expression, I reply, "I need food. I'm withering away from lack of sustenance."

His eyes roam down my body then make their way back up to meet mine. "You are perfection."

I dip my head like I do every time he pays me a compliment. I'm not used to being adored. He raises my chin with one finger until our eyes meet again. When our lips touch, his body collapses onto mine. I wrap my arms around his waist and hold him tight. Maybe my body will forget all about the need for food. But as if the food devil is messing with my night, my stomach growls again.

"You better be glad you're cute. We could combine food with fun. How about it?"

He needs to come up with something more original next time. "It's hard to believe you're a preacher's kid with that one-track mind."

He shrugs. "Man was not meant to live by bread alone."

"That's my point. Even Jesus agrees with me. We need omelets." I squirm out of his arms, scoop up my clothes from the floor, and throw them on. "Chop, chop. I'm hungry."

I lead Tommy by the hand into my peninsula kitchen, and as usual, his knees buckle when he eyeballs my appliances. Before Tommy came along, my Dacor Renaissance range and cooktop barely even got hot. Now they get put to use on a daily basis. My heart swells when I see how content he acts when he's throwing together even the most basic meal.

As Tommy drags out the ingredients, I lean against the counter, taking in this complete package of a man. He's six feet three inches of human yumminess surrounded by two hundred pounds of shyness, sprinkled with an amazing talent for cooking, among other things. And I haven't even started on that brain of his. I'm still baffled by how someone so geeky smart would want me. I mean, he's almost finished with a PhD from the University of Boston. I'm a train wreck compared to him.

It has to be more than a coincidence that he took a break in the middle of a biomedical engineering program to come home and spend time with his brother, who happens to be the long-lost baby-daddy of my goddaughter, Stella. It has to be fate, because otherwise, we would have never run into each other. We certainly wouldn't have been in the same social circles growing up. Mom and Dad made sure of that by sticking me in an all-girls school. *Spare no expense to make a good impression.* And I get the *impression* Tommy's parents are a total one-eighty from mine. My dad's main concern is making money, and my mom wants to show off the money. Tommy's family is more interested in saving souls.

I'm still freaking out that I blabbed to Mom about Tommy, but it was the only way to get her off my back. For two days, I've dodged every conversation, but I can't keep this up for much longer. Brunch with my parents in less than ten hours should be interesting... if Tommy ever speaks to me again.

"I bought you something," I say.

"Frozen omelets, I'm hoping. So we can go back to bed. Hint. Hint." He grabs me around the waist, and his strong hands on my skin almost convince me to give up feeding my hunger.

"Ha, no." I scoot away from him and open the pantry to retrieve a gift bag.

He peeks inside.

"Oh, for crying out loud, just open the dang thing."

He takes too long, so I help him by throwing all the tissue paper out of the sack and onto the kitchen floor. He pulls out his gift and scrunches up his forehead. "An apron?" He unfolds it, and his eyes light up when he reads the inscription. "Real men don't use recipes. Nice."

I scoot around the bar to help him put it on. "It was either this one or the one that said, 'I turn grills on.' I didn't want to give you a big head."

He peers down at the apron then lifts me up to sit on the counter so we are eye to eye. His light-green eyes are intoxicating. "This is perfect. Thank you." He kisses me softly on the cheek and works his way down my neck.

My resistance begins to fade, but if my hunger changes into me being hangry, it won't be pretty. "Uh... the omelets?"

"If you want to call them omelets, it's fine by me."

I stifle a snigger, then my stomach growls.

He groans then winks. "Woman, I wish you had an insatiable appetite for other things besides food."

"Oh, I do, but food almost always wins out, especially when you're cooking."

He raises an eyebrow. "Are you using me?"

I give him a playful push. "Absolutely."

He shakes his head as he pulls out the eggs, cheese, veggies, and the pan. "I should have never told you I could cook."

"I'm worth it, aren't I?" I wiggle on the counter for emphasis.

He clears his throat and shifts the apron. "You better believe it. And that butt of yours is mighty fine." He slides the spatula under my thigh, making me almost fly off the counter.

"Stop it. The health inspector would not approve of using utensils in such a manner."

His eyebrows start wiggling again. "Nonsense. I'll lick it off before I use it again."

Heat races up my neck, and my head feels like it's on fire. "Will you stop doing that and get to work?"

"Yes, ma'am—now that I'm completely awake and it's completely obvious I'm not getting any."

"You got some earlier, and if I have to remind you, then I must not be doing something right."

He chuckles, and a faint blush runs across his face. "I guess I should say I'd like an encore performance."

"Not to kill the mood, but did I mention I kind of, sort of, agreed for us to meet up with my parents today for brunch?"

He flips the omelet in the pan. "You're funny."

"I'm serious. My mom wants to meet you."

He freezes. "Your mom? No. Maybe some other time way down the road."

My heart sinks. "Tommy, please."

He shakes his head. "Don't let me stop you from going."

"No! I can't."

Tommy takes a step backward and bumps into the refrigerator.

I take a deep breath. "My parents are always on my case about my boyfriends. I'd really like to show them I can attract a decent guy."

He runs a hand through his hair. "Okay, fine. I'll go."

Hope springs eternal. "Really?"

"What do I have to lose?"

He may not want me to answer that question.

"I had planned on going to my parents' house in the afternoon," he says.

"I'd love to come too. You go with me—I'll go with you."

He stares at the ceiling. "We like to whip out the board games. You've been warned." He slips my omelet from the pan onto a plate. He then hands me the plate and a fork.

My first bite of anything this man makes is like the first kiss: sweet, satisfying, and leaving me longing for more. I lean back, close my eyes, and groan.

"You all right?"

"I want to marry this omelet."

Tommy's low, sexy chuckle warms me more than the meal. "Glad you like it."

He wipes a crumb from my chin with his thumb.

"Seriously the best omelet I've ever had." I stuff my mouth full of another bite of the omelet. My mother would be *tsking* me from sunup to sundown for talking with my mouth full. She would also despise the fact that I'm sitting on the kitchen counter, wearing nothing but a skimpy tank top and panties. "Thanks for going with me."

He tosses ingredients into the pan to start making his omelet. "You're welcome, but I thought we were still in a more casual phase."

Ouch. I thought we were a little further along than that, but I guess I'm wrong again. "You don't understand my mother. She keeps trying to set me up with Isaac of all people."

He howls with amusement. They met a few times when Isaac stopped by the ICU waiting room to check on Darla, so Tommy realizes that's a lost cause.

"Not funny, but to get her off that train of thought, I mentioned I was already seeing someone." I latch on to his apron and drag him close to me. "I'm so sorry. You don't have to go if you don't want to. I don't want to. I'll make up some excuse like I usually do."

He shakes his head. "It's fine as long as they don't serve me up as the main course. By the way, this cooktop is sa-weet."

"Glad you like it."

"Love it. Why did you buy such high-end appliances if you don't cook?"

I shrug. "When I bought the place, my parents insisted on the best. You'll find out soon enough how they are about everything." *Maybe they will think he's the best too?*

He chuckles. "Are they that scary?"

"Yeah, pretty much."

He tilts his head to the side and crosses his arms over his chest. A near-naked man wearing a sexy apron in my kitchen makes it difficult to concentrate. "You want it to appear like we're still at the hand-holding stage, don't you?"

I smile, and by the way he chuckles under his breath, he knows my answer before I reply. "Let's do a meet-and-greet this time. I'm sure they'll love you."

"Let's hope so, because I'm not so good with parents other than my own." He cages me in, resting an arm on each side of me. Usually, he's an open book, but right now, he's not giving me anything non-verbal.

I take his arm and guide him closer to me. "Mom and Dad can be cold and..." I can't find the right word. "They aren't mean, and they certainly aren't unforgiving. But they are different." I stare into Tommy's light-green eyes, and my heart grows bigger. "They are more corporate. Everything has a purpose to move the company forward. There's not a lot of time for uncalculated decisions."

He slides his arms around my waist and scoots me toward him until I'm on the edge of the counter. I wrap my arms around his muscular neck. He kisses me then whispers in my ear. "I understand. Baby steps. That's completely cool with me."

"Yeah. Baby steps."

He lifts my hands to his lips and kisses them again. I grin and remember yesterday's events. The niece Tommy never knew about was near death, but the latest reports show great improvements. I'm so happy for Theo and Darla. They deserve to be together with their healthy daughter. *Time for a change of subject.*

"Stella's going to be okay."

Tommy holds me closer. "Isn't it a miracle?"

Stroking the back of his head, I say, "Yep, and you haven't really even met her yet. Trust me, you're going to love her. I've never seen myself as a mom, so she's the closest thing to a daughter I'll probably ever get."

The guys I attract haven't been good daddy material until now.

He scrunches his forehead. "You never fathom what the future holds." He pulls away from me with a deer-in-headlights expression then holds his hands out in front of him in a defensive move. "The very, very distant future."

I pretend I'm going to pinch his side, but I take his face in my hands instead and kiss him on the tip of his nose.

He plants another smooch on my cheek. "The biggest problem with meeting your folks is I'm sure after one glimpse, they'll realize I'm shagging their daughter and loving every minute of it."

That's what I'm afraid of. They'll assume I've done it again, that I've met another guy and fallen head over heels for him before I've had time to get to know the real person. And the last thing I want them to do is to scare off Tommy before we get a chance to move past the "casual phase."

CHAPTER SEVEN
Tommy

Theo leads me away from the crowd surrounding his daughter in her hospital room and away from Darla and Shelby, who are giggling like two teenagers. Shelby hands Stella a stuffed teddy bear wearing a pink tutu.

"I wanted to thank you for lighting a fire under my butt," Theo whispers. "You made me realize Darla didn't do anything to hurt me. She did want me to know about Stella."

I slap him on the back, making him stumble forward. I forget that even though he's my older brother, he's much smaller than me. With the stress of Stella's health and his own issues with diabetes, I could have knocked him down with that simple brotherly backslap.

"You'd do the same for me."

He gazes into my eyes, and his well up with tears again. "I'm so sorry for all the things I said to you."

Last week, he spewed some awful accusations my way and even implied that I tried to keep him from the truth. In his right mind, he would have never been so cruel. He's my brother, so I forgave him immediately. That's how we roll.

I squeeze his shoulder. "I don't even remember it."

"You okay?" he asks.

That's my brother, the doctor and the never-off-the-clock preacher's kid. "Yeah, sure. I'm good. I guess so. Why?" I shouldn't have opened the window into this conversation. The only thing worse than talking about my feelings with Theo is doing it with our older sister, Jennifer. She's the mother hen of the group.

Theo scans the room and takes in all the commotion. "Something is a tad off with you."

I shrug and paint a big plastic smile on my face. "I'm good."

He furrows his brow. "Don't close yourself off again, please?"

I shake my head. "I'm good. It's just that…" I peek over at Shelby. We stare at each other and, even though we're surrounded by my family, we share a private moment that says we would rather be jumping each other's bones than be at the hospital. "I'm, uh, meeting her parents today."

Theo's eyebrows rise into his hairline. "Ahh. That should be fun. Are you two that serious already?"

Before answering, I mull over his question. Shelby and I don't seem serious. We're having fun, maybe too much fun, and I prefer to stay at this stage for a very long time. Theo bumps me on the shoulder to pull me back into reality.

"I like her a lot. I realize it's fast and all, but…" Shelby grins from across the room and gives me a cute finger wave that I absolutely adore. "I…"

"You're falling for her, aren't you?"

My neck hurts from whipping my head around so fast to face my brother. "What? No way. Of course not." I roll my eyes, but his words stick in my head. "I don't do love."

Theo raises an eyebrow at my protest. "I loved Darla, and I only spent a few hours with her. She ruined me for everyone else. Years later, I still couldn't move on." He smiles so big, I can see his molars. "And then there she was again. If it's meant to be, it will be. I'm living proof."

All this lovey-dovey talk makes it hard for me to breathe. "Does Darla have you reading romance novels now?"

Theo chuckles then clears his throat. "No. At least, not yet."

"Dude, you are so whipped already. Anyway, Shelby says her parents are pretty stiff. She doesn't want to tell them I've moved in with her already."

Theo's eyes couldn't get any wider. "I'm going to pretend I didn't hear that."

"Thanks, but it's got me wondering." I scan the room to make sure Shelby isn't close enough to hear our conversation. "I really like Shelby, but maybe... you know me."

Theo shoves his hands in his pockets. "Moving in was too soon?"

I exhale. "I don't understand why I thought that was a good idea. Maybe I wanted something real before she figured out I transform into a grade A jerk when I'm in school. And I don't have much money." I lower my voice. "I get the feeling her family's pretty well-off. We're definitely not cut from the same cloth."

Theo pats my back. "You're well-off in other areas." He flicks the side of my head for emphasis. "Besides, you've got to finish school, right?"

That's the other wrinkle. I've spent the last four years in an advanced program that I don't like. Actually, I abhor it, and I've done it because everyone calls me the smart kid. *Tommy's going to make something of himself. Tommy's the genius of the family.* God, I can't stand that label. And every day I spend working on that PhD puts me one step closer to anger-management classes, hence the "pause" I took to spend the summer with Theo. I don't handle pressure well, so I close myself off to keep from angering other people, which usually makes things worse. In the past few weeks, I've even spent time researching other programs of study, but nothing I've found sounds any better.

I stare down at my shoes then clear my throat. "Would it be so awful if I didn't finish?"

When I finally get the courage to peek at my brother, his mouth is open. Ever since Theo was diagnosed with diabetes at the young age of seven, he's wanted to be a doctor, and he worked hard to make it happen. He never wavered. I made one insignificant comment one time about liking math and science, and my teachers jumped on it, encouraging me to pursue engineering. They told my parents that with my high IQ, I could go anywhere I wanted for college. After that, it was all anyone would talk about. Teachers and my parents assumed I was as in love with the idea as much as they were. And since I didn't have anything else in mind as a backup plan, I went along with it.

I graduated from Georgia Institute of Technology and headed straight to Boston after that. My parents enjoy telling people they have one son who is an MD and another working on a PhD. After all they've done for me over the years, I can't let them down, so I will continue to suck it up and do what everyone believes I should do.

The only person who comprehends how much I loathe my life is Heather. Even though she has the policy that the whole world can kiss her butt, she's kept my secret all these years. She came to visit me in Boston every chance she got and gave me the same "figure out what makes you happy" lecture. If it weren't for our daily phone calls, I may have even been in worse shape than I am. She was the one who found me that time I spiraled out of control last year. I'm pretty sure Theo and my big sister, Jennifer, may be aware of my lack of enthusiasm, but they've stayed quiet, which is a huge undertaking for Jennifer, and probably will until they hear it from me.

Theo stares. It takes me a moment to realize he said something because I forgot he was there. "I said, you're so close to finishing."

His response is typical. I glance toward Shelby, who gives me a *come hither* expression that makes my knees weak. I run my hand through my hair to tamp down that anxious feeling bubbling in the pit of my stomach.

I look back at Theo and plaster on a fake smile like I always do. "Yeah, you're right. It would be foolish to quit after all this time."

He squeezes my shoulder. "No need to make a hasty decision."

I'm not sure how I got to this place, and I'm even more confused about how I'm going to get out of it. I am certain Shelby would never want me if she knew the real me. She sees someone who is enamored with her every move, which I am, but I'm so spineless, I can't even stare at myself in the mirror.

A burst of excitement, otherwise known as my two sisters, rush into Stella's hospital room. Their arms are filled with stuffed animals, and they smother Theo with hugs and kisses. Heather tugs on my sleeve to break my blank stare. "Are you okay?" she mouths.

I shrug, but she's not stupid. She may be the runt of the litter, but she's pretty darn perceptive, especially when it comes to me. On the inside, I'm falling apart again, and I don't feel like there is anything I can do to stop it. That squeezing feeling has started, and no amount of calming deep breaths is going to help this time. Once Shelby sees the chink in the armor she presumes I wear, she'll be glad I'll be going back to Boston. But I will be miserable again.

CHAPTER EIGHT
Shelby

My feet would move faster if I were running in a swimming pool. If it weren't for Tommy's gentle nudges, I would never make it across the restaurant parking lot. Meeting my folks for brunch is the last place I want to be. A meal with them is stressful on a good day, and this is not going to be a good day at all. Bringing the new guy to brunch is going to set off a new storm of questions that I don't want to answer, and I certainly don't want to scare off Tommy.

Mom's already asked how long we've been a couple. *Not very long.* Dad will surely ask what Tommy does for a living. *He doesn't have a job.* That's going to go over like a lead balloon. It won't matter that he's got a very good reason for being without a job. They'll figure he should already be out of school and making tons of money. And I'll stick a knife in my eye if my father asks Tommy how his stock portfolio is doing.

At least they won't complain about how he's dressed. He fills out his khakis and light-green polo quite well. If I have any luck, maybe Dad will invite him to play a round of golf. No, wait. That could be an even worse disaster. I should have come alone. It's too soon for them to meet Tommy. Next month's brunch would have been a much better idea.

"Sugar, are you okay?"

I snap back to reality. Tommy's beautiful eyes remove all the tension in my neck by gaping at me like I hung the moon.

He grins, and all of my stress melts away. "Can I hold your hand, or is that a big no-no?"

I latch on to his hand as if my life depends on his strength. "I don't care if it is. Let's go get this over with."

He tugs on the end of my ponytail, understanding that when my stress level rises, so does my ponytail. I squeeze his hand as we wind our way to the private dining section of Sea Salt, my mother's favorite restaurant. She likes it because it brings a taste of the sea to Nashville. Every time we eat there, she raves about the gorgeous blocks of pink sea salt lining the back of the bar. I was always impressed how they constructed the restaurant out of reclaimed wood. Mother would never eat there if she knew that.

Mom and Dad are sitting at their usual corner table already. Mom sips her Teatulia white tea, no doubt, and Dad gulps down his coffee as he checks his phone, probably seeing if he's made money today.

"Daddy."

My fake enthusiasm goes unnoticed by my parents. Dad stands, wearing his perfectly polished Armani suit, and Mom rises right behind him. Her lips form a tight, thin line. Her eyes scrutinize everything from my ponytail to my capri pants. I can't remember the last time I had a pedicure, but Mom will be sure to point out that I'm overdue. *Dang it.* I should have worn a sundress and sandals.

"Hello, Shelby Lynn," Dad says.

I glance back at Tommy, and he winks. If he realizes what's good for him, he'll never call me that. My mom loved the movie *Steel Magnolias,* but my dad had a crush on the country singer with the same name. I give Dad air kisses on both cheeks.

"Mom and Dad, this is Tommy. Tommy, these are... my parents."

Silence. No one moves or says anything for fear of toppling this social Jenga situation to the ground. I'm not sure what to do next. This is where my mother usually turns up her nose like she smells natural gas. Finally, Tommy sticks his hand out, and after too many beats of hesitation, Dad shakes it. My mother sinks back into her seat, and like obedient pups, we follow suit.

"So, remind me. When did you two meet?" Leave it to Mom to get right down to business. She just dives right into the interrogation.

The waiter pours water into our glasses, and Tommy guzzles his down. If he's anything like me, he's wishing his drink was something much stronger.

"Oh," I say as I search for Tommy's eyes, but he trains them on his water glass. "About a month, right?"

Tommy peeks over in my direction. "Sounds about right." His gaze darts around the restaurant, possibly searching for the nearest exit. I know I am.

Mom makes a *harrumph* noise as she sips from her teacup. She places the cup back on the saucer and folds one hand over the other. "Oh, really?"

"Mom, I told you about him."

She sighs. "Yes, but I didn't believe it was *that* sudden."

Dad places a hand on Mom's arm. "Honey, it's not that—"

She groans and takes another sip of tea. "And it's appropriate for us to meet someone who you've fancied for less than a month?"

I roll my eyes. "You invited us, remember?"

She places her teacup down and folds her hands in her lap. "You made it sound like you've been dating for a while." Mom turns to Dad and stage-whispers, "She's done this before, and we all remember how that ended."

I cringe when she does that. What's worse is when she reminds me every day of my failures in the romance department, especially with the one guy whose name I don't even want to pass through my brain.

My mother has a way of making me feel like I'm four years old and she's just caught me drawing on the wall. By the way, that artistic creation was one of my first masterpieces. I was crushed when she had it painted over. Even at that age, I knew what my mother valued the most: her possessions.

Tommy clears his throat. "Actually, I'm glad you invited me. I've been wanting to meet the wonderful people Shelby can't stop talking about." He reaches for my hand, which I am more than happy for him to take.

Dad chokes on his coffee. "Really?" I guess he isn't as clueless as I assumed. He sees right through that fib.

"Yes. You have a remarkable daughter."

Mom lifts her teacup again and peers over it. "Hmm, so what do you do?"

Here we go. The only thing that matters to my parents is what job and, of course, how much money a person makes. They don't care about Tommy's interests or where he grew up. They cut to the chase about what's important to them.

"Oh." He peeks over in my direction.

I grin, hoping he'll continue and be as honest as possible.

"Well, I don't have a job."

Crap. He wasn't supposed to say it like that. I mean, it's true, but it's not for lack of incentive.

Mom slams her teacup down on the table, rattling the saucer. "Excuse me? No job?" She side-eyes me. "Shelby, seriously. This is worse than the drummer."

I hold my hands out to defend Tommy. "Mom, it's not like he's been screwing around."

Mom gasps.

Dad's stern face becomes even colder than usual. "Shelby, your language."

I roll my eyes. "He's in school, for crying out loud." Tommy cringes for some reason, like being in school is worse than not having a job. "He's at University of Boston."

My parents stare at each other then back at me. I dare not brave a glance at Tommy to catch his reaction.

Dad motions for Tommy to continue.

I squeeze Tommy's hand, and I'm not sure if it's some sort of solidarity gesture or to keep my hand from shaking. When he doesn't answer, I do for him. "He's almost finished with his PhD."

His head is down, and he's completely enthralled with the hand-woven, hemstitch napkin in his lap.

"What field?" Dad asks.

Tommy peers up and takes a deep breath. "Uh, computer science and biomedical engineering."

It would have been easier for him to say we were engaged. For some reason, he doesn't like to talk about school. The only reason I know anything about it is because Darla told me.

Dad sits up taller. "Okay, son, tell me more."

He called Tommy "son." He doesn't even call his own son, "son."

Tommy shrugs. "It's no big deal, really."

Dad's eyebrows shoot up. "No big deal? With a degree like that, you could start your own company. Do you hold any patents yet?"

"No, sir." Tommy's hand gives mine a vice-like squeeze. My fingers are going to be a mangled mess before the appetizers are served, if my nerves make it that far.

My dad continues his line of questioning. "Do you own a 3-D printer?"

Tommy shakes his head. Red splotches creep up his neck toward his face. "No. They're very expensive, but my major professor has one in the lab, so I use that one from time to time."

Dad's mouth twitches. I recognize that expression. This cannot be good. "Are you telling me you don't want a 3-D printer?"

My head bops back and forth as I watch the conversation like I'm at a tennis match. My mother smiles like she just caught an insect in her web. That's a far cry from only a moment ago.

Tommy seems to shrink in height with each question Dad lobs his way. My parents have that impact on people, but it's usually when they don't approve. Dad's Cheshire cat grin is an obvious sign he approves. I imagine the marriage-business contract being printed on that 3-D contraption as we speak.

Tommy fiddles with his napkin. "I guess I want one. They're pretty cool, that's for sure, but like I said, a good one is pricey."

"How much?"

I give Tommy an expression that conveys my mental shrug. I have no idea what this is all about.

"Oh, I'm not sure," he says. "Maybe five grand. But hopefully, the prices will start to drop as the demand increases."

Dad whips out his checkbook from his suit pocket. "What did you say your last name was?"

"I'm sorry. What?" Tommy and I ask at the same time.

Dad's eyes flick up to meet Tommy's. "Your last name. So I can write you a check."

Tommy blinks.

My mouth drops open. "Dad, I don't think—"

"Anything to advance your career. Consider it a scholarship. Last name?"

Tommy chuckles while giving me the side-eye. He now understands my angst. "That's very generous, sir, but I'm afraid I'll have to pass. Thank you for the offer, though."

Impressive. Tommy's been around my father for less than ten minutes, and he's already showing more of a spine than I have ever been able to grow.

Dad shrugs and puts his wallet back. Then his fingers fly over his phone screen. He grins at whatever he's pulled up. "Do you work in David Phelps's lab?"

"No, sir."

Dad scrolls through his phone. "Jacob Gentry?"

Tommy shakes his head.

"Jo Alexander?"

Tommy's Adam's apple bobs up and down as his face pales. "Yes, sir."

Dad smiles, not noticing that Tommy went from calm to ghostly white in less than a minute. Dad is actually enjoying this. I stuff a roll into my mouth in hopes of choking on it. Maybe needing the Heimlich maneuver would stop this conversation, which Tommy is clearly not enjoying any more than I am.

My mom smirks at me. "Shelby Lynn, I was wrong about this one. You shouldn't let him get away. He has so much potential." Mom's stage-whispering needs a little work. I can't believe she really said that in front of Tommy. She just met him, and she's gone from giving me the stink eye to talking about snagging him in my web. I sneak a peek at Tommy, who seems more interested in chugging from his water glass.

As soon as his glass touches his lips, I blurt out, "Actually, we're engaged."

Tommy's water gets stuck in his throat, causing him to cough uncontrollably.

Mom backs up in her chair and inspects her silk blouse for water spots. Then she motions for a waiter. "Are you all right?"

With a beet-red face, Tommy swallows and does his best to take in a deep breath. Dad pats him on the back like he used to do to me when I was a kid.

Holy magnolias. I can't believe I said that. The things I'll say to get my mother's approval.

When Tommy regains his ability to breathe and the waitstaff is assured he isn't choking on food, Mom jumps up and runs around the table toward me. Tommy's face is as red as a tomato. My mother hovers over me, smothering me with hugs, and I don't hear her words. I feel as if I'm underwater. Dad gives Tommy backslaps and so many "sons," I want to puke.

"Tell her," Mom says to Dad.

"Tell me what?" This cannot be good.

Tommy and I stand. Through gritted teeth, Tommy mumbles, "Shelby, fix this."

Dad pulls out his checkbook again and begins to write out two checks. He hands them over to me, and I stumble backward. Tommy catches me before I hit the floor.

"Dad, I have a job. I don't need this."

"Your 'job' would never pay for the wedding you deserve. And it's tradition for the father of the bride to pay. So please, take this. It's a gift we've been waiting to give you."

"Hoping to give you for a very long time," Mom interjects.

Thanks for emphasizing the "very" long time.

Dad waves her off before he clutches Tommy's hand. "One check is for your wedding, and one is for your honeymoon, but spend it however you want. It's made out to Shelby since you didn't give me your last name."

Feeling light-headed, I shrink down into my chair and try to hand the checks back to Dad. He holds his hands behind his back, so I give them to Tommy. He scrunches his eyebrows together as he tries to force the checks back to my dad. Dad shakes his head. It's like we're playing a financial hot-potato game.

"Sir, this is generous, but it's not nec—" He peeks down at all the zeros behind the ten on one check and the fifty on the other. His legs buckle, and he stumbles into his seat next to me. Tommy's mouth is open like he's a fish out of water, green around the gills. "I'm going to hurl."

CHAPTER NINE
Tommy

My lungs burn from lack of oxygen. After Shelby said the E word, my autonomic nervous system forgot how to convert oxygen into carbon dioxide. My stomach churns, so instead of eating, I push the food around my plate and keep chugging water, praying the waitress will bring me a shot of whiskey, anything to get me through the most uncomfortable meal of my life.

"Your father and I got married in June, but it may be too hot for a garden wedding. I'm just throwing that out there."

Make it stop.

I place my fork down and give Shelby a stern expression. If she's not going to set them straight, I will. "Actually, Mrs. Williams, the truth is we're not—"

"Mother, we're not ready to set a date yet."

My dentist will need to put crowns on all my molars after this meal. I bob my head at the appropriate times throughout the rest of the meal and say as little as possible. Her parents shower me with so many hugs and kisses when we leave that I'll need a real shower when I get home.

Shelby guides me to her car and pushes me into the passenger seat. After she runs around and slides behind the wheel, she pats my shoulder. "Breathe, Tommy."

I try to suck in a breath, but my internal organs don't want to cooperate. "Are you kidding me?" I plunge the heels of my hands against my eyes. "Of all things, why did you have to say that?"

"It was the first thing I thought of that would change the course of the conversation."

I huff. "Oh, it changed it all right. That was super fun." My voice gets high and girly for emphasis. "We'll have to do that again sometime."

She collapses over the steering wheel. "Argh. Now do you see what I mean? They suck all the life out of the room."

A chuckle erupts from my mouth, even though I am not amused at all. "Just so you understand, that was *not* a baby step. Jeez, Shel."

"I know, I know. It just spewed from my mouth before I knew what I was saying." She mumbles something under her breath then says, "I'm sorry." Her eyes brighten. "At least they took it well."

"You're not helping. Taking it well is an understatement. They took it better than I did." I lean over in order to increase my lung capacity. A bead of sweat trickles down my spine.

She points a finger at me. "Now, that part shocked even me."

"Only because of my 'potential.'" I despise using air quotes, but it seems appropriate this time.

She stares at the steering wheel. "I said I was sorry."

I snort. "If you were really sorry, you'd march back in there and clean up this mess this instant." I point at the front door of Sea Salt, where her parents are exiting.

Shelby cranks the car and speeds out of the parking lot. "I realize we hardly know each other."

That's an understatement.

"Mom will be back to razzing me about my hair tomorrow, but give me one day where she isn't disappointed in me."

My hand taps on the armrest like I'm sending an SOS in Morse code. "Thanks for dragging me down the road of disappointment with you. Did you ever think for a second that she'll never take a liking to me after we tried to trick her?"

Sometimes, I can be such a jerk. I realize Shelby was trying hard to impress her parents for some reason, and when they took a shine to me, she ran with it. I groan. "You have to fix this."

Tears well in her eyes, making me feel like a total schmuck.

I take her hand in mine and kiss it. "One thing you need to learn about me—book smarts doesn't make me wise in these situations. I'm sorry. I have honestly never been engaged before, so I'm not sure how to act."

She swipes a stray tear away. "I'll fix this."

"Fix it now. Today."

"Yes. I promise."

When I rest my head back against the car seat, a slow chuckle bubbles out of my mouth. "I got to hand it to you. Your dad is a piece of work. I was tongue-tied when he offered to buy me a 3-D printer." If I enjoyed my stifling career path even the tiniest, I would have been all over that offer.

She belts out a hysterical round of giggles. "I don't even understand what that is. Does the image jump off the page at you?"

Adorable. "Not exactly."

At a traffic light, she asks, "Why did you get all stiff when I mentioned you were in graduate school?"

My knuckles are white as I grip the door handle. When we drive down Hillsboro Road toward my childhood home, I say, "It's not something I like to talk about."

"Why?"

She just won't drop it.

"I just don't."

She pats my arm. "Oh, I can see why. It's right up there with being a convicted felon and a drug dealer as the three most embarrassing details of a person's life. Dad's personal favorite is rock star."

First her mother mentions something about a drummer, now Shelby says this. Maybe I don't want to know anything about her past because I can't compete with fame. "No chance in that. I'll stick to computers. They don't have the good drugs, but they are pretty dependable."

She stares straight ahead and juts her chin up high. "Your education is much more impressive than some cocky, famous person who has a different girl in every city."

I let out a sigh. It sounds like her last boyfriend was a jerk, and even though she shouldn't have flat-out lied to her parents, I guess I see why. When she compares me to whoever that old flame was, my anger dissolves. But it's hard for other people to understand. As soon as anyone finds out I'm working on my PhD, they start throwing out the word genius. I can't stand being called the G word. I'm smart, but I'm a chump compared to the people at MIT. I would rather be called a dozen other things than be smacked with that label, and it weighs about two and a half gigatons on my chest. Some days, it is all people see, and it smothers me.

"I don't like to be pigeonholed into being one thing. There's more to me than my cerebellum." I tap the side of my head for emphasis.

She winks. "Damn straight."

The rest of the way to my parents' home, we ride in silence. I love the fact that we don't always have to be talking to fill the silence. It's a comfortable quiet that I could get used to. Her parents are going to hate me after this fiasco, and it's not even my fault.

"I really am sorry I blurted that out," she says. "I will fix this."

"Your idea of baby steps is more like one giant leap for mankind."

She groans. "Tell me about it. They liked you so much, which, by the way, has never happened. I figured I should take advantage of the moment."

"I get it, but wow, do they always go willy-nilly with the checkbook?"

Shelby shrugs. "Pretty much, but never to that extent. Holy crap. I'd never spend fifty grand on a wedding. I couldn't live with myself if I wasted that much money on one day." She shivers.

Her words are a relief. I wonder if she realizes how many people can be fed with that amount of money. But it's her money, and she can do whatever she wants with it.

"Glad you feel the same as I do."

Her hand squeezes mine. "Besides, I don't want a big wedding. Just a few friends and your dad marrying us is all I would ever need." She gasps. "I mean, when the time comes. If it comes. I, uh... I'll shut up now."

"Sounds like you're getting cold feet. Now that you kind of proposed to me in front of your parents..."

She smirks at me.

"You weren't assuming we were getting hitched anytime soon, were you?" If she was, I might pass out for sure. I have too much pressure on me as it is.

She gives my arm a playful pinch. "Do I sense some hesitation?"

Yes! "I'm a guy, so of course." *Good deflection, Tommy.* "It goes against all that's good and pure in a male."

"Whatever, Mr. Guy Code. But, no, of course not. I hardly know you. We'll talk about that when you finish school. That is if you haven't gotten tired of me by then."

Oh, thank God.

She taps her fingers on my thigh. "How much longer do you have?"

"I'm not sure. Two years at least. It all depends on my research." There goes that anvil sitting on my chest again, reducing my ability to breathe.

"I can trust you to move all the way to Boston without me, right?" Her eyes dart over to me then back to the road. "I can trust you in Beantown without my eagle eye watching your every move?"

I stare at the roof of the car and wait a beat before I answer if for no other reason than to make her squirm. "Well..."

She smacks me on the shoulder.

"Ow! I'm kidding. Of course. I'm either asleep or in the lab." I stare out the window. Bile rushes up my throat at the thought of school. "Can we talk about something else?" All this talk about Boston and the lab has my nerves on edge.

"You're like a clam about school. I don't get it."

No one does.

"It's just school. A means to an end. I really wish you wouldn't harp on it."

"Oookay. How about, are you going to whip up a tasty treat when we get to your folks' house?"

Thank goodness for the change in conversation. "That would be an affirmative."

"Woo-hoo."

"I gave Mom the list of ingredients yesterday. I'm making my world-famous Jack Daniels brownies."

"You put Jack Daniels in your brownies?"

"Yep. It gives them a bit of a kick."

She nods. "I bet it does, and we both need it after our lovely brunch with my folks. Are you going to make me play Risk?"

I cover my chest with my hand and suck in a fake gasp. "That's not your favorite game?"

She shakes her head. "It's nobody's favorite game." Her voice drops three octaves and she adds, "The game of world domination."

My hand finds hers, and I bring it up to my lips. "See? What's not to love?"

"I'm sorry, sweetie, but I've got to side with Heather on this one. It's too complicated to be fun."

"You're siding with my baby sister?"

She grins as she enters my parents' neighborhood. "Yeah."

"The fake wedding is off."

She sticks out her bottom lip, and I want to eat it. "Aww, please?"

I growl as we pull into my parents' driveway, and the tension rolls off of me before I get out of the car. If it wouldn't be too weird to be in my late twenties and still living with my parents, I would hide in their basement forever. I don't need to grow up. There's no need for graduate school, no need for real life.

Shelby's eyebrows waggle up and down. "Hey. Now that I've let the cat out of the bag, we can tell your folks too."

"Haven't you done enough damage for one day?"

She sticks her tongue out.

"Three weeks, sugar. We met three weeks ago."

She points a finger at me. "Almost four."

I throw my hands in the air. "Oh, in that case, we are behind schedule."

She rolls her eyes then nibbles her bottom lip. "I've never met anyone like you."

"Shelby Lynn, are you proposing to me?"

She kisses me on the cheek. "No, of course not."

I really like her, but I'm nowhere near ready to go so far as putting a ring on her finger, even if I could afford one. I'm not sure if I'll ever be ready for that type of commitment. But when I gaze into her big brown eyes, I get lost and never want to find my way out. However, if we were engaged, even on a pretend level, it could solve some other problems. Those problems are waiting for me in Boston, mainly a certain female. I hope Hazel finally got the hint that it's over.

I kiss Shelby's soft lips. "Whenever you do propose, you have to get down on one knee. I'm old-fashioned."

She gives me a playful shove. "You beat all."

I shrug. "Okay, then the fake wedding is off."

She shakes her head and takes my hand as we wind our way up the sidewalk. "No way, mister. You're stuck with me."

I slide my hands up to cup her face. "You might be sorry you got stuck with me." My lips find hers.

She pulls back and focuses on her feet. "So, we're back to friends with benefits, right?"

Oh yeah. I like the sound of that. With a wink, I say, "Just don't blurt out any news about the 'benefits' part to my preacher father, and we'll be good. I mean, they all get that we're seeing each other, but I'm hoping they're all really naïve and haven't figured out anything else."

"Got it. And as soon as I get home, I'll call Mom and tell her the truth. We are in no way, shape, or form engaged."

The door bursts open, and my mother—the hippie lawyer chick—barrels down the sidewalk, her arms open wide. She must still be riding high from the news about little Stella's good health report.

"I just heard the engagement news."

Shelby and I stare at each other, our jaws dropping to the ground. Nashville is a small big city, but I'm not sure how she found out. I can't imagine our moms being in the same social circles, let alone knowing each other well enough to exchange phone numbers. But somehow, the faux genie is out of the bottle.

Mom grabs me and hugs us both at the same time. I sneak a peek over at Shelby, who seems like she can't breathe any better than I can.

"Uh, news? There's no news. Nope. Not at all. Right, Shelby?" I beg with my eyes for Shelby to correct my mother.

She wrings her hands, avoiding eye contact with me. "Nope. Nothing. Not sure what you mean."

Mom waves off our answers as she drags us up the sidewalk. "Renee just called me and told me the good news."

Shelby's eyes bug out of her head. "My mother called you?"

My mom pats her cheek. "I didn't realize you were Daniel and Renee's daughter. We go way back. Your mother has a gift for organizing charity events."

Son of a...

"Mom—"

"Now don't worry about not telling us sooner. I understand you wanted to ask Daniel's permission first before you announced it to the world."

I back up from my mother. "I didn't ask for anyone's permission to do anything."

Mom belly laughs and flips her gray braid over her shoulder. "Okay, whatever your generation does. You two just met, but it seems like my kids fall in love in a heartbeat, so it's not too much of a surprise." Mom's eyes fill with tears, and she sniffles. "And with all the stress with my little granddaughter... Let's just say we deserve some happiness."

I stare at Shelby, my eyes wide. I mouth, "Help me."

My mother likes to act strong for the family, but she hasn't slept a full night since Stella got sick. She deserves to ride this wave of happiness for a day, but only for a day. Besides, Shelby needs to squirm a little too. If I have to be under the microscope with her folks, she deserves to feel the heat with mine.

Shelby throws her hands in the air in surrender. She started this, and she can end it, but she chooses not to. All she does is take me by the arm and drag me toward the house. But then Shelby screeches on the brakes. "Mrs. Edwards, I forgot something in the car. We'll meet you inside in a jiffy."

Mom gives her another kiss on the cheek before scooting toward the front door. "Take all the time you need, Shelby Lynn. Heather and Jennifer are inside, beating up on Matt in a brutal game of Uno. I'll do my best to hold your news in so you can tell them in person."

That's just peachy. Heather and Jen are going to see right through this farce. I'm not sure how I got myself into this situation, and I certainly can't fathom how I'll get out of it. I tilt my head to the side and stare at Shelby.

She cringes. "Oops."

That's an understatement.

CHAPTER TEN
Shelby

As soon as Mrs. Edwards goes inside the house, I lead Tommy back to my car.

He leans over the hood, almost hyperventilating. The hair falls into his eyes and floats up and down with each exhale. "She believes we're engaged too."

I have no idea what to say that won't make it worse, so I pace in front of the car and pull my ponytail tight. The right thing to do would have been to set her straight, but I couldn't say the words. His mom acted more excited than mine did, and that's saying a lot.

"Let's examine this for a second. We like each other. I mean, being in a relationship wasn't a big stretch for your mom. She's seen us together at the hospital, so it's a positive that she's happy about this. Don't you think?" I try to channel my inner marketing skills, but even I didn't believe a word I said.

Tommy moans and pushes himself off the hood. "That's not the point. My mother has been hounding us all for grandchildren for years. Of course she's happy another of her flock is headed in that direction." He runs a hand through his hair, making it stick straight up in a sexy bedhead kind of way.

"Well, maybe now that she knows about Stella, it gets you off the hook for a while."

He gives me a death stare. "Oh no. It's only made it worse." In a mocking female voice, he says, "Now, Tommy, you want Stella to have cousins, don't you?" He shivers. "This is not good."

"Okay, for the third time, I am sorry. I didn't think this through. I am sorry our parents are under the impression we're going to get married. I am sorry you are fake engaged to me. Am I so hideous that the mere fact of being saddled with me causes you to hyperventilate?"

He rolls his eyes like my brother does when our mother goes on one of her tirades. "This has nothing to do with you."

"But it does." We have a stare down.

He places a hand on each of my shoulders and takes a deep breath. "I like you. A lot. If you don't comprehend that by now, well then, we've got bigger problems. But we are not at that stage yet. We are nowhere near ready to take that step. I mean, speaking for myself, I am not. To you... or to anyone."

My eyes drift down and focus on my shoes. "You're right. I'm an idiot, and we'll—I mean, I—will fix this."

He sighs. "Good." He takes my hand to lead me back toward the house.

"But not today."

Tommy just stops and stares at me.

I pull out my phone and open the text messages from my mother. "This is what my mother said to me yesterday. 'Your hair needs a trim, and you could use some highlights. I wish you would wear something other than yoga pants for crying out loud.' Ooh, and my favorite is this one. 'Have you gained weight?'"

Tommy's jaw drops.

"But here's what she's said to me since the big reveal. 'Sweetie, I'd love to take you shopping.' Here's another one. 'I've found the perfect place to have your engagement party.' And then, this one just came in. 'Tell Tommy welcome to the family. Love you.'" I show him my phone. "'Love you.' I cannot tell you the last time she said that to me." Tears well up in my eyes. "Please. My mother hasn't been this nice to me in years." I motion toward his parents' house. "And then... your mother hugged me like I was one of her own."

He crosses his arms over his chest. "What are you saying?"

Backing away from him, I hold out my hands in front of me. "I realize I said I would set her straight today, but can we pretend for—"

"No."

I hold up my index finger. "One day. Maybe two at the most."

"Shelby." He grits his teeth so much, his jaw clenches. "The longer you wait, the worse the fallout."

"I'll make it up to you."

He chews on the inside of his cheek, pondering my words. "How?"

I wiggle my eyebrows up and down. "Whatever you want."

One of his eyebrows quirks up. "I'm not a paid escort."

The back of my neck is so tense, I'll have to book an hour-long massage to get all the kinks worked out. "I didn't mean to make it sound that way. Just help a girl out."

"There are far easier ways to gain your mother's approval. Wear a dress she likes. Be involved in her favorite charity. Anything is easier than this."

I nibble on a fingernail. "I didn't plan this. I didn't say, 'oh, hey, there's a gorgeous, smart, and funny guy who seems to sort of like me. Let's take him to meet the folks, and while we're there, I'll lie to them, and it will feel so right. He'll be like, okay, let's really do it.'"

Tommy cracks a grin. "Breathe."

My lungs burn from lack of air, and when I take my first breath in what seems like hours, the sensation sends my head spinning. "Please go along with this."

"You didn't give me much choice."

I bounce up and down then slam into him as I wrap my arms around his neck. "Oh, thank you so much."

"But I have to tell my mother the truth tomorrow. She has nothing to do with your mama drama."

"Of course. As long as she can keep it a secret until I can drop the bomb."

The corner of his mouth twitches into a tiny smile. "So, what's our story, Shelby Lynn?"

"First, don't call me that. Second, we'll say we were so overjoyed with Theo and Darla's reunion that it just felt right."

He kisses the top of my head. "That could work, but what about the end?"

I pull back from him and scrunch my nose. "Huh?"

He peers around before he continues. "We have to end it at some point. And saying we moved too fast is too juvenile."

Now I've painted myself into a corner. "Are you saying to end the fake engagement, we have to call it quits for good?" My heart pounds out of my chest, and the chicken salad I had for brunch creeps up my esophagus.

"We'll have to break up for good or do a fake breakup or a soft pause to slow down."

My heart sinks into my stomach. "Clearly, I didn't examine this all the way through."

"Oh, what a tangled web we weave."

"No time for Shakespeare."

He grins. "Actually, it was Sir Walter Scott."

Of course he would know that.

He snaps his fingers. "I've got it. How about you didn't realize I was going back to Boston so soon, and you don't like long-distance relationships."

"When are you going back?"

He glances away and clenches his jaw.

That's an odd reaction. "Your idea might work because I really do hate that. Been there, and it sucks."

He tilts his head to the side. "The little drummer boy?"

"Ha ha. Step one is to get through today. And just so we're on the same page, it will be a fake breakup. Right?"

"Yes, but I might need a spreadsheet to keep up with what's fake and what's real."

I kiss him on the cheek. "Leave it to me."

Tommy chuckles as he takes my hand and leads me to the door. "That's how we got into this situation in the first place." He gestures to the bay window, where someone quickly closes the curtain. "Welcome to the hornet's nest. You have been warned."

He opens the door, and everyone in the house stares at us. I am about to tell a whopper of a lie to a preacher, a lawyer, Tommy's sisters, and his brother-in-law. I'm pretty sure there is a special place in hell with my name on it for being this misleading. This is a tangled web I'm weaving, and if Tommy and I get out of it unscathed, it will be a miracle.

CHAPTER ELEVEN
Tommy

Four pairs of beady eyes stare in my direction when we walk into my parents' house. Heather's squinty-eyed face gives me all the information I need. She's pissed. We tell each other everything, even yucky stuff that's happening with both of us at school.

Jen's mouth changes from open in shock to a big grin. Jen's husband, Matt, mouths "run." My guess is that Mom couldn't wait any longer to spill the beans.

I wave to my family. "What's up?"

Shelby glues herself to my side in solidarity.

Heather stalks over to me and pokes me in the chest with her bony finger. "Maybe *you* should answer that question." She glances over at Shelby. "No offense, but I'm not usually the last to get the details about my brother."

I'm two seconds from caving and telling them the truth, but I lose my courage when the blood drains from Shelby's face. Her mouth opens, but no words fall out. I slide an arm around her shoulders, and the tension subsides a bit.

"Heath Bar, be nice. Guys, we're engaged." Those are two words I never thought I would hear coming out of my mouth.

Jen tackles Shelby in a hug, towering over Shelby's much shorter frame. This is a disaster of epic proportions.

"Oh, this is so exciting." She pulls back a bit. "If you need any help planning your wedding, call me."

"Me too," Mom says.

My mouth goes dry. It is one thing to be fake engaged, but we can't be fake married. I have to draw the line somewhere.

"No, Jen."

She acts like I took her lollipop away. "Why not?"

Shelby and I stare at each other before she breaks the awkward silence. While keeping her gaze on me, she replies to Jen. "I'd love your help."

Seriously? Not helping.

My heart pounds so hard, it's going to leave bruises on my rib cage. Jen bounces up and down. Matt groans. And I'm about to pass out.

"Slow down," I tell my sister. "I've got school to worry about." No time like the present to bring it up. "As a matter of fact, I've been doing a lot of thinking—"

"Speaking of school," Mom says, "Sue Harper from the legal aid society said to tell you how proud she is of you." Mom beams. "I recognize how much you hate it when I brag, but I can't help it. Now I have even more bragging rights. This is such wonderful news. And Heather will help too when she's home from school." She jerks her head toward my baby sister. "Won't you?"

We all stare at Heather, whose expression hasn't changed one bit. She grabs my arm and yanks me away from Shelby, toward the steps leading to the second story of the house. "Excuse us for a minute."

Jen and Mom envelop Shelby in hugs while my little sister ambles up the steps, dragging me by the arm. When we get to her bedroom, she pushes me into the room and slams the door closed behind us. She gestures to her bed. "Sit. You have a lot of explaining to do, mister."

I try my best to act nonchalant by picking at a fingernail. "There's nothing to explain."

She throws her hands in the air. "I beg to differ. You're engaged?" Her voice screeches, probably sending all the dogs in the neighborhood into a tizzy.

"I believe congratulations are in order." If I'm going to lie about all this, I might as well take the opportunity to make my little sister squirm.

Heather punches me on the shoulder.

"Ow."

She slams her hands on her hips and whips her head around to sling a long strand of blond hair out of her face. "Don't mess with me. What's up?"

Rubbing my shoulder to make her think it hurts worse than it does, I stall while I rack my brain for a good answer. "Nothing."

"Do you love her?"

Crap. I can turn into a jerk when the stress of school gets to me, and I have bent the truth to my folks so much I could compete with Pinocchio, but I have never lied to my sister, and I don't plan on starting now. It wouldn't do any good anyway because I swear she has the uncanny ability to read my mind.

"Uh, yeah. I guess." It's as close to the truth as I can fathom at the moment. "Let me back up and say—"

She gasps and plops down in her desk chair. "You don't get married because you guess you love someone, especially after dating that person for only a few weeks. Jeez, you can't even say the L word."

"Theo's probably going to get married soon. Are you going to give him grief too?"

She fixes her steely eyes on me. "That's different."

"How?"

"They have a kid together." Her eyes get big. "Oh crap. Is Shelby—"

"No. God, no." I scrub my face with my hands. This fake engagement is going to be the death of me, especially where Heather is concerned. She'll never forgive me for lying to her. "Could you just go with it, please?"

She sucks in a breath, and I squeeze my eyes closed for fear she read me correctly. When I have the courage to open one eye, Heather has her mouth covered with her hands.

"It's a ruse?"

"Shh." No telling who is standing outside the door, listening to our conversation.

"Why?" She's a terrible stage whisperer.

"Shelby's parents are not like our folks. They're pretty unsatisfied with everything she does. Apparently, she's had a string of bad relationships, and I passed the smell test."

Heather sniggers. "They asked about school, didn't they?"

I try to swat her leg, but she scoots out of the way too fast. "Not funny."

"Yes, it is. It's the thing you avoid talking about the most."

"Yeah. Shelby's mom said she shouldn't let me get away, so without considering all the ramifications, Shelby blurted out that we were engaged, when we aren't at all."

Heather takes it all in and blows out a breath. "Wow."

"Yeah."

"So, when is the wedding?"

"Not funny." I stare up at the ceiling and groan. "Shelby just wants to bask in the glow of her parents' approval for a day or two, then we'll break up."

She pounces on her bed beside me, making the mattress bounce. "Can't you do all that without lying to Mom and Dad?"

I run a hand through my hair. "That was the plan, but word travels fast in this city. And then Mom was so happy. She's been so exhausted worrying about Theo. I couldn't bring myself to pop the bubble she was in."

"I get that, but do you really want to break up? I see how you are with her. You loooove her." She makes kissy sounds, and I push her, causing her to slide off the bed.

"That is not in my vocabulary."

She picks herself up off the floor. "Maybe you need a new dictionary."

I flick her nose. "Stop it, or I'll start harassing you again about the dude at University of Tennessee that picks on you like a fifth grader."

"Fair enough." She stands a little taller and takes a deep breath. "Operation Artificial Fiancée commences." She holds out a hand for me to grab, and I slap it like always. "Let's do this."

"Thanks, Heath Bar. I owe you."

She grins over her shoulder as she gallops out of the room and heads for the stairs. "And as usual, I won't let you forget it."

Chatter from the living room fills my ears as I follow Heather.

Jen smiles at my sister and me when we walk in as she slides a lock of her blond hair behind her ear. "Everything good?"

I wrap my arm around Heather's shoulders. "Yep. All good."

Heather confirms my answer and leans over to kiss Shelby's cheek. Shelby seems as if she's afraid to make any sudden moves for fear of breaking the spell we're all under.

"Welcome to the family," Heather says excitedly.

Shelby lets out a loud sigh of relief, making my mother grin.

Mom squeezes Heather around the waist. "Don't you let this little spitfire scare you," she says to Shelby. "She's nothing but a little bitty love bug."

"Aw, Mom. I have a reputation to uphold."

Matt snorts. "Not working."

Heather gives Matt the evil eye. "We need to finish whooping up on him. Don't you agree, Jen?"

"Absolutely."

I scan the room. "Where's Dad?"

Mom hitches her thumb over her shoulder. "In his study, waiting for his one-on-one with you."

I kiss Shelby's cheek. "Be back in a few," I whisper. "Have fun." I have to pry my arm out of her death grip. Now she understands how it feels.

Faint music coming from Dad's office drifts down the hallway, reminding me of his only rule: music on, come on in. I tap on the door before I open it. I'm about to lie to my father. There's a special place in hell for preachers' kids who deceive their parents.

Dad rests his head back against his chair. His bare feet are up on his desk.

"Hey, Dad."

Dad's eyes pop open, and he grins. Even with the obvious signs he's getting older—the salt-and-pepper hair and wrinkles at the corners of his eyes—it works for him. It makes him seem even more down to earth if that's possible. Sometimes I forget he's also a preacher. "Hey, kiddo. I was wondering how long it'd take you before you escaped your mother's clutches."

I slide into the chair across from him and pull back the outer string of his Newton's Cradle. I let it go, setting the balls in motion. They *tap, tap, tap* back and forth, displacing the energy.

After a long, quiet pause, I say, "I take it you've heard."

Dad chuckles. "Everyone in Davidson County heard your mother squeal when Renee called. This has been one heck of a week to say the least."

"That's for sure. Dad, Heather's already grilled me, so you don't have to lecture me too."

He plops his feet on the floor and leans across the desk. "I trust you to make your own decisions. You haven't flitted between girlfriends, so it's safe to say Shelby is someone special to you."

"She is."

"And you love her?"

My chest tightens at the thought of love, especially the "'til death do us part" kind of love. "Of course." I just lied through my teeth to my father and my pastor. *Or at least, it might be a lie.*

"Let's pray to ask for God's blessings."

I cringe. "Can we skip it and go straight to talking about your sermon?"

He waves me off. "Boring stuff."

As he prays for my engagement, I worry how everyone is going to react when we break things off. It wasn't supposed to go this far. Shelby better have an exit strategy planned, because Boston is seeming better and better with every passing moment, and that's saying a lot.

CHAPTER TWELVE
Shelby

Jennifer, the oldest of the siblings, squeals when Heather forces Matt to draw four cards. I enjoy watching the two of them gang up on poor Matt, but guilt surrounds my heart about what I've asked Tommy to do to his family. They will never forgive me if they find out this is all a hoax just because I want my mother's approval for once in my life. And I can probably kiss any chance of a real relationship with Tommy right out the window. My brother, Vaughan, will have a field day when I tell him about the situation I've put myself in. He'll be glad he's not the sibling giving our parents grief for a change.

Matt picks up his cards and shakes his head. He groans as he mulls them over. "Evil. Everyone in this family is pure evil."

Heather pats him on the back but doesn't act the least bit guilty.

I sit in a lounge chair, watching the three play. My mouth pulls into a smile as I take in all the joyful chaos. I wonder if the house is always full of chatter, playfulness, and stuff everywhere. It's so homey. My parents' house has more of a "look but don't touch" vibe to it.

"What did you mean about a one-on-one?" I ask Mrs. Edwards.

She picks up the newspaper strewn on the floor. "Roman always sits down with each of them individually to talk about the sermon he preached that day. Even if they don't make it to church, they still do it."

"That's interesting." Our family was never the "church every Sunday" kind, but I've always admired those who had that commitment.

She grins. "He started it when Jennifer was too little to sit through a full sermon. She pitched a fit when I tried to take her out of the sanctuary, so he promised they would have their very own sermon at home."

Jen blushes. "I wasn't that bad, was I?"

"Pretty much. My favorite was when Roman said in one sermon that Jesus had to die. It was complete silence in the sanctuary until this cute little three-year-old said, 'Die?' Roman answered, 'Yes. Die.' The congregation erupted into giggles."

Jen cracks up. "See? I was paying attention."

Mrs. Edwards chuckles. "So after that little incident, he decided to sit with her after every sermon and explain it in words she could understand. Then, when Theo came along, he had to be just like his big sister, and so on."

Tommy's mom takes in her flock, and I'm sure they will add Darla, then maybe me. Except I doubt that, especially if Tommy and I stage a breakup soon. They'll determine I'm flaky at best.

"Even after they went off to college, they'd call for their one-on-one sessions."

It must be nice to have conversations like that with a parent. I can't drum up one single example of a time with my dad that didn't include finances.

"Wow. Does Matt do it too?" I ask.

Matt organizes his card collection.

Mrs. Edwards nods at her son-in-law. "Oh yeah. Even when he and Jennifer were on the outs their senior year of high school, Matt would sneak over for his sessions. We tease him that's why they got married, so he could come out of the closet about his sessions."

"Mama Stella!" Matt yells. "Out of the closet means something totally different."

Heather mouths, "Oh my gosh," which makes me grin. She and Tommy resemble each other so much in the face, but she's so tiny. I would be surprised if she was over five feet tall. She's so small, I even feel like a giant standing next to her.

"Want to play?" Heather motions with her head for me to join them. "It's more fun with four."

"Sure." I take a tentative step toward the coffee table. Heather is so protective of Tommy, she could be staging a surprise attack, and no one will ever find my body. She's playing nice all of a sudden, which makes me curious about what she and Tommy discussed upstairs during their private conversation.

Matt deals the cards, and I sit on the floor between Heather and Jennifer. We play a hand of Uno, and I learn quickly that they play for blood, no mercy. The round is loud and merciless, but mostly the girls gang up on Matt.

"You chicks are mean," Matt says as he is skipped from playing a round for the third time.

Jen takes a swig from her tea glass then nods at me. "I'm serious about helping you plan your wedding."

I was hoping we would get more than five minutes without someone bringing up the wedding, but that's not my kind of luck. There is no way it's going to go that far. Soon, all of this will only be a bad memory. My head spins as I try to figure a way out of the mess I've made, but I'm coming up empty.

She holds her hands out. "Now, I realize you probably have a ton of girlfriends to help with that kind of stuff, but I've been down the wedding road. I could help you avoid some major pitfalls."

"Pitfalls?" Matt scrunches up his brow. "Getting married to me had pitfalls?"

Mrs. Edwards whistles through her teeth. "I didn't think we would ever get back to a happy mother-daughter place. I couldn't do anything without making her cry."

"It was awful." Heather pats Matt's shoulder, taking the opportunity to scan his hand of cards. "No offense to you, Matt. Jen was all Bridezilla. I am never getting married. Ever."

Matt winks at his wife. "I figured being married to you had to be easier than getting married to you."

Jen harrumphs. "Don't listen to them, Shelby. The pitfalls I'm talking about are things like finding the right photographer and florist. That kind of stuff."

Tension constricts my throat. "Mother probably already has those things arranged." It wouldn't surprise me if she's done nothing this afternoon except set up one meeting after another. I have to let her down with ease, and pronto. "We're in no hurry to get married. Heather, it's your turn." That's a terrible deflection, but if I can get them to refocus on the game, maybe my blood pressure will have time to return to normal for at least a few minutes. I hide my face behind my cards in hopes they won't notice my reluctance to talk about this touchy subject.

Heather grins deviously. "Why not?"

"Err, I, uh... I believe in long engagements." *Gah. That's so cheesy.*

Heather quirks an eyebrow. "Really? That's odd because Tommy just told me he would like to get married real soon."

Cards fly out of my hands and land all over the table and on the floor.

"Oh dear." Jen bends over to pick them up.

Matt leans over to me and whispers, "I had the same reaction."

"Not funny," Jen says with her head still buried under the coffee table as she searches for cards.

He shrugs. "I meant about my hand of cards."

Heather nudges Matt with her shoulder and takes the opportunity to sneak a peek at his cards again. "At least Tommy's not making us play Risk."

I groan.

Jennifer rolls her eyes. "So he's roped you into playing it too?"

"It's awful. I don't understand what I'm doing half the time."

Jennifer clears her throat, and Heather sits up straight. Together, they say in a deep voice, "The game of global domination."

"Hey," Tommy says from behind them. "Anybody want to play Risk?" He holds up the game box and has the cutest little-kid grin.

"No!" we all yell at the same time.

He pouts, and his shoulders sag. "Come on. It's fun."

Heather shakes her head. "It's too hard to be fun."

Tommy taps the box with his finger, and an evil twinkle shows in his eyes. "No Risk, then no brownies."

We all gape at one another. He wouldn't really hold brownies hostage. That's low.

Matt stands and, with a pained expression on his face, says, "One round."

Tommy practically skips over to the dining room table to set up the game board.

Jennifer shakes her head and has a silent conversation with her husband, who is now in the doghouse.

Heather squeezes my hand. "And you want to marry that nerd?"

I cringe but can't keep the smile off my face. Maybe I do, some-day. Until now, I haven't entertained that line of thought. But if there were someone I would want a forever with, Tommy would be that person. Too bad I mucked it up good.

Heather pats my hand. "We'll pray for you."

"Hey now." Tommy's booming voice reverberates through the house. "Get your butts over here and finish setting this up while I start on the brownies."

I guess if I can make him wait for sex in order to partake of his middle-of-the-night cooking, I should be able to endure a round of his favorite game. I'm pretty sure he makes up the rules as we go. In my mind, I chant "brownies, brownies, brownies." And bless his heart. He's being such a trouper about keeping the fallacy of our en-gagement going. I definitely owe him something.

While the brownies are in the oven, everyone except Tommy pretends to enjoy the game of Risk. His eyes are bright, and he's so excited to be playing this dry-as-Melba-toast game, but we can't fake being excited. I would rather play Scrabble.

Tommy groans. "Come on, guys. Three simple steps. Get and place your army, attack, and then fortify."

I grit my teeth. "I understand the 'place your army' part, but you attack before I get a chance to do anything else."

He winks. "Strategy, sugar. Pure strategy."

I glance over at Matt. He's playing a game of solitaire on his phone that's resting in his lap. Heather and Jennifer are playing Tic-Tac-Toe on a napkin. Mrs. Edwards is relaxing in the recliner and reading the newspaper, while the reverend naps on the couch.

"Boom," Tommy yells.

His father jumps and almost falls off the couch.

"In your face, Heather. I just fortified all of Asia. Bonus points for me."

"Yay," she deadpans as a yawn escapes her mouth. "Does this mean I'm out?"

"Yep."

"Oh, thank the Lord. I'll check on the brownies." She gets up and scoots into the kitchen.

"Don't slam the oven door, or they'll fall. And keep your paws off the second pan. That's for Mrs. Lopez."

"Yeah, yeah, yeah. I hear ya."

Tommy elbows Matt, who jumps and drops his phone. "I'm after your South American armies next."

Matt slumps. "Come on, man. It's all I've got. Take Jen's Australia."

Jennifer pops her husband on the arm. "Hey, now. That's all I have left. What about Shelby? She has Central Africa. You need that too."

I am officially a member of the club now that I've been thrown under the bus during Risk.

"Brownies are done." Heather holds up one of the pans for everyone to see.

"I concede," Matt says as he jumps up from the table.

Jennifer is right behind him. "Me too." She kisses Tommy on the cheek before she runs into the kitchen.

Tommy gives me the side-eye. "What about you, sugar? Going to bail on me too?"

I bite my lip. This nerdy boy is adorkable, but the chocolate aroma wafting over me is more than I can resist. I lunge toward the kitchen, but he grabs me by the waist, making me giggle. He tickles me then kisses my neck. I stop what I'm doing to savor his mouth on my skin. The smell of chocolate combined with his lips on me is intoxicating, and I could easily forget where I am.

Heather clears her throat, interrupting us. "Guys, get a room."

I jump away from Tommy. *Good Lord.* I was only seconds away from making out with him while his parents were in the room. *What is wrong with me?*

"Yeah, gross." Jennifer points at the brownies. "You can do that in a bit. Right now, it's brownie time."

Tommy releases me and pops me on the butt then follows me into the kitchen.

Mrs. Edwards folds her paper and whacks her husband on the arm with it. "Brownie time."

He stretches and stands from the couch.

"Are these special brownies?" Mrs. Edwards asks.

Tommy shakes his head. "No, Mom. Jeez. You're never far from your Woodstock days, are you?"

She shrugs.

He winks at her. "But I did use Jack Daniels."

She rubs her hands together. "Yum. Another winner." She hands me a brownie square, and the moment the treat reaches my taste buds, I'm taken to another level of ecstasy.

I close my eyes and grip the counter with my free hand. "Oh... my."

Tommy whistles. "Shelby, did you just have a cocoa-gasm?"

My eyes flutter open, and I sigh. "I believe so."

"Me too." Tommy winks. "Was it good for you?"

Heat rises up my neck, but I don't care. That brownie was so good. "Definitely."

"Hey, guys." Jennifer smiles, revealing a gooey brownie covering her teeth.

Matt goes in for a chocolate kiss.

"Ew." Heather covers her eyes. "Please, everyone in this house needs to get a room."

Tommy pulls his little sister into a choke hold and gives her head a noogie. I love all the love in this family. It's nonstop razzing, but all in fun. I'm close with my brother, but we tend to get on each other's nerves after a few hours. The Edwards siblings seem to get closer the longer they're together. If I were really marrying Tommy, it's obvious I would be marrying the entire clan, and that thought makes me all warm inside.

"Stop," Heather squeals. "Mom, make him stop."

He pinches her cheek. "You love it."

She lifts an eyebrow. "And just when are you going back to Boston?"

Tommy's smile fades. He releases her and stares a hole through her.

She throws her arms up in a boxing stance. "Chill, bro. Just kidding."

His jaw clenches. *That's odd.* Then he glances over at me, and the playful twinkle is gone. "We should probably leave."

"Okay."

His father slaps him on the back.

Tommy jerks a thumb in my direction. "We're going to stop by to visit little Stella before visitation hours are over."

Reverend Edwards smiles. "Tell Theo I'll be there in the morning but to call me if he needs me to bring anything."

"Sure thing, Dad."

Tommy says his goodbyes, which takes another thirty minutes, and I take advantage of the time by swiping another brownie. With a mouthful, I catch his whole family staring at me. *Busted.* I hope it's only for taking another brownie and not for the massive deceit that is weighing on my heart.

TOMMY IS SILENT MOST of the way back to the hospital. I'm not sure if I should ask why his mood went from playful to almost angry, but something made him flip a switch. He's not the same person he was only a couple of hours ago. But he wasn't deceiving his family then, either.

I stare out the window as he drives my car down Hillsboro Road. "Your family is so... real."

He keeps his eyes trained straight ahead. "Yeah."

"Won't you miss them when you leave?"

He glances my way. "You have no idea how much."

I touch his cheek. "How about me? Will you miss me?"

At a traffic light, he touches my cheek. "You have no idea how much."

I smile. I wish I could beg him to stay, but that wouldn't be right. I begged Blaze to stay, and that didn't end well.

His eyes twinkle. "I have an idea."

"What's that?" I hope it's not another round of Risk. I'm not sure I could take that.

"How about we skip the hospital visit and go back to your townhome? I can do things that will make you moan and clutch the counter again, but this time without food."

My smile consumes my face. "As tempting as that sounds, we need to go see Stella. Visiting hours are almost over for the day."

He pouts like a little boy that just lost his football. Then his eyebrows rise. "But we can make it a quickie."

"Do you mean the visit or the..." I bite my lip.

"I mean the visit."

"Deal."

He floors the gas and screeches through the red light. "And afterward, we really need to figure out how we're going to tell our parents we aren't walking down the aisle."

I groan. "Yeah." My heart sinks a bit. A part of me is going to miss the idea of a forever with Tommy. A big part of me. Maybe it will happen someday. Or maybe never.

CHAPTER THIRTEEN

Tommy

From my perch in the bedside chair, my gaze ping-pongs from little Stella to Theo. She is so much like her daddy in every way possible. Her messy curly hair and deep dimples are the obvious external examples, but she got a lot of her personality from him too. It's weird because she didn't even know him before she got so sick, yet they act like they've been together since birth. And by the way Darla beams, she is thrilled and relieved it's going so well.

After the tenth round of rock-paper-scissors with her father, Stella smiles. "Uncle Tommy, do you want to play?"

My stomach is full of butterflies at her words. I've never been called that before, and it sends a warm, bubbly sensation through me. I clear my throat and smile back at her. "Your dad probably didn't tell you this, but I'm the master at this game."

Shelby is sitting on the other side of Stella's bed and groans.

Theo rolls his eyes. "Shoot, Stella. He used to run crying to your grandmother if I won too many rounds in a row."

I gasp and hold my chest with my hands. "Did not."

Stella covers her mouth with her little hands and snickers, causing those deep dimples in her cheeks to pop out.

I lean toward Theo. "Did too."

"Did not." Our heads almost touch.

Darla slides us away from one another. "Oh my goodness. You guys take your game playing to a whole different level."

Theo takes Darla's hand and kisses it. "My mad game playing won you over, didn't it?"

Darla blushes, and I sneak a peek at Shelby. She watches the happy couple with an odd expression. Wanting, maybe? *Slow down, darling.* A fake engagement is one thing. She'd better not ask me to fake anything else. Her eyes flick toward me then back to Darla and Theo.

A nurse walks in and begins her assessment of Stella. "Stella needs a nap."

Stella yawns. "I'm not tired."

Darla glides a hand down her daughter's cheek. "I'm not either, but we both should try to take a nap. We'll be right outside, okay?"

Stella huffs but can't hold another yawn in.

The nurse holds a device to Stella's ear to take her temperature then smiles down at her. "You take a nap, but remember, all you have to do is push this little sad-face button, and I'll be in here before you can say Jiminy Cricket. Got it?"

Stella pouts but settles in for a nap.

The thermometer beeps, and Theo leans over to see the reading. He nods, so I take that to mean she's doing well. Darla and Theo give their little girl a thousand more kisses before the four of us head out of the room. Seeing Theo in dad mode is unsettling. He's supposed to be untethered like me, only having himself to worry about. Now he's got a daughter, and by the way he can't keep his hands off Darla, I'm guessing he'll have a wife soon too.

It never bothered me when Jen got married because Matt always seemed like part of the family anyway. And Jen was such a romantic. She was planning her wedding day before she had her first boyfriend. But with Theo, it's different. He's a guy and my only brother. I thought we had this silent pact to stay away from romantic stuff.

But look at him now. He slides his arm up Darla's back to lead her out of the room, and his fingers linger on the back of her neck. She leans into him, and they share a whispered conversation.

I glance over at Shelby, and she quickly diverts her gaze away from me. She's giving me the weirdies with the way she's acting. I should be the one on pins and needles.

Theo's phone buzzes, and when he reads the message, he freezes in the hallway. He lets Darla read the message, and they both slowly turn toward Shelby and me.

Darla's jaw drops. "Tommy, do you and Shelby have something to tell us?"

The hole we are digging keeps getting deeper. I swallow hard and dare a glance at Shelby, who has gone pale. It was naïve of me to assume the Edwards grapevine wouldn't extend to the hospital, but I thought I would have a little more time to rectify the situation before confronting my brother.

Shelby shrugs one shoulder. "Uh, surprise?"

Theo blinks and shakes his head.

Darla covers her mouth before she lunges toward Shelby and squeezes her tightly. "Oh my. Why didn't you say something?"

Because there was nothing to say.

"Well..." Shelby bites her lip. "You two had enough on your plate. This is nothing compared to your daughter's health."

"Nonsense. This is fantastic news." Darla pushes Theo, who still looks like a deer caught in the headlights, out of the way and hugs me around the waist. "I'm so happy for you. Shelby deserves someone as wonderful as you." Tears stream down Darla's face. "So, so happy." Her smile fades as she notices Theo's expression. "Aren't you happy?"

Theo scrubs a hand through his hair. "I guess. But just this morning—"

Think fast! "I couldn't let the cat out of the bag before I asked her. Sorry, brother. You're not always the first to get intel." *Big, fat liar.*

He crinkles his brow. "Ooookay." He sticks his hand out for me to shake, but I grab him in a hug. He whispers, "We need to talk."

Shelby's complexion has not returned to her normal tanned color yet. Darla babbles on and on, and Shelby bobs her head up and down, but I have a feeling she's not hearing one single word.

Theo rotates me and gives me a gentle nudge. "Tommy and I are going to grab some coffee. See you in a bit." Then he drags me down the hallway and outside to the hospital courtyard. Several people sit at picnic tables, eating their meals. He plants me on a park bench and paces around me, mumbling unintelligible words, or at least I guess they're words.

"You going to speak anytime today?" I finally ask. "And how about that coffee? I sure could use one."

He throws his hands in the air. "What are you doing?"

I cross one ankle over the other and lean back, watching my brother implode. "Let me explain."

He flings his arms in the air and stomps around like a wet hen. "You have school to consider."

Don't remind me. "Yeah, about that—"

He shakes his head so much, I fear he's going to have brain damage. "Oh no, you don't. You're not going to ruin your plans because of a crush."

The nerve of him talking to me like he's my father. "Weren't you the one who told me just this morning that you knew right from the start Darla was the one for you? Maybe I came to my senses today. What's wrong with that?"

"Realizing who you are meant to be with is one thing. Getting engaged so soon, that's a totally different thing."

"But aren't you and Darla going to get married?"

He crosses his arms over his chest. "Well, yeah, but that's different."

"Why?"

"Because I've thought about her every day for seven years, even when I was dating Mallory. And have you forgotten about Stella? We have a kid together." His eyes get big. "Shelby's not..."

I stare up at the sky. "No. For crying out loud, you're as bad as Heather."

"What about school?"

"School's still on, I guess." Maybe he'll get my subtle hint that I'm having doubts about school, and the reason has nothing to do with Shelby.

His eyes nearly bug out of their sockets. "You guess? Are you serious? You're going to throw everything away?"

Throw everything away? No one in this family will listen to me. If he's going to act this way, then I'll leave him in the dark for a little while. It'll serve him right for busting my chops.

After a serious stare down with my brother, I ask, "Why can't you be happy for me? I'm over-the-moon thrilled for you."

He motions for me to follow him to the other side of the courtyard, where there are fewer people to overhear our conversation. "I am happy, bro. It's just so... out of character, I guess."

I chuckle. "Well, I will give you that one."

"So, it will be a long engagement?"

Shelby better start her exit strategy now, but until then, I'll add some seasoning to the pot of fake stew I'm cooking. "We've talked about her moving with me." That sounded better in my head. I can't believe I said that.

"Really?"

"Yeah. She's ready to cut the apron strings tied to her family. It would be a good way to be without their constant micromanaging. Not only that, they're throwing money around faster than it can be printed." I lower my voice to mimic Shelby's father. "Can I buy you a 3-D printer? Or how about I send you two on a honeymoon so expensive it could feed half the continent of Africa." I run a hand through my hair. "They have that whole 'the love of money is the root of all evil' bit down pat."

The edge of his mouth twitches. "Does she know that?" He motions with his head for me to turn around.

Shelby is standing there. Her skin is even more pale than before, and her mouth is hanging open.

Darla's eyes dart from me to Shelby. "You just told me he wasn't going back to Boston."

Son of a...

Apparently, our stories didn't match up. We didn't plan this all the way through very well, and I'm a grade A jerk. "Sugar..."

She bolts away before I can say anything else. *Crap.* The exit strategy may have started on its own.

Theo motions with his head. "You better go."

Even though I'm a foot taller than her, I have a hard time catching up to my angry spitfire. "Shelby, wait."

She race-walks to the parking deck. Thank goodness for the elevator, because she is ready to leave me behind.

Luckily, I'm able to slip into the elevator before the door closes. "I'm sorry. I didn't have a clue what to say."

"Sounds like you knew exactly what to say." She scoots around me and pushes the number three. Then she bangs her head against the wall. "Not your fault. We didn't get our lies coordinated."

"I don't like lying to my family, so if you don't fix this, I will." I hold up three fingers. "You have two days, then it's going down whether you like it or not."

She huffs, and as soon as the elevator stops on our level, she continues her rush to the car, but this time, I'm by her side. She pulls out her key fob and unlocks the doors.

Before she can open her door, I turn her around. "Look at me."

Her eyes roam my chest, and finally, she makes her way to my face. "You said my parents micromanage me?"

"Yeah, but you say the same thing. Is that what you're upset about?"

"No. Yes." She squeezes her eyes closed. "I don't understand why I'm so upset. This is all my fault, and you're so sweet to go along with it. If we were really engaged, that would have been a good segue into our real breakup."

And it still might. I'm trying hard not to add salt to the wound, but this is more than I bargained for.

I tap her nose. "See? You are a forward-thinking woman. Without even trying, you've planted seeds of doubt about our sudden engagement. And when we tell everyone we've called it off, they'll believe it."

She smiles and gives me a hug around the middle. "You're right. I'm brilliant."

"I would like to remind you that it was your brilliance that got us in the predicament in the first place."

Shelby gives me a playful nudge when her phone buzzes. She pulls it out of her purse and gapes at it with fear in her eyes. "Uh-oh."

Before I get a chance to ask what's going on, my phone buzzes. When I read the text, all the blood drains from my face. "Oh no."

"Please tell me my mother isn't texting you too."

I shake my head. "Nope. It's your father. How on earth did he get my number?"

Her hands shake so much, she almost drops her phone. "Your mother gave it to my mother."

Lovely.

Shelby gulps. "And now Mom wants to meet me tomorrow to shop for wedding dresses."

"Haven't they ever heard of long engagements? I mean long, long, long? So long that you have years to pick out a dress?" My head spins when I reread the text message on my phone. This can't be happening.

Shelby stands on her tiptoes to see my phone. "I'm afraid to ask, but what does Dad's message say? And how in the world did he find out your number?" She cringes as she awaits my reply.

I shrug and lean over the hood of her car to gasp for breath. This is a complete disaster. "He wants to help me pick out an engagement ring."

When I get the courage to glimpse at Shelby, I see her face has turned green. "I'm going to puke."

CHAPTER FOURTEEN
Shelby

In less than a day, this entire fake engagement has blown up in my face. Tommy's family is mostly on board with it. Darla can't stop crying because she's so overjoyed. And then there are my parents, who are creepily happy about it all. The only thing I can focus on is putting one foot in front of the other to get back to my car.

"Shelby?"

Tommy's voice knocks me out of my internal monologue. "Did you say something?"

He raises an eyebrow. "Yes. I asked how we're going to get out of this mess?"

"Beats me."

His hands give my shoulders a squeeze. "That's not the answer I was hoping for."

"I need to talk to my brother. He lies to our parents all the time. He'll have an idea on what to do."

As I hop into the driver's seat, Tommy slides in next to me and adjusts his seat belt. "Call me crazy, but that doesn't comfort me any."

"That's all I've got right now."

"Not good enough." Tommy looks out the passenger window the entire way back to my townhome. From time to time, he shakes his head and mumbles something under his breath.

After another awkward moment, I say, "I'm going to fix this."

"You keep saying that."

"I will." My voice comes out in a high-pitched shrill. "I'll talk to Vaughan and figure out a plan."

He holds his hands out. "I'm going to stay at Theo's apartment tonight."

My heart sinks. I knew this would happen. He believes I'm a freak and my parents are control freaks. I've fricking ruined everything. Tears well up in my eyes. "Please don't do that."

Tommy picks at a fingernail. "It might be good for us. We need some space."

Space is the universal symbol for "I'm tired of you." I've heard that line a time or two in my life. A tear trickles down my cheek, and I do my best to swipe it away without him seeing it.

He touches my face.

I can't stop the tears. "I'm so sorry."

He takes my hand and kisses each knuckle. "So am I, sugar."

"Let me talk to Vaughan, then we'll discuss what to do next."

He gives me a patronizing salute. "I could use a long jog to clear my head."

When we drive up to my townhome, he gets out of my car without saying a word. I unlock the front door, and he shuffles up the steps with me right behind him. He toes out of his shoes, slides out of his jeans, and slips into a pair of running shorts. I hope his shoelaces get tangled so it will delay his leaving, but that doesn't happen. Before I can react to the quick kiss he drops on my cheek, he gallops down the steps and out the door.

The silence overwhelms me. All I hear is my pounding heart. I feel like I've lost someone that I could eventually love, all because of my stupid mouth and my stupid desire to make my mother happy for once. With nothing to lose, I pull out my phone and FaceTime my brother.

On the third ring, he picks up. "What did you do this time?"

His dark, messy hair is all over the place. From my viewpoint, it appears like he doesn't have a shirt on. He chomps down on a slice of pizza. From the Nirvana poster behind him, it's safe to say he's in his own dorm room. At least I won't have this conversation with a random girl in the background.

"First off, do you have on pants, and are you alone?"

"Yes and yes." He moves the phone so it scans down his muscular body until I see boxer shorts then moves back to his face.

"Underwear isn't pants."

"It is when I'm in my own room. Back to why you called. What did you do? Mom sent me a text. I had no idea she could do that. She told me to call her." His voice gets all girly. "She had great news to share."

I almost crack up as I plop down at the kitchen table and prop my phone up on the clay pot holding my succulent plant. "I need your advice."

His laughter rumbles through the phone as he slides another slice of pizza in his mouth. It must be nice to be able to eat that much. He's probably on a carb-load day. "If you want my advice, it must be really bad. Go for it."

"How do you lie to Mom and Dad and get away with it?"

He wipes his mouth with the back of his hand. "Easy. I've had lots of practice. But the main tip I can give a newbie like yourself is to keep your story simple and to remember your lies. Mom loves to ask a lot of questions, and Dad's mind is like a steel vault. He doesn't forget any bit of information. If you say you wore a blue shirt when you went bowling on Thursday, you can't say you wore a green shirt to the movies. He'll remember that kind of stuff."

"Hmmm." I drum the table with my fingers, trying to take all this in. He burps, and I cringe. "God, Vaughan, you're disgusting."

"Maybe so, but you called me, remember? I was content sitting in my boxers, eating pizza, and watching the Braves without anyone bothering me. Now, back to my original question. What did you do?"

"It's a biggie."

"Is it bigger than pretending to be enrolled for a semester and really just hanging out in the dorm room for three months?"

"No way. You did that?"

He picks up his phone and gives me a three-sixty view of his tiny dorm room. "Did you ever wonder why I'm taking classes this summer? I didn't beat the letter informing them I needed to vacate the room if I wasn't enrolled. Rule number one: You can never trust the mail to run slow when you expect it to."

I belt out a chuckle. "Leave it to you to try to be a real-life Van Wilder. You are a piece of work."

"Thank you."

My eyes bug out. "I didn't mean that as a compliment."

"Whatever."

"I cannot believe Mom didn't tell me that. I bet she was peeved." Usually, Mom vents to one of her children about the other. She especially likes to use the phrase, "What will the neighbors think?"

"More like Dad was, but here I am. Fun time is over. It would have been better to just take the courses during spring semester, but live and learn."

"I guess so. You just made it harder on yourself."

"Never mind my transgressions. Spill it. What's your big sin?"

I nibble on a fingernail. "Okay, here goes. So, Mom has never let me forget the fiasco with Blaze."

"The little drummer boy?"

I slump back into my chair. "You and Tommy have to stop calling him that."

He scrunches his forehead. "Who's Tommy?"

I minimize my brother's face and search for a picture of me with Tommy. When I find a good one, I hit send.

Vaughan's phone bings, and his mouth forms a big O as he stares at the picture. "Nice-looking dude. So is this your next victim?"

"Not funny. But I really like him, and it so happens that Mom and Dad love him."

"No joke? I assumed they didn't like anyone."

I snort. "Exactly. So when they went all gaga over him, I sort of... well, I told them we were engaged."

His face is expressionless for a moment. Then Vaughan wipes his mouth with a napkin and swallows hard. "Okay. Congratulations?"

I stare at the ceiling. "If you were here right now, I'd smack you. We aren't engaged. I barely know him. But Mom already wants to go dress shopping, and they've thrown money my way. I'm talking a lot of money. And Dad wants to take Tommy ring shopping. I can't have an engagement ring. I'm not really engaged, and I'm sort of freaking out about all of this, and Tommy is getting cold feet. Not cold feet, like backing out of the engagement—because there isn't an engagement—but cold feet as in going back to Boston to finish school and never seeing me again."

I almost pass out from not taking a breath during my monologue.

My brother sits up straight. "How much? Because I could use a few grand."

"Don't get any ideas of doing this too. I need to fix this without losing Tommy and without giving Mom one more reason to be disappointed in me. It's going to be hard enough as it is."

Vaughan must sense the panic in my voice because he stops the teasing. "I'm assuming you're going to call it off in the near future?"

"I promised Tommy no later than three days."

Vaughan cringes. "A lot can happen in three days. Bite the bullet, pull the plug, forfeit, whatever metaphor works for you. But do it now."

"How?"

"Okay, if you're going to be a chicken about it, then go along with anything Mom wants to do until you grow some balls. When you're with her, let her do most of the talking. Go with the flow, and don't let her suspect a thing. Whatever she orders, you can always cancel later."

I blink like an idiot. "That might work."

"It always works. As long as she gets the impression she's in charge, she gets so wrapped up in everything, she forgets she might be getting fooled. I do it all the time."

"You are one little devil, and for once, I'm so glad you're evil."

He winks. "Can I go now because the Braves are up to bat?"

I blow him a kiss, and as usual, he pretends to dodge it. "Thanks, Vaughan. I hate you."

"Yeah, I hate you too."

He disconnects, and I breathe a sigh of relief. I might be able to do as he suggests, especially since it will only be another day or two before we tell everyone the truth. I hope Tommy doesn't despise me by then, because he is the best thing that's ever happened to me.

I smack my forehead. *Darn it.* I should have asked the expert how Tommy should handle Dad. I redial, but Vaughan's already put his "do not disturb" message on his phone. I cringe at the thought of whoever just showed up at his room.

While I wait for Tommy to return from his run, I take a shower. I let the hot, pulsating water run over my neck and down my back, hoping it will wash away all the stress and let it swirl down the drain along with the shampoo. At least I'm not in full panic mode anymore.

A very tall shadow walks past the glass door.

"Tommy?"

"Hey, sugar."

I squeeze out the excess water from my hair before opening the door. Tommy's dark gaze trails up my body as he holds out a towel for me.

"How was your run?"

"Just what I needed." His eyes hold mine. "I take that back. There's one more thing I need."

I freeze in place, and a droplet of water hangs from the tip of my nose. "Yeah?"

He steps closer to me, letting my wet hair drip over his sweat-covered T-shirt. "I need you, sugar."

All the tension leaves my shoulders, and I am finally able to take in a deep breath. He's not ready to give up on me, on us. I rest my head on his chest and squeeze him around the waist while he kisses the top of my head.

"We'll figure this out," he says in a gentle voice. "Somehow, we'll figure a way out of this."

Right here, wearing nothing but a bath towel, with my wet hair plastered all over my makeup-free face, I am falling for this wonderful man. If I lose him over my stupid impulses, I'll never forgive myself.

CHAPTER FIFTEEN
Tommy

After a hot shower with my steamy girl, there is no better place in the world than being wrapped in a Shelby burrito. She makes me feel safe and loved, and I could stay in her bed with her forever. I realize I can't, so I do my best to savor every moment I have with her. My nice, long run gave me time to sort out my thoughts. While I don't like this fiasco Shelby created, I know her heart was in the right place. Of all people, I should understand the pressure of trying to please the family.

I still cannot believe Shelby wants anything to do with me. Most girls cut and run when I prefer reading a book over going out. And if that doesn't get them running, my odd choices of board games does the trick. It's either that, or I attract women who have a hidden agenda like Hazel. She used me to get back at her old boyfriend, and when I found that out, I backed off. Once I put two and two together about her mother being my professor, it was a no brainer—it was never going to work. I'm so stupid sometimes.

But Shelby is different. She's actually too good to be true. I'm sure I'll mess it up before too long if this charade we're playing doesn't do it first.

"Mmm, that is nice." I'm not sure if she understood my words since my face is covered in her long blond hair.

"Nice? That's it? Just nice?" She pulls my head out of her neck so we're eye to eye.

"Okay, let me try it this way. O-M-G, like, you know, like, it was awesome. Totally."

She pinches my nose. "Stick to just nice. Your valley girl speak is too weird."

"As if."

She gooses me on my right side, in my one and only tickle spot, which makes me giggle like a girl no matter if I'm angry or sad. Not many people have figured it out, and those who have use it against me. Heather knows it, and Shelby found it on day one.

"Stop that." I attempt to pry her hands from my waist.

"As if that's going to work."

I roll her on top of me and stare into those brown eyes that mesmerize me. When I'm tangled up with Shelby, I forget all my problems, especially school and all that it implies.

She peers over at the clock and groans. "It's up-up time. Work day."

My hands roam down her thighs, and she wiggles on top of me. "Are you going to drive me insane with those tight yoga pants again?"

"Yes. And it's so hot outside, I might even wear a skimpy halter top to go with them."

I love her smirk. My head falls back on the pillow. "You're killing me. Can I go to work with you?"

She climbs off of me, and before she covers herself with my T-shirt, I get the best view of her perfect body.

"And do what? Teach a Zumba class?"

I shrug. "I'm a quick learner."

"No. You have a meeting with Dad, remember?"

"Don't remind me. Can't I hold him off for... let's see... three days? Hint, hint."

She leans down and gives me a quick peck on the lips. "You don't understand my father, so no. I'll start the coffee if you want to hit the shower first."

I whimper but understand fun time is over. I head to the bathroom and hear my phone chirp in the other room. "Hey," I call to Shelby. "Do you mind seeing if that's Theo? Or even better, maybe it's your father canceling."

I'm one foot inside the hot shower when Shelby says, "No, it's from Alex."

Shit, shit, shit. My pulse goes into overdrive. Alex is Hazel, the biggest mistake of my life. She hates her old-fashioned name so she shortens her last name from Alexander to Alex. To tick her off, I call her Hazel. I do not want to talk to her. Not today. Not ever. I told her it was over and done, that there was nothing left. I was an idiot for getting involved with her in the first place.

From the bedroom, Shelby asks, "Do you want me to reply?"

"No!" I race into the bedroom, leaving soppy footprints all over the carpet. I grab the phone to delete the text before I even read it. "I mean, it's not important. Alex is, uh, my professor. Professor Alexander. It's just school stuff." First, I lie to my parents about being engaged. Now, I'm lying to Shelby. Alexander is my professor, but Alex is Hazel, Professor Alexander's daughter. Oh, what a tangled web we weave.

Shelby holds her hands up in front of her and backs away. "Okay. Calm down. Coffee will be ready when you get out of the shower, but I'm kind of wondering if you need any caffeine."

She walks out of the bedroom, and I lean against the doorframe, taking deep breaths to force my pulse to slow down. I haven't heard from Hazel in over a month, and I was praying she'd gotten the hint. I hoped she had realized that what happened between us was over, a mistake. It should have never started in the first place.

I get in the shower and turn the water to as hot as I can stand it. The hot water releases the tension in my shoulders, so I let it pound over me. I close my eyes to try to calm down, when a hand slides around my waist. I jump and almost elbow Shelby in the face.

"Whoa, Nelly. It's just me." Her words alone are enough to lower my heart rate to a more normal pace.

I wrap my arms around her and pull her under the flow of water. If I consider her beautiful when she's fully clothed, she's sexy as hell when naked with water sliding down her petite, perfect body. I cover her face with kisses, and when I find her lips, she groans into my mouth.

She pulls back an inch to search my face. "Why so tense?" She rubs my neck, and I swear, I never want to leave her shower.

"School." I lean my head back to get a maximum drenching from the water flow. "Not worth talking about."

"Well then, the next time this Alex dude calls, you let me talk to him."

I clench my jaw. There is no way I'm going to let Shelby talk to Hazel, and there's no way in hell I'm going to let Hazel ruin what I have with Shelby. And I don't even get what this is yet. I'm an idiot. I should have listened to Heather and blocked Hazel's number.

"It wouldn't be wise to sic my girl on my major professor." *More lies.* "Do you want me to get kicked out of school?"

She grins evilly. "Uh, maybe."

Shelby makes me smile. I love her honesty. I lean down to whisper in her ear. "I might take you up on that, sugar."

She pours shampoo in her hand then stands on her tiptoes so she can lather my hair. I nudge her in the chest with my soapy head.

"Watch it, mister, or I'll get shampoo in your eyes."

"I'll close my eyes."

She pushes me under the spray of water. "Rinse. I've got to get to work."

"Yes, ma'am."

After I rinse all the shampoo out of my hair, I slip out of the shower, wrap a towel around my waist, then shake my hair like a dog. When I roam back into Shelby's bedroom, I go in search of a pair of clean underwear. Being the sweetheart she is, she made room in her dresser for some of my clothes last week. But I'm a typical guy, and I can't remember which drawer it is, so I rummage through a few, sliding my hand over her sexy underwear, her socks, and a drawer full of T-shirts.

Buried in the bottom of her T-shirt drawer is a sketch pad. I rifle through the pages as I sit on the edge of her bed. There are pages of pencil drawings consisting of flowers, scenes of the city, various people, and even one of me. I've never seen such gorgeous detail. To think she's been keeping this amazing talent from me is odd to say the least. If I had that ability, I would be showing everyone I knew.

"What are you doing?"

I fumble the sketch pad in my hands until it lands on the floor. Quickly, I pick it up and lay it on the bed. "I, uh... Sorry. I was searching for my underwear and found this."

With a scowl, she snatches it off the bed and stuffs it back in the drawer.

"Those are really good."

"Thanks," she says under her breath. She slings on a T-shirt and yoga pants, slamming all the drawers in her path. *Uh-oh.*

"I wasn't snooping."

She sighs. "I know. Just drop it."

"But they're so good."

It's the first time she's ever given me a resting bitch face. "Tommy, I said to drop it."

I shake my head in disbelief. "Are you embarrassed?"

She shoves her sneakers on, bouncing on one foot at a time. "No. It's something I did a long time ago when I was bored."

"A long time ago? So you drew my picture when you were ten, as in fifteen years prior to meeting me?"

She sits by me on the bed, and for the longest time, she doesn't say anything. Finally, she breaks the silence. "I have to hide my drawings from my mother."

I scratch my chin. "I didn't get the impression she stopped by often."

"I can't take chances."

My jaw drops. "Huh?"

Shelby stares at the ceiling for a long moment. "I wanted to study art. My parents said no way. It was either marketing or business. Or I'm sure they would have paid for law school if I had any interest, but that was never going to happen."

"Seriously?"

"Yep. So I went down the marketing route then decided to get a master's in public health, which ticked them off, but I paid for it myself."

This is crazy. She's so talented, and she has to hide it. It's so unfair.

"Tommy, you've spent one single hour with them, and that's all it took to understand how they are. It's their way or the highway. I've fought with my mother for so many years, it's easier this way. When I get the hankering to draw, I do it. Then I either throw it away or hide the ones I can't bear to destroy."

Unbelievable. I scratch the back of my head, not understanding any of this. I nudge her knee with mine. "Have you ever drawn a picture of yourself?"

She squishes up her face in disgust. "God no. That would be too weird."

I kiss her cheek. "Would you do it for me?"

"No."

Wow. It took her a nanosecond to shoot me down. "I believe you owe me something for going along with this charade." I waggle my eyebrows in hopes I will lighten the mood. Her mouth twitches but fails to pull up into a grin.

"Do you paint too?"

She doesn't answer, so I stare at her until she finally glances my way. "Maybe."

"I want to see."

She shakes her head. "No. I'm not very good."

I point at the drawer in which she shoved her book. "According to those sketches, you're very good, even the one of me. And we both know you didn't have much to go on with my ugly mug."

She rolls her eyes. "I drew that the first day we met. Remember, at Theo's apartment?"

I groan. "Not my finest hour. It's not every day a person finds out they were partially responsible for keeping two people apart for years. Yeah, I'd say that's one for the books."

She touches my cheek. "I meant that was when we first met, and you invited me to stick around for cookies."

I can't help the wicked grin on my face. "Pretty smooth on my part, especially coming from the king of dorks."

She taps the tip of my nose. "It worked, didn't it?"

Our lips meet, and I'm so thankful I was at Theo's apartment that day when Shelby came stumbling in, dragging Darla with her. My life was so messed up, and she made everything balance out again... until she took it upon herself to throw it all out of whack.

Her face flushes. "I couldn't stop thinking about you. I couldn't sleep until I got it down on paper."

Adorable. "Well, I do have that effect on people."

She rolls her eyes. "Got to go. See you later?" She kisses me then jumps up. Before she bounces out of the room, she adds, "Don't forget Dad."

"Can't wait." *Not.*

I sling on my clothes as my thoughts go back to her sketches. I can't believe she's that good and embarrassed about it. My mind goes back to the drawing. She didn't miss a single detail of my face. She even got the triangle of freckles I have under my right eye.

My phone chimes. I pick it up to see that it's another text from Hazel.

Hazel: *Call me.*

She can hold her breath waiting. I delete the message and head out to the hospital so I can sit with Theo for a while before I get to fake it with Mr. Williams. But as I reach my car, my phone rings. Hazel is not going to leave me alone until I talk to her.

I angrily tap the answer button. "What?"

"That's a cheerful way to talk to your professor's daughter."

"Is this a professional call?"

"Not necessarily." Her saccharin voice causes a shiver to run up my spine.

"Then what do you want?" I ask through gritted teeth.

"I miss you."

"We're not doing this. I'm not doing this."

"Whatever. We can talk about that later. When are you coming home?"

I slam the car door shut. "I am home, Hazel." I say her given name just to get under her skin.

"Okay. And you know I hate that name."

And I hate when she patronizes me.

"When are you coming back to Boston?"

I slump down in my seat. "Not sure. Hazel, things have changed. I, uh... I met someone."

"Oh, is that so?"

"Yes, and I'm happy."

She chuckles. "You're trying to convince yourself you're happy. It's only a rebound."

I squeeze my eyes shut. "I'm engaged," I blurt out. *Holy crap.* I can't believe I said that.

This is the first time Hazel has ever been speechless. After a quiet moment, she finally says, "You don't want to get married, and you certainly don't want me to tell Mom what you've been doing with her daughter because she has rules about those kinds of things. But of course, you already knew that. Oops."

"Goodbye, Hazel."

"Can't wait to share with you the little documentary I made. Perhaps your father would get a kick out of it." Her nasal tone makes me want to hurl.

"Whatever."

"I'll see you soon."

She hangs up the phone, and I feel like throwing it out the window. She's going to ruin everything for me, or I'm going to ruin it because I'm an idiot. Either way, everything is about to crumble around my feet. To be so smart on paper, I can make the biggest mistakes in life.

CHAPTER SIXTEEN

Shelby

"Hey, boss lady," Isaac says as I enter the wellness center of the hospital. Had he not been Darla's childhood buddy, I probably would have fired him a long time ago. It takes him ten times longer than most people to do any task because he's such a social butterfly. But as much as I don't want to admit it because it will go to his head, his personality is perfect for this job. Isaac knows most everyone at the hospital, and I haven't met one person who dislikes him. Plus, he has such a killer body, even guys want him as their personal trainer, not caring at all that he's gay.

He raises his eyebrows. "I don't like being the last one to hear juicy gossip."

I slink into a chair at the front desk, hoping the whirring of the elliptical machines will mask my groan. "Did Darla tell you?"

"Duh. Of course." He holds up my left hand. "No ring. I guess there's nothing at the jewelry store in the fake-engagement section."

Snatching my hand away, I sit up straight. "Why would you assume—"

"Cut the crap. I'm not stupid, and I've been around your mother a time or two, so I get why you did it."

My head drifts to the desk. "Does Darla believe it isn't real?"

He waves to another fitness member as she passes by on her way to the treadmills. "She's too much in a dream world to notice, but she did consider it odd and very sudden."

My heart drops into the pit of my stomach. "You didn't tell her, did you?"

Isaac slides his finger over his mouth as if to zip it shut. "Your secret is safe with me."

To give my hands something to do, I fold towels to set out for the members to use. "We'll be officially broken up soon, so it won't matter for much longer anyway."

Isaac crosses his arms over his bulky chest. "And you're happy about that?"

"Of course. It's not like it will be a real breakup." *At least I hope not.*

It's time for a change in topic, something not related to my poor life choices. "Hey, did you stop by to see Stella this morning?"

His face lights up at the mention of his goddaughter's name, and all this talk about fake fiancés is forgotten, at least for the meantime. "I did. She seems so much better, thank God. It seems like Theo and Darla have made up too." He sighs. "It's so romantic."

"That's good. I was so worried if something happened to Stella, we'd have to put Darla in the loony bin."

Isaac shivers. "They'd have to open up an entire suite to put us all in there."

I roll my eyes. "As if I could ever live with you."

He laughs and tilts his head to the side. "Everything good with you, other than the obvious?" He waves to a physician entering the fitness center.

"Sure. Yeah, I guess." When Tommy found my "doodles," as Mom calls them, a whole host of insecurities bubbled to the surface. Now he'll probably bug me about drawing all the time.

Isaac hands a towel to a member and tells him, "Go ahead and warm up on the treadmill. I'll be right over." He turns back to me. "For the past month, you've bounced when you walked. You haven't complained when I take a long lunch, and your hair has been perfect. But today, it's like you just crawled out of bed. And don't get me started on that hair. Girl, you can do better than that."

I stare down then back at him. "Something is off."

"Off? What does that mean?"

"I'm not sure. Tommy's acting weird."

"Maybe he can't figure out how to handle your hair. That, and the fact that he's probably not used to having a fiancée."

I smirk at him. "We met my parents, and I thought that would be a disaster, but they loved him."

"Of course they did. You are the perfect pair, like Ken and Barbie."

I swat his arm. "Stop calling us that."

"Come on, it's true. You both are so darn perfect-looking, and I recognize perfection when I see it."

"Ugh. You're impossible. Anyway, he's acting strange."

Isaac motions to his client to start with seated bench presses. "Like how?"

"He got a text and freaked out when I picked up his phone. It wasn't like I would have read it if he didn't want me to."

Isaac mimes to his client to do a set of lateral pull-downs. "Who do you presume it was from?"

I shrug. "Somebody named Alex. Tommy said it was about school, but why freak?"

He taps a finger to his chin. "Hmm, Al could be a female."

"Oh, please. He said it was his professor."

Isaac is the king of planting seeds of doubt in my brain. Now I wonder if Alex is a female and if it's more than just a professional relationship. When the time is right, I need to ask Tommy. Otherwise, the green monster may get the best of me.

I shake off my doubt. "I really don't believe he wants to go back to school."

"Because of you? Maybe he really does want to get married."

I hand a towel to another client that enters the workout room. "I hope it's not because of me. As much as I will miss him like crazy, I would never ask him to stay."

I've been to Boston a time or two, and all it would take to get me to move there would be the tiniest request from that gorgeous green-eyed man.

Isaac picks up his clipboard and starts toward his client to begin the training session. "Maybe he wants you to ask him to stay." He shrugs and jogs to meet up with his client.

Now that I ponder it, Tommy hasn't said one single time that he couldn't wait to get back to school. He doesn't even talk about what he's studying. It really doesn't seem to crank his tractor. Maybe we're more alike than I thought. Perhaps he does things because others want him to, like me. That doesn't explain why he can't tell me, though. I would never make him do anything he didn't want to do.

On the other hand, it could be more than just school. Maybe he's freaking out because of my announcement to my parents. That was stupid of me, and I should have come clean. But instead of doing that, I perpetuated the lie and didn't give him much choice but to pretend right along beside me. I'm no better than everyone else, forcing my ideas on him. The last thing I want him to do is to wake up one day and realize he doesn't even recognize who he is anymore. He would be just like me.

DURING THE ENTIRE DRIVE to Mina's Designs, I repeat Vaughan's words. *Go along with whatever Mom has up her sleeve. Don't say too much. Don't be argumentative. Everything can be returned.* But I'm so short, anything I like will have to be seriously altered, and I'll be stuck with the bill for a dress I'll never wear.

My mom doesn't take no for an answer, like the time when I mentioned in passing I hoped Phil Carter would ask me to homecoming my freshman year of high school. She left skid marks in the driveway from peeling out so fast in order to get to the dress shop before it closed that day. He ended up going to the dance with Anita Childers, and I watched *Dawson's Creek*. Three years later, I gave that dress away with the price tags still hanging from the neckline.

My mother will never forgive me when she finds out I've misled her. But I'm here now. Tonight, Tommy and I will devise a very public and very ugly breakup. As far as I'm concerned, it can't happen soon enough.

When I arrive at Mina's, Mom's Mercedes-Benz is in the space next to the front door. I park my Prius next to her car and take a deep breath to channel some positive energy. I really should have taken a yoga class before coming here, and I'm sure going to need one after this appointment. The bell above the door announces my arrival, and I notice Mom standing by a lady about my age.

"She's here and on time." Mom gives me a kiss on each cheek and grabs me in a bear hug.

"Hey, Mom."

My eyes gravitate immediately toward the Van Gogh painting of Irises hanging on the wall next to the entrance. It's always been one of my favorites. The fact that he painted such a beautiful painting while he was in an asylum always amazed me.

Mom takes my hand and leads me away from the painting. "Sweetheart, leave the pretty drawing alone."

I would rather stare at the way Van Gogh captures the movement of the plants all day long, but Mom insists I follow her.

She holds her arm out to the young lady I noticed when I walked in. "Shelby Lynn, I'd like you to meet Amara, your wedding planner."

My eyes nearly bug out of my head. "My what?"

Mom stands in between me and my newly appointed planner, I guess in case I throw some punches. "It was presumptuous of me, but I thought it would be helpful since you work so much."

That was kind of her, but I don't need a real wedding planner for a fake wedding. Trying to react the way my brother would in this situation isn't going to keep me from throwing up on this lady's Prada tote bag. I paste on a grin as I hold a hand out to shake Amara's. "Nice to meet you."

"The pleasure is all mine. I look forward to working with you. Normally, we work out the details of the contract first then start on the specifics, but Mrs. William was so insistent I be here today."

Amara's jewel-toned skirt accentuates her olive skin, and I so want to hate her.

Mom leans in and stage-whispers, "She comes highly recommended. I had to snag her while she had a free day."

"That's very sweet of you, and not that I'm ungrateful, but we haven't even set a date yet." *Good thinking. Wedding planners detest that kind of stuff.*

"That's okay. It means you'll be flexible."

Argh. Not what I wanted to hear. I glance down at my watch. "I have a really important work meeting at two o'clock, and I can't be late."

Mom claps her hands. "Then let's get this started. Amara will help you narrow down the choices, and Sophie, the designer, will do the fittings."

As if from out of the blue, a lady appears with glasses of champagne. Mom takes one and hands one to me, but I wave her off. "Better not. I have to get back to work soon."

Sophie examines me up and down like she's scanning my body measurements with an invisible device. "I'd say you're a size two, which means we have tons of styles to select from, but it will have to be heavily altered for your small bust and short legs."

I gasp. *How rude.* I like how I look, and Tommy sure hasn't complained about my lack of height or boobage, so her comment is scathing, especially to a paying customer. I mean, one day, maybe I'll really be buying a dress, but I would never want to pay someone to insult me. Tears prickle my eyes, and I feel a meltdown on the horizon.

Amara's jaw drops, and she looks as if she wishes she could fade into the wallpaper.

Mother slides an arm around my shoulders and gives me a squeeze. "Sophie, you are the best of the best, and it took some serious rescheduling on your part to fit Shelby Lynn into your day, but you are not the only designer in this city. My daughter is beautiful and perfect. If you can't see that, we will be on our way."

My breath hitches, and I fight back happy tears by biting the devil out of my bottom lip. That was totally unexpected coming out of my mother's mouth. She has my back, and the timing is perfect. We can leave, and before Mom has a chance to schedule with another designer, I will have called the wedding off.

Sophie quickly backtracks. "Yes, ma'am. Of course. And to show you how sincere I am, any alterations will be on the house."

Well, crap.

Sophie takes my hand and leads me to the back into the size-two room. Amara is right behind me. I've never seen so much white lace and satin in all my life, and all the dresses are only in my size. It's like a taffeta factory exploded.

"I'll pull out the most popular styles, but please feel free to browse, and we'll go from there." Sophie plucks some of the most god-awful dresses out and hangs them on a separate rack. Some of them, I would never ever be caught dead in. I dare to search for a price tag but can't find one, which means they are so expensive, they're not marked.

Mom's hands fly through the racks. "Nope, nope, never, nope, maybe, possibly." She flings two into the waiting arms of Amara. "Amara, would you be a doll as to help Shelby with those?"

Amara peeks over the material at me, and I cringe as I shake my head. She presses her lips together in a thin line and motions for me to follow her. When we get inside the dressing room, she pulls me close to whisper in my ear. "I'm going to let you in on a little secret. All moms do this. They have a vision for what you're supposed to wear. Try on anything she throws at you, and she'll see how hideous it is. In the meantime, you tell me what you have in mind, and I'll seek it out."

"Can you keep a secret?"

"Of course."

I peek out of the dressing room to make sure Mom is nowhere within earshot then pop my head back inside. I bet a wedding planner sees fake engagements all the time. Maybe she can help me out of this mess. "I'm not really getting married. I'm not engaged. It's a big misunderstanding, but I haven't had the heart to tell my mother yet."

Her smile fades. "Oh. This is new territory for me."

Shoot. "So you don't have any tips on how to get out of this sticky situation without breaking my mother's heart?"

Amara shakes her head. "It's usually the groom trying to get out of the real deal. Sorry. I'm clueless."

Phooey.

"Let's just go through the motions, but understand I'm not buying anything. Okay? And I will pay you for your time. Just don't tell my mother."

She holds out her hand, and we pinkie promise. "Got it. Tell me what you'd like *if* you were getting married."

I close my eyes and try to picture myself walking down the aisle next to my father. He would, of course, be in a black tux. My mother would dress her best in a soft pale blue to match her eyes. Vaughan would be wearing a tux but would rebel and have a sleeveless shirt on underneath and Vans sneakers peeking out of his pant legs. And if I had my pick, my dress would be something very simple and timeless. When I let my imagination go a bit further, I see Tommy waiting for me at the altar. I'm a sucker for a tailcoat, and he would totally rock one.

I blink to come back to reality. "I'd prefer something very traditional, perhaps V-neck with some lace and definitely not a long train. I'd get lost in a big dress. And I realize my mother doesn't care, but I do. I don't want an expensive dress."

"Got it. First, let's try on these that are going to make you seem like Glinda the Good Witch from *Wizard of Oz*." She unzips the bag, and sure enough, a dress springs out and takes up the entire room.

I feel my eye twitch. "Oh dear. My mother likes this?"

Amara smirks. "Yeah. It's a frequent flyer for moms, but as shocking as it may be, it rarely has the same effect on the bride-to-be."

I shimmy out of my yoga pants and T-shirt, and she helps me step into this monstrosity. My boobs are pushed up and almost out of the bodice, and the train is so huge, I would trip and fall within five minutes of wearing the dress. Amara stifles a giggle as I stare at myself in the mirror. "Oh my goodness."

"Just go out there, stand on the podium, and let your mother realize it's not for you."

With Amara's help, I gather up about fifty yards of material so I don't trip on my way out to where my mother sits.

Instead of Mom turning her nose up at it, she clasps her hands over her mouth, and tears well up in her eyes. "Is it possible we found the perfect gown on the first try?"

No!

Amara taps her chin with her finger. "It's beautiful."

Traitor.

She turns me around, making the dress swish. "But it kind of takes away from your daughter's beauty."

Sophie circles me like I'm tonight's kill. "You might be right. The perfect gown complements the bride, not outshines her."

Well, thanks a lot.

Amara mouths, "Say something."

"It's very pretty, but it's not *the* dress. I always pictured myself in something more timeless."

Mom's face prunes up like she smells natural gas. *Ouch.*

"Mother, it's not my dream dress. We have plenty of time to find the right one." Vaughan's advice bounces around in my head. He said to go with the flow. My first impulse is to buck back, but I need to channel my brother to get through the day.

"How about this one?" Amara runs in and hangs another dress on the stand and walks away from it.

I gasp at how pretty it is. The gown is beautiful with cap sleeves, traditional lace, a V neckline, and a simple tulle train. If I were a real bride-to-be, I would snag this one up right off the rack.

Mom takes a swig of her champagne. "Shelby Lynn's speechless."

Amara assists me back into the room as I fight back tears. She lets the monster dress slide to the floor into a pile of taffeta and lace then helps me into the new one. When she affixes the buttons on the back, it's almost a perfect fit. It's only a few inches too long, so I could possibly wear it with heels and need absolutely no alterations. It's so perfect, it's creepy.

Amara claps her hands together. "You are so beautiful in this. If you were really getting married, this would be the one."

I dare a peek at myself in the mirror, and a tear trickles down my face. I envision how my wedding plays out in my head. Dad walks me down the aisle toward my husband-to-be, and I feel beautiful on the most important day of my life. My lip trembles, and I have to bite it to keep from showing all the emotions bubbling up inside me.

My breath hitches. "I love it."

"Show your mother." She guides me out of the dressing room.

My mother is speechless, and her mouth hangs open. "Shelby Lynn, you are so much like your grandmother. Oh my. Do you like it?"

My mother asking me if I like something instead of telling me I like something is surreal. All I can do is bob my head up and down.

My mom looks at Sophie. "We'll take it."

I snap back to reality. "Wait, no. Not yet."

Mom has a hurt expression. "Why not? If you like it—and from the expression on your face, it's the one—why search further? It's almost perfect without touching it."

"But... isn't it a bit early to be buying a dress?"

Mom shakes her head. "I realize you haven't set a date, but this would be one thing out of the way, and I would hate for you to miss out on this dress." She takes my hands in hers. "Please let me buy it for you." Our eyes meet, and I've never seen my mother with so much true happiness in her eyes, especially when it has to do with me. "Please."

Amara stands behind my mother and mouths, "Oh my God."

I know I'm not really engaged, and I realize I have no reason to buy a wedding dress, but the little girl in me comes out. I don't want to disappoint my mother. Plus, it's what Vaughan would do.

And I love the dress.

"Okay."

CHAPTER SEVENTEEN

Tommy

It blows my mind how much Stella resembles Theo. Not only in appearance, but she acts like him too. She has even beat me at rock-paper-scissors three times in less than two minutes. Her father taught her well. It doesn't matter that she's still recovering in the hospital—her competitive skills aren't suffering.

"How do you do that?" I ask in amazement.

She shrugs. "I'm good."

"And modest."

Darla snickers. At this point, Stella could say she was a communist, and Darla would still smile. I love how the three of them mesh so well together. It's as if they've been together all along.

The door swings open, and Heather barrels in, carrying the largest stuffed teddy bear ever made. It's so big, I can't even see my pint-sized sister behind it. I hope Heather is so preoccupied with her niece, she won't have a chance to interrogate me.

"Look what I found." Her singsong voice is something new. Before Stella came into our lives, Heather never talked like that, not even when *she* was the seven-year-old.

"Is it for me?" Stella asks.

Theo grabs it out of Heather's hands. "Nope, it's for me. I love pink."

Stella steals it away from her father.

Heather throws her head back with a big guffaw. "Hey, Stella, he had one like this when he was younger."

Stella doubles over with giggles. It's hard to believe that less than a week ago, she was intubated and fighting for her life. Miracles do happen.

"Did not," Theo says.

I point at Theo. "Did too. You cried like a baby one time when you couldn't find Mr. Fluffy Pants."

Heather fist bumps me. Theo chokes on his coffee when Darla belts out a chuckle. I'll get paid back sometime in the near future for that one, but that's what siblings do. We use little tidbits of our childhood to our advantage when opportunities present themselves. And this one was calling my name to snatch it up and run with it.

Theo harrumphs. "It's time for all of you underlings to exit so my little girl can get some rest."

I glance over at Heather. "Did he call us underlings?"

"Uh-huh. He sure did."

Theo stands and motions toward the door then whacks me on the back.

"I'm going to pay for that comment, aren't I?"

"Yep." He walks out with Heather and me. "Thanks for stopping by. Every day, she gets a little healthier."

"When will she get to go home?" Heather asks.

Theo's face lights up. "Hopefully tomorrow."

I slap him on the back. "Man, that's awesome."

He gets teary-eyed, and Heather hugs him. "See you soon."

I add our usual reply. "If not sooner."

Heather and I leave the hospital, and during the entire walk to the parking lot, she steals glances my way.

"What?"

She nudges me in the side. "Spill it. I see that expression. You've got something playing in the background, and you are going to tell me what it is. And it's got to be more than the fake you-know-what."

I growl. Heather gets me better than anyone. Theo and Jennifer have a sixth sense about each other, and Heather and I have it. We pick up on it in a gaze, an expression, and even over the phone when we're hundreds of miles from each other. We talk at least once a day, sometimes more. She's heard all my secrets, and I know hers. She tells me her fears, and I share my anxieties. I also understand she won't hold back. She'll say what I need to hear.

"She called."

"Haz-hell?" she screams.

I nod.

"Crap. Why?"

"She wants me to come back."

Heather shakes her head, her long blond hair whipping around her head. "Tommy, she's bad news." She winks. "Besides, you're engaged."

"Ha ha."

"Don't answer her calls."

"She called me three times today, but the worst part is Shelby almost answered one time."

"Oh dear." Heather sits down on a bench next to the parking lot.

"Shelby saw the name 'Alex.' You know Hazel likes to be called that. I lied and told her it was from my professor."

Heather watches a bird fly by. "Not good. You should have listened to me. Block. Her. Number."

"I tried, but she's sneaky. What type of person gets a supply of burner phones with a Nashville area code just to trick me into thinking it's someone local?"

"A weirdo, that's who. You realize you don't have to answer the phone if it's an unknown number."

"Yes, but I keep assuming it's somebody I should know."

Heather pinches the bridge of her nose. "There's this really cool invention called voice mail. You should check into it."

I guess I was absent the day my teacher taught common sense. As I thought about the last conversation with Hazel, I remembered one thing she'd said that stuck out like a sore thumb. "She said she had a documentary she wanted to show dad."

Heather scrunches up her brows. "What does that mean?"

I chuckle as I shake my head. "No telling."

"You have to tell Shelby the truth."

I shake my head. "It's too embarrassing."

"Are you going back to school?" Heather doesn't beat around the bush.

I lean over and prop my elbows on my legs. "Yeah."

"Are you going to share an apartment with Tony the Twin again?"

Memories of the last year of living with Tony make me crack up. If it weren't for his crazy antics, I would have pulled my hair out a long time ago. "Unfortunately, he got back with Kate, and they're living happily ever after in some town in Nebraska."

"Well, that's good for him. I guess maybe I should really ask why are you going back?"

"Isn't that what I'm expected to do?"

She flails her arms in the air. "For once, stop doing what's expected of you. Quit school. Work at a diner or a gas station. Get married. Make babies. Anything you want." She pokes me in the chest to emphasize each word.

I stand and walk away from her. "Easy for you to say. You're not Tommy, the smart one. Tommy, who is going to make something of himself."

She catches up to me. "Gee, way to make the rest of us feel real inferior."

"I didn't mean it that way." I run a hand through my hair as I continue through the parking lot.

"Where are you going?" she yells after me, giving up her attempt to keep pace with my long legs.

"I've got to bake something, or I'll explode."

"Can I put in my order?"

I stop and put my hands on my hips. "Cookies or pie?"

She bounces toward me and slips her arm around my waist. "How about cinnamon rolls?"

"Someday, I'll have to share you with some dude. He better be worth it."

She chuckles. "I'm beginning to conclude there is no guy on the planet that can put up with me."

"All losers."

She doesn't answer as we make our way toward the car. Some guy's messed with her confidence, which ticks me off. Out of all of us kids, Heather has the sweetest soul. She's spunky and full of life, but for some reason, guys want drama. If I ever find out who has wilted her personality, he'll have to answer to me. I kiss the top of her head and realize I don't even take my own advice. Hazel is drama. Shelby is everything else. Guys, including myself, are stupid.

My phone chirps, notifying me of a text.

"Is it her again?"

I pull my phone from my pocket and am a little relieved to see a reminder message from Shelby's dad. "No, but there's a big wrinkle in this whole fake-engagement and fake-breakup fiasco."

Heather juts her head to the side. "And?"

"I agreed to meet Shelby's dad for coffee."

When she stops giggling, she pats my back. "I'll pray for you. But still, you need to tell Shelby about Hazel. Girls don't like secrets. Just say, 'I messed up, but I've learned my lesson, and there's nothing going on between us anymore.'"

"That sounds really good coming from you. If I bake a double batch of cinnamon rolls, will you tell her for me?"

She focuses on the ground for a second, and I hold on to hope that she'll help me out. "Sorry, bro. You have to take care of this yourself."

I let out a whimper. "I will eventually."

Heather rolls her eyes. "In the meantime, do something nice for her, something she wouldn't expect, something... spontaneous."

"Have you met me?"

She waves goodbye as she yells over her shoulder. "Girls like that kind of stuff, and it could soften the truth a little."

Heather does have a point.

BONGO JAVA IS MY FAVORITE coffee shop in Nashville, and I'm not sure how Mr. Williams figured that out. It's a little out of the way, and I have to pass three big coffeehouses along the drive, but it's worth it. The purpose of our get-together was vague. It could be to set ground rules about dating his daughter, or maybe he ran a background check on me and found out about that not-so-pretty incident in Boston. If so, this meeting could go south really fast.

When I pull into the parking lot, Mr. Williams is already there. Dressed in ratty jeans and a "Welcome to Nashvegas" T-shirt, he leans against his car—a fricking jet-black Aston Martin—while he talks on his cell phone. Too bad he's already spotted me because I am seriously considering making a U-turn in my Ford P.O.S. and faking an illness. I'm getting good at faking things, so I could probably pull it off.

But as my luck would have it, the car in the space next to him pulls away, leaving me no choice but to park my beat-up crapmobile next to his showpiece. My car sputters as I cut off the engine, and a huge hot flush creeps up my neck. If God is looking out for me, he'll help me get out of my car without dinging Mr. Williams's. I couldn't afford to replace a headlight in his beautiful car.

My car door creaks as I open it, and I slip out without touching his. I scoot past the sick ride with my hands in the air for fear I might touch it and make the car alarm go off.

Mr. Williams chuckles. "Tommy, it's just a car. It has an engine and tires, just like yours."

"I'm pretty sure your engine and tires are a little bit better quality than mine."

"It's nice, but nothing like my grandfather's 1955 Ford Fairlane. I had it restored, and it's a sweet ride."

I feel like I have entered *The Twilight Zone* as I follow him into the coffee shop. Before I can pull out my wallet, he pays for our drinks and offers to buy me a pastry, but I decline. He gets one and leans over to me to say, "Don't tell my wife, but I'm cheating on her with these apple fritters."

I chuckle. "It's the two-to-one ratio of cinnamon to nutmeg."

His eyebrows rise. "You bake?"

My height decreases about a foot. "Yes, sir. It's a hobby. A good stress reliever."

"I should take up baking. Jogging isn't cutting it on the stress re-lief." He motions with his head for me to follow him outside. "Let's go for a ride."

Oh dear. He's going to take me out into the country and cut off my balls for messing with his daughter. All these pleasantries are only a way to cause me to lower my guard.

Mr. Williams holds out his key fob. "Want to drive it?"

I shake my head so much, I might give myself a concussion. "No, sir. I mean, yes, but... that wouldn't be wise on my part."

He jingles the fob in front of my face. "It's just a car."

This cannot be happening. I reach out for the key chain, but my shaking hands drop them. If I had my Fitbit on, the maximum heart rate alert would be chirping like crazy.

"Calm down." He leans down to pick up his keys. "I'm not going to hurt you."

Sweat trickles down my back. There's probably a sweat detector on the leather seats, and it will warn Mr. Williams that I'm stressed. "Okay. Where to?"

"Get on the Natchez Trace Parkway, and let's see how fast this baby will go."

This is not good. I don't feel confident enough to drive one mile over the speed limit, let alone see "how fast this baby can go." I slide into the buttery-soft seat, and he plops down beside me, still eating his pastry. Crumbs fall into his lap, but he doesn't seem to care.

The engine roars to life, and I back out onto the street. I drive like a grandma, puttering down Harding Pike and stopping at every light if it's even close to changing red. Mr. Williams finishes his pastry, crumbles up the paper bag, and tosses it onto the floorboard. At least we have that in common. The car floats along, and I don't feel the tons of bumps in the road that my car seems to be a magnet for. He pushes a button, and the top retreats. My hair whips around in the breeze. *Oh man, I could get used to this.*

Mr. Williams gestures to a street, and I downshift to turn on to it. "After this light, it gets very rural. I want you to punch it."

Punch it. Like what he's going to do to my face when he finds out Shelby and I lied to him.

"Now."

Like an obedient puppy, I shift gears and floor the gas. We go from zero to seventy within seconds, and it is exhilarating. He grins big as we speed down the long stretch of rarely used road. We drive for about fifteen minutes in silence, then he tells me to pull over at the Jackson Falls entrance. Now I see his plan. He's going to shoot me and dump me in the river, and my body will never be found. I pull into the parking lot and cut the engine.

"Come on." He motions for me to get out of the car. "Let's take a walk."

Oh dear. I know better than to go, but I don't have much of a choice, so I follow like a lamb being led to the slaughter. We meander down the trail, weaving back and forth until we reach the base of the falls. A couple is splashing in the water, so I feel at least a little bit relieved that if something happens to me, there will be witnesses.

Mr. Williams takes off his shoes and socks, rolls up his jeans, and wades into the cool water until he is in the middle of the stream, gazing straight at the water cascading toward him. I follow suit and enjoy the view so much, I almost forget who I'm with.

Out of the blue, he breaks his silence. "This is where I proposed to Renee. We were so young and stupid and so much in love. Still are, except for the young part."

With the water rushing over the ridge and the birds chirping in the trees, this is the perfect place to pop the question, but I'm not following why he brought me here.

"I got down on one knee in the middle of the Duck River. Obviously, she said yes, but it wasn't the first time I asked her."

"Really?"

"Yep. I asked her five days after we met. She thought we were rushing things. I knew everything I needed to know about her. But she took off for one of those fancy liberal arts colleges in Maine, and I didn't see her again for four years. I called her all the time, but she was too afraid to even talk to me. That was long before cell phones or email. Somewhere between the dinosaurs and the internet."

Somehow, I'm hearing a story that few people know about, and I feel a little bit uncomfortable with this knowledge. "What was she afraid of?"

"Her parents."

Damn.

"They were stuffy and didn't like me because I didn't come from money."

My eyebrows shoot up. I assumed he came from old money. We have more in common than I thought.

He picks up a pebble and tosses it into the water. "But while she was gone, I finished business school, got a job with my father in his small guitar-manufacturing business that he took over from his father, and I worked my butt off to learn every detail about the business. When my grandfather passed away, Dad was ready to retire, so I inherited the business, and with their vision and my good business sense, it's been very successful. Adding a line of guitar strings didn't hurt anything at all."

The rock I'm standing on suddenly becomes very slippery. After a series of flailing arms, I'm able to gain ground again and manage to squeak out, "Williams Guitars?" Everyone in Nashville knows Williams Guitars are the best. Even I do, and I'm not a musician.

"Yep. And by the way you just reacted, I'm going to say you didn't comprehend that about our family, and so you passed."

"Passed what?"

He pulls out a small velvet drawstring bag from his coat pocket and hands it to me. "You really care about my baby girl. Be good to her."

With a shaky hand, I reach for the bag, praying to God what's inside isn't what I assume it is, and even more so, that I don't drop it in the river. "Mr. Williams…"

"My name is Daniel. Mr. Williams is my father's name." He glances down at the velvet bag that I'm clutching as if my life depends on it. "That was my grandmother's ring. I gave it to Renee right here, and we both want Shelby to have it."

I open the bag, slide the contents into the palm of my hand, and see the most beautiful antique diamond engagement ring I have ever seen. It is exactly what I would imagine Shelby wanting: classy and modest.

A faint smile slides across Mr. Williams's face. "You'll probably have to get it sized. Shelby's such a tiny thing." He clears his throat, and I notice tears in his eyes. "Be good to her and never give up on her. If she's half as stubborn as her mother, you'll need a hefty dose of patience. But she will always be worth it."

A lump forms in my throat. "Sir, I can't take this."

"Please take it."

Instead of bringing me out here to kill or maim me, he's done something worse. He's made it even harder for me to walk away from this situation. There's no way I can drive his car back to town. I wouldn't be able to keep it between the lines with my shaking hands. Shelby and I need to come up with a breakup plan that now includes this ring before her parents give us anything else, like a house or the Aston Martin.

CHAPTER EIGHTEEN
Shelby

Before I even open the door, the magnificent aroma of cinnamon, bread, and all kinds of yummy goodness hits my olfactory nerves. I set my purse down on the end table and make my way toward the kitchen. My geeky boyfriend is at it again. Wearing the apron I bought him, he pulls a baking pan from the oven with one hand and holds the phone up to his ear with the other.

"I don't owe you any answers. It's none of your concern when I get back to Boston. And stop calling."

Wow. I've never heard of a professor hounding a student like this.

As soon as Tommy sees me, he yells "Bye" into the phone then slams it down on the counter. His eyes rake over me, and he gives me a forced smile. *Talk about faking it.* "Hey, sugar." Flour is everywhere, even in his hair. I smile, and he grabs me around the waist.

"Mmm, you smell good," I tell him.

"Not as good as you," he replies.

"Are you all right?"

He nuzzles my neck. "I am now."

"Want to talk?"

"No."

It's really frustrating how closed off he is about school. I wish he would let me help, but it's obvious my assistance isn't wanted.

I take in the state of the kitchen. It looks like a five-pound bag of flour exploded. I wrap my arms around his neck. "What are you baking?"

"Sourdough bread, cinnamon rolls, and snickerdoodles."

"Wow. Not that I'm complaining, but what's the occasion?"

He shrugs. "In the mood." He kisses my neck.

"I love it when you're in the mood."

He takes my hand and guides me toward the stairs that lead to my bedroom.

I stop him and skitter back into the kitchen to grab a cinnamon roll. "We wouldn't want them to go to waste."

"Can't have that, now, can we?"

"Why do you bake? You realize I'm going to eat everything you make."

He focuses on the ground and chews on the side of his mouth. "It clears my head."

What does he need to clear his head about? School? Fake engagement? Me?

I pull his face down so we're nose to nose. "Does this clear your mind?" I kiss his perfect lips.

"Crystal clear," he mumbles into my mouth. "How did it go with your mother?"

I bow my head and stare at my shoes. I was hoping I could say I made a step toward a fake breakup or that Mom changed her mind about him and successfully convinced me to call it off. But all of that would be a lie.

"Shelby, what happened?"

"Don't be mad."

He stares at the ceiling and chuckles. "Spit it out."

I bite my lower lip and attempt to formulate the best response, but there's no way to soften the blow. I let out an exasperated breath. "She bought me a wedding dress."

His eyes nearly bug out of their sockets. "What did you say?"

I back away from him. "It all happened so fast. I'm sorry, but the good thing is I can return it, and that's my plan. As soon as we are officially unengaged, I will take it back. It's the Vaughan method of dealing with the parentals."

"How hideous is it?"

I find his tickle spot, and he squirms out of my reach. "It's actually... it's beautiful. If I was really getting married, it would be perfect for me. Plus, it wasn't ungodly expensive."

His eyebrows waggle. "Do you have it here?"

"No. And even if I did, you couldn't see it."

He leans back against the wall, his eyes twinkling. "Is there a bad-luck rule about seeing the fake dress on the fake bride before the fake wedding?"

"Something like that."

He stalks toward me like a lion closing in on his prey. "Just as well because one glimpse at you in something like that, and I would want to rip it to shreds getting it off you. Isn't that what you're supposed to do on the wedding night?"

My cheeks flame. "Ha ha. I guess we should start planning our exit strategy."

His smile fades. "Yeah. It would be best before we see a not-so-fake wedding announcement in the paper."

I hug him, and he wraps his arms around my waist. I hear his breath catch. "What's wrong?"

"Nothing you need to worry about." He holds me even tighter, if that's possible, then his phone rings. He stiffens in my arms.

"Don't answer it," I whisper.

He lets me go, grabs his phone, and walks outside. Something is wrong, big time, and I am not sure what it is or how to fix it, especially if he won't talk to me about it.

FOR TEN MINUTES, I perch on the edge of the couch, waiting on Tommy to come back inside. When he does enter, he walks past me as if I'm not even there and storms into the kitchen. In silence, I follow him. He tosses dishes into the sink and fills it with detergent. Water sloshes everywhere as he washes the dishes.

"What's going on?"

"Nothing," he says, suddenly very interested in the sudsy water. His lips form a thin line.

"Nothing? You've been acting really strange, and you jump every time your phone rings." I wipe off some flour from the counter and hop up there so I can see his face better.

His molars are going to be ground down to stubs before the day is over. "You're exaggerating a bit."

I cross my arms. "I need to have a conversation with this Alex person." I pick his phone up off the counter. At the very least, I'm going to find out if he is a she.

Tommy snatches his phone out of my hands. "What do you think you're doing?"

I sit there, unable to breathe.

"Trust me. It's nothing."

I bite my lip to hold back tears. "Trust you when you're acting so odd? Something is going on."

He wipes his hands on a dish towel and crosses his arms. "Yes, something is going on, but even though we aren't really engaged, I was hoping you had enough faith in me. Believe me. If I thought you needed to be informed, I would tell you." He slams a dish into the drying rack, making me jump.

I'm not doing a good job at keeping the tears back, and I fight the urge to take the blame for his outburst, like I normally would. "I only wanted to help. That's what couples do." I motion between him and me. "We help each other through difficult times."

He stares at me and sighs deeply. "I guess I don't do this couple thing very well." He motions between us, mocking me. "Good thing you understand that now before this goes any further."

I swipe a tear away. "What happened here?" My voice is shaky. "A few minutes ago, we were all playful. Then your phone rings, and it's like a Jekyll-and-Hyde situation."

"What happened is that your imagination ran away with you, and you got too nosy."

I gasp. "I'm not nosy. Okay, maybe a little."

He chuckles as he rubs his chin. "You are very nosy, and it's cute, but you make it really difficult to keep a secret."

I match his movements by rubbing my chin. "Maybe I don't want secrets. And you were the nosy one poking around in my dresser drawers and asking far too many questions about my drawings."

He stares at the ceiling and groans. "Shelby, I—"

I throw a hand up to stop him. "I'm going to take a hot bath. I've had a long day. I don't even care about how your meeting with Dad went. It doesn't matter. Good night." I rush to the stairs, taking them two at a time as I listen to Tommy clang dishes around in the kitchen. I lock the bathroom door behind me and fill the tub with water so he can't hear my sobs. When I kneel down to rest my head on the side of the tub, I bawl like a baby.

By the time the bathtub is almost overflowing with water, I've forced myself to stop crying enough so he won't hear me. I slip into the hot water, but the tears continue to fall. I don't understand what happened or what I did wrong. I guess I knew deep down that Tommy was too good to be true. Just like all the other guys, he's keeping something from me. I abhor secrets. Secrets lead to lies, and I can't do that again.

But unlike all the other guys, I don't want Tommy to leave. I'm pretty sure I love him. I only wish he loved me back. Realizing all this starts another round of sobs. A knock sounds on the bathroom door, startling me.

"Yeah," I say after clearing the crud out of my throat.

"Shelby, can I come in?" Tommy's voice is soft and almost sounds apologetic.

"I'll be out in a minute." I slosh out of the tub, and while the water swirls down the drain along with my hopes, I wrap a robe around my wet body. Not caring about my appearance, I pile my hair into a big clump on top of my head and secure it with a clip. My reflection clearly shows I've had a major crying jag, but I don't care.

Tommy waits for me in my bedroom. He's sitting on my bed, with his head in his hands. When he senses my presence, he glances up with red-rimmed eyes. I guess I'm not the only one who has had a crying jag. We are about to have our fake breakup, and it feels all too real.

CHAPTER NINETEEN
Tommy

All I was trying to do was set up a little surprise for Shelby, but that went over like a lead balloon. I'm trying to do something nice for her, but I suck at surprises more than I suck at relationships. And when she tried to call Hazel... that would have been a disaster. All I need is for Hazel to fill Shelby's already suspicious ears with half-truths. Then Shelby jumps to the conclusion about who I was talking to when I walked outside. The timing was terrible, but I couldn't take that call with her in the house. It would have completely ruined my surprise. Now we're on the verge of breaking up, and that's the last thing I want.

The fake engagement and this argument, added to all the Hazel mess, is starting to make me freak out. Shelby is too close to learning the truth about Hazel, then she'll realize I'm not the great person she believes I am. And that scares the crap out of me. Something big shifted in my heart today. What started as having a fun time with a cute girl this summer has changed into something more serious and long-term. Having these feelings a few months ago would have made me run like a scalded dog. But now, I'm terrified I've messed it all up. On top of all that, Hazel's cryptic conversations peppered with her not-so-sexy chortle have me confused and concerned.

Shelby quietly enters her bedroom. Her face is red from all the tears I've caused. She drags out a pair of shorts and a T-shirt then goes into her walk-in closet to dress. When she returns, she finally meets my eyes.

I motion for her to sit by me on her bed. From the first time I laid eyes on her, I knew she was different and special. And this is coming from someone who doesn't know squat about relationships. But as soon as I saw her, I knew there was something about her that was going to stick with me forever.

She sits beside me, clutching the edge of the mattress so hard her knuckles are white. I don't have a clue how to smooth everything over without ruining my plans with her.

This whole idea was Heather's, which makes the mess partially her fault. "Do something special," she said. "Show everyone how in love you are. Do something spontaneous." It's obvious my sister is as clueless as I am when it comes to romance.

I clear my throat. "I'm a jerk."

She nods. Wow. She didn't have to agree with me.

"I understand you're trying to help and I shouldn't be so secretive. Soon, things will make sense."

"I'm tired, Tommy. I want to go to sleep." She gets up and stands in front of me. "We're going too fast."

I close my eyes. *Please, please don't break up with me. Please don't leave me.* When I open my eyes, she's still standing in front of me. She fakes a smile.

I swallow hard. "Please don't do this. I promise, you have nothing to worry about."

She takes my hands and kisses them. "You have enough to worry about without an engagement, fake or real, to weigh you down."

My heart sinks, but I agree with her anyway. I don't have the courage to tell her about the ring. Now is not the time.

Shelby clears her throat and takes a deep breath. "I care for you so much. Can't you see that?" Her voice cracks, and so does my heart. "But if you can't talk to me, I don't think I want to be with you. Fake or real."

She motions between her and me, reminding me of my awful outburst. I bow my head and bite my lip to fight back tears. Instead of walking away or telling me to take a hike, she wraps her arms around my head and holds me against her chest. Her strong heart beats against my temple. I don't hold back the tears anymore and let them soak her T-shirt. I hug her tightly.

She picks up my face and plants a kiss on my lips. "I will always love you, Tommy."

Shelby gives me a big bear hug, but it's nothing compared to how her words hold me. No one, apart from my family, has ever said those three words to me.

"I love you too, sugar." Finally, I'm able to say the three scariest words in the English language, but I wish it was under better, happier circumstances.

She sighs as she hugs me tighter. "Oh, Tommy…"

"I am so sorry. I realize I don't deserve this, but can I please stay the night? I'll be gone in the morning if you want me to. I'm not talking sex. I just need to hold you one more night. Please."

She gives me a pained expression. It's too much to ask of her, and I certainly don't deserve it, but I need it.

Her eyes dart away from me before she takes a deep breath. The internal struggle etches across her furrowed brow. "On one condition. Actually, make it two conditions."

"Anything."

"First off, you have to shut off your phone."

I take a big sigh of relief. "Already done. What's number two?"

She puts her finger to her lips and gives me a sideways glance. "You bring me a cinnamon roll."

I smile as I kiss her cheek. "Done, sugar. I'll be right back."

SHELBY'S LEG DRAPES over me as I feed her a sticky cinnamon roll. We haven't spoken in an hour as we cuddle. As promised, I don't initiate anything other than holding her. The only sound is her soft, satisfied moans as I feed her like a toddler. I love that she plays footsie with me without even realizing she's doing it. Her body fits perfectly tucked next to mine, like she's the other half of me—the better half. I don't deserve her, and if I don't get my crap together, I will lose her forever.

I want to confess my sins, but if I tell her about Hazel, she'll be hurt and may not be able to trust me again. She'll want me to stay in Nashville, which I'm more than fine with, but I have to do what's expected of me and hope I make it out alive and sane.

Out of the blue, she asks, "What's your favorite color?"

"Yellow. Yours?"

"Green, like your eyes. Did you have a pet growing up?"

I shake my head and pop another piece of cinnamon roll into her mouth. "No. Mom said she didn't need any more mouths to feed than what she already had."

She lets out a soft snicker. "We always had a dog. No matter how much I tried to make them my dogs, they always followed Vaughan around like he was their mother. He could make them do anything, and they were totally loyal to him. It's a gift. Next question: First job?"

"Ah, that would be lifeguard at the Y."

"Oh, I would have faked a cramp every day so you could give me mouth-to-mouth."

I kiss her cheek. "Fun. And I would have done my duty to make sure you got enough air and plenty of chest compressions."

She pops me on the arm.

I roll her over and lie next to her. I want to be on top of her, but I don't feel like getting rejected tonight. "What's with the twenty questions?"

"I realized how little we know about each other."

I rub noses with her. "We know the important stuff, but I get what you're saying. Dad says you shouldn't marry someone until they've had the flu."

She bursts out giggling. "What?"

"It's true."

"I always get a flu shot to help prevent getting the flu."

"I assume he meant it metaphorically. He's saying not to make a commitment until you've hit a bump in the road. It's then that you see how people act during the 'for worse' part."

"Ah. I get it. Does today qualify as a bump?"

I nuzzle her neck. "Does this mean you aren't breaking up with me?"

After a pause that makes my pulse race, she says, "I am not breaking up with you."

Relief washes over me. *Thank God.* "Thank you for not giving up on me."

"Honestly, I wanted to, but there's something about you that's different from anyone else I've ever met."

"I feel the same way about you. But I will tell you that when I get stressed and feel like things are out of my control, I am not a nice person."

She snorts. "I've noticed. But no one is perfect. You put too much pressure on yourself, and I wish you would open up more."

"I'll try." Breathing in sync with her relaxes me and gives me hope that I haven't damaged what we have so much that it's beyond repair. Plus, it gives me the perfect segue into telling her about my transgressions.

But I chicken out. "Your father is a good guy."

She plays with my hair, causing my eyes to roll back in my head. "He has his moments."

I prop my chin on her shoulder. "He let me drive his car."

She tips her head to the side. "No way."

"I was so scared I was going to scratch it. As much fun as it was to drive, I never want that kind of stress again."

"It's his baby. I drove it one time without his permission and was grounded for a month."

"I learned he's also quite the romantic. He, uh... he gave me your great-grandmother's engagement ring to give to you."

Shelby gasps. "Mom loves that ring." She snorts. "I love that ring."

"They want you to have it." I slide out of her grasp and pull out the velvet bag from my jeans pocket. With shaking hands, I give it to her. "I don't expect you to wear it, and it's your responsibility to give it back to him when the time is right."

She lets the ring fall out of the bag and into the palm of her hand. Then she hands the ring to me. "Just once, I'd like you to put it on my finger. I want to see what it feels like."

Swallowing hard, I take the ring and kneel in front of her. My heart is about to explode through my rib cage, and my legs are so wobbly, I almost fall over. She holds out her left hand, and I slide the ring on her finger. Something changes inside me. Her eyes are fixed on mine like she's feeling it too. My world tilts on its axis, and I have a new center: my Shelby. At this moment, I wish I could really ask her to marry me.

But not tonight. Probably never.

She examines how it sparkles in the light from her end table. Her sad smile changes to a frown as she removes the ring, places it back in the bag, and lays it on the nightstand. I'm not surprised, but my heart hurts just the same. She runs a finger down the velvet bag. "Part of me wishes it was all real."

"The ring is real. The way I feel about you is very real. More real than I realized."

"The other stuff isn't." She snatches her hand away like the velvet bag burns her skin.

"Maybe someday?"

A slight grin slides across her face. "Maybe. But we've got to figure out how to stop this runaway train of lies without our families hating us forever."

"We could elope." I didn't think that thought through before I said it.

Shelby's eyebrows shoot up. "Our parents would never forgive us."

I shrug. "But we would never have to tell them about this mess."

She shakes her head. "Oh no, mister. It would come out one day. I'm having a hard time keeping the lies straight, and it's only been a couple of days. It's inevitable I would mess up at some point."

I slide my arm around her waist and pull her closer. "Got any better ideas?"

"I said I'd tell my parents first, but it might be easier if we start with Heather. She would be a good warm-up for the big reveal. If I can survive her wrath, the rest should be a piece of cake."

When I don't reply, she tilts her head to the side. "Tommy, why are you grinning like you stole the last cookie?"

It's no use lying to her about it. I'm in enough trouble as it is. "Uh, Heather knows."

Her eyes squint almost shut. "Since when?"

"Since the beginning."

She swats me on the shoulder.

"Ow. You have to understand our bond. I can't lie to Heath Bar. She has a sixth sense about things with me."

Shelby pushes away from me and taps her foot. "Will I ever be a person you can't lie to?"

I groan and stand. "Sugar, I promise you, I haven't lied to you." And yet, I lied again to cover up the first lie. The hole I'm digging is getting deeper by the day, and one day, she's going to push me inside it and cover up my body. But if she ever asks me anything specific, I will be truthful with her. I won't lie to her... again.

Shelby stands on her tiptoes and pecks me on the tip of my nose. "I believe you. There is one little thing I guess I should tell you."

No telling what it could be. "Go on."

"I told Vaughan."

She pokes me in my tickle spot and scoots past me. I grab her around the waist, toss her on the bed, and collapse next to her. A girly squeal echoes throughout the room. Maybe we are still a couple. For a moment, she plays with my hair then kisses my cheek. She nudges me away from her and rolls over on her side, facing away from me, then wraps my arm around her waist.

"Good night."

"Good night, sugar." I kiss her cheek and settle in for the night. I'm going to sleep wrapped around the only girl for me and pretend reality doesn't exist. And hopefully when she gets her surprise tomorrow, she'll forget about this bump and won't ever find out about my lies. A guy can hope.

CHAPTER TWENTY
Shelby

My alarm clock forces me out of a deep sleep. I flop over and notice the other side of my bed is cold and vacant. Tommy must have gotten up super early and left. The night ended on a light-hearted note, but something still doesn't feel right. Even though he sort of apologized and told me there is nothing to worry about, I'm still worried. Something is going on, and I need to figure it out before it eats both of us alive. I probably don't want the truth, but I need to find out.

I stumble downstairs in search of coffee, and I find a plate of cinnamon rolls on a plate with a note folded into an origami swan. I stare at the coffee maker and play with the swan, trying to get the courage to unfold it. It kills me to mess up the pretty design, but I unfold the paper swan and read the note inside.

"Dear, sweet Shelby. I am sorry for the mysterious phone calls last night. You have nothing to worry about, and all will make sense soon. You mean everything to me. You're the only thing right in my life. I need you more than air. Love, Tommy."

I swipe the tears away. None of this makes sense, and I'll never understand why he doesn't want to tell me what's going on. I either have to let it eat me alive, accept it, or move on. But I can't move on. I've been burned in the past for being too trusting, so I have to get to the bottom of this. If there is anyone on the planet that's good at uncovering secrets, it's Isaac. He's the best sleuth on earth.

While I dress for work, the drawstring bag holding the engagement ring taunts me from where it rests on my nightstand. It keeps filling my line of sight. I sit on my bed, pick up the black velvet bag, and let the ring slide out into my hand. I slip it on my ring finger and hold my hand out to enjoy the view. It's probably not the best idea to wear it, especially since I need to tamp down my feelings of wanting it to be real, but it's so pretty. And since Tommy and I need to pretend to break up, the fewer people who know what's going on, the better.

But it's so pretty.

I'll regret this later, but I sling the empty velvet bag onto my bed, pick up my purse, and head out to start my day with an art-deco diamond ring decorating my left ring finger. I look down at the old-European-style cut set in the platinum band. I feel better already.

ON MY WAY TO WORK, I stop by the pediatric ward to see little Stella packing up all her balloons and stuffed animals to go home. Darla grins from ear to ear. When Stella sees me, she runs to give me a big hug.

I run my hand over her soft hair. "You take it easy for a bit, okay? Rest up so you can go back to school in the fall."

Her little head bobs up and down. "Yeah. I'm going to be a second grader."

I hug her extra tight. "I'm so proud of you."

She skips clumsily off to find her dad. Having a father must be a new concept for her, but she acts so natural with Theo. It's like they've been a family all along. I catch a glimpse of Darla as she stares at the two of them together skipping down the hallway.

"It appears as if you have two kids to take care of now."

Nothing would be able to slap the smile off Darla's face. "And don't forget Yeti. That is, if I can ever get my dog back from Isaac. They've grown rather fond of each other these last few weeks."

I squeeze her around the shoulders again. "I'm so happy for you."

"Thanks." She pulls away from me, taking in my appearance. I'm sure the dark circles and puffy eyes didn't go unnoticed. "Are you okay?"

I release her and shrug. "I'm not sure."

"Is it Tommy?"

When I don't answer right away, she leads me over to some chairs and sits beside me.

Chewing on my lip, I confide in her. "He's acting really strange. Someone keeps calling him, and he gets super tense every time the phone rings. And every time I bring it up, Tommy gets all pissy."

Darla glances at her child farther down the hall then back at me. "Who do you suspect it is?"

"Alex. Tommy says it's his professor, but it's real stalkerish."

"Hmm. I can ask Theo if you want me to."

"If you think it would do any good, go for it. I'm worried about him. Tommy's already apologized a hundred times, but something is off, like he's dreading going back to school."

"Theo said he was taking a break from school this summer. Maybe it was getting to him."

I bow my head, and Darla takes my hand in hers. "Nice rock."

I groan. "Dad gave this to Tommy to give to me. It was my great-grandmother's ring."

She fingers the ring on my hand. "I was wondering, because Tommy doesn't have two nickels to squeeze together, much less enough to buy something like this. Are you okay with this happening so fast?"

I can't keep the smile from spreading over my face. "I am, but the last thing I want to do is put more stress on him. Not to mention, I don't want to start out a relationship with secrets. That's never good."

"Mommy, let's go," Stella whines, tugging on Theo's arm at the other end of the hallway.

Darla gives her the one-minute signal. "Maybe we can make it a double wedding."

The reality of her statement hits me like a tidal wave, and I can't resist bouncing up and down. "Really?"

She grins and hugs me. "It will be soon too. I'm not letting him out of my sight again."

I give her a big squeeze. "Oh my gosh. This is fantastic. I'm so happy for you. You deserve this so much." I, on the other hand, don't deserve squat. First, I lie to my parents. Now I'm lying to my best friend. *Stop digging that hole.*

Darla glances over at her little girl and her soon-to-be husband. Theo grins and motions for her to join them. The expression they share is one I have to draw when I get home. That exact expression holds so many emotions: adoration, family, hope, desire. They deserve it all.

Darla nudges me with her hip. "Don't worry about Tommy. If it's right, it will work out. You wouldn't fall for someone so easily if it didn't feel right, especially after the dumb drummer smacked you around."

I roll my eyes, but there is so much truth in her words. "I was an idiot. Why do you have to remind me?"

"To make sure you realize that this situation with Tommy is nothing compared to what the little drummer boy put you through."

Ain't that the truth. Nothing will ever be that bad.

I nudge her with my shoulder. "You better get that cutie pie home before I kidnap her."

Her smile fades. "You'll be all right?"

"I will be. Got to get to work before Isaac has them doing line dance moves to Michael Jackson."

Darla nods in solidarity. She understands how much truth there is in that one sentence. "I'll see what I can find out for you from Theo."

"You're the best."

She kisses me on the cheek and scoops up Stella in her arms.

I wave to them as they leave the hospital as one big, happy family. They are going to get married, really married—not a fake, pretend event—but a real-life, 'til-death-do-us-part marriage. And it couldn't happen to a more deserving pair, or trio if I count little Stella.

STANDING NEXT TO THE row of elliptical machines, Isaac grabs my hand. Tears pool in his eyes. Isaac doesn't miss anything. He has this psychic ability to figure out the unspoken. I always thought he knew Darla was pregnant with Stella before she did.

"Is it for real now?"

I snatch my hand back before any onlookers get a glimpse of my ring. "Shh. No, but I had to wear it for one day before I have to give it back."

He gapes like I've lost my mind. "I wouldn't. That thing is gorgeous. The sex must be out of this world."

Heat rushes up my neck. "That's none of your business." I head toward my office, hoping he gets the hint to drop it.

"Cranky woman."

I stare at him. "I'm still your boss, remember?"

He gives me a patronizing salute. "Yes, ma'am."

A Queen song plays over the radio, and Isaac jumps up and down. He grabs me by the hand and leads me to the middle of the weight room to sing along with "Bohemian Rhapsody," knowing how much I love that song. Before the second bar, he's got me into it. Several men lifting weights clap and cheer us on. By the time we get to the Wayne and Garth headbanging part, we have a fan club surrounding us, singing right along. When the song is over, we get a standing ovation, and Isaac and I bow. When I stand back up, I see

Tommy leaning against the front counter with his phone out, videoing us. "That was awesome."

He meets me halfway, and I give him a tentative hug. I hope we're okay, but things between us still feel a little unsettled.

Tommy mimics the headbanging scene and says, "I would have paid money to see that."

Isaac helps a guy doing bench presses while bobbing his head to the next song. "When Isaac channels Freddie Mercury, it gets a little crazy."

Tommy lets me down from the hug, but not before he gives me a kiss.

"What are you doing here?"

"I left before you got up because I had an errand to run. I called in a favor." He pulls out two front-row tickets to Exceed, one of my all-time favorite bands.

I bounce up and down and squeal so loud, the guy doing bench presses can't finish his set. Isaac has to lift the bar off the poor guy's chest. "Oh my God. How did you get these? The concert's been sold out for months. This is fantastic. Did you realize I love them? Oh my gosh. Oh my gosh."

When I have to stop rambling to catch my breath, Tommy replies, "A friend from back in the day works for Universal Records. Exceed is their band. I knew doing his math homework all those years would pay off one day."

I leap into his arms, and he lets out an "oof."

"I took a risk, hoping you hadn't already got a new boyfriend for tonight."

I give him the evil eye. "Stop it." I kiss him on the cheek. "Thank you. Is this what all the secrecy was about?"

"Yep. But here's the kicker." He pulls out backstage passes.

When I squeal, I bet all the dogs in the neighboring county howl. I grab Tommy by the neck and pull him down for a scorching-hot kiss. "You're the best."

Isaac claps and breaks the trance Tommy and I are in. "Yeah, yeah. Love is grand. But you, sir, are not a member of this club." Isaac points at the door. "Get."

Tommy salutes him, making Isaac chuckle. "Yes, sir." Then he locks eyes with me. "See you at your place?"

"Of course. Wait. Did you hear about Darla and Theo's engagement?"

He blushes. "I knew he was going to do it but didn't hear my mother's shrieking celebration yet, so I didn't realize it happened."

"Well, it did. Maybe the focus will be off of us."

He winks, turning me to putty. "Good thinking, right? Especially since your three days are up tomorrow, remember?"

"How could I forget?" I haven't thought of one decent way to make this situation go away, and the clock is ticking.

He waves as he heads toward the exit. "See ya."

I dance around Isaac and squeal again. Poor Isaac might never get the ringing out of his ears.

Tommy shakes his head as he starts to leave. He stops when he bumps into his sister Jen. "What are you doing here?" He seems more confused than I am.

"I came to see both of you." She drags him back to me and claps her hands together. "I have the most wonderful idea."

"Uh-oh," Tommy mumbles.

Jen squeezes my shoulders. "Together with my mom and yours, we're going to throw you two an engagement party."

My hand flies to my mouth to cover the gasp, but it also reveals the ring, the huge ring I'm not supposed to be wearing.

"Oh my lands. That is beautiful." Jen scrunches her brow at her brother. "You picked this out?"

"Not exactly." While Jen focuses on the ring, Tommy mouths to me, "Are you frickin' kidding me?"

"Figures," she says. "It's beautiful. So, about the party..."

I stare at Tommy in hopes he can read my mind. If he tells Jen this was all a misunderstanding, this could be the beginning of untangling the mess I started. He clears his throat. "Jen, uh... the thing is..."

Jen glances from me to Tommy, confusion etched all over her face.

As if a light bulb goes on in his head, Tommy snaps his fingers. "Why don't you plan a party for your other brother instead."

He clearly read my signal wrong.

When his words register, Jen covers her mouth with her hands.

Tommy cringes. "Or maybe I wasn't supposed to say that."

Jen throws her hands in the air. "Praise God. This is fantastic. We can make it a double engagement party. How does Friday sound? At Demos."

Keeping his eyes trained on me, Tommy winks as he answers his sister. "Friday works for us."

CHAPTER TWENTY-ONE

Tommy

After Jen does her hugs and kisses on her way out the door, Shelby ushers me into her office.

"First Mom and Dad put a wrinkle in things, and now your sister?" She flails her arms around as she paces the room.

"Jen's announcement gave me an idea, but first tell me, what in the world possessed you to wear that ring? The last I knew, that rock was tucked away in a velvet bag in your bedroom. Did it magically appear on your finger?" She'd better have a good reason because it already seems mighty comfortable on her hand.

She gazes down at it. "I wanted to see what it felt like. I was only going to wear it one day." She peeks up through the hair that has escaped her ponytail. "What is your idea?"

I sit on the edge of her desk and scrub my scruffy chin. "Let's stage an argument at the party. Make it a huge blowout. Everyone will agree we're moving too fast."

Shelby chews on the inside of her jaw. "That could work."

"You should be thanking me. Tomorrow was your deadline, and now I'm extending it until the party."

I hold out my arms to her, and she wastes no time collapsing into them. "After all this, you'll never want to marry me for real, right?" She sucks in a breath. "Don't answer that."

A warmness works its way up my body and through my chest. Words like that would normally send me scampering away, but something about this trial commitment has helped me see things in a whole new light. Maybe it's the opportunity to get used to the idea of a forever without the obligations that come with it. Or maybe it's because it's Shelby. Really, it's both. And a forever with Shelby doesn't sound so bad at all. I just wish school wasn't looming over me like a black cloud. At least, I hope Hazel got the message after I blocked the burner phone number. I haven't heard from her since last night.

I kiss the top of Shelby's head and mumble into her hair. "You may not be finished with me yet."

She squeezes me tighter. "Thanks. I should get to work before Isaac comes barreling in here. See you later?"

"You bet, sugar. And don't forget the concert tonight."

Her grin spreads across her face. "How did you know I liked that band?"

I bite my lip to keep from smiling. "You like to sing in the shower."

Shelby kisses my cheek. "You haven't seen anything yet."

SHELBY CAN'T SIT STILL in the passenger seat as I drive her car to the concert. She's so smoking hot in her skinny jeans, skimpy top, and leather jacket, I'm going to have to beat off a bunch of gawkers tonight. She's got the rocker vibe down to a science, and I have the scientist vibe going with my khakis and polo shirt. I'm more ready for a round of golf than for a rock concert.

"I haven't been to a concert in ages. And to see my favorite band is unbelievable."

"I'm glad you're glad."

"I hope I don't embarrass you too much. I tend to sing very loud at concerts."

I smile at her. "As long as you don't throw your bra up on the stage, we'll be good."

She sticks her tongue out. "I promise I won't do that... this time."

My jaw drops to the floor. "Tell me you haven't done that."

She cringes as she fidgets in her seat. "Yeah, I went through a groupie stage. My mom hated it when I would leave the house, looking like a hooker."

I cough. "A what?"

"Sorry. Thank God I grew out of it. She was so worried I'd quit school and follow some heartthrob on a worldwide tour. And I would have too."

"What stopped you?"

She gazes out of her window, watching the cars pass us. "Heartthrobs tend to be jerks."

I'll never understand how musicians always get the girls. Brainiacs don't have fans that stalk them. On second thought, I have one stalker, and that's more than enough for me. "I guess I'm not a heartthrob."

"You are more than that."

"Aww, Shelby Lynn, you're going to make me cry." I bat my eyes for emphasis and wipe away a fake tear.

She pops me on the arm. "How dare you call me that."

"Sorry, I couldn't resist. Just promise me you'll give me a heads-up if you plan on getting your boobs autographed."

"I promise."

Before I can shut off her car, she has already bolted out and adjusted the strap of her purse over her neck. "Come on, slowpoke."

I slide my hand in hers, and I can barely keep up with her through the parking deck as we head toward the concert venue. This place could easily hold twenty thousand people, and I don't see one empty seat in the house.

"You are very handsome," Shelby says over her shoulder.

"Uh, thanks?"

She slips her arm through the crook of my elbow and leans into me. "You really don't notice, do you?"

"I'm not sure what you're talking about."

She points at a girl walking by. "That is the third girl in less than thirty seconds who has undressed you with her eyes."

Heat rises up my neck. "That's not true."

A laugh bolts out of her throat as she points at another one. "If I wasn't clinging to you, you would have to peel them off of you."

I roll my eyes. "Sugar, no one sees me like that."

"I do." She takes her arms away from me. "Since you're a science geek, let's do a little experiment." She backs away from me and leans against the wall of the concourse. I move in a circle and bump into a drop-dead gorgeous redhead. Her eyes roam my body, and all of a sudden, I feel very naked.

"Hey there," she says seductively.

"Hi."

"You here alone?" The redhead's fingers dig into my bicep. *Oh dear.*

Shelby steps up and stands next to me with her arms crossed, tapping her toe. "No, he's not."

The redhead's smile deflates. "Can't blame a girl for trying."

When she prances off, Shelby shakes her head. "Told ya."

"Don't ever leave me again. I feel violated." I lean in to whisper in her ear. "Although you have permission to violate me any time."

I love it when she bites her bottom lip. "I'll keep that in mind."

At the entrance my friend John told me to enter, we wave our VIP passes and are directed toward the backstage area. We're met with a sea of people—some in business attire, most in a mishmash of styles—and more musical instruments in one room than I've ever seen. All the people make me feel as overwhelmed as when I'm at school because both there and here, I'm among way too many people who are so different than me. This is so very much out of my league, which is evident by how sluggish my feet are compared to Shelby's bouncy gait. Just as I'm ready to suggest we find our seats out in the arena, my friend John catches my eye. He waves us over, and we shake hands. His black jeans, button-down shirt, and backstage lanyard around his neck make it obvious he's not part of the road crew or one of the entertainers.

"Hey, John. This is Shelby."

Shelby skips over to him and gives him a big hug.

John pulls back from her. "Uh, I guess that means she likes her surprise."

Shelby claps her hands together. "This is so much fun."

John waves to a musician. "Hope you enjoy yourself. Have you ever been backstage before?"

"Yeah, but not for a band this big," Shelby says.

John grins. "Remember, most musicians are really nice, just trying to make a living. But some are pricks. If they don't act friendly, just keep moving."

Shelby smiles from ear to ear. "Of course."

A dude with piercings in his ears, nose, and eyebrow, who has a green Mohawk, meanders down the hallway toward us, carrying drumsticks. The musician appears as if he were transported directly from a bad eighties music video.

John points to the dude. "See that guy? Total loser."

Shelby squeaks and scoots behind me.

"Are you okay?" I ask.

She grabs my hand and squeezes it tight. "I got a little light-headed. Do you mind if we go to our seats and sit for a bit?"

John motions to a room over to the side of the stage. "You can go there and rest a bit. It's where the band hangs out when they aren't on stage."

"No!"

John asks, "What the heck?"

"Beats me," I say as I reach for my girl. "Shelby, let's get you some water and then find our seats. John, thanks so much. We'll see you later."

I slide an arm around her shoulders and guide her to the door when, above the backstage chatter, Mohawk Dude yells, "Well, well, well. If it isn't Shelby Lynn Williams." He whistles. "Damn, girl. You get hotter every time I see you."

I peer down at Shelby. Her lip trembles, and she's gone ghostly white. I give Mohawk Dude a wave and escort my girl out of the hallway as she squeezes the life out of my hand. This is just my luck. The one connection I have in the music business leads us right smack-dab into the little drummer boy.

CHAPTER TWENTY-TWO
Shelby

Blaze stands there with his syrupy grin and that stupid toothpick sticking out of his mouth. He's right in front of me with arms open wide. In the three years since I last saw him, he's aged at least a decade. He has a "rode hard and put up wet" appearance to him, even though he still tries to pull off the same stage outfit of leather and chains. And he's managed to find some real estate on his scrawny body for even more tattoos and piercings.

Blaze scans Tommy and clucks his tongue. "Who's Frat Party Ken?"

I lace my fingers through Tommy's and squeeze our hands together in solidarity.

"Blaze, this is Tommy. Tommy meet..."

Tommy sticks out his hand to shake, but Blaze only stares at it and chuckles. "Whatever, dude."

"He's my fiancé." For once, this fake relationship might work in my favor. I'll try anything to get this creep to back off.

Blaze snorts. "Sure he is." He turns his back on Tommy and slides an arm around my shoulder to drag me into a forced hug. I try to push away, but he pins me up against him. An all-too-familiar marijuana aroma clings to his T-shirt. That's usually his warm-up drug of choice. His mouth grazes my ear, and a shiver runs up my spine. "I missed you."

"I bet you have."

Tommy clears his throat. "Do you mind?" He pulls me from Blaze, and I backpedal into Tommy's much taller frame.

I search for his hand, and when I find it, I grab on for dear life. Tommy towers over Blaze, and his puffed-up appearance causes him to appear even larger.

Blaze ignores him. "We're having a party after the gig, as usual. You're welcome to come. That is, if Ken will let you. It'll be like old times." He winks and zones in on my boobs.

Feeling suddenly underdressed, I cross my arms to cover the girls. He always had this talent of making me feel like I was naked. "Does 'just like old times' come complete with cheating? Or does it come with me getting another black eye?"

Tommy jerks around to face me. "What?"

Blaze rolls his eyes. "She's joking, dude. It was a big misunderstanding."

Tommy's jaw muscles flex. "I bet it was... *dude*."

Blaze chuckles. "Chill, Preppy Paul. You can come too if your mommy won't mind."

Tommy raises his eyebrows and waits for me to say something. I stare back at him. I don't want to be anywhere near Blaze, but everything happens so fast, I can't make my mouth say "hell no."

Blaze lights up a cigarette and blows smoke in Tommy's face. Tommy stifles a cough.

"So, what'll it be?" Blaze asks. "I'll have your favorite nose candy."

I cringe. I only did drugs to fit into his crowd, and I never liked it, but at the time, I could sense I was getting dangerously close to liking it. Thank goodness the smack to the head Blaze gave me knocked some sense into me, along with my brother threatening to really kick my butt if I got near Blaze or drugs ever again.

So I walked away and never answered Blaze's calls. It didn't take long before he lost interest and moved on to the next plaything. I never regretted my clean break, and seeing him right now verifies that I made the right choice. There's no way I could want Blaze after all this time. He treated me like crap, and it took me too long to figure that out. Thank God I did.

By Tommy's irritated expression, he must interpret my moment to recall the bad memories as hesitation or temptation. His hands are clenched in fists. "Why don't I leave you two alone to... catch up," he says, backing away.

"No way," I scream and scamper to catch up to him.

"I'll call you, babe," Blaze yells as Tommy and I make a beeline away from him and down the hall.

"And I won't answer," I holler back as I catch up to Tommy and grab for his arm. "I'm sorry. He's a big jerk. I didn't realize he was in the warm-up band. If I had known, I would not have wanted to come."

He stops walking and cages me up against the wall.

"Tommy—"

"Did he hit you?"

When I don't answer immediately, he growls. "If you say you deserved it, I will flip out. Guys don't hit girls. Ever."

"Just once."

He stumbles backward and scrubs his face with his hands. "I don't believe this."

Blaze leans up against the wall in the distance, staring at us with an evil smirk. I do not need this. He is part of my past, and that's where he needs to stay. I was at my lowest emotionally when Tommy walked into my life. Before then, I didn't let anyone close because Blaze had beaten me down. There is nothing attractive about that guy anymore. Not one thing.

"Kiss me." I don't mean to sound so needy, but dang it, I am.

Tommy's lips slam into mine like he's as much in need of the kiss as I am. When we come up for air, I say, "You went to a lot of trouble to get these tickets, but I feel ill. Can we go home?"

He nods, staring at Blaze. "I've had enough entertainment for one night."

Blaze waves at us and makes a "call me" motion.

Tommy takes me by the hand, and we walk out of the arena. I can hardly keep up with his long strides. Before we get to the parking lot, my phone rings. The sound of Stevie Ray Vaughan's "The House is Rockin'" blares from my phone. I ignore my little brother's ringtone, but as soon as the ringing stops, it starts up again.

Tommy throws a hard glance in the direction of my phone. "Go ahead. Answer it. You're itching to talk to Blaze."

I pull out my cell phone. Tommy is so cute when he's jealous, and I can't help but grin. I rotate the screen toward him. "Oh, lookie here. The calls were from... my brother. I am pretty sure Blaze doesn't remember my number, and even if he did, I don't care. Do you believe me now?"

He slows down enough for me to catch up to him. "Yeah." He blows out a breath. "So that was the little drummer boy in there?"

"Yes, and you don't have to tell me. I have terrible taste in men." I slam my hands over my mouth, realizing I just insulted Tommy. "I meant I used to. Ugh. I can't stand the sight of him. I'm embarrassed I was ever that desperate. I was stupid and lonely and starstruck."

He runs a hand through his hair, making it stand on end. "Are you sure you don't miss the attention of a semi-not-so-almost-famous rock star?"

I shake my head until it hurts. "No, I don't. I like my life now. I love you." I take his hand and squeeze it. "You believe me, don't you?"

"Yes." He chuckles. "Preppy Paul?"

I exhale and fall into his arms. "What a jerk."

"Let's go home. I've got the kind of treat you'll really like."

My eyes roll back in my head. "Yum. That's what I want to hear." We walk hand in hand to the car, and every few steps, I sneak a peek behind us to make sure Blaze is nowhere to be seen. Then I pull Tommy's head down so I can whisper in his ear. "About that treat?"

He grins. "Yeah. Interested?"

I stare at him like he's lost his mind. "Apple tart."

He groans as he unlocks my door. "Woman, you are killing me."

"Okay. I wonder if Blaze can make apple tarts." *Shelby, that was tacky.*

He grabs me and pushes me up against the car. "Trust me, my... tarts are way better than his."

I kiss him softly. "No comparison."

His hands roam under my jacket, and I wrap my arms around his neck. Then my phone rings again, but this time it is not my brother's ringtone. If it's Blaze calling, I may go back in there, and this time, I'll be the one to get arrested for assault. Tommy stares, waiting for my next move. I don't want to go down the Blaze road again. I gape at Tommy.

He raises an eyebrow. "What's it going to be?"

"I don't want him."

"You sure?"

"You're being ridiculous." My voice screeches through the parking lot.

He hands me the backstage pass. "Go on. It's killing you. Go have... fun. You want to. Every time your phone rings, you get tense, like it's reminding you of what you're missing out on."

"That's not true. And to prove it to you..." I pull out my phone and power it down.

He points at his head. "Are you sure? Because this hair is never going to be dyed green. Ever."

A lady walking by us stares as I crack up. "So you're not ruling out the Mohawk?"

The edge of his mouth twitches, and he bites the inside of his jaw. "I'll leave that one on the table for now."

I smooth out a lock of his hair that doesn't want to lie back down. "Don't. I like it just the way it is." Once I get all his hair smoothed down, I mess it up again. "What was your name again? Ken? Paul? I can't remember."

"Not funny. I want to deck him so bad."

"Oh my, Tommy. This is a side of you I haven't seen yet."

He leans forward until his forehead rests on mine. "The thought of having to share you with anyone makes me see a little green, but I should trust you."

"Are you going to block Alex's calls?"

His jaw clenches. "I can't do that. It's school. I wish to God I could."

"Me too, Tommy. Maybe having to share you has me seeing a little green too."

"It's not the same."

I shake my head. "It feels the same."

His phone alerts him to an incoming text, and I jut out my chin as I hold out my hand. "I showed you mine."

His brow furrows as he reads the message. I stand on my tiptoes in order to read his phone, but he backs away.

"What does Alex want tonight?"

He shoves the phone in his back pocket.

"Tommy, what are you hiding? If it's school, just say so. Or is it something else? Or someone else?" I'm tired of walking on eggshells about Boston. He needs to spit it out. I may not like it, but it has to be said.

"No. Stop asking."

I swallow hard, and for the first time since I met him, I really don't believe he's telling me the truth. There's nothing I can do to change his mind, so I say, "If it's all the same to you, I really want to be alone tonight."

His jaw drops, then he throws up his hands in frustration. "Fine."

Things are far from fine.

CHAPTER TWENTY-THREE
Tommy

When I get to Theo's apartment, I sling my keys across the room and let out a huge groan. I'm so glad Theo moved in with Darla because I don't want to deal with having to explain anything to him. I'm the biggest dork on the planet. It's clear that I don't have much girlfriend experience. Even though I'm supposedly a smart dude, I failed the chick test, big time.

I head into the kitchen, but since I haven't stayed here in weeks and Theo lives on hospital food, there are no ingredients to even make toast. Trying to figure out another way to calm down besides bake, I pace through the living room then pull out my phone to dial my professor. I need to give her an answer.

"I was beginning to assume you were ignoring me," Professor Alexander says.

"I've been thinking."

"And?"

I stare at the ceiling, not believing what I'm about to say. "I, uh, I'm coming back to Boston. Might as well, right?" These last few days have been so stressful, even Boston is sounding pretty good.

"Oh, Tom, that's wonderful. I've got some great ideas to share with you about the next steps on your project. Just tell me when you'll be here, and I'll have your lab space ready."

After a deep sigh and a quick kick to my own ass, I say, "Give me a few weeks to find a place to live."

"Sounds good. See you soon."

I hang up the phone, and it immediately rings. Assuming it's Alexander again, I answer without checking the caller ID.

"I just happened to be getting a free meal with the folks and overheard you talking to Mom. So, you're coming back. Can't wait to see you."

Son of a...

"No, Hazel. I said no."

"Stop calling me that hideous name."

Thus the basis for me using it.

She huffs into the phone. "We need to catch up."

I slump down on the couch. "No. I'm coming back to school. That's all. It's over between us, and I'm engaged, remember?"

"You're engaged?" Her high-pitched shrill sends shock waves through my eardrum.

"I'm pretty sure I told you, but since you don't listen to anyone other than yourself, I assume my words fell on deaf ears."

"And you can survive a long-distance relationship?"

Nope. "Of course."

"Sure..."

I run a hand through my hair. "Listen, Hazel. There is no 'us.' That was over before it started. If I come back, I'm a student only. Got it?"

"No. I do not get it."

"Back off, or I will tell your mother." I should have done that when it all started, but Professor Alexander has a "no drugs, no drama, no daughter" policy. At least I didn't do drugs. Hazel tried to get me to, but it was one of the many reasons I needed to get away from her.

I don't like school, but if I'm going to be there, I certainly need to have my major professor on my side. She could make or break my entire career. If Professor Alexander refuses to sign off on my work, all my time there would be for nothing.

"Don't threaten me. Two can play at this game."

I sit up straight. "What are you talking about?"

"Let's see. Besides sleeping with the professor's daughter, there's the part about getting arrested. Does any of that ring a bell in that big brain of yours?"

I chuckle. "Only you can stir up trouble and walk away unscathed. I got to hand it to you. It's a gift."

"Or maybe some incriminating photos getting into the wrong hands..."

"There's not even a selfie out there on the cloud. Nice try."

Hazel remains silent for a beat. Then in a singsong voice, she adds, "I wouldn't be so sure about that."

A shiver runs up my spine. There are no photos. *Are there?* My phone buzzes to tell me I have a text from my sister.

Heather: *WTF did you do?*

"I have to go."

"Bye, Thomas."

My blood boils when she calls me Thomas, and I'm sure it's a dig because I use her real name.

"Whatever." I hang up in the middle of one of her hyena cackles.

Instead of texting my sister back, I do the old-fashioned thing—I call her.

My voice trembles as I give her the news. "I'm going back."

"Where are you?"

"Theo's."

"I'll be there in ten."

I hang up and throw the phone across the room. The cover pops off and skitters under the table. Boston is the last place I need to be. Hazel is up to something, and it can't be good. I also don't want to leave Shelby on a bad note. Regardless of the engagement being fake, I don't want to mess things up with her for real.

THIRTY MINUTES LATER, Heather knocks on the door. I sling it open, ready to be mad at her for taking so long, but I can't because she has four bags full of groceries. *Bless her heart.*

"That's the longest ten minutes in history."

"You are lucky no one was at the store at this hour, or it would have been longer. You'll agree that this was worth the wait." She waddles into the kitchen and hoists the bags onto the counter then waves her hand around the supplies she bought.

"Since Theo's been eating at the hospital for weeks, I assumed there was nothing in the pantry worth consuming. Surely you can make something out of these random items."

I grab her into a bear hug. "Thank you."

"No problem. Now, tell me what's going on."

For the next hour, I talk as I start a loaf of bread and whip up a batch of cookies while she reassembles my cell phone. As the cookies are still in the oven, I plop the bread dough onto the floured countertop. As I knead the dough, I fill Heather in on the events of the last few days: the calls from my professor and Hazel, the mess with Blaze, and the last call from Hazel.

Heather's jaw drops a little farther with every event I tell her. "I'm confused. Sometimes the calls were from your professor, and others were from Haz-hell calling herself Alex, the crazy daughter?"

"Yes."

"Did I ever mention that her rationale for calling herself Alex is the dumbest thing ever?"

"Yep. I think you've mentioned that a time or two." I fold the dough again for good measure.

"It's like insisting that people call me Ed because my last name is Edwards."

"I'm not arguing with you."

"Why does your professor keep hounding you?"

"She's like that. Works twenty-four, seven. When she has an idea about a project, she calls and texts. It's easy for her to forget most people have lives outside the lab."

Heather pretends to choke me. "Why didn't you say that to Shelby? She thinks you're cheating."

"Because she'll say 'just say no' to the calls, and believe me, nobody says no to Alexander. She's the best in the field."

Heather makes a *pfft* sound. "Never mind that part. Hazel has fatal attraction written all over her face. She's mental. Do you really believe she has damaging pictures of you?"

Trying not to make eye contact with my sister, I focus on the task in front of me and press the heels of my hands into the dough. "If she does, she must have a secret camera hidden in my apartment."

Heather acts like she's going to throw up. "I wouldn't put it past her."

After another punch to the dough, I let out a huge sigh. "You aren't helping. I've been racking my brain, trying to remember one incident when she could have staged something like that, and I come up with nothing."

Heather cringes. "To think you did it with her makes me want to throw up. You could have your pick of girls, and you get involved with a person who starts fights just to make someone else jealous. What is wrong with you?"

"A moment of weakness. And any guy worth their weight would have stepped in to protect an inebriated girl at a bar. How was I to know I drew the short straw? I happened to be at the bar the night she decided to make her ex pay for breaking up with her. Now she's doing the same with me."

Heather groans. "It's tough being noble. You should teach a course on that topic."

I wallop the dough one more time before I place it in a bowl and cover it with a towel. "Can we talk about something else?"

"Yeah. Let's talk about Shelby. She considers you to be the greatest thing since sliced bread. Pun intended. In my opinion, she needs an attitude adjustment, but whatever."

My head hangs low. "Yeah, I know."

"You need to fix this. Don't leave anything unsaid. It will fester. Explain to her you have a crazy ex and a workaholic professor. It's pretty simple. You are the one who's making this difficult."

Heather makes it sound so simple, but I'm the one who has to live with the consequences.

The oven dings, and I pull out a cookie sheet full of perfect chocolate oatmeal cookies. Heather puts a flaming-hot one in her mouth and has to spit it out. "Hot."

I smile. "You never can wait."

"I can't help it. They're so good. So tell me more about you and Shelby. She called me in tears."

"Why did she call you?"

She shrugs as she attempts to eat another hot cookie. "Between sniffles and sobs, I am pretty sure she said she tried her brother, Darla, and somebody named Isaac, but no one picked up. Normally, I would be miffed at being fourth in line, but it took a lot of guts to call the sister."

I slump. "I'm an idiot, and I'm jealous, and oh yeah, did I mention I'm an idiot?"

Heather cups her hand around her ear and leans close to me. "I'm sorry. I didn't hear that. Did you say you're an idiot?"

"Shut up." I chomp down on a cookie. Another perfect batch.

"Shelby adores you."

"Yep."

"And you love her."

The corners of my mouth tip up in a slight grin. "All this love stuff is so new to me. There is no law of physics to help me figure it out."

Heather rolls her eyes. "Don't let that crazy Boston chick mess this up."

I hand her another cookie to keep her mouth from making words. "What am I supposed to do?"

She shrugs. "Transfer to Vanderbilt. You could actually walk to campus from this apartment."

"I've thought about it. But..."

"But what? You'd be accepted in a heartbeat."

"I'm not sure if I want to be accepted anywhere."

She scrunches up her nose as though she's trying to read my tone. "Your heart isn't in it anymore, is it?"

I stare down then back at her. "My heart has never been in it."

She wraps her arms around my waist. "We put pressure on you, don't we?"

"I realize y'all don't mean to, but every time someone calls me 'the smart one,' my blood pressure rises twenty points."

"What can I do? Anything but play Risk every day." She gives me a cheesy smile.

"Just help me stay sane. Maybe it'll only be one more year. Probably two." Bile rises in my throat. "I just gave myself indigestion."

Heather dusts the crumbs off her hands. "Quit."

"I can't."

"Why not?"

I sink my hands into another gooey ball of dough, the best ingredient for frustration. "The thought of all the money Mom and Dad have spent on my education... I can't let it be for nothing. And it's what is expected of me."

Heather grabs another cookie and points it at me. "This is what I expect of you."

"What? Make cookies all day?"

"No, but why not? It makes you happy, and you're so good at it."

I sigh. "It would be a waste of an opportunity to improve myself."

She swallows another cookie down in one big gulp. "Better than wasting your sanity. Tommy, figure out what makes you happy and run with it. That's all Mom and Dad really want for you."

"Shelby makes me happy."

"Duh. Don't mess around with Hazel. If you feel like you have to go back to school, it has to be completely professional."

"No doubt about it. I am not interested in Hazel. Not at all." I glance at my watch, realizing it's late. "Heather, why don't you call Mom to tell her you're hanging with me tonight? It's too late for you to be on the road."

"I already told her."

"Good. Please do me one favor," I say as I hug my baby sister. "No snoring."

She pinches my arm.

"Ow. The way you snore, it's no wonder you don't have a boyfriend."

She goes in for another pinch, but I put my hand on her head and straighten my arm so she can't reach my body. It's hilarious watching her swing at air, trying to hit me.

"I don't have a boyfriend because most guys are buttheads."

I agree with her. They can't see past her cute-as-a-button appearance to notice her huge heart. "And they wouldn't pass the triple Edwards test."

She cringes. "Nope. No one can pass that."

"One day, it will happen."

She hugs me. "Tommy, you're very special. All I want is for you to be happy."

"Me too, Heather."

"You should call Shelby. Dad says we should never let the sun go down on our anger."

I stare at the ceiling and sigh. "You're right. I hope she'll talk to me. I have to tell her I'm sorry again and that she can trust me."

Heather slides my phone over to me. "She'll talk to you. But now that you've heard about the skeleton in her closet, you should tell her about yours. No more secrets."

She's right, but I don't want to lose Shelby, and I especially don't want her to think I hop from bed to bed. The less she hears about Hazel, the better.

"I'll try."

CHAPTER TWENTY-FOUR
Shelby

My fingers itch to call Tommy. I don't like how we left things, and I already miss him. The townhome is too freaking quiet and lonely without him, and it is already losing that yummy baking aroma that follows him like a cloud of confectioner's sugar. I rummage through the refrigerator and come across one last remaining cinnamon roll that he made last night. I peel back the plastic wrap, taking in the gooey goodness just waiting for me to dive in. Instead of swallowing the pastry whole, I warm it up in the microwave, sending the delectable scent throughout the kitchen. Forgoing the table, I hop up on the counter, my favorite place to sit while Tommy bakes.

There is an art to eating a cinnamon roll, and it doesn't involve chowing down on it. The delicacy is more delicious if I peel the roll apart to savor the buttery cinnamon sugar within the roll. I pop a strip into my mouth and moan. Even though I watched Tommy use normal ingredients, he always ends up creating something so much better than anything I've ever eaten.

I lick the sugary icing off my fingers, wishing Tommy was here to feed it to me. There is nothing like Tommy's large hand serving me something he made and his eyes lighting up when he sees I love what he made. Nothing I ever had with Blaze would compare to that. I don't miss Blaze one bit, and I never want to go down that road again. Ever. I could kick myself for giving Tommy the slightest impression that I do.

But he didn't help matters any with his mysterious phone calls. I'm still miffed at him for that. The last person I should have called was his sister. I bet she considers me more drama than I'm worth. She's probably scolding him right now for getting involved with me. But when Vaughan, Darla, and even Isaac didn't answer, I wasn't sure who else to reach out to. Even though I said I wanted to be alone, I needed at least one human to validate my feelings. Heather did her best, but I really put her in an awkward position.

I slide out of my shoes at the front door and climb the stairs at a snail's pace, heading up to collapse onto my bed. It is way too big and empty without my big teddy bear, Tommy, lying next to me.

My thoughts go back to the evening's events. And the more I think about the evening, the sicker I feel. Just hearing Blaze's voice again made my skin crawl. It wasn't always like that. There was a time when his voice, whether it was singing me a love song he'd lied about writing for me or whispering my name in my ear, would make me weak in the knees. But that was three years ago. Three years that included seven drunken fights, two confirmed cheating incidences, and one very memorable night in the emergency room. I beat myself up mentally for lying to my parents about the black eye. Only my brother knew what really happened, and I had to beg him not to beat the crap out of Blaze. In hindsight, I should have let him wail on that idiot.

By the time I had decided enough was enough, his band had a semi-decent following and Blaze moved on to greener pastures, thank goodness. I was left licking my wounds, both physical and emotional. I rarely dated after that because my self-esteem took a huge hit. My sassy attitude and laser focus on work helped to hide the pain, and I decided all men were jerks because up until that point, they were.

Then Tommy came along. He's different in so many ways, and it's not only that he's not violent or a cheater. He's certainly cut from a different cloth in those characteristics, but he's also kind, loyal, and multilayered.

Even though I should call Tommy, I pick up my phone and dial my brother instead. If anyone can knock some sense into me, it's Vaughan. And he'd better answer this time.

"'Sup, sis."

"Where are you? I tried to call you."

"You didn't answer when I called either."

"I need your help. It's Blaze. I saw him tonight."

"Why?"

I sigh. "Tommy took me to a concert. He had no idea who would be in the warm-up band."

Vaughan snorts. "Let me get this straight. You can't decide between a cokehead, violent asshat and a smart, decent-looking dude who believes you hung the moon." He whistles through his teeth. "That's such a tough decision."

"You don't understand. I don't want anything to do with Blaze. It's that..." I meander down the stairs to the front window and peek out. "I've blocked his calls, but I'm afraid he'll stop by. I live in the same place."

"Where's Tommy?"

I nibble on a fingernail because the truth sounds so stupid. "We had a fight."

"The way you talked about him, he sounded like a keeper."

"He is, but he thought Blaze was calling when it was you."

"Yeah, about that—"

"And then he gets mysterious calls and gets all weird."

"Are you in high school? Now, back to me."

"Please come home this weekend. I miss you."

"Actually, Mom called to tell me about this massive engagement party. I can only assume you haven't broken it off yet."

I bang my head against the wall. "It's complicated."

"That's an understatement. I'm coming home, but I'm butting heads with Dad again. I can't stay at home. I might get arrested."

Vaughan and Dad are always butting heads. They're both too hardheaded to see that they're more similar than they realize. "You're always welcome at my place."

"I'll be there tomorrow, but not sure you want me at the party unless you need a distraction from all your drama, because Dad is bound to start something with me."

I feel bad from my brother. He has as hard a time pleasing the folks as I do. The only thing different is that he doesn't care. "It wouldn't hurt my feelings if you weren't there. I don't want to be there either. Everyone is taking this way too far."

A ruckus in his dorm room tells me his roommate must have barged into the room. "Got to go. Call Tommy."

My phone buzzes just as Vaughan disconnects. A text from Tommy pops up.

Tommy: *I am sorry.*

Without wasting another second, I call him, and he answers immediately. "Hey, sugar."

"Hey. Uh... where are you?"

"I'm at Theo's apartment."

"Oh." I pull on my ponytail. "I said I wanted to be by myself tonight, but that was a mistake. Is it too late to ask you to come back?"

All I hear over the phone is his breathing. I wish I could feel his breaths on my neck. "I'm in the middle of something right now."

"Can I come over?" *Please say yes.*

Tommy hesitates. "Hmm. Heather's here."

I crash onto the sofa, and tears begin to well up in my eyes. She's probably told him to run away as fast as he can.

Over the phone, Heather says, "Hey, Shelby, come on over and help me eat all this stuff."

Tommy's baking.

His laughter puts me at ease. "Of course you can come over as long as you don't mind Heather being here."

"Not at all. I'll be there in a jiffy."

"I was pretty frustrated when I got here so... I hope you're hungry."

My mouth cracks into a huge smile. "Always."

The talk we need to have will go down easier with a full stomach.

THE TRAFFIC GODS SMILE upon me because I hit every green light and make it to Theo's apartment in record time. Tommy jerks open the door before I can knock and grabs me around the waist. He kisses me all the way back to the kitchen.

"I'm so sorry, sugar."

Heather clears her throat in an overly dramatic way. "Guys, I'm right here."

Tommy pulls back, and I already miss the contact.

"Sorry, sis. I couldn't help myself."

She hands me a cookie. "It's all right."

The minute the cookie touches my lips, I let out a groan.

Tommy's eyes twinkle. "The bread should be out of the oven soon."

I clutch the edge of the counter. "Have mercy."

"It's hard to stay mad at him when he whips out the baked goods." Heather chomps down on another cookie. "At least I can't."

After another bite of the scrumptious cookie, I say, "Heather, I shouldn't have called you. I'm sure I put you in the middle. It was wrong of me, but I really do appreciate you listening."

With a full mouth, she replies, "It's okay. It's time both of you cleared the air." She waves a hand toward me. "Why don't you show my brother how it's done?"

"Nothing is going on with me and Blaze. I do not want him. I want you."

He cups my face in his hands. "Shelby Lynn." Tommy kisses me on the cheek. "I don't deserve you."

Heather groans. "It's your turn, bro."

He swallows hard and takes a deep breath. "A lot of the calls were from my professor, otherwise referred to as the biggest workaholic you'll ever meet." Tommy glances over at Heather, and she nods. "And others were from a girl I saw briefly."

My heart sinks. Way down deep, I knew this was it. He still has feelings for her, and he doesn't want to tell me.

"Nothing is going on. I promise. It was over before I met you and it's going to stay that way."

I've heard that before.

Tommy's hands bear down on my shoulders, but not as much as his words.

"You could have told me from the get-go," I tell him. "We all have a past that's less than flattering."

Heather claps her hands. "That went pretty darn good. Don't you agree?"

Not really, but I reply, "Sure. Maybe while you're here, you can help us figure out a fake breakup. We were planning on doing something at Theo's engagement party."

Tommy whispers in my ear, "She's had plenty of experience with real breakups."

Heather's face becomes white, and she swallows hard. I ache for her because I understand exactly how that feels. "Tommy, apologize to your sister."

"Sorry, sis. That was low."

She rolls her eyes at me. "You have a brother, so you get how they can be."

"What do you suggest?" I ask.

Heather paces through the small living room of Theo's apartment. With every move, her hair swishes around her waist. "Since Blaze was a bit of a misunderstanding between you two, you should incorporate that into your fake spat. Make it during the meal or something. Bring something up about it to stir the pot."

I ponder that idea for a moment. "That could work. My parents despise Blaze, and I mean hate with the fire of a thousand suns. If we hint that I'm having second thoughts about the engagement, and he's in the mix, they would believe it. They won't like it, but it will be believable."

Tommy points at me. "And remember, we had a little misunderstanding at the hospital. That could help with the believability."

Heather nods. "You have to really beef up the idea you're going back to graduate school. You're not sure how long it will be or when you'll be home to visit. School is all-consuming, yada, yada, yada."

He never discusses school. "How long will it be?" I ask.

He shrinks about six inches in height. "I don't know. Can we focus on the issue at hand?"

Heather claps her hands together. "Hey, you two. This planning isn't supposed to plant seeds of doubt. Don't make it more than what it is, okay?"

Tommy winks. "She's right. Let's just get through this part."

It rubs me the wrong way how he dismisses every conversation about school.

Heather yawns. "I'm going to bed. You two lovebirds try not to be too loud. The walls in this crappy apartment are very thin."

Before she leaves the kitchen, I pull her back to me. "Thanks."

"Don't give up on him," she whispers in my ear. "He really cares about you."

"I realize that." Even though he cleared some of the air tonight, I get the impression there's a whole lot more he's not saying.

Heather snaps her fingers. "Hey, I almost forgot. Since Theo and Darla's real wedding is going to happen sooner rather than later, I got hornswoggled into finding places for their rehearsal dinner. Do you two feel like helping me out? It would involve sampling menus."

Tommy ponders her words. "I could be talked into food. It might give me some new recipes to try."

If it means spending more time with Tommy, I'm up for it. "Sure. When?"

"The day after tomorrow. But you'll have to help me in secret since, by then, the two of you will be in Splitsville."

I don't like the sound of that. I don't even want to pretend to be broken up with Tommy. I glance over at him for guidance.

He shrugs. "What do you say?" He acts like everything is fine and dandy, and from his point of view, it might be.

But I have to sort things out in my mind and decide if he's giving me the full picture of his secrets or if I'm just being paranoid. Instead of pushing the issues further, I say, "Sure. Why not?"

CHAPTER TWENTY-FIVE

Tommy

Our engagement party is going to be worse than Boston, worse than graduating with honors from Tennessee Tech, and worse than getting mixed up with Hazel. I don't know how we're going to pull this off, especially since most people can read me like yesterday's news. It's my hope that Heather will play along and make our act realistic. Shelby clenches my hand as I drive toward the party at Demos restaurant. I would bet she feels the same as I do. We are going to hurt people because we didn't squash the misunderstanding earlier.

She clears her throat and stares straight ahead into the dark night. "I've said this a thousand times, but I am really sorry about all of this."

"What's done is done. They'll get over it. I hope your parents aren't so angry that they ban me from seeing their daughter ever again."

She snorts. "It's not the 1800s, and I'm not some lady-in-waiting, needing my father's permission for everything. Haven't you figured out by now that I pretty much do what I want?"

I raise an eyebrow. "I also understand you want to please your parents so bad, you'll concoct a web of deceit to get in their good graces." No telling how my parents are going to feel about her when all is said and done.

Shelby's grip on her purse is so fierce, I worry she might break the strap. "I wish my brother was going to be there tonight. It would be nice to have one person in my corner."

"You have Heather, and you have me."

"Yeah. I hope when this is over, you'll still be in my corner."

We drive up to Demos, and a valet is waiting for us. "That's odd. Demos is very casual." I get out of the car and hand the keys to the valet driver.

"Special event tonight, sir. Are you an invited guest to the engagement party?"

Shelby's eyes grow wide. "I guess so."

We walk hand in hand up to the restaurant as Shelby fidgets. "I thought this was going to be a small get together," she whispers.

When we open the door, the hordes of people filling the restaurant yell, "Surprise," making us jump back. *So much for a small get together.* They are all going to wish they'd never shown up. People from Dad's church, some neighborhood friends, and tons of people I've never met surround us. I receive so many backslaps, I'm sure there will be bruises across my shoulders in the morning. Shelby gets whisked away by Darla and some other girlfriends as I spin around, hoping to find one of my sisters. Heather waves from the corner then points at Jen. I raise an eyebrow as Jen makes her way through the crowd. She wraps her arms around me in a hug.

"I thought this was going to be just a few friends," I whisper.

"It got out of hand."

I canvas the crowd. The number of people here makes my lungs squeeze shut. "I need to talk to you for a second in private."

Jen smiles. "Sure. But then you must mingle for at least a few minutes before we sit down to dinner."

Shelby catches my eye, and I wave her over. She and Jen hug and do the air-kiss thing that girls do. "You look so pretty tonight, Shelby."

"Thanks." Shelby glances at me. "Uh, Jen, we need to tell you something."

I didn't want to confront my big sister alone about this, but she put so much effort into this party, the least I can do is prepare her for when the dung hits the fan.

Jen looks at both of us inquisitively. "Okay."

Shelby leads us to an empty back room used for storing restaurant supplies and starts pacing.

Jen gives me a death stare. "What's going on?"

I clear my throat. "Jen, there isn't an easy way to say this, but—"

"You eloped?"

I take a step back. "No. Why would you say that?"

"Because the two of you are acting very strange."

Shelby takes Jen by the hand and sits her down at a table covered with silk flower arrangements. I wedge myself between a box of Christmas decorations and a portable steam table that, from the inch of dust on the lid, hasn't been used in years. "We are not engaged. Never have been."

"But..."

"My mom told your mom what I told her, but the truth is I lied."

Jen's mouth drops open. "Lied? Tommy, how could you do this?"

"He didn't do anything wrong," Shelby answers before I can say anything. "It was all me. I blurted it out one day because for once, my parents approved of my choice in men, and I'm very sorry. It's all my fault."

Jen's gaze shifts from Shelby to me. "But why not?"

"What?" Shelby and I yell at the same time.

"You could be. Take a gander at the two of you. You're perfect for one another."

I stare at the ceiling, hoping the tiles will give me some divine intervention. "Jen, not yet, okay? We just met."

"But—"

"Jen, no. Stop. We aren't engaged, and that's that." I scrub my face with my hands. "We're going to stage a fight tonight so people will believe we've broken up. It's the only way for Shelby to not seem like a fool to her parents."

"There's got to be a better way."

I have to admit I'm a bit worried about the staged breakup. "Shelby, there are way more people here than we expected. We need to rethink this plan."

Shelby shakes her head. "I wish I had a better idea. I hope you'll forgive me for embarrassing your family."

Jen smiles. "You've been around my family enough to know they don't care about other people's opinions. Theo just found out he had a baby six years ago out of wedlock. Quite the scandal. But we don't care. We love his child and Darla. So don't worry about us. After the shock wears off, it will be nothing but another story we'll tell at Thanksgiving."

I chuckle, and relief washes over me. She's taking all this way better than I ever imagined. "That's probably the most accurate statement anyone has ever said. So, Jen, just play along, okay? No matter what we say, it's just acting to put doubt in people's minds."

She meets my eyes, and her smile fades. "Okay. Does anyone here know?"

Shelby bites her lip, and a drop of sweat trickles down my back. "Heather does."

Jen gasps and pops me on the shoulder. "You told her and left me in the dark?"

I scoot out of her range of fire. "Not on purpose, but we didn't plan any of this."

She jabs a finger at me. "The next time you stage a fake engagement, you better let me in on the secret. Do you understand, mister?"

"Yes, ma'am."

Shelby tugs on my sleeve. "We better get this over with."

"Jen, once we get settled at the table, could you text me? Anything. Just make sure no one sees you do it."

"Okay."

I take Shelby's hand and lead her back to the crowd. "Let's get this over with." I lean in to her and whisper, "I am not good at lying, so I hope this works."

She closes her eyes as she takes a deep breath. "It will all be over with soon."

That's what I'm afraid of.

As we sit, Mr. Williams clinks his glass to get everyone's attention. "Thank you all for coming tonight to celebrate Shelby and Tommy's engagement. A toast to Tommy and Shelby. May they live happily ever after."

"Hear, hear." Everyone around the large table clinks glasses. If I take a sip of my wine, I'll choke on it.

My phone chirps, and I pull it out. I give Shelby a sideways glance, and she motions for me to continue. When I read the text from Jen, I bite my lip to keep from snickering. *Colossians 3:9.* Only a preacher's kid would send a Bible passage. *Do not lie to one another, since you laid aside the old self with its evil practices.*

Shelby lets out an overexaggerated groan and stares at the ceiling. "Can you put that thing away for one hour?"

"It's important."

She guzzles her wine then slams the glass back down on the table. "What does *Alex* want this time?"

I slide my phone back into my pocket. "If I've told you once, I've told you a dozen times, it's about school."

Mr. Williams places his glass down and leans over the table. His eyes never leave Shelby's face. All the guests around the table halt their chatter to listen to us.

Shelby rolls her eyes. "Have you ever heard of a professor who stalks their students endlessly? This so-called Alex calls all the time.

Sounds like it could be more than just school." She faces me. "Tell me, Tommy, is Alex a female?"

Heather gasps, and my anger rises. "Does it matter? The gender of my major professor is none of your concern."

Mom takes Dad's hand. Her knuckles are white from her death grip. Theo wraps an arm around Darla as she nibbles on a fingernail.

Shelby waves over the waiter to fill her glass again. "That's rich. What are you hiding?"

"Nothing." This is beginning to sound very real. "If you want to talk about who's hiding something, tell me how many times you've seen Blaze in the last few days."

"No," Mrs. Williams says. "Shelby Lynn..."

"Oh, Mother. He's exaggerating. We saw him at a concert the other night." She flails her hands in the air like a perfect drama queen.

I snort. "The instant we bumped into that sorry excuse for a human, you started developing your plan to get me out of the picture."

Shelby's jaw drops. "That's not true."

My guffaw shocks even me. "Right. He asked you to stay for the after-party, and what did you do? You hesitated. You actually had to ponder before you answered."

Theo stands. "Tommy, why don't you step outside with me for a minute?"

"No, thanks."

Everyone around the table freezes in place, listening to our very public breakup, while Darla tugs Theo back into his chair.

Shelby squeezes her eyes shut and takes a deep breath. "Tommy, you need to let it go."

I scoot my chair out and stand. "Let it go? Fine. I will... let it go. Excuse me." Before I lose it, I hightail it toward the bathroom with Theo, Heather, and Jen right behind me. I throw up a hand to stop them. "Guys, not now." I slam the door to the bathroom behind me and turn on the sink. The swirling water racing down the drain reminds me of my hopes that this breakup was going to be easy. I'm so busy splashing water on my face that I don't hear anyone enter. When I see Theo's reflection in the mirror, I jump. "Crap, Theo. Make some noise next time."

"Those were some theatrics out there."

I stare at his face in the mirror. His mouth forms a straight line. He rarely pulls a serious face, so I'm sure he's upset with me. "Just an act to lead to a fake breakup."

"Fake? What do you mean fake?"

I take a few steps back until I bump my head against the wall and squeeze my eyes shut. "We were never engaged."

"You're kidding."

"Nope. So we needed to pretend to be mad. It's not real."

Theo scratches the back of his head. "Sounded pretty real to me."

"I guess I'm a good actor."

"You suck at lying. That was more real than you want to let on."

To keep others from hearing our conversation, I mash the button on the hand dryer. "It was the only way to stop this freight train of a fake engagement. We'll be fine tomorrow."

He scrubs his face with his hands. "You laid out all your insecurities in less than two minutes. School, Alex, Blaze, whoever he is."

A knock on the bathroom door makes me jump. "Son, can I come in?"

I groan. If there is anyone in this world I don't want to disappoint, it's Dad. "Sure."

He opens the door and wraps me in a hug. "Your mom is sorry."

"For what? She hasn't done anything."

He pulls back and takes in both of his sons. "She wants you to be happy and got a little crazy when she heard you had found someone. You shouldn't feel pressure from anyone, especially us, to get married before you're ready. You'll recognize it when the time is right." He winks at Theo then pats my shoulder. "Right girl, right time."

"Yeah," Theo says. "You should go home. You probably don't have much of an appetite anyway."

I couldn't agree more. "I need to talk to her parents first. I need to tell them I never meant to hurt her."

Dad stops me from leaving the bathroom. "Not tonight, son."

Theo nods. "Let things calm down tonight."

My heavy sigh is so loud, I'm sure everyone in the restaurant hears it. "Okay."

Theo helps me find the rear entrance of the restaurant and gives me a pat on the back. As I round the corner toward my car, our pre-arranged post-breakup place, I see Shelby sitting next to my front tire with her head in her hands.

"Sugar?"

She snaps her head up, and even in the dimly lit parking lot, it's easy to see she's been crying. She wipes her eyes. "Can you take me home?"

"Of course."

I help her into the car, but before I can even get out of the parking lot, she loses it. Deep guttural sobs make her body shake. I slide one hand to the back of her neck to caress it.

"Oh, Tommy."

"Shh. It's over."

Her breath hitches. "Is it? Us, I mean?"

I'm not sure. "No, of course not."

She buries her face in her hands and moans. "That was awful. You realize I didn't mean any of that."

"Of course, and I didn't either."

"All of our words, they sounded so much like pent-up frustrations. Tommy, I am so sorry for all of this."

"Me too."

We ride in silence all the way back to her townhome. It's so quiet, my ears hurt from the silence. When I walk her to her front door and unlock it, she stops me from entering. "We're broken up, remember?"

I give her a partial smile. "Fake, remember?"

She stares at her feet. "Yeah, fake. Mom said she might stop by tonight, which means she definitely will, so I need to do a sweep around the place to make sure I didn't leave any drawings lying out. You know how she is. Plus, you shouldn't be here."

"I guess not. I'll see you soon." I give her a light peck on the lips. Fake breakup, my ass. This feels all too real, and I don't like it.

Shelby said some things I knew were on her mind. She may have thought her words were only pretend, but I'm confident there was a lot of truth behind them and that one day soon, that truth will break us for good.

CHAPTER TWENTY-SIX
Shelby

Barely inside the door, I collapse, and the tears pour down my cheeks again. None of my real breakups hurt this bad. It's only been thirty minutes since our faux split, and I already miss Tommy. I don't know how I'll deal with it when he leaves for Boston. That won't be pretend at all, and there's nothing I can do to keep it from coming.

"Shel, you okay?"

I squeak, forgetting my brother is in my townhome. Before he can ask any other questions, I wipe my face and paint on a fake smile. "Yep. Right as rain."

"You look it." He plops down on the couch and rests his hands behind his head. "Tell your wise younger brother everything."

"Wise? Since when?" I drag myself off the floor and sit on the coffee table in front of him. "It was awful."

He clicks the remote, flipping through channels. When he lands on the Atlanta Braves game, he stops. "Was it believable?"

"Too much so." I swipe another tear away. "I, uh... I may have lost him. The hurt in his eyes from the things I said to him to incite the breakup was terrible."

Vaughan doesn't take his concentration off the baseball game. "Was there a hint of truth to what you said?"

My voice is so quiet that I can barely hear my reply. "Yes." And Tommy's words cut close to the truth too.

He clicks the remote to shut off the television. "If your ugly cry-ing face is any indication, you wish the words weren't so candid, right?"

I groan. "I can't help that I'm an ugly crier. But yes, I completely regret it. This is all my fault. If I hadn't told Mom we were engaged, I wouldn't have had to say those terrible things to Tommy."

He stares at the ceiling as he ponders his next words. "Maybe, but then maybe those words would have come out at some point in the future anyway and this spared you from the pain later on."

I plop down next to him on the couch. He rests his arm behind my neck and strokes my hair. There have been so many times over the years that my little brother has consoled me just like he's doing right now. He's not a great philosopher, but his touch comforts me, assur-ing me he cares and he's there for me.

"You should let him stay the night. You both need that."

"It's good to have some space. We both have a lot of things to sort out. Plus, Mom said she would stop by."

"Well, thanks for the warning." He gets up and stretches. "I'm going to call it a day. Night, sis."

I try to smile at him as he lumbers up the steps. As I straighten up the living room, a knock on the door makes me jump. Maybe Tommy decided we needed to talk. I fling open the door to find Mom stand-ing there, still wearing her seafoam-green Badgley Mischka cocktail dress. I try to hide my disappointment behind a weak smile, but I'm terrible at it. She pulls me into a hug, and my crying jag starts all over again.

"Oh, Shelby Lynn, I'm so sorry." She leads me to the couch, and for the first time in forever, I collapse into her arms. She holds me and peppers my face with kisses. "I thought he was a good catch."

My breath hitches. "He is a good catch. I'm the idiot."

Her hand slides my hair off my forehead. "Give it some time. These things sometimes have a way of working themselves out." To my relief, she doesn't mention Blaze.

Vaughan ambles down the steps. "Sis, where's the—" When he sees Mom, he does his best to tiptoe back upstairs.

"Not so fast, young man."

He freezes then swivels around, revealing that gorgeous smile he uses to trap the ladies. "Hey, Mom."

She motions for him to enter the living room. "Hiding from your father again?"

He scrubs the back of his neck. "Something like that." He plops down in the recliner and stares up at the ceiling. "We'll never see eye to eye about school."

"Not seeing eye to eye is one thing. Lying that you are taking classes for an entire semester is another. Sorry, kiddo, I can't help you this time."

"I realize that."

Mom squeezes me around the middle. "But lucky for you, we have bigger issues to deal with."

Vaughan winks. "Thanks, sis."

I roll my eyes. "Glad I can help."

Mom claps her hands together. "Let me tell you a little story about how I met your father."

Vaughan and I both groan. We've heard this story a thousand times. Dad was learning the guitar-design trade from his father, and Mom's boyfriend wanted a custom guitar built. I guess we will have to sit through this story one more time.

"Now, now. Did I ever tell you what part of your dad first got my attention?"

Vaughan chuckles, and I throw a pillow at him, whacking him in the face. I answer my mom before he can make a wisecrack. "I'm assuming it was his smile because he has a very nice smile."

"He has a very nice smile," he says, mocking me. Vaughan doesn't sound anything like me.

Mom shrugs. "Yes, he does, but it was his hands. He has these strong hands, and when I met him, he always had at least one Band-Aid wrapped around a knuckle. I'm sure woodworking is hard on the hands. Anyway, Peter, my boyfriend at the time, ordered a custom-designed guitar and refused to pay for it because it had one tiny flaw on it, one simple place where the varnish was a tad too dark. I was embarrassed for Daniel at how Peter treated him, like he was low-class, but your father took it in stride even though he spent weeks making that guitar. It was beautiful." She points at Vaughan. "You have that guitar now."

His eyes bug out. "Wow. I had no idea."

A fluttery feeling settles in my stomach. "Mom, I'm going to cry, and I mean a good cry this time."

She grins. "Needless to say, Peter and I broke up that day, and I vowed I would make it up to Daniel. Every day for months, I would stop by and bring him lunch. Sometimes, he would take it. Other times, he would pretend to not be in the shop. He was obviously embarrassed, but I kept getting glimpses of the great man he was. I mean, he still is. One day, I begged him to teach me how to play the guitar. He agreed, and for the next month, he gave me lessons." She gets a faraway expression and sighs. "My first song I learned to play was—"

"'I Can't Help Falling in Love With You,'" Vaughan recites. "You told us that part."

Mom's tale is so romantic, I wonder if I'll ever have stories like this to tell my future kids one day.

"Daniel wanted to scrap that guitar for parts, but I begged him to keep it. Even though he didn't make the guitar for me, because of it, we've never been apart."

I blow out a breath. "What's this got to do with my situation?"

"Two years. It took two years from the time I knew he was the man for me to the time we actually figured out a way around our differences. He was embarrassed at how my old boyfriend treated him in front of me, but how he handled the situation sealed the deal for me. And he was worth the wait."

In less than ten minutes, my mother has given me more romance advice than she has in my entire lifetime. This is the mom I always hoped she would be.

Vaughan clears his throat. "Mom, I like you better when you're busting my balls about something."

She shrugs. "If you want me to—"

He jumps out of the recliner and kisses her cheek. "On second thought, never mind. And I'll talk to Dad tomorrow, okay?"

"Sounds good."

Vaughan takes the steps two at a time to get out of the estrogen-induced walk down memory lane.

"Shelby Lynn," Mom continues, "I'm not saying to take Tommy back. I am saying to stay away from Blaze."

"That is not hard to do at all."

"Good, and Tommy is worth waiting on. That might mean a few years until he finishes school. Do you consider him worth waiting for?"

She stares, and I couldn't lie to her even if I wanted to. "Yes, Mama. He is."

"Great. My work here is done. Now, I better get home before your father sends in the cavalry."

I walk Mom to the door and give her a big squeeze. "Thanks, Mom. And I'm sorry for embarrassing you."

She waves me off. "This is nothing."

My chest tightens as I rehash the deceit I've been living with. I very well may pop the mother-daughter bubble we're in, but I have to set the record straight. I squeeze my eyes shut, and before I chicken out, I say, "Tommy and I were never engaged. I only said that because I wanted to make you happy. Please don't be mad at Tommy. It was all my fault." Forcing my eyes open, I take a much-needed breath.

Mom's jaw drops, then she covers her mouth with her hand as a slight snicker escapes. "Did Vaughan tell you to do that?"

"I heard that," Vaughan yells from upstairs.

Mom busts out a laugh and cups my face in her hands. "Oh, honey, you always make me proud."

If she's not going to bust my tail about the big reveal, then I should be completely honest with her. "What about painting? You've never supported me about that."

Mom glances down and rakes her teeth across her bottom lip "Your father told me I've been too hard on you about that. And the other day at the dress fitting, you were fixated on the Van Gogh painting. I saw the hurt in your eyes when I shooed you away from it. You're a talented artist, and you should be proud of it. As long as you don't quit your job and decide to be one of those starving artists. You're better than that."

This has been the most bizarre day of my life. My emotions have ping-ponged from grief to shock to elation. Mom opened the door to accepting my artistic side, and I can work with that. It's not the full-blown welcome wagon I was hoping for, but with her, I have to take what I can get. Not able to form words, I wrap my arms around Mom's neck and cry more tears, but this time, they're happy tears.

She pulls away from me and kisses me on the cheek. "Bye, sweetie."

I watch from my front door until my mother's taillights can't be seen anymore. Before I enter my room, I knock on the door of my spare bedroom.

Vaughan opens the door then flops back on the bed. His big muscular frame makes the mattress bounce.

"Pinch me. I need to make sure I'm not dreaming."

He reaches over to grab my arm, and I swat him away.

"It was a metaphor."

He blows out a breath. His face looks ashen.

"Vaughan, what did you do?"

He covers his face with his forearm. "I might have, uh, given that guitar to a girl."

I pop him on the leg. "You didn't."

He holds his hands out in front of him as if I'm going to smack him, which I just might. "It's stupid, but there's something about that guitar. It must be covered in fairy dust or something. I couldn't resist. Then..."

I flop on the bed next to him. "Let me guess—she doesn't want anything to do with you."

"Pretty much."

"Can you get the guitar back?"

He groans. "It's complicated."

I roll onto my side and notice his face is flaming red. "Are we talking about a guitar or your love life?"

He nudges me until I slide off the side of the bed. "Go to bed, sis. And call Tommy. You guys need to clear the air."

After I whop him with a pillow, I leave his room and fall into my own bed. My mind races, and there's no way I'll be able to rest without hearing Tommy's voice one more time. I've gotten used to it being the last thing I hear before I drift off to sleep every night, and tonight, of all nights, I need it. I pull my phone from my purse and call his number.

"Ex-fiancé speaking," he answers.

My shoulders relax, and I let out a sigh. "Hey. I couldn't sleep."

"Me either."

I settle back into my pillow. "Mom told me a big, sappy story, and she wants us to not give up on one another."

"I like the way your mom thinks."

"I also told her about the fake engagement. She took it really well."

"How do you feel?"

How do I feel? "Relieved, sad. I guess more than anything, I'm very overwhelmed right now."

"Yeah. I may be baking for the next few days to work through everything that's happened." His voice trails off as if he's reliving our argument like I am.

"At least Heather will enjoy the results."

A moment of awkward silence passes.

"I should let you get some sleep," he says. "Are you still going to help Heather with the food tasting next week? You don't have to if it's too soon."

"I hope I'm still invited."

"Yeah, sure. I mean, of course you are."

My stomach tenses because his words are not very convincing. There is so much left unsaid, but I am too emotionally drained right now to discuss it further.

"See you in few days?" I ask hopefully.

"Sure. That should be enough time to let the dust settle, especially since the cat is out of the bag with your mother. I hope my parents take it as well as your mom did."

"We can tell them together if it would go over better that way."

"Maybe." He pauses. "I... I'll see you soon."

Tonight may have been exactly what we needed to slow us down. I only hope we don't slow to a standstill.

CHAPTER TWENTY-SEVEN

Tommy

For the past two days, I did my best to stay busy without thinking of Shelby too much. I should have been researching rental properties near campus, but I procrastinated by mowing the neighbor's yard and fixing her rickety porch. That was way more satisfying, and I accomplished it all without one single call from Hazel. After finding out I will be back in Boston soon, she seems to have backed off. I need to take the small victories while I can.

But today, I get to see Shelby again. It's too bad I have to share her with Heather, but we promised to go food sampling with her for Theo and Darla's rehearsal dinner. Since I want a few minutes alone with Shelby, I decide to show up earlier than our agreed-upon time. I need to see her in order to keep myself from going into another baking frenzy. After two days, I'm all jittery without her. It's worse than caffeine withdrawal. I'm not sure how I'll ever go an entire semester without seeing her. I can't do it, and I'm sure I don't want to.

I unlock her townhome door with the key she gave me. My hands shake so much, I have a hard time getting the key in the lock. "Shelby Lynn?"

"I'll be down in a minute, and don't use my middle name, mister," she yells from upstairs.

I make myself at home, when I hear a crunching sound from the kitchen. There's a guy sitting at the kitchen table, wearing nothing but a tight pair of boxer briefs. His biceps flex as he scoops cereal from his monster-sized bowl to his mouth while he reads the sports page of the newspaper. His hair is super short on the sides and longer on top, making the messy front fall into his eyes. And he has the perfect scruffy beard. Yeah, I'm a bit jealous of that beard. I scratch my chin, wishing I could grow something like that. With my blond hair, any beard I attempt always ends up looking more like a teenager's peach fuzz rather than anything sexy.

I clear my throat. The dude, who seems completely at home, peers over the paper at me. "'Sup." Then he dives back into his paper and cereal as if a guy showing up during his breakfast is an everyday occurrence. I've got at least six inches of height on him, but damn, it would be nice to have some of that bulk. He's big, but not in an "I can't bend my elbows" kind of way.

He must sense my stare because he glances up and motions to his bowl. "Want some?"

I shake my head. "I'm sorry. Who are you?"

Shelby bounces down the steps, making me go weak in the knees. I've missed her so much. Damn, I'm one lucky man.

She pauses a foot away from me, and after several false starts, she gives me a tentative sisterly hug. "Hey."

God, she smells good.

She gives the guy in the kitchen the evil eye before she swats him on the back of his head.

"Ow."

"Put some clothes on, you caveman."

He scans his body. "I've got on underwear."

She rolls her eyes. "Thank God. Tommy, this is my pain-in-the-butt baby brother, Vaughan. Vaughan, this is Tommy."

We knuckle-bump. Thank goodness he's not competition.

"Vaughan is crashing here for a bit. Mom and Dad are driving him crazy."

"Ah."

He smiles. "I needed a break."

"I hear ya. Are you in school?"

He bobs his head up and down and puts up a finger for me to hold that thought while he swallows a huge gulp of cereal. "Sorry, man. UT Knoxville."

Someone knocks on the door, and Shelby says, "I'll get it. It's probably your sister."

"Really? My sister goes there," I say to Vaughan. "Any chance you've heard of—"

My words are cut off by Heather's screeching voice. "Oh my stars."

Vaughan drops his spoon and gets a shit-eating grin. "Hey there, Heaven."

Through gritted teeth, Heather replies, "How many times do I have to tell you, it's Heather?"

"To-ma-to, to-mah-to."

I glance at Shelby. "I guess they've met."

She shrugs. "Seems that way."

Heather, still with a deer-in-headlights expression on her face, backpedals toward the front door. "I just remembered I have to do something for Mom." She throws the list of restaurants into my hands. "Can you take care of food sampling without me?"

Vaughan perks up. "Food sampling? I want to go."

"No!" Heather and Shelby say.

My jaw drops. "Heather, this was your assignment, not mine. We were only going along to help you, remember?"

"But... that thing."

"What thing do you need to do for Mom?"

Her eyes are about to bug out of her head. It's clear she is not comfortable being in the same room as this near-naked dude. "You remember... that thing."

Vaughan stands and stretches. Heather's gaze doesn't go unnoticed. "Aw, Heaven, let's do this. I won't bite... this time."

She gasps, and I chuckle. Shelby smacks me on the arm. Soon, I'll make Heather spill the beans, but now I'll help out my little sister.

"Okay. I guess Shelby and I can handle it. You take care of that... thing."

She turns her back on Vaughan and mouths "thank you" to me. Over her shoulder, she gives Vaughan one last evil glare as she bumps up against the door. "Text me where you'll be, and I'll meet you there as long as *he* isn't there." She sneers at Vaughan. "He is not invited."

I glance over at Vaughan in time to see him wink at her. She spins around so fast and practically runs out the door.

I stare him down until he glances at me. He clears his throat as he tries to dispose of the grin that is permanently fixed on his face. Then he buries his head in his newspaper again.

"I don't know what you did, but you ticked off the wrong girl," I say.

"Heaven?" Shelby asks him.

I reply for him. "She's a preacher's kid. Not very original."

He shrugs and chomps down on another spoonful of cereal.

Shelby groans. "Vaughan, please put some clothes on."

"All right. I'm going. But can I go sample food with you?"

"Yes. It would be nice to have another opinion. Is that okay with you, Tommy?"

Not really. It seems like she doesn't want to be alone with me. I was hoping for some time to get back on the right track with Shelby, but I guess it's not going to be today. Heather would make herself scarce if she thought we needed alone time, but I get the feeling Vaughan will stick close by as long as the food doesn't run out.

"I don't care as long as you have on clothes," I finally say.

He pushes past us toward the stairs, pumping his fist in the air. As he walks away, I can't help but stare at his deltoids.

Shelby snaps her fingers under my nose, breaking my spell.

I turn my attention to her. "What?"

She rolls her eyes. "Not you too."

WHEN I TEXTED HEATHER about Vaughan tagging along, she faked an illness. Her rationale for ditching had better be a good one. So, the three of us spend most of the day going from one restaurant to another, trying to find the perfect place for Darla and Theo's rehearsal dinner. Since they want to get married in a month, many restaurants are already booked. But some still have openings. Every few minutes, I'll catch Vaughan's eye, and he quickly finds something else to stare at. He needs to explain why he made my sister scamper away like that.

I slump in the booth of the fourth restaurant of the day and gape at Vaughan tossing back chow mein. I thought I could put away food, but that boy tries every Italian, Indian, and French meal put before us and even has room left over for dessert. While sitting in a Chinese restaurant, he lets out a belch, earning him the stink eye from Shelby.

She narrows her eyes at him. "I can't take you anywhere."

"Sorry, but it was all so good. You forget I've been stuck eating dorm food all summer."

"I have to agree with him." I rub my swollen belly as I fight back the urge to let out my own burp.

Vaughan holds out his fist for me to bump. When I don't knuckle-bump him, he shrugs. As soon as a tall, sassy waitress prances by, he loses interest in me. Shelby snaps her fingers under his nose.

He blinks. "What?"

"Stay on target. What was your favorite?"

"Italian."

She shakes her head. "Mine was French. Tommy, what was yours?"

"I'm glad Heather narrowed down the choices for us, or I would be in a food-induced coma right now. Honestly, they were all good."

She groans. "That's a cop-out."

I sigh. "I get that, but here's the problem. All this fancy food is really excellent, but Theo would be happier with good old-fashioned barbecue or burgers instead of a stuffy sit-down meal. Plus, there will be a little one running around."

"Yeah," she agrees. "You're right."

Vaughan perks up. "Barbecue? We haven't sampled that yet."

Shelby stares at him. "Stop talking."

Out of the corner of my eye, I see Jen walk into the restaurant. "Oh no. My sister is here."

Vaughan's eyes widen. "Heather?"

"No, worse. It's Jen, and she's with my mother. I haven't had a chance to tell Mom about our engagement being fake. Mom told me I needed space away from the situation. Shelby, you need to hide."

Shelby gasps. "Jen knows I'm doing this for Darla. You hide."

Vaughan shovels in another mouthful of kung pao chicken. "I'm not hiding."

"Oh, hush." Shelby grabs me and shoves me under the table until my knees are bent up next to my ears. It's not easy for someone my size to hide underneath a table only covered with a white tablecloth. "Don't speak." Her chair screeches as she stands. "Hey, Jen, what are you doing here?"

"Doing some shopping and wanted to pop in for a late lunch, but it appears pretty busy."

"Yeah. This is my brother, Vaughan. He's helping me sample food for Theo and Darla's rehearsal dinner."

"Oh, what did you decide on?" My sister steps closer to the table and almost stomps on my foot. Another chair screeches away from the table, and Jen plants herself in my seat.

I scoot so far away from her that I sit on Shelby's feet. Vaughan kicks me in the ribs, and I nearly hit the table with my head.

"Everything was so good, but we need to focus on what Theo and Darla would like. I'm sure they would prefer something more casual." Her words come out fast, like she's been running a marathon.

Jen snorts. "That's for sure. And with little Stella, a fancy sit-down meal probably wouldn't go well unless they served chicken fingers."

Mom's familiar shoes appear next to the table. "Jen, sweetie, we'll never get a table here before I have to be back in court. Let's grab a sandwich down the street."

"We can eat with them," Jen says.

No!

Vaughan chuckles. Shelby reaches under the table and runs a hand through my hair. At least it had better be her hand.

"Where's Heather?" Mom asks. "I thought she was going to sample food."

Vaughan coughs. "Oh, she had a *thing* to take care of."

If it wouldn't blow my cover, I would kick him in the balls.

"Oh. Shelby, I'm sorry things didn't work out with Tommy." My mom's tone is compassionate. "Maybe you two can work it out after you've had some space apart."

"Space?" Vaughan asks. "As in more than a few inches?"

I'm beginning to see why Heather ran from him.

Shelby grabs a handful of my hair, and I am seconds away from letting out a yelp. "You're right, Mrs. Edwards. We were probably moving too fast. But I still care about him very much."

I wish I could kiss her right now.

"I understand, and he cares about you too." Mom is the best. "We should go."

I see feet shuffling around, and it sounds like Shelby gives them hugs. A few leg-numbing minutes later, Shelby lifts up the tablecloth. "The coast is clear."

"That was close." I face Vaughan as I dust off my pants. "You are going to get your face punched in one day, and I can't wait to witness it."

He smirks at me. "Sorry, but back to the issue at hand. Barbecue is a fantastic idea."

Shelby glances around the four-star restaurant we're standing in the middle of. "But this is so pretty."

"Sis, you're thinking too much like Mom and not about what your best friend would want."

She pouts. "You're right. Let's go." Shelby bolts out the door and down Division Street, leaving Vaughan and me to catch up with her. She pulls out her phone.

"Oh no." Vaughan glances over at me with fear in his eyes. "I've seen that face before. She's got a plan."

"Is that bad?"

He lifts one shoulder. "It could go either way."

While Shelby mumbles into her phone, I take the opportunity to grill Vaughan about the encounter with Heather. "So it appears you and my sister have met before."

He nibbles on the side of his mouth. "You could say that."

I take a step forward, towering over him. "Choose your next words carefully."

He backs away, holding his hands out in front of him in defense. "We've met a time or two. I'm on the baseball team, or *was* on the team, but that's a totally different story for another day."

Shelby shoves her phone into her purse and stomps toward us. "What did you do?"

He waves her off. "Heather automatically assumes I'm a player."

"She's usually right about these things," I say.

Vaughan shakes his head. "Not this time. Besides, she can't stand me. It was a big misunderstanding, and I haven't had a chance to do anything about it."

"Man, don't mess with her. She will kick your butt, and I'll sit on the sidelines, cheering her on."

A flush runs up his neck. "I, uh... never mind." He runs a hand through his messy hair.

Talking to a guy who likes my little sister is foreign territory for me. She doesn't put up with crap, so he must really see something in her that most other guys miss. "You like her, don't you?"

He fights a smile but isn't winning. "Maybe. But like I said, she doesn't like me at all, so the only time I can interact with her is when I annoy the heck out of her like a third grader." Country music blares through one of the honky-tonks, catching Vaughan's attention. Vaughan points down the street, toward where the music is coming from. "I haven't been to the Wildhorse Saloon in ages. Tell the planner I'll take an Uber back to her place."

Shelby walks back to us and latches on to Vaughan's arm. "Where are you going?"

I pop Vaughan on the back. "Sorry, man. Seems like Shelby's not done with us yet."

She bounces up and down. "I've got the best idea."

Vaughan steps away from her. "Calm down, sis. I see those brain cells smoking."

"The dinner's going to be at my parents' house."

I shake my head. "We're supposed to be mad at each other, remember?"

"I already thought of that. Mom agreed. She said it would be a great step toward us reconciling. Her words."

My eyebrows shoot up, and Vaughan whistles.

She points at me. "And you are going to prepare the meal."

I shake my head. "I don't think so." By that time, I'll be up to my neck in school-induced stress. I'll be lucky if I make it home in time for the wedding.

"Sure. Like you said, it will be something simple. I'll be your assistant, and I'm sure Isaac will help too. It'll be fun."

I stare down at the sidewalk. Now is as good a time as any to tell her. "I'm heading back to Boston next week."

Her face loses its color, and she freezes in place. Neither one of us breathes. Tension builds between us, thicker than the summer humidity.

"Uh-oh," Vaughan says. "Can I leave now?"

"Go," she replies without blinking,

"Whew." He scoots down the sidewalk toward Second Avenue, and I wish I could go with him.

"I was trying to find the right time to tell you, but I couldn't. Plus, I didn't want to ruin today."

"You're not coming back for the wedding?" Her voice cracks.

"Of course I am, considering I'm the best man, but I can't plan a meal and get things done while focusing on my studies."

She swallows before she speaks. "I'll do all the legwork. You tell me what to buy, what the menu will be, and I'll get it all ready for you. All you have to do is show up and boss me around."

I grab her around the waist and draw her close. "Me boss you around?"

She smirks. "It will be a first." She pokes me in the chest. "And don't get used to it, mister."

I stare up at the sky for some divine intervention. There's no way I can refuse this beautiful woman. And with this party to look forward to, it might help me get through the next semester of hell.

I concede. "Okay."

She dances around me and squeals. Several tourists walking by give her a wide berth as they stroll down Division Street.

"You should get it approved by Darla."

"I already did. I'm a fast talker." She cringes. "There's one more thing Darla wants you to do."

I narrow my eyes at her. "What?"

"She wants you to make her wedding cake. Again, very simple."

I groan. It's a good thing Shelby is adorable. "Add it to the grocery list." Secretly, I was hoping Darla would ask me to make it because I've been itching to try out a Mad Hatter cake ever since I saw one in Mom's *Southern Living* magazine, and it would be perfect for them. The playful topsy-turvy design symbolizes what they've gone through, but they have still come out in one piece.

She jumps into my arms and wraps her legs around my waist. "You're the best boyfriend slash ex-fiancé ever."

I savor the feel of her in my arms. "I get that a lot."

She finds my tickle spot, making me squirm. "What am I going to do when you leave me?"

I rest my forehead against hers to breathe in her intoxicating peach scent. "I'm not leaving you."

"It sure feels that way. Ever since the fake breakup, it's been awkward, and I'm afraid when you're gone, you'll forget about me. Maybe find a smart girl..."

I pull back from her so we can see eye to eye. "Hey, stop that."

A tear trickles down her cheek. "Now that I know when you're leaving, I'm really nervous." She locks eyes with me. "I'm scared."

I hold her so tight, I'm not sure how she can breathe. "I'm scared too, but we'll be okay. I promise."

"Will you tell me the truth about something?"

"Of course." I kiss her cheek. *Please don't ask about Alex.*

"Do you have a girlfriend in Boston waiting for you?"

I kiss her lips. "I do not have a girlfriend in Boston." I'm not telling the whole truth, but I answered her question truthfully.

She lowers her gaze. "You're so agitated and tense lately."

I sigh. "I don't handle stress well, and I've taken it out on you. I am so sorry. There are all these expectations."

She wraps her arms around my neck and whispers in my ear, "Then why do you do it? Why are you going back?"

I nuzzle her neck. "That's the million-dollar question."

And I don't have an answer.

CHAPTER TWENTY-EIGHT
Shelby

Vaughan stumbles in from his honky-tonk shenanigans and collapses into the recliner to watch a super hero movie with Tommy and me. I'm not sure which *Avengers* movie it is, but Tommy tries his best to out-do Vaughan on Marvel Comics trivia, which is next to impossible.

"I don't like this Hulk as much as the original," Tommy says.

"Do you mean the original movie or the one in the TV series that my dad loves to watch on one of those oldies channels?"

Tommy huffs. "TV series, of course. Bill Bixby and Lou were the original hulk. And my dad watches that channel too."

"I guess, but Lou was hard to understand, and he's got to be about a hundred now."

"True," Tommy says.

"I like this one," I say, trying my best to interject myself into the conversation. They both stare. "What?"

Tommy motions for me to continue.

Vaughan groans. "Please don't tell me you think he's cute." He makes kissy faces, and I shove his ugly mug away from me as fast as I can.

"Well, now that you mention it..."

My brother rolls his eyes. "Oh God."

Tommy stands and stretches his long legs before he goes into the kitchen. "That's not the point at all."

"Sis, maybe you should keep your opinions to yourself."

I pout. "But it's the correct opinion."

"Hey, Tommy," my brother calls. "Can you bring me another beer?"

I pop Vaughan on the leg. "Get your lazy butt up and get it yourself."

"Sure," Tommy says as he comes back into the living room with a homemade, fresh-out-of-the-oven pizza in one hand and three beers tucked under the other arm.

Vaughan relieves Tommy of one beer and pops it open. "Thanks." He takes a giant gulp. "Ah, this hits the spot."

Tommy slices the pizza, and my mouth salivates when I catch a whiff of the crust. He hands me a slice then turns his attention to Vaughan. "But you've got to tell me what got my sister's panties in a twist."

Vaughan spews beer out his nose. Thank goodness it only soaks his shirt and not my carpet. He coughs, and I pat him on the back.

"You okay, little bro?"

He muffles another cough. "Sorry. It was an interesting choice of words, that's all." Vaughan reaches for a slice of pizza, but Tommy snatches it out of his reach.

"You want to explain that comment?"

Oh dear. Tommy's very protective of his baby sister. If my brother did anything to hurt her, he may not live to see the morning.

Vaughan puts his hands up in surrender. "It's nothing really. We have a few friends in common, and things got out of hand at a party this past spring."

Tommy takes a step toward him, and Vaughan shrinks into the chair. It's funny to see my massive brother actually afraid of someone.

"Nothing happened. I swear. But some people got the wrong idea that... something did happen, and they gave us a hard time about it."

Tommy sits back down without losing eye contact with Vaughan.

"But you did the right thing and set everyone straight. Right?" I ask. *Please say you did.* He's a pain in the butt, but he's the only brother I have, and I really don't want his nose broken.

"Uh, sure. Of course. At least I'm in the process of making it right." He inches toward the pizza.

Tommy picks up the pizza slicer. "You better, or I'll find interesting uses for this thing."

Vaughan swallows hard. "So... how about that Hulk? He's cute, huh?"

Tommy chuckles. "Just stay away from her. She's a good girl."

"Yes, she is." Vaughan chomps down on his slice of pizza, and his eyes roll back in his head. "This is the best pizza I have ever had. And you don't have anything to worry about. Staying away from Heather is not going to be a problem. She pretty much gives me the death-ray stare any time I'm near her."

"Good," I say, causing Vaughan to throw daggers at me with his eyes.

"Thanks a lot, Shelby. For the record, I happen to like her. A lot." He squeezes his eyes shut and takes a deep breath. "Forget I said that."

Tommy's face is red, and if he isn't careful, he's going to break the neck of the beer bottle he's holding. But Heather is exactly what Vaughan needs, and judging by his little truth bomb, she's also what he wants.

Vaughan straightens in the recliner. "Not like-like. I mean she's funny and spunky." He gets a far-off gaze in his eyes, one that I've never seen on him before. This cannot be good. "And she doesn't care what other people think about her. I like that a lot."

"That's my girl," Tommy says.

"It's kind of hot."

Not a good thing to say in front of her protective brother, who happens to be rubbing his temples.

But Vaughan keeps going. "Most girls are clingy and whiny. 'Do you miss me? I texted you five seconds ago. Why didn't you text back? Hey, Pookie Pie.' Ugh."

I bite my lip to keep from smiling. "Pookie Pie?"

He points a finger. "Don't repeat that."

Tommy snatches another slice of pizza from the pan. "Aw, we're eating with Pookie Pie. Heather will love that."

A flush runs across Vaughan's face. It's a good color on him. *Poor guy.*

As his big sister, it's time for me to intervene. "Not to change the subject—"

"Please, sis. Please change the subject."

"Have you talked to Dad about your problem with school?"

His face becomes as hard as stone. "Nope. Time to change the subject again."

I tap his foot with mine. "Come on. With my drama, he might let you off with a warning."

He takes another swig from his beer then pauses for a long moment before speaking. "Maybe."

"Good."

Vaughan rubs his face with his hand. "Let's watch the movie. All this talk is going to make me miss Stan Lee's cameo."

I wink at Tommy and snuggle in next to him to watch the cute Hulk. He rubs my shoulders, and I don't want the movie to ever end because that means it will be closer to the time when he leaves. I don't want to lose him, but I am, and it's breaking my heart a little more each day. Sneaking around to keep our parents in the dark is wearing me out.

Fortunately, Tommy likes to watch the entire movie and all the credits. He says his favorite part of the movie is the hidden scene after the credits. Vaughan crashes in the recliner, softly snoring. I rest against Tommy's chest and close my eyes, trying to remember his brown-sugar scent, the mole on his neck, and the flecks of gold in his eyes. Before I can stop it, a tear escapes and trickles down my cheek. I don't have a chance to wipe it away before Tommy does.

He kisses my cheek. "I better go."

"Yeah." I walk him to the door and wrap my arms around him. "Please don't go."

"Tonight or..."

"Both." I bury my head in his chest as he rubs circles on my back. "I don't like pretending to be broken up with you, and"—I take a deep breath—"I feel like we really will..."

"Break up?"

"This is way harder than being fake engaged, especially since I still care about you so much."

He kisses my neck and hums as he slides his hands to my waist. "Well, I've heard of makeup sex. How about breakup sex?"

My jaw drops. "That sounds awful and pretty darn good at the same time."

He takes me by the hand and leads me to the stairs. Before we can make it to the second step, someone knocks on my door.

"Shelby, it's Dad."

"Oh crap," I mouth to Tommy. I gesture to the upstairs. "Be quiet, okay?"

He salutes me and tiptoes upstairs. Dad knocks again.

"Coming." I open it, and paint on a happy face. "Hey, Daddy. Come in. It's kind of a mess."

"I heard another voice." Dad canvasses the living room.

I point at the recliner, where my brother yawns and groans at the same time. I've never been so glad for Vaughan to be here in all my life.

Dad's spine stiffens. "Son? I heard you were in town. Avoiding me?"

"A little." He pushes the recliner to a sitting position and starts to rise.

Dad points at Vaughan. "Stay right there. I'll deal with you in a minute." He turns his attention back to me. "Are you okay? I haven't had a chance to talk to you since the blowup. Your mother says you are, but I had to see for myself."

I kiss him on the cheek. "I'll be fine, Daddy. Better to find these things out now rather than later, right?" I keep digging that hole of deceit, and eventually, it's going to bury me alive.

"I really thought he was a keeper."

"He might be, Daddy, but the timing is off."

He scans the room, landing on the coffee table, which is littered with drinks, a pizza stone, and plates, three of them to be exact. *Shoot*. He picks up the plates and hands them to me. "Vaughan must have been real hungry."

"Uh-huh."

Dad glances down at my ring finger, which is now void of the beautiful engagement ring.

"It's upstairs. I can get it for you if you want."

He takes a step toward the stairs, and my lungs forget to work. This feels worse than telling him I was engaged.

Vaughan clears his throat. "I'll get it for you." *I owe you one, bro.*

Dad shakes his head as he admires a painting on the wall. "No, you keep it. It's for you."

I let out an audible breath, and Dad winks at me.

"Do you want your money back?" I ask.

He blinks. "Of course not. I only came here to make sure you were all right."

I cross my arms. "I'm not getting married now, so you can have the money back if you want it."

"Money?" Vaughan pipes up from behind me. "Oh yeah, the money. How much?"

I sneer at him over my shoulder. "Go back to sleep."

Dad takes my hands in his. "That money is yours to do with whatever you want. I don't want it back."

"I'll take it off your hands," Vaughan says.

Dad kisses my cheek again and gives me an eye roll then points at Vaughan. "It's your turn now. Why did you lie to me?"

Vaughan shrinks back into the chair with nowhere to hide. "I was having too much fun for school. Lots of distractions. It was baseball season, and it got too easy to skip."

"And those distractions cost you your baseball scholarship."

Vaughan covers his eyes with his forearm. "I'm an idiot." He moves his hand away from his face, and the sarcasm and snark are no longer there. "I'm very sorry, Dad." He bows his head and picks at a fingernail. "Maybe I need to transfer to a different school."

Dad shrugs as he sits down on the couch. "Different geography, same problems."

He shakes his head. "Nope. I promise it will be different, and I'll buckle down on my studies. Summer school wasn't so bad, especially since most of my bad influences were gone." Vaughan gives me a quick glance, hoping I will throw in my two cents.

"It's a great idea," I say. "If he wants to go to a local university, he can stay here as long as he picks up after himself." If Tommy and I ever get back to a good place, having my brother here might get awkward, but Tommy would do the same for his sister.

Dad scratches his chin as he ponders my proposal, then his mouth twitches with a partial grin. "I bet he could be a walk-on to Bellevue's baseball team."

Vaughan's eyes brighten. "I could. And they have a top-notch music business program."

Dad shakes his head and blows out a disgusted breath. "You have to be serious this time. And until I'm convinced, you'll have to apply for student loans. Prove it to me that you're serious this time, and after the next semester, we will reevaluate."

"I'll take it." Vaughan rests his head back against the recliner and breathes deeply. "Thanks, Dad. I'm not going to screw up this time. I promise."

Dad pats Vaughan's knee. "I believe you. I better go."

I give Dad a hug and walk him to the door then watch him drive away. Vaughan stares at the ceiling.

"You want to explain what happened?" I ask.

He shakes his head. "Not really. Let's just say you women are going to be the death of me."

I chuckle. "I knew it had to be about a girl. Does it have anything to do with Heather?"

"Kind of."

I roll my eyes. "You'll never learn."

He points at the stairs. "Neither will you."

Tommy peeks his head down the stairwell. I forgot he was here. "Is it safe to flush the toilet now?"

"Yes, please." Taking the stairs two at a time, I race toward him. "Why do I keep lying? Mom knows. In fact, I can't believe she didn't say anything to him."

"We'll figure something out. I thought this was going to be the easy part, but neither of us want to disappoint our parents."

Later on, while I'm tangled up in Tommy's legs under a sheet, reality hits me. I only have a few more days before he leaves. I don't want him to go, and he doesn't act like he wants to go either. When he comes back, I'm afraid things will never be the same.

But we do have tonight.

CHAPTER TWENTY-NINE
Tommy

I don't have to check the calendar to know that I only have one more day before I'm back in Boston. My acid reflux is a bitter reminder. Mom and Dad thought a family game night might perk up my mood, but not even a good old game of Risk could do it today. When I invited Shelby, I told her I was going to tell my parents we weren't broken up anymore. It's way past time to set the record straight.

Theo barges into my parents' house, carrying Stella. He hardly places her feet on the floor before she races off to hug her grandparents. It's hard to believe that only a few weeks ago, she was knocking on death's door. Theo wraps his arm around Darla, and the two watch as their daughter chases our father around the living room. Right behind them, Jen and Matt waltz in.

Heather gallops down the stairs and captures Stella, making her squeal. "Want to see if you can beat me in a game of Trouble?"

"Bring it," my niece challenges.

We all get a kick out of this pint-sized teenager in training. Stella already acts like an Edwards with her competitive board-game mentality.

Heather guides her to the corner of the room and dumps the contents of the game box on to the floor. After that, the two don't even remember the rest of us are in the house. At some point, I need to get Heather's side of the situation with Vaughan, but I don't want to ruin her fun today.

Theo rubs his hands together in anticipation. "Who wants to get their butt kicked in Battleship?"

"Me." Shelby's voice has me turning my head toward the door. The room becomes quiet as we all watch her standing frozen, like she's afraid of moving away from the door in case she has to make a quick getaway. I hoped she would show up, but I was afraid it would be too awkward for her. And it is.

Heather rises, walks over to Shelby, and takes her hand to lead her into the room. "Theo, you said you were ready to get your butt kicked. Shelby, please be my guest."

Theo clears his throat and motions to the kitchen table. "You've been warned."

I lean over and whisper in her ear. "Kick his butt."

The tension in her face releases as a giggle bubbles out of her mouth.

Mom and Dad stand frozen, not sure what to make of Shelby being here. I gesture toward Dad's study, and the three of us leave the chaotic kitchen for the sanctuary of Dad's office. "I'm guessing you'd like an explanation."

Dad props a hip on the side of his desk as Mom sits next to me on the sofa. "Well, yes. Your dad and I are a bit confused."

"It is confusing." I take a deep breath. "Shelby and I decided we aren't ready to be engaged, but we're not ready to call it quits either."

"Son, the things you said to one another..."

If I tell them it was fake, it would confuse them even more, and since some of those words had a great deal of truth to them, I would be lying if I went down that road. "We're taking a step back to see how things go while I'm away." My stomach lurches at that thought.

"That's probably wise." Mom squeezes my hand. "You'll feel it soon enough if it's meant to be."

I scrub my face with my hands. "Can I count on you to not make her feel uncomfortable tonight? I want her here. I still care about her. A lot."

Dad stares at me for a second, like he's trying to read between the lines. "Of course. Now let's go have some fun." He pats my back as he leads us into the kitchen.

Theo's hair sticks up in ten different directions. He's met his match in Battleship because Shelby sits back, calm and collected, evaluating her fleet. When our eyes meet, she bites her lip. I wink at her, and she blows out a breath of relief.

Darla walks up to me. "Want to play Risk?"

"Seriously?"

Darla shrugs. "Sure. I mean, I have no idea how to play, but I'll get Matt and Jennifer to play too. It'll be fun."

She is so perfect for Theo. I'm glad things worked out for them.

"Okie dokie. Let's do it," I reply before she has a chance to change her mind.

Darla pumps her fist in the air. "Yay! Jen, get your butt over here. We have a country to conquer."

"Noooo," Jen says.

Matt laughs and points his finger at her. "You have to play Risk."

Darla taps him on the shoulder. "You too, mister. This is Tommy's send-off, and he wants to play Risk."

"Oh. One game. And that's only because you're leaving tomorrow... and because you baked."

Without even trying too hard, I win, as usual. Darla got conquered early on, even with the help of little Stella. Jen and Matt tried to form an alliance, but it still wasn't enough to surpass my brilliant moves. *Bwa-ha-ha.* I'm the master of world domination.

After games and burgers, we settle in to watch a Stella-approved movie. Shelby sits far away from me, which is probably a good idea since the couple of times I brushed against her body tonight, I wanted to forget my family was in the room. If she's anything like me, she's trying to get through this night without falling apart.

I catch her staring, and I wink at her. She smiles, but it doesn't reach her eyes. Then she picks up Stella and holds her. My mother tickles Stella's foot. Mom is so happy to have a granddaughter and is itching for lots more. Maybe Jen can help her out in that department. I can't get my head out of a book long enough to cultivate a healthy relationship. Hazel is not what I want. Shelby is, but I'm sure she'll get tired of waiting for me.

Like her uncle Tommy, Stella has to watch the entire movie, including the credits. After she wakes up her dad, they get ready to leave. I kiss Stella and give Darla a hug.

"See you in about a month at the rehearsal dinner?" Darla's voice falters.

"Yep."

Theo and I stare at each other. Concern etches his face. "I'm just a phone call away. Call me if you need anything."

"You have your hands full right now."

"Never too full, Tommy." If I weren't biting my lip, I would have lost it, but I manage to hold back the tears. He grabs me in a hug. "Please let me help you if you need it," he whispers.

"I will. Love you, bro."

Theo smiles. "Love you too. See you soon..."

"If not sooner."

The happy couple leaves, and Heather picks up the games, arranging them back into the proper boxes. Mom and Dad say their goodnights and make their way upstairs, but not before Mom gives Shelby a kiss on the cheek and squeezes my shoulders. Shelby sticks around to help me clean up the kitchen. I'm pretty sure she's stalling.

I bump her with my shoulder. "You all right?"

"Nope." Her head stays buried in the dishwasher as she rearranges forks for the third time.

"Me either."

She stands straight but keeps her eyes trained on the floor. "Are you staying here tonight?"

I nod. "Dad's taking me to the airport tomorrow, very early. I shipped most of my stuff yesterday so I wouldn't have to lug it on the plane."

She bows her head. "You'll call me when you get settled?"

I brush a strand of hair away from her face. "Of course."

Her lip trembles. "Will you miss me?"

"I already do." All she has to do is say, "don't go," and I will change my plans immediately.

She backs away, wipes her face, and picks up her purse. "I better go."

"Let me walk you out."

In the humid night, the only sound is the cicadas chirping in the nearby trees. Shelby stands at her car door with her back to me. I reach out to touch her shoulders, and she trembles as her body slumps. She sniffles.

"Come here." I turn her around and hug the life out of her. "I'm going to miss you so much."

Her breath hitches. "I should leave, but first I have something for you." She opens her trunk and pulls out a gift bag. "Don't make fun of me, but you inspired me to give it another try."

I remove the tissue paper and retrieve a silver five-by-seven picture frame containing a pencil drawing of us baking in her kitchen. The detail is incredible, and I can't keep the smile from forming on my face. "It's beautiful. I mean your half of the picture is, but mine... Well, you did your best with what you had to go on."

She rolls her eyes as another tear trickles down her cheek.

I wipe the tears off her face and touch my lips to hers in a soft, quick kiss. "Bye, sugar."

And just like that, she's gone from my life. Or I'm gone from hers. I watch her drive away until I can't see her taillights anymore. Then I go back in the house, close the front door, and scan the quiet living room. I mosey into the kitchen to make sure it's tidy before I head upstairs.

As softly as I can, I climb the stairs and knock on Heather's door before I open it. She's lying in her bed, scrolling through something on her phone.

"Hey, bro."

"Would it be too weird if I slept in here tonight?"

She slides over and pats the empty side of her bed. "Do you want to lie head to toe like we used to?"

"Thanks, sis." I peel out of my shoes and flop onto her bed, making the mattress squish in. She throws me a pillow. After I get situated, we fall into silence.

Heather clears her throat. "I don't normally offer my opinions..."

Her words make me chuckle. They could not be further from the truth.

"You're making a big mistake," she says. "Your heart isn't in school anymore."

I close my eyes, trying to remember every detail of Shelby's face. "I realize that."

If I have any luck left, going back won't be a mistake that can't be fixed. Only time will tell.

CHAPTER THIRTY
Shelby

The last three days have been utter misery. I check for text messages and voice mails so much I wear out my phone. Poor Isaac and Darla have been at the wrong end of my bad temper today. I snapped at them so many times, they've gone into hiding. A knock on my office door makes me jump. I glance up to see them tiptoeing into my office.

Isaac gets on his knees and shuffles over to my desk. "I'm sorry. Whatever I did wrong, I didn't mean it. Please don't flog me." He always has a way of making me smile.

Darla schleps in behind him and sinks into a nearby chair, appearing a little green. "I need you to sign my FMLA paperwork." She slides it over to me.

As I read over the form, I gasp. "Oh my gosh. You're pregnant?"

Darla blushes. "Again."

I run around my desk and give her a hug. "Why didn't you say anything?"

She shrugs. "Uh, I didn't want to make a big hoopla about it."

Isaac pokes her cheek with a finger. "Couldn't you tell? Her green complexion says it all."

Darla gives him a death stare, making him take a step backward.

"But green is a good color on you. At least this time it's combined with a happy glow."

She rolls her eyes. "Right now, I'm too exhausted to argue, so don't mess with me."

I slide back into my desk chair and read over the FMLA form. Tears prick my eyes. I'm a terrible friend to be envious of Darla, especially since she's gone through so much to get where she is today, but I want what she has—the house, the guy, the kids. I focus on the form in silence. When I glance up, Darla and Isaac stare at one another. Then Darla gets up, and they start to back away.

"Okay, stop. Sit. Both of you. I'm sorry. I'm stressed to high heaven. Tommy's gone. It's been three days, and I haven't heard a peep out of him."

Darla scrunches her brow. "Three days? That's odd. He called Theo on Mon—"

Isaac slaps a hand over Darla's mouth. He gives me a cheesy grin, and my heart sinks. He called his brother as soon as he got back to Boston, but not me. I force back tears and put on a fake smile, hoping they buy it. "He must be really busy."

Darla pats my arm. "I'm sure he is. He's getting settled in, and he's probably already up to his neck in lab work or whatever crazy stuff engineers do." She nudges Isaac in the ribs.

He mouths, "What did I do?" She gives him the evil eye until he obviously gets her message. "Sure. Of course. He probably has a lot of catching up to do." Isaac looks back at Darla for approval.

"Tommy always has to be the best," Darla says.

I bow my head, trying to extricate the negative thoughts from my brain. He was always so secretive about school. There has to be more to the story. "I suppose. I broke down and texted him yesterday, but I got nothing back. I just miss him."

She rubs my shoulder. "Of course you do. Would you like to keep me and Stella company tonight? Theo's got to work. It'll be fun."

Isaac shakes his head. "I have a better idea. You could take my night shift. Staying busy is what you need to do."

He doesn't deserve an eye roll. I shake my head. "That's okay. I'll be fine."

Darla prods me. "Come on. You haven't spent much time with Stella since she got out of the hospital. She misses you. You don't want her to presume you don't like her anymore, do you?"

"Can't have that," Isaac says. "Can I come?"

I shake my head. "You have to work."

He pouts for a second then gets a happy face again. "We close at nine, and that's still early in the sleepover time zone."

Darla looks at me. She'll go with anything I want. Finally, I concede. Isaac can even put fun in a funeral.

"Sure," Darla says. "It'll be a sleepover like the good old days."

"Except with wine?" Isaac and wine are a dangerous combination.

"I'll bring the wine." I point at Darla. "But you will have to drink water."

She smiles big. "Yep. And thank goodness I'm not as sick this time. Maybe I'm more relaxed for this baby."

I shoo them out of my office. "Get out so I can finish these reports, or I'll have to spend the night here."

Isaac smiles. "You could take my—"

"Go!" I point at the door.

"Yes, ma'am."

Darla and Isaac leave, and I take one more glance at my phone, but I still don't have any messages. *Tommy, why are you doing this to me?* If he's not going to text me, I'll reach out to him again.

Shelby: *Thinking of you.*

I delete it.

Shelby: *Hey.*

Delete.

Shelby: *Miss you*

Delete.

Shelby: *Call me*

Delete.

Shelby: *Are you ignoring me?*

After deleting my fifth message, I finally give up and throw my phone back into my purse. All of those options made me sound like a pathetic teenager. The one thing I've learned about guys is the more I push, the more they run.

I pick up my things and walk out of my office. *Screw the reports.* They'll be here waiting on me tomorrow.

I FORGOT HOW MUCH FUN sleepovers at Darla's house can be. And even though Isaac invited himself, he's like one of the girls. He even lets Stella paint his toenails a hideous fuchsia color. I snap a photo of them to add to my Facebook Timeline. While I'm on social media, I check Tommy's page. He hasn't posted anything in two years, so that's not going to be helpful at all.

Darla, Isaac, and Stella do their best to keep me occupied so my thoughts aren't consumed with Tommy. He only crosses my mind when we're making dinner, or taking out the trash, or watching the movie, or hugging the pillow, to name a few minor times his image passed through my brain. I need him so bad, and there's nothing I can do about it.

During the movie, I draw a picture of Stella sitting in Isaac's lap. He adores her, and I capture the moment on paper perfectly. When I slide it over to Darla, she scurries out of the room in a fit of hormonal tears. After she composes herself, she joins us again and gives me a huge hug. "That is adorable. I didn't realize you could do that."

A blush creeps up my neck. "An old hobby. Tommy brought it back to the surface."

She gazes over at her daughter then down at the drawing. "Don't ever bury it again."

Stella jumps out of Isaac's lap. "Mommy, I want to see."

Darla shows the drawing to Stella, and she gets the biggest grin. "Hey, Uncle Isaac, it's us."

Isaac's jaw drops. "Don't let Mommy Dearest see it."

I laugh. "We've made some strides toward an appreciation of my creative side."

Isaac gives me a thumbs-up. "It's about time she came off her high horse."

Stella scrunches up her brow. "Mommy, I want a horse."

"Thanks a lot, Isaac," Darla says.

I had so much fun drawing the picture I gave Tommy. It took me a while to get the dusting of flour in his hair just right, but it was worth it. "It feels good to sketch after such a long time not doing it. And it feels liberating sharing my talent with the people I love."

Darla points at Stella. "Anytime you want to get your frustrations out and need someone to pose for you, just stop by. Stella is a big ham."

The little girl makes me smile. "That she is."

Darla doesn't see any more of the movie because she's too busy studying the drawing. When Stella's eyes close, Darla carries her to her bed, leaving Isaac sacked out on the couch. Darla and I lie in her bed to have girl-talk time. She places the drawing on her nightstand, and it means the world to me that she likes it so much.

"I cannot believe you're going to have another baby."

She chuckles. "Me either. For a guy who thought he was infertile, Theo sure can pack a punch."

"I'm so happy for you. You're such a good mama, and this time, Theo will be here for you. It's what you always wanted. You deserve it."

"Aww, thanks, Shel. It's still such a shock. If you would have told me six months ago that all this would be happening, I would have said you were a blooming idiot."

"Oh, I'm the idiot all right."

"You are not. Theo's pretty tight-lipped when it comes to his family, so I don't have any more information than you do. Tommy's only called Theo that one time, and all I heard was 'Hey, Tommy,' then Theo slipped outside. But he does that with Jennifer and Heather too. He's pretty protective of his family."

"He lived with Mallory, so can you blame him?"

"Oh, I'm sure he did the same when she was around, so I don't take it personally."

Maybe I shouldn't have brought up his ex-girlfriend's name. Mallory was Darla's old college roommate, then she was Theo's girlfriend for a lot of years before he moved back to Nashville.

"Sorry if she's still a sore subject."

"No, it's okay. I've seen her a few times, and she's been really nice. She seems genuinely happy that Stella's going to be okay." Darla snickers when I gape at her like she's crazy. "I'm not saying we're best buds or anything, not like we were in college, but at least we're friendly."

I play with the comforter, pulling it up to my neck. "Was I too clingy?"

"Of course not."

"Not clingy enough?"

She bops me with a pillow. "Will you stop it? He's busy. You remember what graduate school is like at the master's level. Imagine what it's like working on a PhD."

I sigh. "I guess you're right."

"Maybe by the weekend, he'll be able to catch his breath."

"I suppose." A big yawn stifles my speech. I hope Darla's right. All I can focus on is the multitude of phone calls from Alex he got the last few weeks. Maybe this Alex *is* a girl like Isaac suspects, and maybe they are spending time playing catch-up or having makeup sex. Tommy never clarified the gender of this person when I spewed my hateful comments during our fake-breakup scene. He sure has a way of skirting around the complete truth.

Gah. Maybe he's really busy—busy studying, busy working, busy being with smart people. Or worse, maybe he's too busy baking for someone else.

CHAPTER THIRTY-ONE

Tommy

Walking into a snake pit would be more exciting than Jo Alexander's lab. It is just like I remember. The drill press has metal shavings all over it, and drill bits litter the workbench. Storage bins overflow with tiny parts, and the microscopes attached to computer stations have bleary-eyed graduate students staring into them. When Mike, my old lab buddy, sees me, he plucks the earbuds out of his ears and shakes my hand.

"Hey, wasn't sure you'd come back."

"I wasn't sure either." I scan the room. "Any progress on your thesis?"

He grins. "So close to being done. Stan is analyzing my data to make sure I didn't miss anything, then I should be ready to present the prelim data to my committee."

"That's great. Is Alexander around?"

Mike motions to the office within the lab. "Probably on the phone, as usual."

"Thanks. I'm not eager to have our status meeting."

"May the force be with you."

We knuckle-bump.

Professor Alexander is probably going to chew me out for taking so much time off, but it wasn't nearly enough. I rap my knuckles on the doorframe, and Alexander pops her head up from her computer screen. "Well, look what the cat dragged in. Come in."

Her office hasn't changed since I last saw it. Manuscripts litter her desk, and the picture of her and Hazel with their arms wrapped around each other is perched on her credenza. On the wall hangs her Notre Dame doctorate diploma. But what grabs my attention the most is the plaque next to the photo that states her motto: No drugs, no drama, no daughter. I have two huge strikes against me.

"Hey, Doc. How's it going?"

She slides her reading glasses off and shrugs. "Some projects are going well. Others, like yours, are stalled." Her eyebrows rise. "If it was anyone but you, I'd be all piss and vinegar about it."

I stare at my feet as I sit in the chair next to her desk. "I appreciate your understanding. I've got some time to make up."

"How was your summer break? Was it all you thought it would be?"

I bust out a belly laugh and train my eyes on the ceiling. "Hardly. Let's see—my brother reconnected with an old flame and found out he had a six-year-old daughter who almost died." I snap my fingers. "Oh, I did meet someone, and we got fake engaged. That was real fun."

My professor chuckles as she leans back in her chair. She balls up her dark hair into a bun and uses a pencil to keep it in place. "I see you were busy. The whole fake engagement must have been interesting."

My face feels like it's on fire. "Parts of it were."

She points at me and waggles her eyebrows up and down. "You're in love."

A warm feeling consumes my body. "I am."

"Love is grand with the right person." She adjusts her wedding ring then clears her throat. "Ready to get back on the computer sci horse?"

My eyes land on the picture of her and Hazel. "Sure. Mike said he's close to presenting his data."

Alexander quirks an eyebrow. "You could be next if you buckle down. A new grad student has started. His name is Craig Phillips. I'd like you to mentor him."

I jab a thumb at myself. "Me? The guy who flaked out and ran home to his mommy?"

She belts out a very unprofessional guffaw. "Yep. And you needed that break. It obviously did you some good. You're glowing."

Her words make me cringe. "Dudes don't glow."

Professor's eyes twinkle with an expression that seems almost happy, and she is never happy unless we are discussing Boolean logic or integrated-design engineering analysis software. This warm and fuzzy side of my professor is something I've never had to deal with. It's easier when she's grumpy and work-oriented. This part of her is almost human. If Hazel was more like her mother, she would be at least tolerable. But she's still not the one for me.

"Of course dudes glow." She scribbles down something on a sticky note and slides it across her desk to me. "This is Craig's contact information. Show him the ropes."

"Yes, ma'am." I like helping others. Plus, it will keep me super busy in case *she* comes around.

"Don't call me ma'am. Check your Southern manners at the door."

I salute her as I get up to leave and slam right into Hazel. The warm feeling is replaced with an ice-cold death grip. "Hey, Thomas," she whispers as her hands roam up my chest.

I immediately push them off before my professor sees. "Hi, Hazel. I need to go."

As I scoot around her, she yells, "Call me, and we can discuss the you-know-what."

Not on your life. I sneak a peek at Mike on my way out. His shiver conveys my feelings exactly. *Time to bake.*

MY CRUMMY FURNISHED apartment is such a small space, I had to scoot the tiny bistro table up against the wall in order to maneuver in and out of the kitchen. It's a gloomy place to live, but thank goodness I have bread dough to punch because I couldn't feel more lost. Maybe it is better that Tony's not my roommate anymore so he doesn't have to witness the flour fiasco. He was starting to get pudgy around the middle, a fact that infuriated his girlfriend.

So I stand in my kitchen, drowning my anxiety in flour, yeast, and sugar. Today, I'm working on Italian. Yesterday, it was sourdough, and Monday was whole-wheat bread and a batch of chocolate chip cookies. My apartment overflows with baked goods, from pastries, to cookies, to every type of bread in the book. I guess I need to bring all of it to the lab because I am running out of room here. Craig could stand to put on a few pounds, and I'm more than happy to help in that department. That's what mentors are for.

I feel like a heel for not calling or texting Shelby. When I saw her sweet words in the text she sent, I came close to calling it quits up here. I promised I would call her when I got settled, but it's just too hard to hear her voice and not be able to hold her. When I get back in town for Theo's wedding, I'll make it up to her.

Someone knocks on the door. The only person it could be is Hazel, and I don't want that girl in my place. I didn't give her my new address, but she's a sneaky one. There are at least a dozen ways she could find out, not the least of which would be to follow me here from the lab. I wouldn't put it past her.

I tiptoe to the door and squint through the peephole. Instead of seeing my worst nightmare, I spy an elderly woman standing there. Her gray hair is pulled back in a braid, and her hands are propped on her hips as she taps a toe. *Thank goodness.* I can handle this.

"I don't have all day, Sonny."

I whip open the door, and her scowl morphs into a wrinkly grin. "Aren't you a handsome boy? I heard we had a new student in the building, but I thought he'd be another wiry, feeble mama's boy. You aren't any of that."

I catch about every third word because of her thick Boston accent. Even though I'm not new to the area, every time I come back from being down South, I have to listen extra carefully at first to the locals. And today, it's obvious I am out of practice. I dust off the flour from my hands, sending particles trailing through the air, before I stick a hand out for her to shake.

"Tommy Edwards. Nice to meet you, ma'am."

She gives me a handshake so firm, I'm sure she bruised some knuckles. "Don't call me ma'am."

"Don't tell my mom. If she heard I wasn't showing you respect, she'd have my hide." I show her inside.

Her nose wiggles as she gets a whiff of my baking. "The name's Sarah Kennedy. I live in the apartment below you. These rusty old vents send your baking smells right to me, so I had to investigate."

"I'm so sorry. Please, take some of this off my hands." I lead her over to the kitchen counter, where I have taken out my frustrations.

"What are you studying?"

"Engineering."

She shuffles over and nibbles on a cookie, smacking her lips with every bite. "Yum. That's good."

"Thank you. So, are you from Boston?"

She glances over her glasses like I'm the dumbest person on earth. "The name's Kennedy. Fill in the blanks, Sonny."

"I'm not sure I... oh. The Kennedys? As in John F.?"

She smirks as she crunches down on another cookie. "Yep. Distant, but nonetheless, Hubby was a cousin, twice removed."

"Wow." I'm not sure if I should believe her, but anything is possible, I guess.

"I bet you're wondering if that's the case, then why am I living here in this drafty, old apartment instead of the Compound?" She shudders. "That humid, salty air. Too many tourists. I like the city."

"Okay."

She points at her cookie. "I should take you to the Union Oyster House, the oldest restaurant in the country. We could sit in the Kennedy booth and eat lobster ravioli."

Yum. That sounds good. "Uh... sure." I cut a loaf of bread and hand her a piece.

Her eyes roll back into her head when she takes a bite, making me smile. "You missed your calling."

"Thanks."

She smacks her lips to catch some crumbs in the corner of her mouth. "Where you from?"

"Nashville."

"Never been there. Yee haw!"

I chuckle. "It's not that bad."

"If you say so. You bake a lot?"

"A lot." I punch the dough again, not that it needed it, but it feels good. "And you are always welcome to take some of this off my hands. Lord knows I'll never eat all this."

She grins. "I could do that. Could I trouble a sweet Southern boy into changing some light bulbs from time to time?"

"Absolutely." I start a pot of coffee. I guess she'll be sticking around for a while, so I might as well get comfortable. We get acquainted for the next hour, and while she sips her coffee, she watches me over her cup.

"Son, you need to get laid."

I stop and stare at her. "Huh?"

"Not that I mind eating your goodies." She lets out a big chortle.

I jump up, rush into the kitchen, and stick my head in the freezer to cool off the embarrassment. This elderly lady has such a youthful soul.

"What I mean to say is—"

"I'm not sure I want to hear what you meant," I say before I close the freezer door and take a swig from my water bottle.

"I see what you're doing. Some people are stress eaters. You're a stress baker. And you need a girl."

After I am sure my face has returned to a semi-normal color, I sit beside her at the table again. "I've got a girl."

"Really?" She scans the small apartment. "I don't see her. She's not one of those blowup dolls, is she?"

I run my hands through my hair. Mrs. Kennedy is a pistol. "No, ma'am. She's real." I motion with my head toward the counter, where the framed picture Shelby drew for me sits propped up next to the bag of flour.

"She's a pretty little thing." Then, out of the blue, she pops me on the shoulder. "Don't you ever call me ma'am again."

"Sorry, ma'am. I mean sorry, Sarah. Remember, I'm not from around here."

"Ah, yes. A Southern gentleman. I forgot. Anyway, tell me about her."

I proceed to tell her about Shelby and how wonderful she is and how she makes me feel. I even confide in Sarah that I don't want to be here and tell her about the Hazel complication. She reminds me of an elderly Heather in that I can tell her anything without fear of judgment.

"So, are you certain Shelby's the one after only a short time?"

"Yep."

"And you're willing to risk losing her to go to this brainiac school?"

"It's what my family expects of me."

"Did you tell her about that whacko?"

"No. That was a fling." I hold my hands out to defend myself. "It was over before I met Shelby, so there wasn't anything to tell."

She kicks back in her seat and stares at the ceiling. "So, if this psycho chick wasn't part of the trouble, would you still be this uptight?"

"Uh…" I shove the plate of cookies across the table toward her. "Cookie?"

She shakes her head. "You should have told Shelby. What's Hazel got that this sweet Southern thing doesn't?"

"Nothing. Here's the thing. I'm pretty sure Hazel will try to blackmail me into doing things I don't want to do anymore."

"Any basis to her scheme?"

"Not at all, but my father's a pastor, and I don't want anything to taint his reputation. She said something about pictures."

"Pictures? Hmm. Anything kinky?"

I choke on my coffee. "Not hardly."

"Then are you flattered she's stalking you?"

I snort. "Shocked and confused is more like it. I thought she'd get the hint when I left for the summer. I don't date. I don't even have time to give a girl any attention, let alone have a relationship. Shelby was an outlier for sure."

"That's a waste." She wags her head. "Have you faced a mirror lately? You are a catch."

"Miss Sarah, are you hitting on me?"

She huffs. "Shoot, you couldn't handle it."

I chuckle. She's probably right.

"Tell me this. If you had no pressure on you and could do anything with your life, what would you do?"

I think for a moment. "I have no idea. I do like helping people."

"Helping others helps you, right?"

I nod.

"And let's not forget you like to bake, and you're very good at it."

"It's my happy place."

"You could feed poor people while you feed your soul."

I stare at her. She's like my new angel in this crap pile of a situation. With her around, I may be able to handle the pressure. Heather will be happy when she hears she doesn't have to fly up here all the time to keep me from banging my fist into a wall.

"In a perfect world, that would be awesome, but reality is engineering. My parents have put a lot of money into my education, and it's all I'm trained for. I wouldn't have the foggiest idea how to run a nonprofit."

"Suit yourself, but don't let the world dictate your path for very long, or else you'll end up losing your way. You don't want to get so lost, you end up blowing your brains out."

Boy, she doesn't hold back. "I have to keep my head down and finish without going down the rabbit hole."

"Yup. And the whacko will drag you down so fast, it will make your head spin."

My phone chimes. It could be Mom checking in on me or Heather ready to bless me out for not calling Shelby. And I deserve every bit of it. I just figured if I heard Shelby's voice, it wouldn't be enough.

"You might want to get that," Sarah says.

"Yeah. Just a sec." Shelby's face lights up the screen and brightens my mood. Unable to wait any longer, I press the phone to my ear. "Hey, sugar."

"Tommy. So your phone does work."

I love that sassy voice. "I'm sorry. I'm an idiot, but you already knew that."

"Yes. It's been almost a week. That's an eternity in Shelby years."

I chuckle. "I'm so sorry. I have done nothing but work in the lab, focus on data, and sleep. What little down time I do have, I've spent baking and beating myself up for not calling you."

Silence on the other end causes my heart to race. When she doesn't respond, I add, "I'm terrible about this stuff. I speak better with flour and sugar."

When she finally speaks, her voice is soft. "I guess..."

"It's no excuse." I let out a deep breath. "I tend to close myself off when I get overwhelmed, and I'm going to work on that."

"And I need to work on trusting you."

My heart breaks because I've caused her to mistrust me. "That's one thing you can do completely. I'm just really busy, but I'm not so busy that I can't call you at least once a day."

"Really?" Hope fills her voice.

"Absolutely." My voice becomes soft and low. "I wish you were here."

"Me too."

Sarah leans in close to me. "Tell her you love her," she stage-whispers.

"Who is that?" Shelby asks.

"It's... it's my neighbor, Sarah."

"Give me the phone," Sarah says, grabbing for it before I have a chance to walk away. She's right behind me, doing her best to snatch the phone away from me.

"Shelby, Sarah wants to talk to you." I relinquish the phone to Sarah.

"Shelby, this is Sarah Kennedy. I want you to understand I'm going to take good care of your Tommy for you." Her eyes get big. "Oh, heavens no. He's all yours. I'm just using him."

I cringe and try to pry the phone away from Sarah.

"Well, somebody's got to eat all the bread and goodies he's been making. Without you, all he does is bake, bake, bake." Sarah grins. "Yeah." She snickers then hands me the phone.

I let out an exasperated sigh. "Hey."

"Is Sarah your fairy godmother?"

"Something like that."

"And you're baking for her?"

"Not for her, but I'm glad somebody can take everything off my hands. She's pretty spry for eighty."

Sarah smacks my arm so hard, it's going to leave a mark. Then she strikes a bodybuilding pose. I have to fight the smile off my face.

"I'm seventy-five," she says in a haughty voice.

"Sorry."

Shelby laughs. "Is it safe to say she's not your type?"

"Yes, it is, but you are."

"Aww," Sarah says.

I blush. "I'll call you back later."

"I miss you."

I close my eyes and lean back against the counter. "I miss you too." I hang up the phone and smile at Sarah. "That was Shelby."

She shakes her head. "Boy, why are you here?"

"Because I'm an idiot."

Sarah doesn't argue with me, and I get the feeling she would if it were necessary. I should enlist Sarah in a plan to rid Hazel from my life for good. Maybe Hazel will listen to Sarah. I know I should.

CHAPTER THIRTY-TWO
Shelby

Tears flow down Heather's face, and her entire body trembles with laughter as I tell her the story about Sarah. Just when it seems as though she's got it together, she starts up with another gigglefest. It's a good thing she came over to my place for coffee instead of meeting at Bongo Java because her outbursts would have gotten a few harsh stares from the other customers.

"She said she was using him?" Heather has a hard time spitting out her words.

"Uh-huh. She sounds like a doll."

"If Sarah is your biggest problem, you'll be fine."

I become stoic. "Is his lack of communication because I'm not smart?"

Heather's jaw drops. "Never, ever say that again. It's not true, and Tommy would never think that of anyone, especially you."

I pick at my nail polish—I need a manicure in the worst way. "That's got to be it. I don't fit in with his life, at least his Boston life."

"You don't fit there, and neither does he. Trust me—he doesn't want to be there. He's super stressed, and when he gets this way, he shuts down."

"Yeah. He mentioned that when I spoke to him last."

"There was one time none of us heard from him for over a month. Mom was going insane, assuming the worst. Theo was the closest in Baltimore, so she flew him to Boston to check on Tommy. He was fine, but he had locked himself in his apartment. Theo said by the time he got there, the entire apartment was filled with cookies and pastries."

I smile, but it's not funny. "I'm sorry, but there are worse things to do when you're overwhelmed."

"Theo talked him down off the proverbial cliff of dough, and then this summer, when Tommy called, wanting to spend the summer living with Theo, we knew he was going down the rabbit hole of stress again." She glances up, and her face lights up. "Then he met you."

I couldn't stop smiling even if I wanted to. After nothing but duds for boyfriends, I assumed I would never meet anyone great. And right when I stopped searching, I found Tommy.

"I've never seen him more alive." Heather hugs me. "You saved him."

Tears fall from my eyes and drip down my cheeks. "Why in the world did he go back?"

"He doesn't want to let anyone down."

I scrub my face with my hands. "But he's letting himself down."

"Ding, ding, ding. We have a winner!"

We sit in silence, and I let her words sink in. Everyone labels Tommy "the smart one," and they want him to make something of himself. It sounds like if he keeps going the way he is, he'll either become a bitter old man or he won't live long enough to care.

I have to ask the dreaded question. It's now or never. "Who is Alex?"

Heather stares down and fidgets as if she's contemplating something. Finally, she sighs. "This is going to sound worse than it is. His professor's name is Jo Alexander, who is a female."

I knew it. My heart sinks.

She grabs my arm. "It's not like that, but she is a complete control freak. You don't have anything to worry about with her except the demands she puts on Tommy to finish his projects and publish papers. It drives me crazy, and believe me, I've made my opinions known."

"I bet you have. I don't want to lose him."

"You won't. I won't let that happen. Try to relax and focus on your work until you get to see him again."

"So he wasn't involved with anyone?"

Heather scrunches her brow. "Well..."

"Never mind. I have to learn to trust him. It's hard for me, but I need to, because unlike all the other guys, I have faith in Tommy."

Heather blinks, and her lips quirk up. "You can trust my brother. I promise."

She's right, but it's hard. Even though we haven't known each other very long, I've never felt like this before, and I don't like having a single day away from him. I feel a connection to him, and I don't want to ruin it with childish jealousy and distrust. This is nothing like being away from Blaze. I felt like I needed a deep whole-body cleanse and soul scrub when he would leave to go on tour. With Tommy, it feels more like I'm missing my right arm. I should be ashamed of myself for concluding he had another girlfriend. I've got to keep my chin up and trust him. He is cognizant of where I am and how I feel. Maybe if I give him space, he'll figure things out. But he's a guy, so he may think I don't care. Surely he's not that stupid.

"When are you going back to school?" I ask Heather.

She shrugs one shoulder. "Not sure. Let's just say I don't fit in at UTK. I'm taking my own break, and maybe I'll transfer to a local college."

I raise an eyebrow. "Does my brother have anything to do with it? Because I can fix that in an instant."

She purses her lips and takes a deep breath. "He's not the cause, but he didn't help the matter either. Mainly, he's just a pest."

"Yep. You got that right."

Heather is clueless about Vaughan's feelings for her, but it's his own fault. If he didn't act so prepubescent all the time, she might realize he's a great guy. Next to Tommy, he's the best guy ever.

"Sometimes Vaughan acts like a ten-year-old little boy, especially around girls."

Heather chuckles. "I totally agree with you on that one. The only thing he hasn't done is tug on my ponytail."

I bite my lip to keep from smiling as I remember Vaughan's confession: "I like her a lot." He's never said anything like that about a girl, especially to me, so he must really have it bad for her.

"He's a good guy. Deep, deep, deeeeep down, he's good."

Heather throws her head back and belts out a chuckle. "It must be really deep."

"I'm not sure if he wants anyone to hear this yet, but he may be sticking close to home next semester."

Heather's eyes brighten for a slight second, then she recovers. "Good for him. I mean..."

"Don't be quick to judge him."

She juts her chin out. "I could say the same about my brother."

Ouch.

My phone chirps, announcing I have a text message.

Heather's eyes dance. "Ooo, is it from Tommy?"

My heart skitters in anticipation. I nod as I swipe my phone to see Tommy's message. My face hurts from the huge smile.

Tommy: *I'm low on sugar a.k.a. you.*

Aww. That is so adorable.

Shelby: *Nashville has a ready supply of sugar, and it only accepts Tommy currency.*

He sends me a winking smiley face and a pink heart.

I send him a text with pink lips. This is more like it.

CHAPTER THIRTY-THREE
Tommy

A knock on my apartment door wakes me from a fitful night's sleep on the couch. Without Shelby hogging the covers and using me as a human pillow, I don't sleep worth a crap. Most nights, I crash on the couch, not even bothering with the bedroom. I drag myself to the front door. Fearing it's Sarah wanting me to kill another spider, I have the good sense to fling on a T-shirt before I open the door.

I wish I had left it closed. And I'm very glad I have clothes on because in waltzes Hazel like she owns the place.

"What are you doing here, and how did you find out where I live?"

She rolls her eyes. "Mom's passwords are always one of three words, so I logged into her system and checked out your file."

Noticing the time on my watch, I say, "How impressive. Your mother must be so proud, but I need to get to the lab. It's already seven."

"I'm well aware of that." She looks around my puny apartment, taking in my measly existence. "We need to talk."

"I have nothing to say to you except goodbye."

She shakes her head and sits on the couch. She pats it for me to sit next to her. I remain standing with my arms folded.

"Why so grumpy?" she asks, pouting. Her glossy dark hair falls over one eye.

"Not grumpy. I'm also not playing anymore." I scrub my face with my hands, not believing the mess I've gotten myself into. "You lied to me about who you were. Let's get this straight right now. If I haven't made it clear before, I will today. You have done nothing but cause me trouble since the day we met at that godforsaken bar. It's over. Got it?"

She flings her dark hair behind her shoulder and bites her lip, trying to appear bashful. There is nothing bashful about Hazel. When she first waltzed into the lab to visit her mother and I realized she was the girl from the bar who I had been seeing, I thought I was going to pass out. Everyone in the room stopped what they were doing to stare at her. She had her head held high, was sharply dressed, and she had the biggest sultry smile on her face. I'd never really had a serious girlfriend, and before I knew it, I had broken two of Alexander's golden rules: no drama and no daughter. If my professor had found out, she would have blackballed me at school. If she puts her stamp of disapproval on a student, the other professors in the department follow suit and any semblance of a reputation in the field is history.

Hazel bats her eyes. "Didn't you miss me while you were gone doing whatever you needed to do in Redneckville?"

I can't help but grin. "You're a piece of work. I'm not interested." I blow out a breath as I walk into the kitchen to put space between us. "God, I was such a fool."

She picks up a pastry and nibbles on the edge. "Foolish for leaving for the summer. We had a good thing going." She lets out a wicked laugh. "We could have had a great time, but no, you had to visit your family." She flips her hair out of her eyes and takes me in like she's ready to eat me for dinner. "So what do you say?"

I shake my head and lean against the kitchen wall. "Nope. Not interested anymore. Besides, your mother would have me neutered." And I certainly didn't want to be forced to beg a new advisor to take me on in their lab. That would only make my time here longer.

Hazel puts her half-eaten pastry back on the plate. *Ew.* As sexy as a nineteen-year-old can, she glides her way over to me, and I press myself against the wall. Alexander always brags about how smart her daughter is. If she could see how dumb and reckless Hazel is with guys, she would be furious. Her stalker ways are very unattractive and stupid.

She closes in on me. "I thought you liked me."

I try my best to make that frickin' wall behind me move. When she finds my tickle spot, I squirm and push away from her. "Stop." I open the refrigerator to grab a bottle of water and to bring down my body heat. "Everybody likes you, Hazel. Now that I'm back, I need to focus on my studies. You need to find someone interested in you."

She snorts. "You are. You just forgot how interested you are."

"And I'm a preacher's kid. Maybe I've decided to be celibate from here on out until I get married." That's a big, fat lie, but I'm not above fibbing to get her off my scent. Hazel scans my entire body, and on instinct, I cover my crotch because I feel very naked right now.

"We both know that's a lie."

Crap. I point at Shelby's drawing of us. "Plus, I'm not available."

Hazel runs a finger over the frame and flips it over so the drawing is face down. "Has she heard about me? About us?"

My molars are going to be ground down to dust. "There is no 'us.'" I slide away from her and guzzle some water.

She claps and bounces like a cheerleader. "I have the best idea. You could be my tutor. I mean, I don't need one, but it will keep my mother off our trail in case she sees us together."

Dear God. Send help now. Love, Tommy.

I point at the door. "Leave."

Hazel taps a finger on her chin and grins evilly. "You realize Mom would be furious if she got wind of our relationship."

"Your word against mine."

Her evil grin tells me she's up to something. "Or it's your word against mine plus some well-timed photos."

I try to keep a poker face. "There aren't any photos."

She quirks an eyebrow. "You sure about that?"

Dear God. That help I asked for would be greatly appreciated right about now.

We're at a standoff, and she has the upper hand. This could be bad if she really does have photos. It's impossible, but she acts pretty sure of herself.

"Prove it."

Someone bangs on my door, making Hazel jump in surprise and me jump for joy. *Yay for answered prayers.*

"Thank God," I mumble under my breath as I push past her.

"Tommy, honey," Sarah says from the other side of the door. "Can you help me reach something at the top of my closet?"

"Unbelievable." Hazel huffs as she stomps to the door. "This isn't over."

"Yes, it is."

She snorts. "We'll see about that." She slings open the door then storms past Sarah and down the stairs.

Sarah points in the direction Hazel went. "Tell me that thing isn't Shelby."

"No. That's my professor's very manipulative daughter. Anytime you see her stop by, please find something for me to help you reach or a bug to kill. Anything."

Sarah bows. "That's my job. But, Sonny, you don't really want her, do you?" She cringes.

I shake my head. "She gets under my skin. And she's trying to blackmail me."

Sarah chases after Hazel. "Ooo, you let me have a swing at her."

I grab her arm. "Save your rage. I may need it another day."

"Whacko," she yells down the stairwell.

"Sarah," I say with a *tsk*.

"Half-baked," she adds as she shuffles back to her apartment.

"I sure am glad you're on my side."

She winks. "You better believe it."

I shut the door and collapse onto the couch. Staying away from Hazel is going to be harder than I thought, especially now that she knows where I live. I'm kicking myself for flirting with her last year. She makes my skin crawl and plays me like a fiddle. Even if Shelby wasn't part of my life, I would never want Hazel. She's toxic.

I can't take another year of this game she's playing. If I could work under another professor, I would. I thought of that before my little break, but no one has an interest in the work I've done so far. Plus, Alexander is the best. It's not her fault she has a horny, out-of-control daughter. I am still holding out hope that a new grad student will catch Hazel's eye, but so far, I'm the one she wants caught in her web.

And I need to figure out if the photos she mentioned really do exist. If she rears her ugly head again, I'm going to force her to give me evidence. I made it abundantly clear I didn't want any photos of myself, good or bad. I am practically nonexistent on the internet. All of us kids try to steer clear of a strong social media presence to keep Dad's reputation pristine. The worst that has happened is Theo having a child outside of marriage, and no one knew that, not even Theo.

Perhaps Sarah and I can develop a secret code for when I need help. Or I might have a better idea.

"YOU WANT ME TO DO WHAT?" Sarah asks, her voice screeching off the walls. She sounds more like a teenager than a septuagenarian.

"I want you to move in here until I leave for my brother's wedding. I have to keep away from the—"

"Whacko?"

"Yeah. If I can keep her away from my apartment that long, she'll get the message that I'm serious."

"Doubt that will help. If you were gone all summer and it didn't click, why would you assume a month more will?"

Sarah has a point. For a while, I thought Hazel had moved on, but when she got wind of me coming back, she started up again.

"You saw how she hightailed it out of here when you showed up at the door. It upset her plan. So you can be my Hazel repellant."

Sarah taps a finger to her lips. "What's in it for me?"

"It's just a thought, but I could cook—"

"Done."

I chuckle. "Really?"

"You had me at homemade bread, omelets, spaghetti…"

"Wow. I said all that?"

"Between the lines."

I shrug. "Okay."

She pats my hand. "You get ready for school, son. I got some grocery shopping to do."

"Oh, here. Let me give you some money." I pull out my wallet and hand her some bills.

She crinkles them up and shoves them back in my hand. "And don't get any ideas about me doing your laundry. As you Southerners say, 'ain't gonna happen.'"

"Yes, ma'am."

She pops me on the arm. "And don't call me ma'am."

"Okay, Sarah." I point at the bathroom. "I need to get ready for the day." Before I forget, I run to the kitchen and pilfer through the top drawer. "Here's the spare key."

She takes it and shoves me toward the bathroom. "Now get. I won't have you late for school, mister."

"Thanks." I kiss her on the cheek then hustle down the hallway. I can do this. I pull out my phone and text Heather.

Guess what? I've got a roommate. She's real cute.

Immediately, my phone rings. When I answer, Heather yells into the phone. "What the heck?"

"Calm down. My new roommate is Sarah."

"Oh. My. Gosh."

"Shut up. Hazel showed up today, and I needed a defense plan."

"Bro, that just might work."

It had better work.

CHAPTER THIRTY-FOUR

Shelby

Isaac slides out of the desk chair and onto the floor, laughing at my story about Sarah, especially the part Heather told me.

"She moved in with him?"

I hold a hand out to help him up. "Apparently, there have been some break-ins, and she didn't feel safe on the first floor. It probably has something to do with his massive cooking skills."

"It's hysterical," he says, wiping his eyes. He crawls back into the chair and lays his head on my desk. His whole body quivers with laughter.

Darla enters my office and jerks a thumb toward Isaac. "What is wrong with him?"

Isaac throws his hand up in the air like a first grader. "Ooo, ooo. Let me tell her."

"Go ahead."

"Tommy's got a girl living with him."

Darla whacks him on the shoulder.

"Ow."

"Why are you laughing?" She turns her attention to me. "And why aren't you crying?"

"Because he's got his very own Aunt Bea, like on the *Andy Griffith Show*."

Her mouth gapes open. "What?"

"Yep. He fixes stuff for her, and she eats all the food he bakes."

"Are you sure she's... old?"

I laugh. "Positive. Over the phone, it sounds like she's pushing eighty. Real feisty, though. I'm surprised Theo didn't say anything."

Darla rolls her eyes. "They are so tight-lipped, it ticks me off." She grins wickedly. "Although I've recently learned that when Theo's real tired, like after a double shift at the hospital, he talks in his sleep. He answers me too. It's like truth serum."

Isaac's evil side rears its ugly head. "Did you ask him something good and juicy about Mallory? Like do her farts smell like lilacs?"

"Don't start with me this morning. I'm a little queasy. Even the mention of her name or her lilac-smelling farts could send me running to the bathroom."

He snaps his fingers. "This could be useful at times. How about asking Theo who Alex is?"

I throw a pencil at him. "No."

Isaac butts in. "I still believe Alex is a female."

Ugh. I don't have time to hear 'I told you so' from Isaac, so Alex will remain gender neutral to him for now. I say to him, "This person texts Tommy all the time, like a stalker."

"Hmm," Darla says. "Theo works all night tomorrow. He'll be good and tuckered out when he gets home. If you want me to, I could mention it."

"No, don't. It's none of my business, and if I need any information, Tommy will tell me. I have to have faith in him."

"Do it," Isaac says. He's such a little troublemaker.

"No!"

Darla puts her hands up. "I won't. I promise. But you've got some vacation days you need to take, or you'll lose them. You could go to Boston to surprise him."

I haven't been to Boston in ages, and I am already having Tommy withdrawal. I could easily be talked into visiting him. "I'd love to, but it feels awkward going without telling him first, like I'm trying to catch him cheating or something."

"Do it," they both say at the same time. Isaac knuckle-bumps Darla.

Seeing Tommy again would relieve me of some of my insecurities. Even if I only go for the weekend, it might be all I need to put my fears to rest.

"Why not?" I bob my head up and down like I've finally figured out the world's most pressing issue. "I'm going to do it, but don't tell Theo or Heather. I want it to really be a surprise." A flush rises up my neck. "I painted him a picture of the Nashville skyline. I could bring it to him."

Darla's mouth drops open. "If it's anything like the drawing you made for me, he'll love it. Does it feel good to let that side of you out again?"

A slow smile plays on my lips. "It does, and now I don't feel the need to hide my drawings from my mother."

Isaac groans. "I never understood her problem anyway. She loves going to art galleries."

I hold up a hand to shut him down. "That is art. Mine were... doodles."

"Doodle on, sister."

I smile. "Thanks."

MY KNEE BOUNCES SO much that Vaughan presses his hand on it to make it stop.

I point at the steering wheel. "Two hands on the wheel when you're driving my car."

"You are more nervous than a whore in church. What is your problem?"

I stare out the window, trying to find the right words. "It's stupid, but I'm so nervous about going to see Tommy without telling him first."

"Don't go." He gives me a sly smile, as if he's already aware I'm going no matter what he says. "Sis, if a girl went out of her way to make a surprise visit for me, I'd be... touched."

"Touched."

He shrugs as he exits the interstate and heads toward the airport. "Touched as in impressed. I'll tell you the correct word if it ever happens to me." Vaughan slows the car as he rounds the curve and heads toward the unloading zone.

"No, Vaughan. You can't drop me off. It's tradition."

He groans. "Shel, you're getting too old for this."

"Never. I have to say my last goodbye at the security gate."

"You're going for a long weekend, not off to war."

I stare at him until I catch his attention.

"Okay, you win." He pulls out of the unloading lane and makes his way to the parking deck. "Are you going to Boston so you can catch Tommy doing something inappropriate?"

"No, of course not. Because he's not Blaze. That's not Tommy's style. He's honest, and trust me, I can spot dishonesty a mile away. I want to surprise him, but in the back of my mind, I'm afraid the Tommy I know isn't the real Tommy."

"Sounds like you don't trust him."

"I do. Never mind."

My brother licks his index finger and sticks it in my ear like he used to do when he was seven.

I shove his hand away. "You are disgusting."

"Just trying to stop the runaway freight train called your insecurities."

"But what if—"

"Stop. Maybe you really shouldn't go."

I focus on my lap as he pulls into a parking space. "I need to see him. I miss him."

Vaughan pinches my cheek. "That's what I wanted to hear. Everything else is just meaningless."

NOW THAT I'M STANDING outside of Tommy's second-floor apartment, I can't figure out what I'm going to do when I see him. I'm not sure if I should let him make the first move or just jump into his arms and let our emotions take over. I took a huge leap of faith coming here unannounced. He could be asleep, tangled up with some Yankee chick, or he could be slumped over a computer, pecking away at the keyboard. One thing is for sure—nothing is going to happen if I don't knock on the door.

After the third, harder knock, I bite my lip to keep the tears away. I've come this far, and he's not even here. Of course he's not here. I forgot about the different time zone. It's the middle of the morning in Boston, and like all dedicated students, he's probably been on campus for hours.

Walking backward, I slink away with my tail tucked between my legs. Just as I'm about to descend the first step, his door creaks open, and an elderly lady appears. "You searching for Tommy?"

I recognize her voice from our phone conversation. The smell of fresh pastries swirls through the hallway. "You're Mrs. Kennedy, right?"

She stomps her foot. "You darn Southerners with your prissy manners. It's Sarah, and get over here and give me a hug."

I run toward her, drop my bags, and fall into her arms. "I'm Shelby."

"Of course you're Shelby, and you're even prettier in person. Come in."

I scoot back to grab my bags. "My flight was delayed, then I never thought I'd find his apartment. I forgot how big Boston is."

She waves me in. "You just need to figure out how to work your way around it. Sorry you missed Tommy. He just left a few minutes ago."

My shoulders sag. A few frickin' minutes made all the difference.

"If I knew you were coming, I would have tried every excuse in the book to keep him from leaving." She leads me to the kitchen table. A plate of scones sits in the middle.

I stare at the scones, and Sarah chuckles as she hands me the plate. "You miss his cooking, don't you?"

A hot flush runs up my neck. "Among other things. What am I going to do now?"

Sarah stares at me like I'm an idiot. "You go to plan B. You've come too far to go back now. Plus, he needs to see you."

A warm sensation fills my heart. I needed to hear her words to confirm my feelings. "I don't want to bother him. Maybe I'll just hang out with you until he comes back."

"Nope. He'll be there for hours. You get your butt up and get on over to the engineering building."

My mouth drops. "How would I find it?"

"Do your feet work?"

"Yes, ma'am."

"Then walk out of this building and go five blocks. The engineering building is the big glass one on the other side of the road. You can't miss it. And don't call me ma'am."

I fight back a grin. "That's it?"

"Yep. Not sure what floor Dr. Alexander's lab is on, but someone should be able to help you when you get there."

I blink. The little I've heard about his professor terrifies me. The possibility of seeing the source of Tommy's stress sends a trickle of sweat down my back.

"Go!" Sarah urges. "And if his mouth isn't bruised from all the kisses you give him, I'm going to smack the both of you."

I throw my head back and howl with laughter. Before I walk out the door, I grab the older woman in a big hug. "Thank you, Sarah."

"My pleasure. And I noticed you didn't call me Mrs. Kennedy."

"What can I say? I'm a fast learner."

I wave to her as I take the steps two at a time. When I reach the floor below, I hear her yell down to me, "Hope you brought a box of condoms."

Goodness gracious. She's a piece of work.

CHAPTER THIRTY-FIVE

Tommy

I stayed clear of Hazel's grasp for almost a full week. She usually only stops by the lab when her mother is in class lecturing, so I guess Hazel avoids her mother as much as I avoid her. My hope is that she's become interested in some poor undergrad schmuck and forgotten all about me. I just need to make it to Theo's wedding unscathed, which is only two weeks away.

I tiptoe into the lab and find Mike looking through a magnifying glass, focused on microelectrical components. His curly dark hair falls over his forehead as he leans forward. Mike's grungy USC sweatshirt is going to bring out the worst in the professor considering her alma mater, Notre Dame, is a long-standing rival. She's serious about her football team, even if she is a stick-in-the-mud professional.

"Hey, Mike," I say.

He jumps and drops the component on the ground. "Crap."

"Sorry, man." I pick up the component for him. "Why so jumpy?"

With the tweezers, he gestures toward Alexander's office.

"Is she in a mood?"

He shakes his head. "Nope." On a scrap of paper, he scribbles a note and slides it over to me. *"Just Hazel."*

Son of a...

"You might want to try this capacitor." I scribble a note back to him and tap my pen on the paper. *"Rescue me ASAP."*

He reads my note and fist-bumps me. "Are you sure I can... trust that component?"

I give him a thumbs-up and add to my note. *"Leech."*

His eyes get wide. "I get it now," he says as Hazel pokes her head out of the office doorway.

I rip out the page we're writing on from his notebook and toss it in my backpack. "If you need more help with that component, just holler."

"Hi, Thomas. You've been avoiding me." Hazel's syrupy singsong voice grates on my nerves. She crosses her arms over her chest, pushing her cleavage out of her low-cut blouse.

"I had class. You should try it sometime."

"Well, you're not in class right now. Besides, I have something really important to show you." Using her index finger, she motions for me to come to her.

I glance over at Mike, and he gives his head one slow shake. "I was helping out Mike. I can meet you in the conference room in an hour."

She gestures to her mother's office, which occupies the corner of the lab space. "This really can't wait. It's time sensitive." She spins on her heel and marches away.

I lean down to Mike and whisper, "Give me two minutes. If I'm not out by then, make up any excuse to get me out of there."

He chuckles.

"I'm dead serious. Anything. Pull a fire alarm if you have to."

I walk toward the office, my heart racing in my chest. This is the first time Hazel and I will have been alone since the time she pulled a fast one on me at my apartment. I check to make sure my T-shirt is tucked in and my zipper is up. I even button my plaid shirt all the way up to my neck for an extra layer of defense. The grip on my backpack strap is so tight, I might rip it in two. I stop at the doorway, afraid to go any farther into the room. Maybe if I hear her out and she doesn't get a reaction out of me, she'll move on.

"What are you doing here?" I glimpse over my shoulder. "Your mother could be back any minute."

"Mom's having a root canal, so we've got plenty of time."

"I don't."

She points at a chair. "Sit."

"I prefer to stand, but thanks anyway."

She walks to me and grabs me by the collar. The unexpected force sends me off balance, and I tumble into the chair. *Dang, she's strong.* She hovers over me, giving me a view down her low-cut blouse. She licks her lips. "You like what you see?"

"Hazel, no." I attempt to get up, but she pushes me back down then gooses me in the side.

An involuntary nervous giggle pops out of my mouth. "Stop."

"You still like it, don't you?"

I shake my head.

"And stop calling me that hideous name."

From out in the lab, Mike yells, "Tommy, I need your help out here. Right now."

Again, I try to stand. "I need to help Mike."

"You need to help me." She tickles me again and unbuttons my plaid shirt. She untucks my T-shirt, and I latch on to her hand. But instead of yanking her hand away, she sees it as permission to grope my crotch. I groan. *Dammit.*

"Seems like I need to help you."

"Oh my God!" a startled voice says from the doorway.

I snap my head around and see Shelby standing there with her hands covering her mouth.

Mike pulls Shelby back into the lab. "Sorry, man. I tried."

I push Hazel away from me. She stumbles backward and bumps up against the desk. "That's Shelby? Oh, Thomas. Seriously? Ew."

I storm out of the office and into the lab just as Shelby runs out into the hallway.

"Shelby, stop."

"Get away from me," she yells over her shoulder while rushing to the elevator. The doors close right before she gets to it. She frantically pushes the down button while she scans the area. When she spies the exit sign for the steps, she pushes past me and flings the door to the stairwell open. This cannot be happening.

I am right on her heels. "Shelby, please stop. It's not what it looks like."

"I don't care. Just leave me alone." She races down four flights of steps, just out of my reach.

"Please, let's talk."

"I said get away from me."

I grab her arm before she exits the building. She keeps her eyes trained on the floor. Tears stain her face. Her lip quivers. I take her face in my hands, but she swats them away.

"You don't get to touch me ever again."

"Shelby, please."

"No." Her eyes are slits. "I believed in you, Tommy. I trusted you. I thought you were different."

Tears cloud my vision. "Let me explain."

She shakes her head. Buckets of tears stream down her face. "Your professor? God, I'm such a fool."

"No."

She backs away from me. "Goodbye, Tommy." She storms out of the building.

I lean against the wall as she runs away. I wipe my face and take the elevator alone back up to the lab. There's no use chasing her down. She's too upset to listen to me, and I can't form coherent words. None of it will make a bit of sense to her anyway.

Inside the lab, Mike stands there with his hands in his pockets. His complexion is as white as a ghost. "I'm sorry, Tommy. I tried to warn you."

I pat him on the back. "It's not your fault." I take two long strides to the office, where Hazel is sitting at her mother's desk with her feet propped up on it. Alexander would have a fit if she saw that.

Slamming the door behind me, I say, "I hope you're happy."

She smiles, and if I wouldn't get arrested for assault, I would smack that smirk off her face. "Actually, I am. Now maybe you'll get back to what we need to talk about."

"And just what is that, Hazel?"

She grins evilly. "Oh, you'll like this." She pulls out her phone and shows me the screen. "That's us getting it on in your apartment."

The photo is dark, but there is no denying it's her lying on her back, naked, in my bed, with my buck-naked body on top of her. Her hair is splayed across my pillow. The clock and the picture of my family on the nightstand are displayed prominently. Yeah, this is bad. Really bad.

My pulse races so much, I'm about to pass out. I shake my head, and it takes me a moment to form words. "When did you take this?"

"Right before you left over the summer."

"Delete it."

"Nope. And if you stop avoiding me, I won't send this to your preacher father and everyone at your church. I hacked into the email system." She smirks as she flips her hair off one shoulder. "Tommy, the preacher's kid, getting it on with the professor's daughter. Then there are the rules. Don't you remember Chris Franklin?"

My mind races, trying to organize the facts I heard about Chris when I first started in Alexander's lab. He transferred to Michigan. I assumed it was to finish his research, but maybe there was another, darker reason.

She points at the plaque in Alexander's office. "He's the reason for this. Mom flipped and refused to support his research when she found out what we were doing." Hazel pouts. "Too bad because he was adorable."

My head spins, and the palms of my hands become sticky with sweat. "This is impossible."

"Oh, it's so possible."

I stumble backward and knock into the door. "Are you blackmailing me?"

"Call it what you want." She leans down to pick something up off the floor. "Oh, looks like your little Shelby dropped this paint-by-numbers set when she caused a scene." She pouts. "Oh no, the dollar-store frame broke." She chucks it into the garbage can.

"You malicious child." I snatch it out of the trash and storm out of the office. Mike looks like a deer caught in headlights as I rush past him and out of the lab.

It only takes me five minutes in my anxiety-ridden state to walk back to my apartment. I fling open the door to my apartment and throw my backpack in the corner. I pace from the living room to the kitchen and back again. My heart beats so hard and fast, I'm afraid it's going to explode.

If Shelby had walked in two minutes earlier or later, things would have been completely different. I kept this part of my life a secret from her, and now it has come back to haunt me. I'll never win her back, not if she won't even look at me. And if Hazel sends out that photo, I'll never be able to show my face in Dad's church again.

I pull out my phone and dial Shelby's number for the tenth time in ten minutes. Again, she doesn't answer, and all my texts go unanswered as well. This is unbelievable. I'm losing it all. I'm losing Shelby.

I throw my phone on the counter and scrub my hands through my hair. I lean against the wall, and tears burn my eyes. I'm going to lose the love of my life, and I'm going to lose my sanity.

My front door clicks, and in walks Sarah. "Dear Lord, what happened? Did you see Shelby?"

I take two deep breaths and nod. "I lost her."

She gestures to my kitchen. "You, in the kitchen. Bake. Now."

SARAH SITS WITH HER head in her hands as I throw another cookie sheet full of snickerdoodles into the oven. She jumps when I slam the oven door.

"She wouldn't even let me explain. She saw something out of context and thought the worst of me."

"Sonny—"

"To be clear, I'm not screwing around with Hazel. I have no idea how she took that picture."

"Sonny—"

"The hurt in Shelby's eyes." I run a flour-doused hand through my hair before I fling a hot cookie sheet across the kitchen. "I have nothing now. I don't want to be here, and I have nothing to go home to." I slump into a chair. What a difference a few minutes makes. If I had waited thirty seconds more to answer the door that day, I would have never met Shelby to begin with. "She got a surprise all right." I rise from my chair, turn off the oven, and head toward my bedroom. "I need to think."

"I'm so sorry, Sonny. So very sorry."

"Me too."

In total darkness, I lie on my bed. My phone buzzes, and I grab it in hopes that Shelby's calling me. Instead, I realize I have two emails from my professor, asking where I've been, and one from Hazel with the infamous picture attached. But there's nothing at all from Shelby. I shouldn't have expected it to be her. The grip on my phone tightens enough to break the screen. I channel my last bit of frustration into the loudest scream of my life and slam my phone into the wall.

CHAPTER THIRTY-SIX
Shelby

My puffy red eyes don't conceal my heartbreak. The person at the ticket counter will never forget me: a Southern gal in the middle of a crying jag. She exchanges my ticket for a flight out today and even upgrades me to first class, bless her heart. The glimpses I get from the airline attendants when I board the plane make it clear my mental state was shared among the crew.

I collapse into my oversized seat and scroll through my text messages before I have to power my phone down for takeoff. One message after another is from Tommy, begging me to call him. I can't. I don't think I ever can. Another tear slides down my cheek. From the main entrance to the plane, a girl squeals, jolting me out of my depressed bubble. I certainly hope that bouncy bottle of energy doesn't sit by me because I might have to smack her. Trying to block the noise, I lay my head back on the headrest and close my eyes, hoping to find a happy place that probably doesn't exist. The squeaky girl's voice fades, so I hope that means her seat is way in the back of the plane.

A person clears his throat, and assuming I must be taking up too much space, I scoot as close to the window as possible.

"Where's Preppy Paul?"

No fricking way. My eyes snap open. If I weren't already buckled into my seat, I might have been removed from the flight due to me punching him in the face. Of all the flights in all the airports, Blaze has to be right here, towering over me in the aisle, on the worst day of my life, taunting me.

"I'd say it's nice to see you again, but I was taught not to lie."

He snorts and gives me the once-over. "You look like hell. I've been meaning to call you."

"Sure you have. Go away."

Behind me, a drop-dead gorgeous girl clears her throat. She has stunning auburn hair and is wearing a dark-blue Anne Klein pantsuit.

Blaze turns and faces the biggest resting bitch face ever.

"You're in my way. That's my seat." She points at the seat next to me.

He holds his ticket out to her. "Want to trade?"

"No, she doesn't." I lean over and push him out of the way then take the woman by the hand and help her into her seat. "Hi. I'm Shelby."

She shakes my hand and smiles. As she buckles her seat belt, she glances up at Blaze, who hasn't moved an inch. "Something on your mind?"

He chuckles. "You don't recognize me?"

I didn't realize he had risen to the "don't you know who I am" status, but apparently he assumes so.

With a straight face, the woman next to me replies, "No. And since I've made it thirty years without that lovely pleasure, it's safe to say I'll survive at least another thirty. Scoot."

Blaze throws his head back and belts out a laugh. Another passenger slides past him. He pulls out his wallet. "What will it take to get you to switch seats with me? Shel and I go way back."

He holds out a fifty-dollar bill. I grab my purse and pray to the God of all that is good and decent in the world that I have some cash on me. I find three twenty-dollar bills and wave them in front of the girl's face. "Sixty if you don't let him have it."

She rotates her head so I alone can see her wink. "Sold."

He rifles through his wallet again, but she stops him. "Auction is over, Mr. Full of Himself. If you think I'm giving up my first-class ticket, you're stupider than you appear. Now move along."

With a thin-lipped smile, he says to me, "I'll see you when we land."

She shoos him away. "Don't count on it."

He moves to the far back of the plane, and when I hear the squeal of his latest fan again, it's obvious he's found his companion for the night.

I let out a deep sigh. "Thank you so much."

"No problem." She hands me my money back. "I don't need your money, and just for the record, I'm well aware of who he is."

"You are?"

"Yep. I used to work for Mecca Records. He's hit on me a time or two, but I guess he was too high at the time to remember faces." She rolls her eyes then frowns. "Those tears aren't for him, are they?"

I shake my head. "Oh, heavens no. I... it's a long story."

She rotates her arm to check her watch. "We've got about two hours to kill." She slides her hand over the soft armrest. "And really comfy seats. By the way, I'm Layne."

For the entire flight, I spill my guts, telling her how Tommy and I went from strangers to a couple, to being fake engaged, to fake broken up, to really broken up. I show her pictures on my phone of Tommy and me, and I cry more tears than I ever thought possible, all without one glass of alcohol. Every now and then, we hear Blaze and his new plaything. Lord only knows what they're doing. Thank goodness it's a night flight and most people have their lights off. The best part of it all is that Layne lives less than ten minutes from me. On the saddest day of my life, I may have met a new friend.

After a long silence, Layne asks, "Are you sure of what you saw? From what you described, he seemed like a keeper before what happened today."

"It seemed that way."

"You need to sleep on it. No hasty decisions. And stay away from you-know-who."

I shiver. "I'd rather live alone for the rest of my life than be around the likes of him again."

The flight attendant ruins our conversation to prepare us for landing. As we begin our descent to Nashville, Layne gives me her phone number in case I have a weak moment and want to talk to Blaze. She said she'll knock some sense into me. Somebody needs to.

When the plane lands, Layne sees the worry on my face as I glance back to where Blaze is sitting. "Leave this to me," she whispers. She motions for me to leave ahead of her, and as I reach the cabin door, I hear her let out a string of curse words. "I can't believe I spilled everything out of my purse." Several passengers behind her groan.

Bless you, Layne. As I scoot out of the terminal, I peek over my shoulder. Blaze gets bombarded with adoring fans. He's already forgotten I was on the plane, thank goodness.

THE UBER LETS ME OUT in front of my townhome, and I drag myself up the walkway. The hot, muggy air is a far cry from the crispness in Boston. It's like the atmosphere weighs as much as my heart does. When I open the front door, I flip on the ceiling fans and open the windows for ventilation. My bags drop to the floor, and I collapse onto my couch. The tears flow again for the thousandth time.

I'm not sure how long I sit there, curled up into a ball. It could have been five minutes or five days. A hand touches my shoulder, making me shriek.

"Hey," Vaughan says, backing away. "I didn't mean to scare you." When he gets sight of my red, puffy eyes and runny nose, his eyes get big. "What in the world happened to you, and why are you home already?" He kneels in front of me and takes my shaking hands in his. "Talk to me, sis."

"Oh, Vaughan." I fall into his arms. He holds me and lets me cry it out again. I'm not sure where to begin. After what seems like an eternity, I finally find the words. "He's cheating on me."

He shakes his head and leans away from me. "What? No way."

I blow out a breath. "I walked in on him."

"Sis." He stands and paces in front of me.

"It was awful. I went to Boston to surprise him, but boy, I'm the one who got the surprise."

He crinkles his brow. "Are you sure? It doesn't sound right."

"Yeah, Vaughan. I'm sure."

Vaughan scrubs his face with his hands. "Tommy's not a cheater. It's not in his DNA. Trust me. I can spot a cheater when I see one." He gestures to himself.

"I thought that was all an act."

He shakes his head. "It's all an act now, but it wasn't always that way." He blushes. "That sounds worse than it really is. Anyway, Tommy... I can tell he's one of the good ones. It must feel messed up right now, but there has to be an explanation."

"Of course there is. I'm an idiot. I promised myself I wouldn't let it happen again, and it did. I'm such a fool."

"You are not a fool. Did you let him explain? Sometimes we guys get into situations that seem worse than they really are."

"Actions speak louder than words." I cover my face with my hands, and another round of tears starts.

Vaughan holds me and lets me cry myself out, then he curls me up on the couch and places a quilt over me. Before my eyes close from exhaustion, I see Vaughan walk into the kitchen. He pulls out his phone and calls someone, speaking in a hushed tone. I'm too exhausted to care.

I ROLL OVER ONTO MY back and stare at the ceiling, trying to figure out what time it is. All the events of the night flood back into my mind. Pizza boxes and beer bottles line the kitchen table. My sweet brother chomps down on a slice of pizza as he debates something with… Heather? I pretend I'm still asleep, hoping they'll say something about Tommy, but all they do is carry on with their usual banter.

"Heaven, all I'm saying is she's a babe. What am I supposed to do?"

He'll never learn. I scratch a tickle on my nose.

I open my eyes in time to catch Heather punching him on the arm. "Ugh. Stop calling me that stupid name. And do you have to be such a Neanderthal when it comes to girls?"

He snorts and gulps down a swig of beer. "She wants it. I got it. End of story."

Heather puts her hands over her ears. "Stop, please. Do you have any idea where her mouth has been?" She shivers. "She's disgusting."

He snickers like a girl. "I love making you squirm. And everything I just said is one-hundred-percent a complete lie." He smiles at her with a gotcha grin.

She smacks him repeatedly on the shoulders until he captures both of her hands.

"Let go. I hate you."

"I hate you too."

Uh-oh.

He frees her hands, and she crosses her arms over her chest. "One day, Vaughan, you are going to meet someone who is going to give you a run for your money, and I hope I'm around to see you squirm." She sticks her tongue out at him.

He pinches her cheek, and she quickly swats his hand away.

"What makes you think I haven't already?" he asks suggestively.

She gasps. "You should stop acting like a—"

I let out a sneeze. They both snap their heads in my direction. Heather shoves Vaughan once more for good measure before she tiptoes over to me.

"Hey," she says like she's tending to a wounded puppy, which she is. She gives my arm a squeeze. "I'm going to get to the bottom of this. I promise. This situation is a little complicated."

I blow out a breath. "Don't bother."

Heather sits beside me on the couch, and Vaughan comes over to rest on the arm. "I'm close to Tommy, probably closer than anyone else, and I know how he feels about you. I'm also privy to some stuff he got involved in at school."

I shake my head. "I knew something was going on with his professor. I just knew it. And you flat-out lied to me about it."

She blinks. "What? No, I didn't. Is that what you think?"

"Yeah. I saw—"

"Regardless of what you say you saw, believe me, it's not Jo Alexander." She bites her lip and stares up at the ceiling as if asking for some divine guidance. "It was the professor's daughter."

"What?" Vaughan and I ask at the same time. I'm not sure if this makes the situation better or worse.

"Her real name is Hazel. She likes to be called Alex because she hates her name. I call her Haz-hell because, well, it fits."

Vaughan holds out a fist, and they knuckle-bump. Heather blushes then adds, "I promise you, it is way past being over. He is not interested."

I wipe my nose on my sleeve, grateful that my mother isn't around to scold me. "He sure appeared... interested to me."

"Tommy is not interested. Not even a little bit. He's so messed up. Hazel lied to him, and it got real complicated, but I promise you he is not cheating on you."

I snort and wipe my nose on my sleeve. "You could have fooled me."

Heather's phone rings, making me jump. She pulls it out of her pocket and reads the display. Her brow crinkles. "I've got to take this," she says as she leaves the room.

I stare at Vaughan as he watches Heather leave. He side eyes me and does his best to conceal a smile. "What?"

"Why did you call her of all people? Why?"

He sits beside me. "Because I don't like seeing you upset, and like she said, she understands Tommy better than anyone."

My brother is more amazing than he'll ever realize.

Heather rushes back into the room. "Guys, I have to leave."

"Are you safe to drive?" I point at the empty beer bottles.

"I had water. He drank all those beers." She kisses me on the cheek. "Everything is going to be fine. Trust me."

I don't trust anyone anymore.

CHAPTER THIRTY-SEVEN

Tommy

"Tommy, your mother's here," Sarah whispers to me.

I blink my eyes a few times to focus before I sit up in my bed. I haven't changed clothes in three days, but I have gone through six pounds of flour, eight packets of yeast, two dozen eggs, and two bags of sugar. My hair probably still has flour in it, making it appear prematurely gray, and I have so much dried dough caked under my fingernails, it will take a sandblaster to remove it all.

Sarah pats my shoulder and walks with me to the living room, where Mom and Heather are waiting for me. Mom crosses the room and envelops me in a big hug. I motion for Heather to join us. She wraps her arms around me, and we all cry together. I'm so sick of crying.

"I'll leave the three of you alone," Sarah says as she shuffles out of the apartment.

Mom wipes the tears from her eyes. Heather spies all the baked goods sitting on the counter, table, and every other horizontal space in the apartment.

"Good Lord, Tommy. You could open up your own bakery." Mom motions for me to sit on the couch. "Let's figure this all out."

I cover my face with my hands. "Mom, I'm so embarrassed."

"Oh, hush. Start at the beginning. I'll figure out what I can do from the mom end."

I peek over at Heather, who has her mouth full of an apple tart. She motions for me to spill everything. "It's time. Don't hold back."

"How is Shelby?" I ask her.

"Hurt. Confused. Sad. Very sad."

I sigh, then I tell my mother everything. I tell her about the relationship with Hazel and the intimidation. Then I finally have the nerve to say what I've needed to say for a long time. "Mom, I don't want this anymore. I'm not sure if I ever did."

"You don't want what?"

"This." I wave my hand around at the apartment. "Boston. School. Engineering. I don't want it."

She wraps an arm around my shoulder and gives it a good squeeze. "I thought you liked it."

I glance down at my feet and shake my head. "I don't, but I liked making you and Dad proud."

She sighs. "It's about time."

I snap my eyes up at her. "What?"

"I've always felt that your heart wasn't in it, but you had to decide that for yourself."

Heather winks. "Told ya."

"You wouldn't be disappointed if I quit?"

"I'd be disappointed if you kept doing this to yourself. Quit school. Come home and reexamine your life. You're young, bright, and... you're my kid, so I believe you'll succeed in anything you do."

"What about Dad? I don't want to embarrass him with this mess."

"He loves you. Here. Tell him yourself." She calls Dad and holds it out for me to speak to him.

"Bud, are you okay?"

"I'm better, but I've been talking with Mom... and I don't want to finish school. My heart isn't in it."

"Son, you only get one life. Don't waste a moment being miserable. I'm sorry if I contributed to any of your pain."

The truck full of bricks speeds off my chest. If I needed to, I could fly. Either that, or I now have the energy to kick my own butt for keeping all this to myself for so long. "Thanks, Dad."

"I love you," he says.

"Love you too." I hand the phone back to my mother, and she takes the phone in the kitchen to have a hushed conversation with my dad. Heather scoots onto the couch beside me.

I kiss her on the cheek. "Thanks, Heath Bar."

"You're worth it. Can I tell you a secret?"

I nod.

"I'm transferring from UT. I want to go to school close to home. I'm researching Bellevue University."

I give her a big hug, scooping her up so high, her feet dangle off the floor. "And with me in town, I could keep the riffraff away."

"Absolutely. Don't tell Mom yet. I've got to work out some things with my scholarships to make sure they transfer with me."

Being back home with my brother and sisters will make everything right again. Well... almost everything.

Mom claps her hands as she enters the living room. "Okay, the three of us are going to see your professor and her smut-britches daughter to set them straight."

Heather doubles over in a fit of giggles. "Mom, where did you learn to talk like that?"

She points at Heather. "From you."

My sister gasps. "Uh-uh. My brothers taught me everything I know."

"Mom, I'm worried I could be in a lot of trouble," I say. "That photo..."

She holds out her hand. "Let me see it."

My heart sinks. The only thing worse than having a photo taken of me having sex is having to show it to my mother and sister. After a painful silence, I open the email with the photo and show it to Mom.

Her brow scrunches as she peers at the phone then back at me. "And you're one-hundred-percent sure this is you?"

"Well, yeah." I stand next to her. This situation is so humiliating, I don't think it can get any worse. "See the picture of us on the night-stand? That's my room. That's me on top." I wish there was a hole that could swallow me up right now because any level of hell would be more satisfying than this crappy conversation.

Then something in the photo catches my eye. I suck in a huge breath. "Wait a second." I snatch the phone from my mother and en-large the extremely embarrassing photo. My face splits with a huge grin. "That's not me. That's my old roommate, Tony the Twin."

Heather peers over my shoulder and examines the shot. She bobs her head so much that it might fall off. "It's him. I walked in on him one time when I was visiting you. I thought it was you and was terri-bly creeped out at the thought of seeing you naked. I mean, he does favor you, except..."

I point at his butt. "He's got his fraternity symbol tattoo. He told me he lost a bet one time." I let out a deep breath, and months of pressure and anxiety float away like sifted flour. "That's him."

"Son, did Tony have anything to do with blackmailing you?"

"I seriously doubt it, but there's only one way to find out."

I call Tony, and after ten minutes of catching up, I get to the meat of the conversation. "You remember Hazel, right?"

"You mean Hazed and confused? You're not still with that beast, are you?"

"No, but she's trying to blackmail me with a photo. I'm pretty sure it's you in the naked pic and not me."

"Uh-oh."

"Tony?"

He sighs. "She set me up. She was going to ruin my relationship with Candace. Why do you think I moved to Nebraska of all places?"

"So you weren't a willing partner in this?"

"Hell no."

I pump a fist in the air. I knew better than to think Tony had anything to do with this.

"She came over one day, and she was spitting mad at you. She stormed around the apartment like she owned the place. She claimed she was searching for something in your room. To get her to chill, we had a few drinks. One thing led to another, and boy, that girl can drink a sailor under the table."

I've seen that side of Hazel, and it isn't pretty.

"She threatened to show the picture to Candace if I mentioned anything to you. By that time, you had moved home for the summer, and I got the heck out of town. I'm real sorry, man."

"It's okay. I appreciate you telling me now."

"Now that I think back, I was pretty hammered, but I vaguely remember her picking up her phone from your desk. Maybe she had the video rolling the whole time and took screen shots?"

"Yeah. Sounds like what she would do."

"Tommy, the photo..."

"Don't worry. Did I ever tell you my mother is an attorney?"

Tony whistles. "Hazel messed with the wrong guy."

After I relay the conversation to Mom and Heather, they high-five each other. I feel like the most fortunate man alive right now. Heather gives me a thumbs-up.

Mom picks up her purse and says, "When we get back from our meet and greet, you need to pack your bags because we're leaving in the morning."

Mom and I head toward the door. Heather sneaks into the kitchen.

"Aren't you coming with us?" I ask Heather.

"I better not. Mom's way more tactful than I am, so I'll wait right here."

"Don't eat it all in one sitting," Mom says to her.

Heather fakes a shocked expression. "Me? You would say that about your baby girl?"

Mom laughs. "Every day and twice on Sunday."

That's my mom. She tells it like it is, and Hazel is about to get schooled.

When I open my apartment door, Sarah falls into my arms. "Sorry, Sonny. You guys should talk louder so an old fogey like me can snoop easier." She rights herself then heads to the kitchen and points at Heather. "I'll keep this little filly company while you put that hobag in her place."

MOM AND I WALK IN SILENCE to the university campus, and right before I open the door to the engineering department, I freeze.

My mom smiles in a way only a mother can. "You can do this. I've got your back."

"Thanks. I don't want you to take this the wrong way, but I need to handle this myself. If I end up needing legal counsel, I'll squeal 'uncle,' okay?"

"That's my boy."

We take the stairs to the third floor, where Alexander's lab is. It's time to be honest about what happened and about my change of plans.

Mike is sitting in his usual chair with his eyes trained on the microscope in front of him, soldering microfilaments together.

"Hey, Mike. I want you to meet my mother. Mom, this is Mike. He's from Atlanta."

They shake hands, and my mom gives him a friendly smile. "Ah, two Southern boys up here in the North. Nice to meet you."

Mike grins. "Yeah. We band together and try not to pick up the accent."

I gesture to my professor's office. "I need to speak with Alexander. Can you keep my mother company for a few minutes?"

He motions to a seat next to him. "No problem."

"So, what are you working on?" Mom asks as she sits.

Mike clears his throat and goes into geek mode as he explains his project. I stand outside Alexander's closed door and pray that she doesn't flip out about me breaking her rules. This could go very badly very quickly. After one deep breath, I knock on the door.

"Enter."

I open the door and close it behind me.

Alexander's eyes flick up over her computer screen, and she arches an eyebrow. "What happened to you?"

I run a hand through my hair, and flour particles drift through the air. "A little culinary accident. Do you have a minute to talk?"

She closes her laptop and takes off her reading glasses. "This sounds serious. What's up?"

"I need to tell you some things, and I hope you don't think poorly of me after what I have to say."

She props her elbows on her desk. "I seriously doubt that could ever happen, but go on."

Trying to figure out which thing to tell her first is a hard decision: I'm quitting school, or I was seeing her daughter, and she's blackmailing me. Neither is going to soften the blow for the other.

"I took the summer off because there were some things weighing me down, school only being one of them."

"And?"

I focus on my shaking hands. "Before I left, I had been seeing someone here, and she wasn't who I thought she was. It shouldn't have happened at all."

Alexander leans back in her chair and crosses her arms over her chest. "Tommy, why are you telling me this?"

I close my eyes and say a silent prayer for guidance. "The girl was Hazel." I open my eyes, and Alexander's expression doesn't change. "I tried to end it."

"You were seeing my daughter? Right under my nose?" She stands and starts pacing around the room. "I can't believe it. How did I not see this?"

"She only stopped by when you were out lecturing."

Alexander slams a balled-up fist down on her desk, and I jump. This is not going well. Perhaps I do need my mother in here.

"I can't believe she tried this again," Alexander says.

My head snaps up. "What?"

She stares at the ceiling and groans. "Hazel and I have never been close. I focused too much on my career, and she rebels every chance she gets. Her favorite move is to... make a move on my students. Let me guess. Did she say she'd get you kicked out of school for messing with her?"

I swallow hard before I nod. "But it's worse. She has photos. She says she's going to make them public."

My professor gasps.

"It's not me in the picture. It's my room, but it's not me. I can prove it."

She bites her lip. "I'm assuming these are less than flattering photos of my daughter."

"Yes, ma'am. I'm pretty sure she planted the phone to take a video. It looks like the still photos were screen shots. I'm just guessing on that part."

She shoves the heels of her hands against her eyes. "Are they on social media?"

Good question. "I have no idea."

Alexander lets out an exasperated groan then holds up a finger. "One minute." She scoots around her desk and opens up her laptop again. I hear a *bing*.

"Make it fast, Mom," Hazel says. "I'm on my way to class."

Yeah, right.

"Quick question," Alexander says in a hard voice. "Have you been harassing one of my students?" She swivels the laptop toward me so I'm in view.

When Hazel sees me on the screen, she scowls. "Don't believe him, Mom. He seduced me."

She turns the laptop back to her. "I'm not buying it this time. Young lady, you are not allowed in this lab ever again."

"Mom, he—"

Alexander holds up a hand. "Stop. Tommy's a good guy. I trust him, and he came clean with me." She points at me. "You are going to apologize to him and never contact him again, or I will stop paying for your tuition, your car, and your apartment."

"You can't do that." Her voice screeches through the laptop speakers.

"Try me."

When Hazel doesn't respond, Alexander waves me over to her side of the desk. "Tommy, do you have anything to add?"

I walk around the desk so Hazel can see me on the screen again. With a wide grin, I say, "Actually, I do. Tony has a tat on his butt."

Hazel's face fades from an angry red to a sickly pale green.

Alexander, with anger I have never even heard her unleash on the dumbest of students, yells, "And never contact him again. Do you understand?"

Hazel scowls. "Fine. Your loss, Tommy." She logs out of the connection with her mother.

I fall back into the chair and stare at the ceiling. "Wow."

"Yeah, wow. You should have come to me."

"You're right, and I'm sorry."

She sits back down and crosses one leg over the other. "Now that we have that out of the way, is there anything else we need to discuss?"

My head spins from her support. I owe her so much. She believed me over her own daughter. And I'm going to reward her by giving up my position as her graduate student. Only an idiot would do that.

"My heart isn't in this anymore."

My professor lets out a deep sigh. "Ever since you came back, I knew it was only a matter of time before you decided to hang it up. Tommy, you are one of the most easygoing, friendly, genuinely kind-hearted people I have ever met. It could be your upbringing or where you're from, but no matter the reason, it's a good thing. You should follow your heart. I'm going to miss you and everything you have to offer to the program. But you need to find what's right for you."

The heavy burden I've been carrying on my shoulders for so long is gone. I feel like I can fly all the way back to Nashville. I stand and shake Alexander's hand. And in order to keep my emotions from getting the best of me for the tenth time today, all I can do is nod and say, "Thank you."

I exit the office, and Mom stands. Her hands are fisted by her sides. "And?"

"You don't have to play the attorney card. It's all good."

She spreads her arms wide and welcomes me into them. I am more than happy to oblige her.

Mike slaps me on the back. "Good luck." Then he leans in to whisper in my ear. "I've considered transferring to Vanderbilt. Can I contact you if I do?"

We fist-bump. "You better believe it. And you have a place to crash anytime."

We wave goodbye to Mike, and as soon as we are out of the building, my professional-lawyer mother does an Irish jig around me on the sidewalk. "Let's go home."

Home sounds good to me.

I OPEN MY APARTMENT door and catch Sarah and Heather with their hands literally in the cookie jar.

"How did it go?" Heather asks between bites.

"Better than expected."

Heather throws her arms around me, and I kiss the top of her head.

Mom plants her hands on her hips. "Did you leave any food for me?"

Sarah points at a cookie. "I sure am going to miss this boy."

"You could come with us," Heather says.

"Nah, I can't do that. This is my life."

Mom wraps her arms around Sarah and kisses her cheek. "You saved him from being all alone up here. My family and my home are yours."

A tear trickles down Sarah's cheek.

"Sarah, are you all right?" I ask her, helping her to a chair.

"It's just... I'll miss you."

"We can visit each other. Have you ever flown in an airplane before?"

She gets a far-off look in her eyes. "It's been a long time, but my husband and I used to fly all the time when he was CEO of Delta."

My mouth drops open.

She taps the tip of my nose with her finger. "And my Delta perks only allow us to fly first class. Would you accept the offer if I was able to fly you guys home like that? It would make an old gal happy."

"Uh..." I peek over at my mother and Heather. "We can handle that."

Sarah fishes out her phone, and with the swiftness of a teenager, she arranges all our flights back to Nashville.

"I'll reimburse you for our flights," Mom says.

"Nonsense. I have unlimited lifetime sky miles for up to four people per flight." Her eyes twinkle.

We all crack up. Sarah is a piece of work, and she's certainly been my guardian angel. I'll miss her more than words can say.

A knock on the door makes us all freeze.

"I'll get it." I open the door to see Hazel standing there, but I no longer fear her threats. I shake my head. "You just won't let it go."

Hazel saunters in, her head held high. She stops in her tracks, and the blood drains from her face when she sees the other people in the room. "Uh, can we go somewhere to talk in private?"

"Nope. You've already met Sarah. This is my mother, who happens to be an attorney."

Hazel gulps, making Heather giggle.

"If you think my mother is scary..." I point at Heather. "That's my little sister, and she can squash you like a bug with one tiny glare."

Heather gives her a finger wave.

Hazel backs toward the door. "I'm not sure what I saw in you in the first place. You are such a graduate school dropout." She spins on her heel and storms out of my apartment.

Sarah throws her hands in the air and shouts, "Woo-hoo!"

I hug her. "I really wish you would change your mind about moving to Nashville."

Her eyes sparkle. "Well, there are four tickets. I should at least find out what all the hoopla is about Music City."

Mom, Heather, and I wrap Sarah in a group hug. The day just keeps getting better.

"Should I bring my cowboy boots?"

Heather kisses her cheek. "Sure. Why not?"

I survey the room and three of the most beautiful women on the planet. They only want what's best for me. They love me no matter what. But there's one woman missing from the picture, and I have no idea what to do about it.

"How do I get Shelby back?"

Sarah taps my nose again. "Oh, I am pretty sure you know how."

Mom and Heather agree.

I grin from ear to ear. "You are absolutely right. Of course I do. I hope it works."

CHAPTER THIRTY-EIGHT
Shelby

Darla and Isaac try their best to keep me occupied. They have jammed my work schedule with meetings and filled my nights with errands. Darla's wedding is only two weeks away, and there are a ton of things to do. But when I think of weddings, I never envision having one. Darla offered to change the venue for the rehearsal dinner, but I insisted it be at my parents' place. I'm a big girl, and no matter where it's held, I'll have to run into Tommy anyway.

It's fun watching Isaac in his element. He is good at picking out flawless floral arrangements, and I have to admit, the dresses are perfect, not too "foo-fooey" as Darla instructed. He even agreed to share the planning with Amara. I owed it to her after the fiasco with my fake engagement.

Darla steps out of the changing room, wearing her wedding dress, and Isaac gasps. She spins in a circle, getting a view in the mirror from all angles.

"Does that mean it's pretty? I hardly even wear a sundress, much less something this fancy."

Tears well up in his eyes. "You are so beautiful."

She glances over at me. "What do you think?"

Her dress is a soft-white tea-length gown with just the right amount of antique lace that her sister, Diane, saved from their mother's wedding dress.

"Theo won't be able to contain himself when he sees you in it."

She blushes. "I feel pretty."

Isaac sings "I Feel Pretty" and twirls her around.

I throw my head back and laugh. Of course Isaac never misses an opportunity to pop out a show tune.

Amara brings out the bridesmaids' dresses, and I'm close to losing it. For Heather, Diane, and me, Darla chose tea-length dresses in the faintest shade of pink. Stella's flower-girl dress is just like Darla's but in the same shade of pink as ours.

"Wow," I exclaim. "Isaac, if it didn't mean losing you as an employee, I'd suggest you go into the wedding-planning business."

He kisses me on the cheek. "I knew you loved me."

Darla takes one more glimpse at herself in the mirror and exhales deeply. "Isaac, you've done so much for me and Theo, but I'd like to ask you for one more thing."

Isaac leans over to me and whispers, "She wants me to catch the bouquet."

Even in my somber mood, I chuckle.

"Would you walk me down the aisle and give me away?" Darla asks.

The only time I have seen Isaac not cracking jokes was when Stella was sick—until today. He swallows hard and stands up. With wobbly knees, he walks over to Darla and buries his face in her neck. Deep sobs come from his throat. "I'd be honored. Thank you so much."

I have to avert my attention from the sweet scene in order to keep from losing it. I can't imagine anyone else doing the honor.

Darla backs away and wipes a tear from her face. "You sure this is okay?" she asks me as she looks down at her dress.

Isaac stuffs a calla lily under my nose as if it's a bottle of smelling salts, making me jump back into reality. "It's beautiful. The pink edges match our dresses perfectly."

Isaac rolls his eyes. "Hello? Of course."

Darla giggles. "Okay, dresses ready. Flowers picked out. Photographer arranged. What am I forgetting?"

We stare at her, and finally she says, "Oh yeah. Cake." She lowers her eyes. "Tommy's making the cake."

The mention of his name sends a whole host of emotions through me: sadness, regret, longing. But this isn't about me. I hand her a card. "Open it."

Tears well up in her eyes as she reads the contents. A pregnant bride has enough emotions to fill a football stadium.

I give her a kiss on the cheek. "My parents love you like you're one of their own. They want you to have anything you want for your reception. It's all on them except for the aforementioned cake."

"Wow," Isaac says. "Can I be adopted?"

I roll my eyes. "You wouldn't be gaining anything since both of our parents are old money, remember?"

He snarls. "Yours are way cooler than mine."

I stare a hole through him. "Your father owns a baseball team. It doesn't get any cooler than that."

Isaac cringes. "Baseball is so manly."

"Exactly."

Darla snaps her fingers under his nose. "Focus. Reception. Help me. I'm clueless."

Isaac stage-whispers to me. "I tried to get her to do all this weeks ago, but she kept going home and falling asleep." He makes a *pfft* sound. "You can't plan all this in two weeks."

Amara holds her arms up and out, striking a "ta-da" pose. "Thank goodness for me. I have connections and am willing to call in some favors."

Darla bawls into her hands.

Isaac pats her back. "Oh dear. This is going to be harder than I expected."

Amara points at herself. "Leave it to me. A friend of Mrs. Williams is a friend of mine."

The rest of the afternoon, we zip in and out of bakeries, caterers, and restaurants. Darla finds everything she wants, and with some elbow grease—in the form of ever-flowing cash from Isaac—everyone is able to have things ready by Saturday. Money talks, and Amara seems to have a reputation at every place we go, so they are more than happy to arrange things on such short notice. All this running around keeps my mind so busy, I hardly have time to be sad about Tommy. He only crosses my mind a few dozen times.

Exhausted, we crash at an Italian restaurant for an early dinner. Darla's complexion is an eerie green due to her pregnancy, but she's a trouper. She sips on water and nibbles on a sourdough roll while we wait on our food. "I can't believe we got it all done so fast."

Amara beams. "Told you I had connections."

"I may be calm on the outside, but I'm totally freaking out inside. I cannot believe this is really happening."

I squeeze Darla's hand. "You deserve this. I'm so happy for you."

"Thanks." Her smile fades. "This must be really hard for you."

I shake my head. "Nonsense. This is your day. It's all about you and Theo. I couldn't be happier for the two of you." It's completely true, however, I want my happy day too. Seeing Darla try on her wedding gown took me back to the day I went dress shopping with Mom. Even though it was pretend, I let myself fantasize about walking down the aisle toward Tommy. Now there will be no dress and no Tommy, and all I want to do is curl up into a ball and cry my eyes out. As soon as I get home, I'm going to do just that.

Isaac clears his throat. "This is probably not the right time, but have you heard from him?"

I shake my head. "Nope. I can only assume he's still taking care of the rehearsal dinner."

"Yeah he is," Darla says. "But we can move the venue from your parents' house if it will be too awkward for you."

I wave off her comment. "Of course not. If it gets weird, I'll just lock myself in my old room like I used to do." Avoidance is my plan. But there is no way I'll be able to avoid being escorted down the aisle by him. I'll have to keep my eyes trained on Darla and focus on not breaking down in front of everyone.

"Drama, drama, drama," Isaac says.

Darla throws her napkin at him.

As much fun as today has been, I'm exhausted. I can only imagine how Darla must feel. After we eat, Isaac drives us back to Darla's house, and she lets out a dozen yawns on the way. She's so snoozy, it takes both Isaac and me to help her into her house safely. She zonks out on the couch before we can even wave goodbye.

While Isaac drives to my townhome, I sense he's itching to say something by the way he can't sit still, but I don't want to talk about anything important.

"Darla is so fortunate to have you in her life," I say.

He gives me a quick glance, then his eyes move back to the road. "Two nice compliments in one day? Are you about to kill me?"

"Jeez. Am I that bad?"

"No. I'm only giving you a hard time. But sometimes it's difficult for you to take off your boss hat and remember we're friends too."

"Good friends."

"Yep. Darla's lucky to have you too."

"Aw, but I'm being serious. You filling in for her father... that's the sweetest thing."

He swallows hard. "He wasn't a good man. He was downright mean to her. I'm glad he's not here to see this, to be a part of this. She's the best friend I've ever had."

"Me too."

He pulls up to my townhome and cuts the engine, but I don't get out. We sit and stare out the window. Finally, I break the silence. "I miss him."

He sighs. "Of course you do. Sometimes things don't work out like we hoped they would. Sometimes they do. We only understand after we think back. You're a great person. I'm glad I have you in my life."

My breath catches in my throat as I exit his car. "Thanks." My voice is a bit shakier than I want it to sound. "See you at work."

He zooms away, and I walk toward my front door. On the porch is a baker's box. I kneel down and open it to find a dozen red velvet cupcakes with cream cheese icing. Each cupcake has red sprinkles in the shape of a heart on the icing. There's no note, but it's a no-brainer who they're from. Tommy has some nerve assuming I can be won over by sweet confections.

Balancing the box in one hand, I open the door with the other. For ten minutes, I stare at the cupcakes, debating whether to call Tommy and thank him. If I open the line of communication, he'll try to apologize, and it's too late. He lied to me, and I'm not going down that road again.

In the end, I take out my phone and stare at the screen. My finger hovers over my contact list, and seeing Tommy's name makes me miss him even more. But instead, I call Vaughan.

"Yo, what's up?" He pants as he speaks.

"What are you doing?"

"At the gym, running on the treadmill."

That's what I should be doing after all the food I've eaten and all the goodies staring at me right now. "Are you hungry?"

"I'm always hungry. What do you have in mind?"

I peek into the box again. "Oh, someone left me a box of cupcakes, and I won't be able to eat them all."

"Did Tommy make them?"

"There wasn't a note, but I assume they're from him."

"I'll be there in ten minutes. If you start without me, I'll tell everyone you used to kiss your Leonardo DiCaprio poster."

He wouldn't...

In less than ten minutes, Vaughan bolts through the door as promised. He inhales deeply. "I smell them. Give me." He charges through the living room toward the kitchen and sees a single cupcake resting all by itself on a plate on the counter. His shoulders drop. "Man, you were supposed to wait."

I cringe. "I couldn't." I walk backward toward the refrigerator. "But there are a few left over." I fling open the fridge door.

He peeks inside and eyes ten more cupcakes waiting for him. He kisses my cheek then grabs them along with a gallon of milk and jumps up on the counter.

I slide up beside him, and we gorge ourselves on cupcakes. We don't even waste time using glasses for the milk. We take turns drinking straight from the jug to wash down the delicious treats.

I never knew the taste of certain foods could bring back so many memories. Thoughts of Tommy making cookies or kneading dough swirl through my brain. But the memory that sticks is the way he would feed me cinnamon rolls like a bird. On instinct, I lick my lips.

Vaughan leans back and pats his distended belly. "Tommy has outdone himself this time.

Are these 'forgive me' cupcakes?"

I shrug. "I guess they are."

He swallows the last of the cupcakes and taps my knee with his. "That means two things. One is that he's back in town. And two, he wants you to forgive him."

I shake my head. "I can't do that."

Vaughan licks cream cheese icing off his fingers. "If he keeps this up, I may want to date him."

I belt out a huge laugh. "You're not his type."

"Of course not." He winks. "He only has eyes for you."

If only that were true. Leaving mystery treats on my doorstep is one thing. It's going to take way more than sugary carbs to change my mind about him.

CHAPTER THIRTY-NINE

Tommy

Relaxing on my parents' back porch, I feel free for the first time in ages. Free from the bondage of a program I didn't have the desire for anymore. Free from the pressure and fear that I was going to regret my stupid actions for the rest of my life. My ex-professor texted me to say that if Hazel ever contacted me again, I should let her know. She wished things had turned out differently but understands I have to do what's right for me. That's a huge load off my mind.

But I'm also still free of Shelby, and it's going to take some time for her to even hear me out. When she walked in on Hazel and me, it appeared way worse than it was. But I didn't trust her enough to tell her the truth to begin with. And that's probably the biggest hurdle I have to overcome. I hope my sugary peace offerings help.

Last night's cupcakes were no doubt inhaled, especially when I noticed on my last drive-by that Vaughan's car was there. I'm sure all twelve cupcakes have been metabolized by now. Since I didn't get a phone call or a text, I need to up my game and do something she can't resist. Before I dive back into pounding dough or making pastries, I need to pay a visit to Dad at his church.

When I tiptoe into the vacant church, memories of growing up surrounded by the wonderful families here flood through my mind. So many times, Theo and I would chase each other around the altar or play hide-and-seek, driving the church secretary crazy. Heather liked to shout from the balcony to see if her voice echoed. It did.

296

Now, with no one else to distract me, I kneel at the altar. It's just me and my God. I need guidance about what my next step should be.

I am confident leaving school was the right thing to do because the anger and frustration was left behind in Boston, and I don't ever want to find it again. That part of my life is over, but I am uncertain what to do next. And in my typical style, I put stress on myself to figure it out within four days of being back in town. Mom keeps telling me things will work out. Dad smiles a lot. With no pressure from them, I shouldn't put any on myself. If they're proud of me even though I'm an unemployed graduate school dropout, I shouldn't be ashamed of myself either.

It's not shame. It's lack of direction and lack of purpose. I guess that's what I hope to gain from my silent alone time with God. I have no idea what I want to do. I like to help others. The one thing that keeps tickling my brain is what Sarah said: feed others while I feed my soul. Maybe I can find a charity to get behind. Even if I volunteer for a while, it will help me figure out my purpose in life.

In his quiet, unassuming way, my father enters from the side entrance and kneels. He bows his head in prayer alongside me. I close my eyes and soak in the moment of being here at the altar, like I've done so many times before, right next to the greatest man who ever lived. I feel his hand cover mine, and peace washes over me. I'm not afraid of the future or of what people might think. I'm meant for something more than making money or having a string of degrees after my name. Helping people is a much sweeter way to live, and somehow, I'm going to use what I'm good at to help others. No one has ever turned up a nose at my cooking. Surely, I can do something with that.

Dad stands, and I follow him out of the sanctuary and toward my car in the parking lot. "Thanks, Dad."

He shrugs. "I didn't do anything except raise a fine young man who makes me proud every day."

"Dad, did you know that Shelby and I were never really engaged?"

He bows his head. "Yeah. Theo blabbed. But the way you gazed at each other... the title might have been fake, but the feelings weren't."

"It doesn't matter. I pretty much messed that up. I doubt I will ever have a second chance."

He pats me on the shoulder and chuckles. "All is not lost, my doubting Thomas. Don't give up hope. But like Thomas in the Bible, you'll have to see it with your own eyes before you believe it, right?"

"I guess so."

"How did working with Open Table Nashville go this morning?"

My achy back doesn't keep me from smiling. I love the hard, back-breaking work, especially if it's for a good cause. "Awesome. I delivered welcome-home kits to five families who have gotten off the street."

"That's great, son."

My heart swells as I remember how the one lady who had been homeless for two years hugged me so hard, I thought she was going to break a rib.

"Dad, the faces on those people who have a place to call home, something they can afford. They won't have to sleep outside in the cold anymore. And I promised I'd help tutor them so they'll have some new skills to add to their job applications. Plus, I never realized until I met Sarah that I'm a pretty good handyman too. I'll keep an eye out for any easy repair I can tackle when I deliver meals."

"That's my boy. Any chance they have a paid position available?"

I shake my head. "I wish, but they're underfunded as it is. I'm going to search other nonprofits in the area to see what's available."

Dad's face beams. "I'm so proud of you, no matter what. And I'll keep my ears peeled on any opportunities that come my way."

That's all I want out of life. I want to do something good and make my parents proud at the same time. I never felt this way about school, and to hear my dad say those sweet words means the world to me.

"Thanks, Dad. I better go. I've got some penitent baking to do."

Dad fist-bumps me. "Make a double batch of everything you bake. I'd be happy to pray over them if it would help."

"It never hurts."

If I could figure out which item would make Shelby's hurt melt away, I would stay up all night making it. I want her back so bad. But sometimes we can't have what we want. Sometimes we can only watch and admire from afar.

That's not good enough.

CHAPTER FORTY
Shelby

Vaughan calls it stalking. I call it observing. From across the parking lot, I peek through binoculars to watch Tommy help load boxes of food onto a truck. Today, he's working at Second Harvest Food Bank. Yesterday, he was at Open Table Nashville. He certainly isn't being lazy. Thanks to Vaughan's slick talking, he managed to get some intel out of Heather. I'm shocked she's giving him the time of day, but I'm glad she is. As expected, Heather reports that Tommy can't stop helping others.

Vaughan drums his fingers on his steering wheel. "Seen enough? The guy's a poster child for doing good deeds. Are you satisfied he's not hooking up?"

I gasp. "I never for one second thought that."

"Then why all the secrecy? Just go up to the guy and talk to him."

I shake my head. "I can't. I'm not sure I'll ever be ready to talk to him."

"You need to get over that because I highly doubt he's going to miss his brother's wedding just so you don't have to see him. That's next week, right?"

"Yes." I watch through the binoculars again. His biceps flex when he picks up box after box. I miss those arms around me. "At least the wedding will be a public event. It's the rehearsal dinner, which by the way, I talked him into catering, that worries me."

Vaughan snatches the binoculars away and peers through them. "He acts happy. I mean, as happy as he can be without you."

I punch him on the shoulder. "I noticed too. What is he doing back in town?"

He lowers the binoculars from his face. "Go over there and ask him yourself."

"No."

"Sis." He slams the binoculars against the steering wheel, causing the horn to honk.

Tommy looks our way.

I slink down in the seat and drag Vaughan with me. "Crappity crap."

"And you have the nerve to say I act like a middle schooler. If you're not going to talk to him, can we please leave?"

I take one last sneak peek and catch Tommy walking into the main building of the food bank. "Let's go while we can without being noticed."

Vaughan drives away and chuckles under his breath. "You'd make a terrible James Bond."

"I prefer Jason Bourne, thank you very much."

"Can we go back to your place to see if the sugar fairy paid you a visit?"

My stomach growls with the thought of treats made by Tommy. My brain may be in denial about my feelings for him, but my stomach will always be a traitor.

Vaughan pokes me in the side. "I'll take that as a yes."

TODAY, THE TREAT DELIVERER leaves chocolate chip cookies. Vaughan, Heather, and I sit in my living room, gorging ourselves. I can't tell if she is trying to be the intermediary or if she likes my brother more than she wants to let on. It might be a little of both. Vaughan unbuttons his jeans to let his non-gut relax. Heather lies on the love seat, moaning. I dunk a cookie in milk then let it fall apart in my mouth. It's so moist and delicious, I think I've died and gone to heaven.

Heather sits up, holding her stomach. "I'm such a traitor."

Vaughan chuckles. "You're going straight to hell for fraternizing with the enemy." He reaches over to the coffee table, doing his best to grab another cookie without moving his body. Heather scoots the plate out of his reach, and he falls off the couch with a thud.

"That's not nice," I tell Vaughan.

"So you're telling me he's dropped off his goodies every day this week?" Heather asks, making Vaughan chuckle.

I pop him on the shoulder. "Yep. The cupcakes had 'I am sorry' spelled out in the icing, and the crème brûlée—"

"You realize that's just burnt pudding, right?" Vaughan asks.

I glance over at him. "Did it taste burnt to you?"

"Yum. It was fantastic."

He doesn't deserve an eye roll. "Tommy's very stealthy. No matter how hard I try, I never catch him in the act."

"What was after the burnt pudding?" Heather asks.

"Cinnamon buns."

She gasps. "He knows I love cinnamon buns."

"Each one had a sweet note sticking out of it that he wrote by hand."

"My brother is romantic?"

Vaughan grins. "Yeah. I almost ate the one that said, 'You are sweeter than anything I bake.'"

"Aww." Heather is so cute about this mushy stuff.

Vaughan shivers. "I almost got a cavity from reading it."

The notes were adorable, and after Vaughan left, I retrieved all the strips of paper and stored them in my nightstand. Every night since then, I've reread them and spilled tears all over them.

Heather scoffs. "Tommy has some explaining to do the next time I see him. He has a lot of nerve to not make me a batch."

I cringe. "Sorry. I would have saved you one, but that muscular glutton over there got to them."

Vaughan sits with his back against the couch. "I do not apologize for my actions. You snooze, you lose. Although I better start hitting the gym extra hard, or I'm going to transform into Dad before long."

With a mouthful of cookie, Heather says, "Oh, you're fine the way you are." She gasps, and a piece of cookie goes down the wrong way.

Vaughan pops her on the back as she has a coughing fit.

She waves him off. "I'm good."

He nonchalantly stretches his arms over his head, making his Nirvana T-shirt rise to expose his six-pack. It doesn't go unnoticed by Heather. She shakes her head as if to clear her mind of impure thoughts. I wish the two of them would grow up and admit they have feelings for one another. They are so cute together. If any good came from this whole mess with Tommy, it's that Vaughan is acting almost like an adult around a girl he likes. At least he's not tugging on her braid, so that's a huge accomplishment.

Heather looks longingly at the remaining cookies. "I love my brother, but if he keeps this up, he's going to make me fat too."

Vaughan gives her the once-over. "I like girls with a little meat on them."

I shove him so he falls over like a turtle. "You're going to make me throw up."

Heather's face flushes. "You do realize that Tommy's trying to ask for forgiveness?"

"Yes, but I just can't. I've been cheated on too many times."

Heather makes her way from the love seat to the couch, where I sit. Vaughan slides a hand up her thigh, which earns him a swift smack. She sits by me and pushes Vaughan away. "I shouldn't get involved, but I know how much he cares about you." She takes a deep breath. "I'm going to break my promise. He never cheated on you. Before you met him, he got mixed up with his professor's daughter, which was completely against his professor's rules. He's so shy—he was clueless how to handle her advances. When she tried to make her ex-boyfriend jealous by making out with Tommy at a bar, the dude punched him. But my brother can hold his own and got in a few licks before he hightailed it out of there. He tried dating her for a while, but she was a train wreck. So he headed back home for the summer because he wanted no part of that hot mess."

Vaughan whistles. "Wow. Wish I had a professor with a daughter that would hit on me."

Heather stares at him. "Stop talking."

He holds his stomach. "Yes, ma'am."

She rolls her eyes. "Anyhow, it gets worse. Hazel was blackmailing him with nude photos, but it was actually someone else. Besides, she's like fatal attraction. Super creepy."

Vaughan whistles. "Boy, when you break your code of silence, you let it all out."

Heather balls up a fist to show him how tough she is... or isn't. "Mom was ready to draw up a restraining order against Hazel, but it wasn't necessary. The professor put the kibosh on Hazel's folly."

When I don't say anything, she adds, "Let me be perfectly clear. He. Did. Not. Cheat. On. You."

Oh my gosh. No wonder he was so jumpy every time his phone rang. All that on top of not wanting to be in school was more than anyone would be able to handle. And I made it worse. I wouldn't let him explain when he finally got the courage to do so.

I stare into my glass of milk as the cookie disintegrates into the liquid. "I believe you. I wished I had begged him to stay in Nashville. I almost did so many times but figured it would be selfish of me."

"He had to quit for himself."

"How is he?"

"He's okay. Sarah's here, visiting. She's staying in Theo's old room until the wedding. It's like we have another grandmother. And she adores Stella, obviously. But her favorite will always be Tommy."

"Sarah is amazing. I can't wait to see her again."

"She asks about you constantly, and Tommy misses you big time."

"I miss him too, but he could have been honest with me from the start. I wouldn't have liked it, but I cannot deal with secrets and lies." I stare down at my cookie, and suddenly I'm not hungry. "What's he going to do now?"

Heather shrugs. "Whatever he wants."

"Really?"

She smiles, and a gem of an idea starts to form in my brain. Tommy quit school. Helping people makes him happy. Even though I may not ever get past the lies, he deserves to find something that makes him happy, and I know just the thing that could do that for him. It's a long shot, but I have to at least do some research to see if it's possible.

CHAPTER FORTY-ONE

Tommy

If it weren't for Mom and Heather's help with the dinner prep, I would not have gotten everything done in time. And Sarah stepped in as if she's been a member of the family all along. She chops tomatoes as Heather tosses the salad.

"Did I tell you about my husband's relatives?" Sarah asks.

Heather steals a glimpse in my direction. "I think you have."

"He was a Kennedy. *The* Kennedy if you catch my drift."

"Uh-huh."

Sarah slides the rest of the tomato slices into the salad bowl, then she and Heather take the bowl to the buffet table. I throw another slab of meat onto my cutting board to shred the pork. The aroma fills the room and makes my stomach growl. I rip a piece off the bone, and it slips out of my hand and lands on the floor. Darla's dog scarfs it up before I can do anything about it. That's the fifth time I've dropped something today. My fingers keep fumbling because I know I'll see Shelby tonight and I'm not sure how to act around her. She won't return my calls, and it's obvious my secret treats didn't do the trick, so I'm all out of ideas on how to win her back. I really thought the angel food cake would have done it.

"Hi, son."

The knife slips, narrowly missing my index finger. Mr. Williams stands in the doorway, his hands hanging by his side. I lower my gaze as he walks toward me.

He inhales deeply. "If that tastes half as good as it smells, I am going to love what you're cooking."

"I, uh..."

"Tommy, I don't have all the facts, but you're a good person."

"Thanks. I appreciate it. And I'm real sorry for lying to you about the engagement."

"Actually, Shelby is the one who lied. You cared enough about her to help her out."

"I do care about her. So much."

Theo enters the kitchen with little Stella on his back and Mom right behind him. He's all smiles, which only makes me smile. I'm so happy he's finally happy.

Mr. Williams leans in and whispers, "Don't stop telling her that." He winks as he steals a slice of pork. Then he shakes Theo's hand and walks out of the kitchen.

"Stella Bella, do you want to help me set the table?" Mom asks.

"Yay," she says as Theo puts her down. She runs off with her grandmother.

"Need any help?" Theo asks as he steals a piece of pork. His eyes roll back in their sockets. "This is so good."

"Thanks. Can you write me a prescription for Xanax?"

He chuckles. "I'm the one getting hitched, not you."

"That's true."

"This has to be hard. You're standing in her parents' kitchen, and you'll have to see her."

I cut down harder on the pork. "Not helping. Her father just had a chance to throw kitchen knives at me, and he didn't. I'm not sure what to make of that."

"Just breathe. And thank you for doing this." He pats me on the back. "Love you, bro."

I'll be fine. All I have to do is stay focused on the food and not chop off a finger. I need to find a way to talk to Shelby alone, but with a house full of people, that's not going to be easy.

As if she knew I was thinking about her, she enters the kitchen with her mother at that moment. She's beautiful, even barefoot and wearing no makeup. Her eyes meet mine then dart away. She has a private conversation with her mother before she goes to visit with Darla.

Isaac enters along with my parents, Jennifer, and Matt. Vaughan skips down the stairs, steals a petit four from the tray, and inhales it. He gives Darla a kiss on the cheek, hugs Shelby, then walks my way. He sticks his fist out for me to bump. "You've outdone yourself."

I smile. "Thanks. I thought you were staying at Shelby's."

He growls. "She forced me to come home for the weekend to help set up for the dinner. All four of us under the same roof all night, and we survived. I'm as shocked as you are."

"Miracles happen every day."

"The cinnamon rolls would have won me over."

I chuckle.

He steals a glance over his shoulder at Shelby, who folds and unfolds linen napkins, then focuses back on me. "Don't give up, okay?"

I shrug.

He peeks over at Heather, who sneers at him. "I can't stay. I've got a date."

"You better get out of here while you can still walk."

Vaughan guffaws. "I'm already regretting this date." He takes in all the food, then his gaze lands on Heather, who turns her back to him. *Ouch.*

"I'll make you a plate for later," I tell him.

He claps his hands over his chest. "You're the best. Can I marry you?"

I smile but step back. "No."

After he leaves the kitchen, it suddenly feels like the rapture came and Shelby and I are the only ones left on earth.

Quit being a wimp. Talk to her.

"Shelby."

She spins around to face me, and three napkins flitter to the floor. We both kneel down to pick them up. When our eyes meet, I finally get the courage to talk to her. "I am so sorry for everything. I should have been honest with you from the get-go."

She springs to a standing position and race-walks to the kitchen door. "I have to get dressed," she says over her shoulder.

At least she gave me five words. That's progress.

When it comes time to sit down for the meal, Heather pushes me toward my seat. "You'll thank me later."

"I don't understand."

"You will."

As I get situated, a familiar peach scent wafts my way right before Shelby settles in beside me.

Ah, Heather the matchmaker.

Shelby's light-pink sundress shows off her toned arms and shoulders, and I want to kiss the lipstick off her mouth so bad. She juts her chin up and stares straight ahead. When everyone is seated, I stand and clink my glass to get their attention.

"As the best man, I'm supposed to propose a toast."

The room gets quiet. I survey the table and make eye contact with each person. Shelby fidgets with the napkin in her lap.

"Uh, I guess I should have written it down, but here goes." I clear my throat and try not to focus on the sweat trickling down my back. "First to Darla—you are everything my brother ever wanted. And if it weren't for me..." I cringe, and our families enjoy my big goof, understanding the massive mix-up that caused Theo and Darla to be apart for seven years. "I'm really sorry about that, and to make sure it never happens again, I've changed my email address to 'Tommy the Doofus.'" A round of laughter erupts. "Welcome to the family."

Glasses clink together. "Hear, hear."

I stare at Theo. "There aren't words in the English language to convey what I'm feeling, so I'm going to rely on the Bible. First John, chapter two, verse ten. 'Whoever loves his brother lives in the light.' My life is so much brighter because of you." With a shaky hand, I hold out my glass to clink Theo's.

Tears well up in his eyes. "Ditto, bro."

I'm shocked I can make my wobbly knees bend to sit back down. Shelby smiles and whispers, "That was very sweet." Maybe there's a slight chance my relationship with her is not completely over. I got four more words out of her.

"Thanks."

I make it through dinner without choking on anything or dropping my fork, so all in all, I consider it successful. Afterward, I need air, so I find a secluded place on the back deck to hide. If I were a smoker, this would be a great place to sneak a puff or two. Soft footsteps catch my attention. Shelby tiptoes my way. Of course she would find me. This is the house she grew up in after all. My sweet angel stands before me, barefoot and beautiful.

"You found my favorite hiding spot," she says, sliding onto the bench beside me. "I'd come out here when my parents were bickering or when they were trying to make me do something I didn't want to do." She smiles. "I stayed out here so long the day of my debutante ball after-party, I almost missed the whole thing." Shelby tucks her knees up to her chin and lets out a sigh. "I miss you."

I bow my head as my hopes rise. "I miss you too."

"But I can't take you back. I can't. I'm sorry."

My heart sinks, but I brave a nod. Vaughan's words still ring in my ear. *"Don't give up."*

She nudges my shoulder with hers. "Will you take a ride with me?"

I snap my head around. "Huh?"

She stands and holds out her hand for mine. "I want to show you something."

I take her hand, and it molds with mine, like it has always been there. I could stand there, holding it all night, but she's on a mission. She slips on her sandals, picks up her purse, and without saying goodbye to one single guest, she ushers me to her car. We drive in silence to the west side of town, where she parks next to an old building with boarded-up windows.

Confused, I look at her. "What's this?"

She gets out of the car and leads me by the hand to the front door. She pulls out a key from her purse and opens the building. After Shelby flips a switch, the florescent lights buzz as they flicker on. She walks to what used to be a bar, hops up onto it, and dangles her legs like always. She makes a sweeping motion with her arm. "I see a bunch of café tables and chairs over there. And in this corner, some comfy mismatched couches." She swings around. "That back area could be an art studio and a tutoring station." She gestures toward a back room and winks. "Back there, a yoga studio."

I smile at her. She hops down from the bar and takes my hand. "It's going to be a sandwich shop and bakery."

"That's great, but what's this all about?"

"There's more. The best part is that there will be no set prices for anything. People pay what they can. If they don't have money, they won't get turned away. They'll still be served a meal or get help with their homework. But for payment in return, they will help make the bread or tutor a kid with spelling... anything they're able to do." She grins. It's been so long since I last saw that infectious smile. "They pay whatever, and they do whatever they can. I may call it the Whatever Café." She lifts one shoulder. "What do you think?"

I walk around the room, seeing in my mind what she described. My heart explodes with happiness. With the biggest grin on my face, I say, "I love it. What a fantastic idea."

She wipes her forehead. "Whew. Considering I used our honeymoon and wedding money for the down payment, you deserve to be my business partner."

I snap my head around so fast, I see stars. "What did you say?"

"A little blond birdie told me you're at a crossroads and searching for a new direction in life. I think..." She shakes her head. "I take that back. I am confident you would be great at this. That is, if it's what you want."

"Really?"

"Yeah." She holds up her hands. "Business partners only."

I fight the urge to sweep her up into a big hug. Seeing her every day without being in her life might be the hardest thing I've ever done, but I can't let her go completely. I'll take what I can, and maybe one day, when the time is right, we can be more than business partners.

"Thank you."

"No. Thank you. It's your devotion to helping others that inspired me. And you are a mighty fine baker. The crème brûlée was my fav, by the way."

I lean up against the bar and scrub my face with my hands. "Shelby Lynn—"

She pokes me in my tickle spot. "You had to call me that, didn't you?"

"I'm so sorry for everything. I never cheated on you. I promise."

She holds up a hand to halt my apology. "Stop. I know. Heather told me. I believe you."

The weight of the world is lifted off my shoulders.

"But I can't be with you like that again. I'm sorry."

"You deserve to be happy, and for you to offer this to me... I can never repay you the kindness."

She gives my bicep a tentative squeeze. "Promise me you'll be happy and be yourself. That's all I ask."

I stare at my feet. "I realize you don't want me anymore, and I understand, but I will always love you, and I will always try to regain your trust."

"I appreciate that. The trust thing may never happen, but we can work well together." She holds out a hand. "Partners?"

Even though I would much rather grab her into a big hug or kiss those luscious lips, I'd better not. Instead, I shake her hand. "Partners."

CHAPTER FORTY-TWO

Shelby

Piano music filters through the church and up into the room we are using to get dressed. While I put the finishing touches on my makeup, Stella bounces down the hallway as she practices dropping rose petals on the floor. Darla's sister, Diane, fusses over Darla's veil, and Isaac relaxes in a wingback chair, already on his third glass of champagne.

Mom knocks on the doorframe. "Everyone decent?"

Isaac snickers. "Never."

Mom kisses him on the cheek. Behind her, Dad pats Isaac on the back. "You're doing a great thing here."

Isaac takes one last swig from his glass and groans. "I hope I don't pass out or pee on myself, or pee on myself when I pass out."

I cringe. "That's one way to leave an impression."

Mom's gaze lands on me. She covers her chest with her hands. "Shelby Lynn, you are gorgeous."

"Thanks, Mom." I need to do something with my hands to keep me from messing up my hair and makeup, so I hug my stomach. "Can we go somewhere and talk?"

Mom scrunches her brow. "Sure."

I motion with my head for Dad to join us, and they follow me out of the room and down the hall to another room used to store handbells and other musical equipment. I need to tell them about my business plan. I guess the little girl in me will always want their approval. I can't face them because I don't want to see their reaction.

"Tommy and I are going to be business partners in a café I want to open."

Over my shoulder, I notice Mom glaring.

Dad stares at the ceiling. "Shelby Lynn…"

"I appreciate that you're worried I'll get hurt again, but I won't. Besides, he never hurt me. It was a big misunderstanding."

My mother takes my hands in hers. "Sweetie."

"Darling." Dad wraps an arm around my shoulders. "Tommy is a good guy. And if you believe you can make a go of being a small-business owner, then go for it. I understand better than anyone how satisfying it is to be your own boss."

Mom smiles. "But you're wrong if you think you can keep it just a business relationship."

"I can."

Mom rolls her eyes. "*Pfft*. Honey, I'm not blind."

Dad agrees. "He has this expression of adoration all over his face. He's in love with you."

Mom nods. "You can see it in his eyes. There's no denying his feelings."

Tears well up in my eyes, threatening to ruin my perfect makeup. Isaac is going to have my hide if I'm a smeary mess. "Past tense. It's over."

Dad shrugs. "Don't be so hasty. It's not only his eyes. It's in yours. And the longing in your eyes tells me you're not over him."

"But I am."

He throws his hands in the air. "Okay. If you say so."

It's now or never. Mom has to either support me one-hundred-percent or not at all. "I'm going to start selling my paintings too. I'm good at it, and I'm not going to be ashamed of my talent anymore."

Dad cups my cheeks with his hands. "That's wonderful. Don't you think so, Renee?" His expression dares Mom to dispute his words.

She chews on her bottom lip for a moment then takes a deep breath. "Yes, you are, Shelby. You're talented and should share that with others."

Dad lets out a belly laugh at my startled expression. "That wasn't so hard, now, was it?"

He winks at Mom, and I let out a sigh of relief.

I snap my fingers. "One other thing. About the money."

He shakes his head. "It's yours to keep."

I fight back a smile. "Good. Because I already spent it."

DARLA IS SUCH A BEAUTIFUL bride. She doesn't even act scared, but Isaac does. He's in total father-of-the-bride mode, and if he doesn't calm down soon, I'm going to find a double shot of whiskey to pour down his throat. Diane and I get the honor of holding Darla's dress while she goes to the bathroom one last time. Heather plays rock-paper-scissors with little Stella. They are so freaking cute together, it's not even funny.

Jennifer runs into the room. "It's time."

We line up at the back of the sanctuary, and I peek inside to see Theo standing at the front next to his father, who will officiate the ceremony. They both can't stop smiling. When I go to take my place, I bump into the best man, Tommy. He looks mighty fine all dressed up, and I suddenly can't breathe. His smile melts my heart. *Darn you, Darla, for insisting he escort the maid of honor, me, down the aisle instead of being at the altar with Theo.*

Jennifer and Matt walk down the aisle arm in arm, then Heather with her escort, their cousin. Next is Diane, Darla's sister, with one of Theo's work friends. The only people left in the back of the sanctuary are Tommy, Darla, Isaac, and me.

I can't stop staring at Tommy, just like I did the first time I met him. The only things missing are the flour in his hair and the chocolate chip cookies in the oven. Last night ended with an awkward truce, but I tossed and turned all night, unable to get his face out of my dreams.

He leans down to whisper in my ear. "You're beautiful."

"So are you."

He laughs. Isaac shushes us and motions for us to make our way down the aisle. I give Darla one last kiss on the cheek before I take Tommy's arm. He covers my hand with his and chips away the last bit of ice from my heart. He takes a step down the aisle, but I don't move. He gapes at me, confused as all get out.

After I swallow the frog in my throat, I whisper, "I forgive you."

"Thank you," he mouths, then he motions for me to walk with him.

We start down the aisle again, but about halfway to the altar, I freeze. He peers down at me then jerks his head toward Theo, eyes wide.

"Are you okay?" he asks me.

I nod, but I can't make my feet move. I glance back at Darla, who motions for me to continue down the aisle. Isaac gestures to the front of the church. I start down the aisle again, but not before I whisper in the faintest voice possible, "Tommy, will you marry me?"

Tommy stubs his toe, and I latch onto his arm before he makes a nosedive into the pew where his mother and Sarah are sitting. A slight giggle runs through the sanctuary. He straightens, and his face is all flushed and blotchy. Then he mouths to Theo, "I'm sorry."

Theo throws his head back and laughs.

I didn't mean to open my mouth and spill all kinds of craziness. I only wanted to ask him if we could start over, but when I saw him and felt his hand on mine, I knew I wanted more and for real this time.

"Did you hear me?" I whisper.

He trains his eyes on his father at the altar and mumbles so only I can hear. "I heard you."

His lack of response has my heart skittering. He was supposed to take me in his arms and swing me around, yelling at the top of his lungs how much he loves me. When we get to the altar, where we're supposed to go separate ways, he takes my hand and plants a quick kiss on it before walking to his side of the church. I walk stiff-legged to my position because if I bend my knees, I'm going to be the next one to tumble.

The organ announces Darla's entrance, and we all look back to watch Darla and Isaac enter with little Stella right in front, placing rose petals along the path for her mama to walk to her daddy. Isaac is all smiles, and when he gives Darla a hug at the altar, he acts like he doesn't want to leave her side. He may never really give her away to her husband. Darla hands me her bouquet then takes Theo's hand.

I feel Tommy's eyes on me, and when I get the opportunity, I sneak a peek at him. He's smiling like a Cheshire cat, and not once during the entire ceremony does he take his eyes off of me. Heat rushes up my neck, and I feel like the worst best friend in the world because I cannot wait for this ceremony to end.

After Theo and Darla exchange vows and the reverend announces Dr. and Mrs. Theo Edwards to the congregation, I am only seconds away from getting next to my man again. Darla and Theo exit the church, then Tommy takes me by the hand, and we sprint down the aisle right behind them. As we wait for the rest of the bridal party to exit, Tommy and I stare at each other. As if on cue, we both let out a huge breath.

People mill around the parking lot, wishing the newlyweds good luck, but Tommy and I stand frozen in time.

He rocks back and forth on his heels then waggles an eyebrow. "Did you mean it this time?"

I glance over his shoulder to the happy couple, and Darla catches my eye. Her eyes get wide, and I give her the thumbs-up. She blows me a kiss before picking up her daughter to include her in the celebration.

"So?" he asks with hesitation in his eyes.

"You better believe I meant it."

He lets out a sigh of relief. "My answer is yes. A thousand times, yes. For real. Forever." He grins. "I am the worst brother in the world, but I cannot wait for the reception to be over."

"Me either."

We do our obligatory best man and maid of honor duties and mingle with the guests during the reception, but Tommy's gaze is always on me, making me feel warm and fuzzy all over. When Darla throws the bouquet, I scoot out of the way on purpose to make sure it hits Heather smack-dab in the face. She tries to bat it away, but it's like her hands have superglue on them. Sarah crosses her arms and huffs. I don't need the bouquet tradition to figure out who will be getting hitched next.

Tommy has other plans. His tall body and long arms make it a no-brainer on who catches the garter. He twirls it around his finger and lets out a "woo-hoo!"

Theo and Darla aren't much for small talk, and as soon as the opportunity arises, they dart off for their honeymoon while little Stella skips toward Heather's car for a weekend adventure with her aunt.

In the middle of the parking lot, Tommy watches me as if the rest of the world stops existing. His infectious smile captivates me again, like it did the first day we met. He takes me by the hand and whisks me back inside the church and up a staircase. We climb four flights of stairs that lead to the church steeple. When we get to the top, which overlooks Nashville, he pulls me toward him. The setting sun over the cityscape with the rolling hills in the background is definitely going to be in my next drawing.

"Did you mean it?" he asks. "You really forgive me?"

I can't form words, so I grin like an idiot. He pulls me into a hug, and my ear squishes up against his heart, which is beating about a hundred beats per minute.

"I love you." He kisses the top of my head. "I'll never let you down."

"I believe you."

He takes my face in his hands. I nestle into his chest, and we watch the sun set over the city. "Are you sure you want to marry me? After all, I'm a graduate school dropout."

I push away from him and take one long, sultry gander at this hot mess of a man. "You are one-hundred-percent right for me." I gaze down at the guests as they drive away from the church. What a perfect day for a wedding and a new beginning for us.

Tommy backs me up to the railing and presses his entire body against mine. When his mouth falls on mine, I forget where we are. I can't wait to start the rest of my life with this man. I don't care what we do. I'll even play the game of Risk with him, as long as he's always by my side.

"So, Shelby Lynn... what do we do now?"

I lean into my beautiful, real fiancé, and when his eyebrows shoot up, it's obvious he's reading my mind. "I have an idea."

At the same time, we say, "Let's bake."

Acknowledgments

To Jymie Smith and Kelly Ann Hopkins. I couldn't have done this without your support.

To the entire Red Adept family, in particular:

Lynn McNamee — Thanks for believing in this story and in me.

Erica Lucke Dean — You are the best mentor ever.

Alyssa Hall & Neila Forssberg, my awesome editors — I'm honored to be able to work with you again.

Jessica Anderegg – The cover is so pretty.

To Mark — Thanks for putting up with me for 30 years.

To Maddie — You are the coolest person on the planet.

Also by Cindy Dorminy

Left Hanging
Right for Me

Watch for more at www.cindydwrites.com.

About the Author

After several decades of writing medical research documents, Cindy Dorminy decided to switch gears and become an author. She wanted to write stories where the chances of happy endings are 100% and the side effects include satisfied sighs, permanent smiles, and a chuckle or two.

Cindy was born in Texas and raised in Georgia. She enjoys gardening, reading, and bodybuilding. She can often be overheard quoting lines from her favorite movies. But her favorite pastime is spending time with Mark, her bass-playing husband, and Maddie Rose, the coolest girl on the planet. She also loves her fur child, Daisy Mae. She currently resides in Nashville, TN, where live music can be heard everywhere, even at the grocery store.

Read more at www.cindydwrites.com.

About the Publisher

Dear Reader,

We hope you enjoyed this book. Please consider leaving a review on your favorite book site.

Visit https://RedAdeptPublishing.com to see our entire catalogue.

Don't forget to subscribe to our monthly newsletter to be notified of future releases and special sales.